---------------- ★ ----------------

"A thorough job," the sheriff observed. The single bullet had passed obliquely through the victim's skull, exiting along with a large chunk of skull from behind the right ear. "The weapon is under his chair."

Enriquez's body rested like a sandbag in the modern fabric-and-fiberglass swivel chair. His left arm hung straight down, index finger extended as if he'd been pointing at the large revolver that lay between two of the swivel chair's five black legs. His left shoe rested flat on the clear plastic carpet protector under the chair, and his right leg was extended under the desk.

"It's supposed to be a pretty standard picture," Torrez said, and Estelle looked up at him quickly. He didn't elaborate but let the remark pass with a shrug.

---------------- ★ ----------------

"...exciting police procedural thriller. Steven F. Havill is a talented writer who is an expert at creating believable characters and plausible plots."

—Harriet Klausner

D0556578

Previously published Worldwide Mystery titles by
STEVEN F. HAVILL

SCAVENGERS
BAG LIMIT
DEAD WEIGHT
OUT OF SEASON

A DISCOUNT FOR DEATH

Steven F. Havill

W★RLDWIDE.

TORONTO • NEW YORK • LONDON
AMSTERDAM • PARIS • SYDNEY • HAMBURG
STOCKHOLM • ATHENS • TOKYO • MILAN
MADRID • WARSAW • BUDAPEST • AUCKLAND

For Kathleen

A DISCOUNT FOR DEATH

A Worldwide Mystery/February 2005

First published by St. Martin's Press LLC.

ISBN 0-373-26518-2

ACKNOWLEDGMENTS

Special thanks to David Martinez

ONE

UNDERSHERIFF Estelle Reyes-Guzman stopped the unmarked county car at the curb on Bustos Avenue directly in front of Kealey's Dry Kleaners and Laundry. Even as she pushed the gearshift toward Park, Estelle saw Julia Kealey appear at the shop's door, hand reaching for the OPEN-CLOSED sign, ready to call it a day.

Julia flipped the sign but held the door open and watched with a sympathetic smile as the undersheriff pulled herself out of the patrol car and crossed the sidewalk. "You look like you've had an interesting Monday." She greeted Estelle in a voice husky from the mixture of cigarette smoke and dry-cleaning fumes.

"Interesting but endless." Estelle grinned, and then her dark face sobered. "How's Royce?"

"He's...what would be the best word...he's *okay*. Just okay." Julia let Estelle slip by into the shop. "He has some good days and some bad days. I keep kidding him that it's a victory if he can remember enough about the day to decide whether it's good or bad." She closed the door behind them and turned the bolt, adding with resignation, "Alzheimer's is nasty stuff, Sheriff. I wouldn't wish it on my worst enemy."

Julia leaned against the counter as her only concession to fatigue. A stout, powerful woman, she looked ten years younger than the sixty-four that she was. She riffled through the ticket file and located Estelle's stub before the undersheriff had fished her half out of her pocket.

"Three pants suits," she said. "Just a sec."

Estelle's fingers drummed an unconscious beat on the Formica counter, and as the parade of bagged and tagged clothing hummed around the endless track she glanced at the clock. She had wanted to be home by five p.m. at the latest. That deadline was three hours and four minutes dead. She took a slow, deep breath and relaxed. Francisco and Carlos wouldn't care that she was late, although they'd be in a lather about the presents. The two little boys had no sense of time in the first place.

With any luck, the boys' father would be home to keep them occupied, but Estelle couldn't remember the last uninterrupted day that her physician husband had enjoyed. Still, it had been nice to imagine that the small, modest birthday party planned for that evening *could* happen without interruption.

The guest of honor would be the most philosophical of all. Bill Gastner, the *padrino,* or godfather, for Estelle's two little boys, had turned seventy-two—not a bad accomplishment for someone who knew the inside of a hospital nearly as well as he knew his own home. But he certainly wouldn't mind if Estelle was late to slice the cake. Thirty-two years as first undersheriff and then sheriff of Posadas County, New Mexico, had taught him all he needed to know about the vagaries of best-laid plans.

"Here you go," Julia said, and hung the plastic bags on the small rack beside the cash register. "There are movie stars who would like to look as elegant as you do, young lady," she said. "If anyone had told me that it was possible to look so good in a tan pants suit…" She let the rest of the sentence drift off and smoothed the nearest plastic bag with her hand. "Well," she added before Estelle could reply. "That's twenty-three ninety."

"I really appreciate this, Julia," Estelle said. "If I get any behinder, I'm going to meet myself."

Julia laughed and handed the undersheriff her change with one hand while she lifted the hangers off the hook with the other. "And here I thought it had been dead quiet these past few days. I haven't heard any new juicy gossip in weeks."

Estelle took the clothing with another round of thanks, not rising to the light bait Julia had tossed out. "Thanks again, Julia."

The woman waved her hand in easy dismissal. "I'm usually here until eight-thirty anyway, before I get everything squared away." She turned the bolt and held the door. The cool October evening was crisp, welcome after the chemical atmosphere of the cleaners. "You take care now," Julia said, "and have a good week." She closed the door. As she stepped across the sidewalk, Estelle heard the door bolt click into place behind her.

Traffic was light on Bustos, the main east-west arterial through the village of Posadas. A single car approached in the curb lane from the east, and Estelle paused to let it pass before stepping out around the front fender of the patrol car. She recognized the driver as Maggie Archer, wife of the school superintendent, and lifted a hand in greeting as the Volvo station wagon passed. Across the street, a pickup with a rattling stock trailer pulled out of the Chevron station, eastbound, with a loud clatter of diesel.

As she reached for the door handle of her unmarked car, the cry of tires reached her on the light breeze. At the same time, the sound of two engines joined in, one the characteristic strangled bellow of a late-model V-8 working hard, the other the high-pitched warble of a motorcycle's two-stroke.

Estelle opened the door to toss the clothing on the seat. For a moment, she stood with the door open, leaning her weight on the window frame, listening. The eastbound ranch pickup had clattered into the distance. Somewhere off on the side streets to the north the two racing drivers were having a grand time. They'd roar through enough neighborhood stop signs that eventually someone would call the village police and complain. As Estelle listened, both vehicles turned south, heading toward Bustos.

Maggie Archer's dark blue Volvo continued west at a sedate pace, its taillights receding under the halo of street lamps. Six blocks separated the spot where Estelle then stood from the intersection of Twelfth and Bustos, and as clearly as if they were homing missiles, the sounds of the two racing vehicles headed south toward that intersection.

The approach to Bustos Avenue on southbound Twelfth Street included an aging metal bridge, one of those structures with silver-painted steel lattice sides and a grilled roadbed that made tires hum. In deference to its years, the bridge was posted with a plethora of weight-limit warning signs. The trusses spanned an arroyo and an abandoned irrigation ditch, both of which would have been adequately served with a simple metal culvert. Whether functional or not, the "Bridge by the Don Juan" was the last of its kind in the county, preserved as a historical landmark. Even Estelle's young sons had learned to howl in unison with the tire noise for that brief instant of harmony whenever the family car crossed.

As more than one driver had proved in the past, the old bridge also doubled as an effective takeoff ramp if a vehicle hit the approach too quickly.

Two heartbeats before Maggie Archer's Volvo station wagon arrived at Twelfth Street, Estelle saw the motorcyclist rocket through the Stop sign and into the intersection. The streetlight by the Don Juan de Oñate Restaurant flashed on the bike's yellow fenders. The machine was still half airborne, its front wheel pulled high and crossed wildly as if the rider was attempting to recover from a showboat motocross jump.

Instead of continuing straight through the intersection and diving onto South Twelfth Street, the rider attempted a turn left onto Bustos, crossing directly in front of Maggie Archer's station wagon. Estelle saw the flare of the Volvo's brake lights, and then the motorcycle was down.

A tire or foot peg grabbed asphalt and the machine flipped wildly across the street, shedding parts and its rider. At the same instant that the bike crashed into the southeast curb of Bustos Avenue and the unseated rider slammed into the base of the steel utility pole, a Posadas Village patrol car shot into the intersection, tires squealing. The car narrowly missed Maggie Archer's Volvo and continued across Bustos, skewing to a stop on Twelfth Street. The motorcycle finally crashed to a halt halfway across the front yard of the vacant rental house on the southeast corner of Twelfth and Bustos.

"Ay," Estelle gasped. She ducked inside, twisted the ignition key, and yanked the unmarked car into drive before the door slammed closed.

Even as she accelerated down the street toward the carnage, she palmed the mike. "PCS, three ten. Be advised of an MVA at Bustos and Twelfth involving a motorcycle. We'll need an ambulance. And notify Chief Mitchell."

"Three ten, PCS. Ten four." If dispatcher Ernie Wheeler said anything else, Estelle didn't hear him. She was watching the village patrolman as he clambered out of his car. She snapped on the grill lights of her own unit, and the officer stopped in his tracks the instant that he saw her approaching. His left hand drifted to the roof of his car as if he needed the added support to remain upright. The emergency lights in the roof rack hadn't been on when the police car rocketed into the intersection, and they remained dark now. Like a deer caught in headlights, the village officer froze.

Estelle swung her car broadside so that its bulk protected the tangled motorcycle from eastbound traffic. Maggie Archer's Volvo had drifted to a stop, its nose poking into the Twelfth Street intersection. The lump that had been the bike rider lay motionless, head down in the street, body awkwardly sprawled up over the curb near the base of the utility pole.

As she opened the door of 310, Estelle turned at the sound of another vehicle accelerating toward them from the east. Sheriff's Deputy Thomas Pasquale braked hard, stopping the county Expedition in the center of the westbound lanes, forming a "tee" with the back of Estelle's unit.

The village patrolman, Perry Kenderman, remained rooted in place as if he were a bewildered tourist frozen in a photograph. Estelle ignored him and sprinted to the biker's side. The sprawled figure was hardly larger than a child, twisted with hips up on the lip of the sidewalk and upper torso in the street's drainage basin.

The body had that tragically limp, deflated appearance of a flung doll, without a twitch, without a moan. Dreading the answer, Estelle knelt and reached out to touch two fingers to the soft skin of the victim's throat just below the helmet. Not a tremor stirred the large carotid artery, a vessel that should have been pounding with the excitement of the chase or racing with the trauma of broken bones.

One of the support bolts at the base of the utility pole had torn a chunk out of the side of the helmet. The wrenching impact had been violent enough to snap the cyclist's neck as the force of the collision wrapped her body around the base of the pole.

Estelle gently slipped her fingers behind the biker's head, under the margin of the heavy helmet. She closed her eyes and felt a fracture so catastrophic that she could trace the irregularities of the shattered vertebrae.

The undersheriff sat back on her haunches and let out a long breath.

"Ambulance is on the way," Pasquale said. He had sprinted across from his vehicle and dropped to his knees beside Estelle. He reached out toward the cyclist's shoulders, but Estelle held up a hand sharply.

"Her neck's broken," she said. "Don't touch her. The EMTs are on the way."

"We got a clear airway?" Pasquale crouched down. The beam from his heavy flashlight reflected from the cracked plastic face shield as he bent forward to double-check for a pulse. Estelle felt her stomach churn. To pound the cyclist's heart back into motion, they'd have to move the body, straighten it out to clear the airway, support the neck. With the brain disconnected, there was no point.

"If you can figure out how to put her spine back together so the air will do some good," Estelle whispered.

"Well, Christ," Pasquale said. "It is a girl, isn't it."

"Yes." Estelle pushed herself to her feet and looked across at Patrolman Perry Kenderman. The officer had moved a step or two further away from his car and now stood in the middle of the street, hands locked behind his head as if he expected someone to slap handcuffs on his wrists. "Ay," Estelle said. "This is all wrong."

"Pardon?" Pasquale looked up at her, but she shook her head.

"Stay with her," she said. "And call in for some help. We need to perimeter this entire intersection." She nodded toward Maggie Archer as the deputy reached for his radio. The woman had gotten out of her car and now stood by the door, arms folded and hugging herself, not daring to move. "And make sure Mrs. Archer doesn't drive off." Far down the street to the east, she heard the wail of the ambulance as it pulled out of the Posadas General Hospital parking lot, less than a minute away.

TWO

PATROLMAN Perry Kenderman's angular face was pale, and as Estelle approached, she could see his deer-in-headlights gaze shift from the motionless form under the utility pole to the dark figure of Maggie Archer across the street, and then to the rapidly approaching ambulance. Only when Estelle reached out and touched him on the shoulder did he turn and acknowledge her presence.

"Perry, tell me what happened." She watched his face. His heavy lips moved, but whatever it was that he wanted to say stuck in his throat. Estelle waited. Kenderman had been hired as a full-time village patrolman just months before by Chief Eddie Mitchell, but he'd served long enough as a part-timer to know the job. Perry Kenderman had proved himself steady and dependable. No particular flame drove his ambition—just what the village fathers appreciated.

Estelle glanced back over her shoulder as the ambulance pulled to a stop and the two EMTs bailed out. Deputy Pasquale had been kneeling by the fallen rider, and he rose to step out of the way as the two EMTs approached. Estelle turned once more to the patrolman.

She knew that Kenderman had seen his share of accidents. Less than a month before, he'd responded to the scene of a pickup truck rollover that had killed a two-year-old. Estelle had arrived in time to see Kenderman working frantically with the EMTs trying to save the child's life. He hadn't frozen in his tracks then.

But tonight, he'd been struck dumb. There was nothing anyone could do for the motorcyclist, Estelle knew, but Kenderman didn't. From such a spill, the norm would have been broken bones, pavement burns, maybe some lacerations from the bolts at the bottom of the utility pole. Kenderman could have handled any of those injuries as a first responder. But he had not taken a step. With a sinking feeling in the pit of her stomach, Estelle could guess why the patrolman had been stunned into silence.

His patrol car, askew in the street, was effectively blocking Twelfth, and Estelle moved past him and leaned inside the vehicle. She turned on the red lights and paused before straightening up, looking at the radio.

"Perry, talk to me," she said quietly. "I want you to tell me what happened."

"She wouldn't stop," Kenderman said, finally finding his voice. This time he looked fully at Estelle, and she could see that he'd returned from whatever mental hideout he'd initially chosen.

"This started out as a routine traffic stop?" Estelle kept her tone neutral, noncommittal, hoping that the leading question would serve to prime the officer's pump.

Kenderman's head bobbed a bit, as if he couldn't decide whether to nod or shake.

"Where did you first see the bike?"

"Up...up on..." and he paused. "She was comin' down toward the bridge, there, on Twelfth Street. She run the stop sign at Highland."

"You were parked there, or coming up behind, or what?"

"I...I was comin' out of Highland the other way."

Estelle turned and looked north, past the Don Juan de Oñate Restaurant, toward the small silver bridge. Highland Court, a narrow lane that was actually only five or six blocks long, crossed Twelfth Street a scant two blocks before the bridge. She looked back at Kenderman. His Adam's apple jumped as he gulped air.

"You knew who the cyclist was?"

He shook his head quickly, and Estelle saw his eyes dance away. She regarded him silently.

"I need to make sure I understand," she said finally. "Where were you when you first saw the motorcycle?"

Kenderman frowned at the pavement. "I was eastbound on Highlands."

"On which side of Twelfth?"

"West." He nodded as if the image had finally coalesced in his mind.

"You were coming up on the intersection of Highland and Twelfth, then?" He nodded again. "And where was the motorcycle?"

"It was comin' down Twelfth toward me. Southbound."

"And you said it ran a stop sign?" The question obviously jarred Kenderman, since Estelle was sure he would know as well as anyone that there was no stop sign posted on the through street.

Kenderman ran a hand over his face in frustration. "She was comin' west on Highland. That's what I mean. Christ, all this happened so fast." He put both hands over his face, shuddered a deep breath, and then extended them toward Estelle. "She was comin' west on Highland, got to the stop sign at Twelfth, and ran right through, right there in front of me."

"And that's the first time you saw the bike?"

"What do you mean?"

"You hadn't been in pursuit earlier? This was your first encounter?"

"The first time." Kenderman's voice had firmed up some, and he gazed off into space, his head shaking slowly.

Estelle heard a clatter behind her, and saw one of the EMTs unloading a gurney from the ambulance. "Stay here," she said, and Kenderman nodded.

Deputy Pasquale stood on the sidewalk just beyond the utility pole, a dozen feet from the wrecked bike, conferring with a second deputy, Sgt. Tom Mears. Across the street, a black and white state police cruiser slid quietly to a stop behind Maggie Archer's Volvo. Bustos Avenue was effectively corked, with what little traffic there might be forced into a single lane.

As Estelle approached, Mears walked to the motorcycle and knelt down beside it. Pasquale followed, hands thrust in his pockets. The "two Toms," as Chief Dispatcher Gayle Torrez had dubbed them, frequently worked the same shift—Mears methodical and meticulous, the younger Pasquale still tending toward impetuosity.

"Banged it up some," Mears said to Estelle. He reached out a hand and squeezed the front tire. "You saw it happen?" His right index finger traced over an arc on the tire's sidewall, high near the edge of the tread. The tire's black rubber was scuffed and bruised. Mears brought his flashlight close.

Estelle dropped to her hands and knees, focusing her own light. "I was parked in front of the dry cleaner's, standing beside my car. The bike looked like something caught on the pavement just as she crossed in front of Mrs. Archer's car. I think the rider was trying to turn left onto Bustos."

"Foot peg, probably," Mears said.

Estelle turned and looked across the street. "When the bike entered the intersection, the front tire was off the ground." She held her hands as if she were pulling up on the bike's handlebars. "It was cocked. Then the front tire planted and everything went crazy."

"It's a dirt bike," Pasquale offered. "Those knobby tires can be tricky as hell on pavement."

Mears stood up, hands on his hips. "The bike just sort of somersaulted over itself, then? Tripped over itself?" He looked over his shoulder toward the utility pole. At its base, the two EMTs conferred quietly, all urgency drained from their pace. "If she hadn't caught the pole, she probably wouldn't have done much more than skin an elbow."

Estelle sat back on her haunches, head twisted so that she could see Perry Kenderman. He leaned against the village patrol car, a two-year-old Ford Crown Victoria that sported a fancy blue, white, and gold paint job, including the large dare emblem flagged across the rear fenders. During his last year on the job, the former village police chief had been so proud of the unit that he'd talked the village into buying another one just like it.

"Sheriff, you about ready?" One of the EMTs had stepped close, and he nodded toward the black-shrouded body. No amount of high-tech medicine was going to put the cyclist back together.

"No," she said quickly. "Not until the coroner gets here."

The EMT nodded and turned away. "We need to tape this area off," she said. "Did you call Linda?"

"She's on the way," Tom Pasquale said. "And Bobby's on his way down."

"We're going to want really careful pictures." Linda Real would take careful and perfect photos, she knew, in black and white, color, and video. She stood up with her hands on her hips, and Mears followed her gaze as an ancient, rumbling pickup truck pulled to a stop across the street behind the state police cruiser. She took a deep breath. "Let's see what the sheriff wants to do," she said and glanced at Mears.

"This ain't going to be pretty," Mears said. "What do you want to do with him?" He leaned his head in Kenderman's direction.

"Just make sure he doesn't take off," Estelle replied. "And make sure he doesn't talk to anyone else. Not even Chief Mitchell when he gets here. There are some questions he needs to answer."

Posadas County Sheriff Robert Torrez stepped slowly out of his truck, lingering for a moment with one hand on the door as he surveyed the scene. He saw his undersheriff approaching and waited.

"Who is it?" he said without greeting.

"We don't know yet. We're waiting on Perrone." She shook her head. "She broke her neck."

Torrez slammed the door of the truck. Something clattered inside, but he ignored it. "*Her* neck?" he asked quietly.

"It appears that way."

"So tell me."

"Right now, it appears that Kenderman was chasing the bike," Estelle said. "A close chase. They entered this intersection less than a second apart. But there are some inconsistencies with his story. He says the chase began just a block or two north of this intersection, up by Highlands. I know that's not true."

"Oh?"

Estelle nodded down the street toward the east. "I was standing on the street in front of Kealey's. I heard both the car and the bike. They were quite a distance to the north and east. Much farther than two blocks.''

"You heard the patrol car?"

"Yes, sir. Then I saw the bike enter the intersection and heard the chase car close behind. A split second later, the village unit entered the intersection. The bike hadn't even stopped moving. The village unit stopped where you see it now."

Torrez's face remained impassive as he took a step toward the front of his truck so that he could see around the bulk of the ambulance. A tall, broad-shouldered man, he moved carefully, as if reluctant to intrude. "You heard Kenderman's siren?"

"No, sir. It wasn't operating."

"But his lights were?"

"No, sir. I turned those on myself just a minute ago, when I first went over to talk to him."

"What does he say?"

"Only that he was eastbound on Highland, near the stop sign at Twelfth. First he said the bike was southbound on Twelfth, then he corrected himself to say that it was westbound on Highland when it ran the stop sign and then *turned* southbound on Twelfth. That's when he says he initiated pursuit."

"But you don't think so?"

"No, sir. I know that's not the case. Unless there was a sudden switch in cars just before the bridge, that's not what I heard."

Torrez muttered something to himself, then said, "I was workin' on this," and he patted the primer gray front fender of his truck, "and I had my radio on. Kenderman wasn't talkin'. Not to Dispatch, anyway."

"No, he sure wasn't. His radio wasn't turned on, Bobby."

Torrez looked sharply at Estelle. "You're sure about that?"

"Yes, sir. I checked his car."

"Let's go take a look," Torrez said.

"And there's another inconsistency that bothers me," Estelle said. "From the first exchange I had with Kenderman, he referred to the cyclist as *she*. When I asked if he knew who she was, he said no. He's lying, Bobby."

Torrez glanced down at Estelle as a grin touched his broad face. "He is?"

"Sure he is. First of all, she's got short hair, or at least it's all bundled up under the helmet. She's wearing blue jeans, running shoes, and a black quilted down jacket, all over a petite build. How is he going to know it's a girl when she flashes by on the bike? Especially at night. If the bike was coming toward him through the intersection, its headlights would be in his eyes…assuming the incident happened the way he said it did."

"Fifty-fifty chance," Torrez said.

"I don't think so. Besides, motorcyclists are *he* until proven otherwise."

Torrez grinned again. "Always?"

"Absolutely always."

They reached the back door of the ambulance and one of the EMTs appeared at Torrez's elbow. "Sheriff, Dr. Perrone's on his way, but it's going to be a few minutes." The sheriff didn't reply but stood with his hands in his pockets, looking down at the shrouded figure under the light pole and then at the crumpled motorcycle beyond. Off to the right, Mears was in the process of marking one of the digs in the pavement where the bike's foot peg had struck.

"Did someone call the chief?" Torrez asked.

"Dispatch says he's in Deming," Mears said. "They're trying to reach him. Kenderman was the only village officer on duty, Bobby."

Torrez nodded and twisted at the waist, looking across the intersection toward the bridge. "Did Maggie see all of this?"

"Yes," Estelle replied. "She drove past me on Bustos as I was coming out of the cleaners. I heard the chase during the entire time it took her to drive from there to this point. That's six blocks. And she wasn't in a hurry."

"So the chase could have been over a considerable distance," Torrez said. He shrugged. "How long does it take to cover six blocks at thirty miles an hour? That's about what Maggie was driving? If they were after each other the whole time she was moseyin' down the street, they could have covered ten or twelve blocks, maybe more."

"The chase sounded like at least that," Estelle said.

"Then someone saw it," Torrez shrugged. "No doubt about it. Has anyone talked to Maggie yet?"

"No, sir."

"And what's he doing?" Torrez jerked his chin in the direction of Kenderman's patrol car. Deputy Tom Pasquale was walking slowly around the village unit, flashlight in hand.

"I told him that he needed to check for contact between the car and the bike, sir," Mears said.

"Kenderman's unit collided with the bike?"

"We don't know that," Estelle said, and Torrez looked at her with interest. "At least not yet," she added.

"Well, shit," Sheriff Torrez said. "He's runnin' after her without any of his emergency equipment on, he's not talkin' to Dispatch…what does he think he's doin'?"

"That's a good question," Estelle said.

Torrez nodded and ambled toward Kenderman's patrol car. "Let's see what he's got to say."

Lights from Alan Perrone's BMW flashed across their faces as the assistant state medical examiner tucked the car in behind the ambulance. The coroner's dapper figure joined the shadows under the utility pole.

"Impound the bike and the car both," Torrez said.

"Impound the patrol car?" Pasquale asked.

"Yep," Torrez said. "And somebody find Chief Mitchell and tell him that he needs to hustle his ass back here."

THREE

THE PHONE RANG six times before the receiver was picked up. No one came on the line immediately, but Estelle could hear her husband's soft voice in the background, sounding as if he was explaining something to a small set of stubborn ears. Her mother's voice surprised her. Normally, Teresa Reyes didn't bother with the telephone; the modern gadget was a chore for clawed, arthritic fingers.

"Hello?" Teresa sounded as if she were cautiously exploring the inside of a dark, unfamiliar closet.

"Hey there, *Mamá*," Estelle said. By looking south, she could see the corner fence a few blocks away that marked the front yard of their house on South Twelfth Street.

"Are you all right?" Teresa asked, switching immediately to Spanish.

"I'm fine, *Mamá*. There was a nasty accident up here on Bustos, so I'm going to be a while."

"We heard the sirens," Teresa said.

"I bet you did. From where I'm standing, I can see the front yard. We're right in front of the Don Juan. How are *los hijos?*"

"Carlos went to bed about ten minutes ago," Teresa said, and Estelle smiled. Her youngest son, not yet four, "enjoyed his dreams," as her husband Francis was fond of saying. "Francisco is learning how to play chess with the grand master."

"It's hard to imagine that little anarchist following the rules. He drives Francis crazy."

"He's inventive, *hija. Padrino* deserves a medal for patience."

"He's playing with *Padrino?*"

"Yes. The three of them are in the dining room."

A voice in the background, intending to be heard on the phone across the room, was unmistakably Bill Gastner's. "Ask her if she's going to be home in time for some cake, or if we should finish it up."

"Tell him to finish it," Estelle said. "We've got a mess."

"There's always something," Teresa said. "We thought you'd be home earlier."

"So did I, *Mamá.*"

"Here's your husband," Teresa said abruptly. "I'm going to bed now."

"Okay, *Mamá.* I…" Estelle started to say, but the receiver was already in transit. Dr. Francis Guzman stopped what he was saying to his son in mid-sentence, and Estelle pictured him standing beside the kitchen table with the chess pieces strewn here and there, one hand on top of little Francisco's head, ready to steer the child if necessary.

"Where are you, *querida?*" Francis asked.

"If you step outside the front door, you could look up the street and see me," she replied. "Right in the intersection by the Don Juan. It's going to be a little bit longer, I guess."

"Bad?"

"One fatal. A girl riding a motorcycle hit the utility pole."

"Ouch."

"*Verdad,* ouch. It looks like there was something going on that involved a village policeman, so it's getting complicated."

"Which cop?"

"Kenderman."

"Huh. He was chasing her, you mean?"

"I'm not sure. But it looks that way."

"Have you talked with Chief Mitchell?"

"That's who we're waiting on right now," Estelle said. "He's on his way back from Deming."

"And sometime soon, we hope." She heard her son's voice again in the background, plaintive and high-pitched, and then Francis said, "The kid wants to know when you'll be home."

"I have no idea," Estelle said. "And I know how he loves answers like that."

Francis chuckled. "We miss you, *querida*. Want to talk to birthday boy?"

"Of course she does," Bill Gastner said. "Hey, sweetheart," he added, and his voice boomed into Estelle's ear after the quiet, almost-whisper of her husband. "Thanks for all the goodies. But no more birthdays now."

"You're declaring a moratorium?"

"I should have, about thirty years ago. What do you have going on up there?"

"A motorcycle smacked the utility pole on the corner of Twelfth and Bustos. A young woman was killed."

"Anyone we know?"

Estelle looked down at the driver's license that Deputy Pasquale had handed her a few minutes before. "Colette Parker," she said. A small, almost elfinlike face stared up at her, and Estelle turned the laminated license slightly to cut the glare from the flashlight held under her arm.

"Colette Parker. The name rings a really faint bell," Gastner said.

"She's twenty-two, worked in the supermarket," Estelle said. She remembered a slight, quick-moving figure, blonde hair cut in a pageboy and hooked behind jugged ears, a small neat girl in her old-fashioned white apron, far more fetching in person than she appeared in the motor vehicle department photo. "In that little deli the new owners put in." She turned the license over and saw the motorcycle endorsement.

"Don't remember. But I don't hang out in delis much, either. I probably know her folks."

Estelle heard the small voice in the background again, and Gastner said something unintelligible. "Your bonehead son thinks his bishop is a rook," Gastner added. "There's something about diagonal moves that escapes him." Estelle heard a giggle and then a conspiratorial conversation between the little boy and his father.

"Don't let him con you, sir. He plays with Francis all the time. He knows what the rules are."

"You'd never know it. And they're playing two against one, so that tells you how fair the whole setup is in the first place.

Anyway, you about to wrap things up down there? Are we going to see you this evening?''

"Ah, no...probably not. We've got a problem or two."

"There's always those," Gastner said, and Estelle grinned at the broad implication in his tone—*they're your problems now, sweetheart.* "I'm about to wrap up this important tourney and head for the hills. Anything I can do for you?"

"I don't think so. I'm sorry I got held up. I had the best intentions."

"Don't give it a second thought. I know how these things go. Give my regards to Roberto."

"I'll do that." She turned to glance toward where Sheriff Robert Torrez had been standing talking to Perry Kenderman, and was startled to see that two additional figures had arrived and were hunkered over the motorcycle. "I'll see you tomorrow, probably."

"Sounds good. Be careful."

Estelle switched off the phone. She looked across the intersection again and saw that District Attorney Daniel Schroeder had turned his attention from the bike to her. He regarded her thoughtfully from across Twelfth Street. If he was actually listening to what the man standing beside him was saying, he gave no indication. Estelle started across the street, and Schroeder reached out a hand to contact Chief Eddie Mitchell's shoulder. Mitchell looked up and saw Estelle. The two men waited by the motorcycle as she approached.

Mitchell stood with both hands on his hips, blunt jaw clamped askew as if daring his opponent to throw his best punch. At one point, both Estelle and Eddie Mitchell had been sheriff's deputies before roads diverged. Mitchell had left to join the Sheriff's Department in Bernalillo County, an area that included the huge metroplex of Albuquerque. He had passed the lieutenant's exam and then abruptly quit to return to the village of Posadas to take the chief's job when Eduardo Martínez retired.

Whatever forces drew Mitchell, a native of Pittsburgh, to the tiny New Mexican village was anyone's guess. Other than innocuous remarks like "Pretty country," he'd never bothered to explain.

A stocky bear of a man, Mitchell was as quick on his feet as a dancer. He waited, hands on his hips, brows furrowed.

"Evening," Schroeder offered. As usual, Schroeder's suit was immaculate, and the light from the street lamp winked off the polished gold rims of his glasses. The same height as Mitchell, the district attorney gave up a good fifty pounds to the chief of police.

"Hello, sir," Estelle said. "Chief." She nodded at Mitchell, and he extended his hand. His grip was firm, and he didn't let go. His light blue eyes locked on Estelle's, and for a long minute, he stood silently, as if trying to read her mind.

"Bobby says he's going to impound the patrol car," Mitchell said finally. His voice was a light tenor. He released his grip.

"Yes, sir."

"Is there something to make you think that there was contact between the car and the cycle?"

"No. It's just a very good possibility."

"A possibility?"

"Yes, sir."

Mitchell searched Estelle's impassive face for a moment. "Kenderman tells me that the cyclist ran a stop sign at Highland, right in front of him."

"That's not true, sir."

"Tell me what's true."

"She may well have run a stop sign, or half a dozen of them, during the time he was chasing her. But it didn't happen the way he says it did."

Schroeder ran his right hand through thinning blond hair. "Did the Volvo lady see anything?"

"Her name's Maggie Archer. The bike crossed directly in front of her, but she had time to stop. There was no contact. Even as the bike hit the pavement and started somersaulting, the patrol car entered the intersection, right in front of Mrs. Archer's car. She had a grandstand seat. Mears is talking with her right now."

"I see he is," Schroeder said. He thrust his hands into his pockets. "Tell me what you think happened, Estelle."

Briefly, Estelle recounted what she had first heard, and then seen. "It was a chase over several blocks, sir. If Mrs. Archer traveled six blocks during the time that I heard the police car and the bike, then they could have covered twice that distance."

"You heard them turning this way and that?"

"Yes, sir."

Mitchell shook his head and gazed down at the bike. He toed the back tire with his boot. "So if Kenderman says that he initiated chase at the corner of Twelfth and Highland, he'd be lying."

"Yes, sir."

"And you can't see any way around that."

"No, sir."

Mitchell puffed out his cheeks and exhaled slowly. "And no lights or siren."

"No, sir."

"And no conversation with Dispatch."

"No, sir. The radio in the patrol car was turned off when I looked inside. Even if he had it on during the chase, he didn't use it. The sheriff was home, monitoring the channel. He says that Kenderman wasn't talking to Dispatch."

The chief rocked the cycle's back tire back and forth against the small amount of slack in the drive chain. "I think we all need to confer with Officer Kenderman," he said finally. "I'd like both you and the sheriff in on it."

"Certainly."

"Right now, Kenderman thinks that it's his word against yours…and I assume he doesn't know where you were standing when you heard the chase—or even *if* you heard it, for that matter. Is that correct?"

"I don't see how he could."

"Good. Then let's leave it that way for a little while," Mitchell said with a curt nod. "There's always a chance that there's a great big unknown in all this mess. We need to give Kenderman every opportunity." He looked hard at Estelle. "After all, there is the possibility that what you heard wasn't related to this accident."

"No, sir, that's not a possibility," Estelle replied, but Mitchell shrugged.

"We'll talk to the officer again and see. Is it all right if he rides down with me?"

Estelle hesitated. She liked Eddie Mitchell and trusted him, but she wanted nothing to inadvertently bolster Perry Kenderman's confidence. "I'd prefer that he rode in with one of the deputies, sir."

"In custody?"

"That's not necessary."

"All right." Mitchell pivoted at the waist to survey the intersection. "Let's get this mess cleared up."

As the chief stepped away from the bike, Dan Schroeder held out a hand and touched Estelle on the arm. "I need to talk with you for a minute." So far, he hadn't said a word about the fatality, and it was evident to Estelle that he'd been patiently waiting for that business to be wrapped up.

Schroeder watched Mitchell's blocky form retreating across the intersection toward Bob Torrez and Perry Kenderman. For a moment he remained silent with his thoughts. "Are you ready for grand jury tomorrow?"

Estelle sighed. "If I fall asleep on the stand, poke me."

Schroeder managed a tight smile. "Long day, eh."

"Very."

"I had a call from George Enriquez last night."

Estelle raised an eyebrow but said nothing. A long-time Posadas resident and owner of an insurance agency for more than twenty years, George Enriquez qualified as a town father as much as anyone. But beginning at nine o'clock Tuesday morning, a grand jury would start reviewing evidence that Enriquez had engaged in fraudulent insurance practices for more than a decade. District Attorney Schroeder would be seeking indictments on twenty-eight separate counts of insurance fraud, including one count that involved deputy Thomas Pasquale as a victim of the scam.

"Enriquez wants to deal."

"Deal? I wouldn't think he had much of a bargaining position, sir," Estelle said.

"In part, it's the same old song and dance...give him a few weeks, and he'd clean up the mess, make financial amends—the

same sort of nonsense that we've heard from him too many times
before.''

Estelle nodded and waited.

"And then he said that he wanted to meet with me today."
Schroeder turned toward the utility pole and looked at his watch.
"At two p.m. in my office in Deming. That was seven hours
ago."

"What did he have to say?"

Schroeder straightened his sleeve carefully over the watch.
"He never showed."

"Maybe he changed his mind."

"That's possible. But he's not home, and the answering machine at his office says that they'll be closed until Friday. It gives
an 800 number for emergencies."

"You mean he skipped?" The idea of George Enriquez up-
rooting himself and fleeing Posadas was ludicrous. Whenever she
saw him, Estelle thought of stuffed animals. Enriquez had the
same hugability, the same sort of flannel personality, as a favorite
old polyester pet. He wasn't the kind to go furtive, slipping
across the border to life on the gold coast. After state insurance
investigators had finished pawing through his office files during
the past months, there wasn't much left to hide.

Besides, nearly every incident of fraud that Estelle and state
officers had investigated had been penny ante, the sort of incom-
prehensible crime for which the monetary rewards were counted
in occasional hundreds. In Deputy Pasquale's case, George Enriquez had told the young man that his motorcycle policy was
held by a major company. Each month, the financially naive
Pasquale had paid his premium directly to Enriquez. When Pasquale had made a minor claim, Enriquez had made prompt set-
tlement with a personal check. Pasquale was pleased, and completely nonplussed to discover later that he had no policy, that
in all likelihood his monthly insurance payment was going directly into Enriquez's pocket. Other instances with other customers were sometimes lesser, sometimes greater in financial risk.

"Skipped, schmipped," Schroeder said with a shrug. "We
don't know. Neither does his wife. He left the house this morning. That was the last time she saw him."

Estelle had talked with Connie Enriquez several times and had found the woman an enigma. She wasn't the kind who would sit home and twist rosary beads around her knuckles as her husband's world fell apart. At one point in the investigation into her husband's affairs, she had simply shrugged her gargantuan shoulders and said, "He made his bed. Let him lie in it."

"He didn't give any hint about what else was on his mind? When he talked to you on the phone? You said 'in part' it was the same old story."

"Uh huh." Schroeder made a face. "Let me just tell you what he said, word for word. First, I said that I didn't see that we had anything to talk about, that he could ask to testify before the grand jury if he wanted to but that he didn't have to. I made it clear to him that he didn't need to be there, that his attorney didn't need to be there. He understood all that. I told him that the grand jury session would probably take most of the week and that he had at least that much time to put all his ducks in a row. That's when he said, 'I can give you something.' I said, 'Something like what?' And then he went off on this long song and dance about all his little shenanigans being so inconsequential."

"The Popes would have liked to have heard that when their house burned down," Estelle said. "Had anyone survived to file a claim."

"I know, I know," Schroeder said impatiently. "And we've been through that. When he finally wound down, I said again, 'Something like what?' And this time, he said, *'I can give you Guzman.'*"

Estelle heard perfectly clearly, but out of stunned reflex said, "Give you what?"

"'I can give you Guzman.' That's what he said. *'I can give you Guzman.'*"

"I can give you Guzman," Estelle repeated.

"Correct."

"And then what did he say?"

"Nothing. He said he couldn't talk on the phone. That he'd see me at two p.m. in my office in Deming. End of story. He never showed. Like I said, he's not home now." Schroeder looked at his watch again. "Or at least he wasn't fifteen minutes ago."

"So what did he mean by that?" Estelle regretted the question as soon as it slipped out.

"I don't know," Schroeder said. "I was hoping you could shed some light."

"I'm the leadoff witness tomorrow for the grand jury. He'd be able to figure that out."

"Of course. You're the officer who put the case together before my office horned in." Schroeder managed another half smile. "The implication is obvious—that he knows something about you that I need to know—something that throws your grand jury testimony into question."

"Or that he was just bluffing."

"That's possible. Unlikely, but possible." He took a deep breath and hitched up his slacks, then smoothed his suit coat back into perfection. "Keep me posted on what happens with Kenderman," he said. "And we'll take Mr. Enriquez one step at a time. Maybe he just buried himself in a hole somewhere with a good bottle. Being told that you're the target of a grand jury investigation is a fearsome thing, Estelle. It shakes lots of scary things out of the tree. Run and hide isn't an unusual reflex."

Estelle nodded, her empty stomach still clenched in a knot. She watched Deputy Tom Pasquale slide into the village police car, start it, and pull away, headed toward the county maintenance barn and the secure bay the sheriff's department kept there. Perry Kenderman stood and watched, flanked on one side by Sheriff Robert Torrez and on the other by Chief Eddie Mitchell. The ambulance had already departed with the pathetic bundle that had been Colette Parker.

"Shake the tree," Estelle muttered as she stepped off the curb.

FOUR

ESTELLE GLANCED IN the rearview mirror as she eased the county car to a stop just south of the Highland Court—Twelfth Street intersection. Chief Mitchell's sedan idled up behind hers, followed by the sheriff's rumbling, disreputable pickup truck. Kenderman rode with the sheriff, and Estelle knew that the village officer's mood wouldn't be soothed by comfortable small talk. Torrez favored silence.

The intersection was illuminated by a single streetlight on the northwest corner. Estelle switched off the ignition and sat quietly. If Colette Parker had been westbound on Highland Court, racing pell mell toward the intersection, she would have clearly seen Kenderman's village patrol car head on across Twelfth Street. That the girl would blast right through the intersection, ignoring the village patrol car and inviting a chase, was not beyond the realm of possibility. But that didn't jibe with what Estelle had heard.

She glanced in the rearview mirror and saw the huge form of Sheriff Torrez, followed by Kenderman's slender shadow. Estelle got out of her car and closed the door. Chief Mitchell had been jotting something on his clipboard, but after a moment he tossed it on the seat. He glanced at Kenderman as he stepped out of his car but said nothing. "This is as good a place to start as any," Estelle said.

Across the street, a porch light flicked off. "That's nice," Mitchell muttered but didn't elaborate.

"Show us exactly where you were when you first saw the motorcycle," Estelle said to Kenderman.

His gaze shifted across the intersection, flicking this way and that as if he was uncertain about which version of the incident to embrace. "Right there," he said. He walked to the middle of the street and pointed at the eastbound lane of Highland Court. "I was just pulling up to the stop sign here."

"You hadn't stopped completely yet when you saw the bike?"

"Well, hell…I guess I was just comin' to a stop. I was putting on the brakes when I saw it."

"And where was she?"

Kenderman turned and looked over his right shoulder. "Comin' that way."

"So she ran the stop on the east side of the intersection?"

"Yes."

"And then?"

"Well," Kenderman said, "she turned on down this way," he pivoted in place, looking back down Twelfth Street the way they had come. "Right for the bridge."

"And that's when you initiated the chase?"

"Well, I wasn't pushin' it too hard," Kenderman said lamely. He glanced at Chief Mitchell.

"How well do you know Colette Parker?" Torrez asked. He tossed the question out casually, as if he really didn't want to know.

"I know who she is, all right."

"But you didn't know it was her when you started the chase?"

"No."

"You didn't recognize her bike, or anything like that?"

"No. The light wasn't all that good, and she was movin' kind of fast, anyways."

"I see," Torrez said, sounding as if he clearly *didn't* see.

Estelle's telephone chirped. "Guzman."

"Estelle," Sergeant Mears's matter-of-fact voice said. "We've got us a little tangle here. I've been talking with Maggie Archer, and she tells me that she knows Colette Parker. In fact, Colette was one of her students about five years ago."

"Okay." She turned her back on her three companions and walked toward the rear of her car.

"The thing is that according to Mrs. Archer, Colette has two little kids."

Estelle groaned. "Where are they, Tom."

"With the grandmother, apparently."

"*The* grandmother?"

"Colette's mother. Her name's Barbara Parker. Lives over on Third Street, north of the park. That's the address on Colette's license, too. They all live there together, apparently. Mrs. Archer said that she's known the Parker woman for years. She's got some counseling job at the school."

"You're going over there now?"

"Yes, ma'am."

"How old are the two kids, did Mrs. Archer know?"

"She guessed that the oldest might be four. Something like that. Maybe four. Colette had the first one the spring of her senior year of high school. That's when she dropped out."

Estelle sighed. "Small favors."

"Pardon?"

"I was thinking that at least the kids are with someone right now, Tom. That's all. Let me know when you've talked with Mrs. Parker, all right?"

"Yep. Linda and I are headed that way right now."

"What's the street address?"

"Just a second." After a brief rustling, Mears said, "Seven oh nine Third Street."

"Thanks." Estelle switched off the phone. She didn't turn around immediately but stood silently, leaning against the back fender of the unmarked car. She closed her eyes, allowing the memory of the distant chase to replay. The Third Street address for Barbara and Colette Parker would be in the distance to the north, approximately where car and cycle were when she first heard them.

She turned and walked back toward the other three. "Perry," she said, "are you sure that's the version that you want to go with?"

His eyes were both frightened and wary. He glanced sideways at Chief Mitchell, but Mitchell's gaze was noncommittal.

"It ain't a *version*, Undersheriff," Kenderman said. "It's what happened. I don't know why you got such a problem with what I'm tryin' to tell you." He gestured up the street. "I was there, she run the sign, I went after her. She dumped it just past the bridge." He took a short breath, as if a sharp pain had jabbed him in the solar plexus. "Christ, you was on Bustos yourself. You saw."

"Yes, I did," Estelle said gently, refusing to rise to the indignation in his tone.

"Tell you what," Mitchell said easily. "We'll check in with you tomorrow, Estelle. Give you a little time to talk with some folks. We'll go from there. Fair enough?"

Estelle nodded.

He reached out a hand as if to take Kenderman by the shoulder but stopped just shy of contact. "I'll run Perry over to the S.O. so he can make a formal statement and then take him on home. Pasquale is going to take the deposition?"

Estelle nodded. "He'll be at the office. We'll be back in a little bit."

"Nothing else right now, then?"

Estelle shook her head.

"Come on," Mitchell said, touching Kenderman's elbow. He managed to sound sympathetic. Estelle watched them leave, and as the taillights faded toward the bridge, shook her head in disgust.

"You're sure Kenderman's lying, aren't you." Sheriff Torrez moved out of the middle of the street to allow another car to pass. Two elderly faces peered out at them as the sedan shuffled by.

"Yes, I'm sure," Estelle said. "He's lying, but I don't know why."

"To save his sorry ass, obviously," Torrez said. "He didn't follow any kind of procedure, and he forced a fatality."

"Maybe that's it."

Torrez looked askance at her, then grinned. "Let me know when you're ready."

Estelle took a deep breath. "I just want to be sure."

"You *are* sure. So where do you want to start?"

"Half the people in Posadas either heard what happened tonight or saw a part of it. It shouldn't be hard to retrace a pretty fair approximation of the chase route.'' She glanced at her watch. ''I hate to let any of this wait until tomorrow.''

Torrez grunted what passed for a chuckle. ''Pasquale and Mears are on until midnight. Jackie's on after that. It'll give them something to do. Like I said, where do you want to start?''

Estelle turned and looked across the street. ''How about two ten Twelfth,'' she said. ''They turned out their porch light just after we drove up. That means they're home.''

''And don't want to talk to us,'' Torrez said.

''All the more reason.'' She reached into her car for her clipboard and double-checked the tape inside the microcassette before sliding it into her jacket pocket. She'd taken two steps back toward 210 Twelfth when the phone on her belt awakened once more.

''Guzman.''

''The two kids are home with their grandmother,'' Tom Mears said without preamble.

''They're all right?''

Mears hesitated. ''They're in bed, asleep. I guess they'll find out in the morning.''

Estelle heard a sound in the background that could have been a yelp of pain, a sob, or both. ''Mrs. Parker's with you?''

''Yes, ma'am. What I wanted to tell you was that she says Kenderman stopped by earlier this evening to see Colette. They've been going together for a little while.''

''How long?'' She looked across at Torrez and shook her head wearily.

''For about six months, the mother says. Colette wanted to break it off. Kenderman came by this evening, while he was on duty. He wanted to talk to Colette, and she didn't want to see him.''

Estelle backpedaled as if she'd been shoved and slumped against the side of her car. ''Ay,'' she murmured.

''Mrs. Parker tells me that sometimes after Colette puts her daughters to bed, she likes to take a short ride on the bike. No traffic, all by herself—that sort of thing. That's what she did tonight.''

"And Kenderman followed her."

"Mrs. Parker doesn't know about that."

"She didn't hear anything?"

"Apparently not. She had the television on and wears earphones so the noise doesn't disturb the kids."

"Thanks, Tom. You're going to get a statement from her tonight?"

"If I can. She's not doing too well."

"Do what you can. Bobby and I are going to talk to some neighbors at the other end of the racetrack." She switched off and then pushed the phone's autodial. "Wow," she breathed. She looked at Robert Torrez and rolled her eyes heavenward. "Looks like it started as a domestic," she said. "Nothing's going to be simple."

Sheriff Torrez waited patiently, arms folded across his chest. Dispatcher Ernie Wheeler answered Estelle's call.

"Ernie, I need a name and number for two ten North Twelfth Street."

"It's Luis and Maria Rubay," Torrez muttered just loud enough for Estelle to hear.

"The sheriff says to check a listing for Rubay," Estelle added. "R-U-B-A-Y." She waited for a moment and then jotted down the number. "Thanks. The sheriff and I will be at that address for a few minutes."

As she was pocketing the phone once more, Torrez nodded across the street at the small brown adobe on the northwest corner, directly across Highland Court from the Rubay's at 210. "If Maria didn't see or hear anything, then we can talk to Mrs. Corning. She's been watching us all the time we've been here."

Estelle grinned. "You know everybody in every house? You sound like Bill Gastner, the walking gazetteer of Posadas County."

"Not quite," Torrez said. "I don't know who lives over there, for instance." He jerked his chin at the two-story cinder-block monstrosity on the northeast corner of the intersection.

"Maybe we'll find out," Estelle said. "Somebody knows exactly what happened."

"Yep," Torrez agreed. "Perry Kenderman, for one."

FIVE

ESTELLE GUZMAN pushed the doorbell button in the center of an enameled tin design that looked like a flattened, road-killed lizard. Inside, they heard the first notes of "Ave Maria" on the chimes. There was no response, no movement or shuffling from within. No dog yapped greeting or warning.

Estelle turned and lifted an eyebrow at Torrez. "Tell me I wasn't dreaming when I saw the porch light turned off," she said.

"Maybe on a timer. Or not. Maria marches to her own drummer."

"She an aunt of yours?"

"One of the cousins."

"She lives by herself?"

"Yep. Her husband Luis died a month or so ago."

"I'm sorry to hear that." She pushed the button again, wondering how much information she could pry out of the sheriff, one isolated sentence at a time. She listened to the six soaring notes of the doorbell once more. With no response, she stepped back and drew out her telephone, dialing the number Dispatch had provided.

In three rings, a woman's voice answered with a warbling "Yeesss?" that sounded as if she was holding the phone in one hand and a dripping egg beater in the other, interrupted midrecipe.

"Mrs. Rubay?"

"Yes." The reply was guarded, then brightened. "And whatever you're selling, I'm really glad you called. I just declared bankruptcy and can't find anyone who'll take my checks."

Estelle glanced at Torrez and grinned. "Mrs. Rubay, this is Undersheriff Estelle Guzman with the Posadas County Sheriff's Department. Would it be possible to talk with you for a few minutes?"

"I don't see why not."

"We're just outside your address. Is this a good time?"

"Sure. Hang on just a minute. I'm just cutting up my husband, and I don't want the pieces to blow all over the dining room floor."

The phone clicked off. "She's butchering her husband," Estelle said, and Torrez nodded.

"I'm not surprised."

In a moment the dead bolt clacked. When the woman opened the door, Estelle realized that she knew Maria Rubay as one of the part-timers who worked at the post office. No doubt Cousin Robert would have dredged up that basic information eventually if pressed hard enough.

"Evening, Maria," Torrez said. He ducked his head in greeting, both hands firmly in his back pockets.

"I was about to call the police because of all the vagrants standing around out in the middle of the street a little bit ago," Maria said, and favored them with a warm smile, an expression that illuminated her classic oval face. She looked at Estelle. "You have an awfully nice telephone voice," she said. "You could be one of those phone solicitors who keeps me such good company in the evening. Come on in."

"Thank you."

She held the door for them, looking up as Torrez slipped past her. "You've grown another inch or so," she said, and her cousin actually laughed. "How did a family of runts produce you and your sister," she added. She shook her head and then waved at the sofa in the living room. "Let's sit."

"We're sorry to bother you, Mrs. Rubay," Estelle started, but the woman interrupted.

"*Maria* works just fine. And it's no bother. I'm glad for the company. You know, I just don't answer the door after dark. Especially with Luis gone now. I just ignore it."

"I understand."

"You want to see what I'm putting together, Bobby?" Before
the sheriff could answer, Maria Rubay rose quickly to her feet.
"Of course you do. Come into the dining room."

On the table, a vast sea of family photos lay in no obvious
order, with the scissors and glue holding down a pile of scrap.
"I'm cutting Luis out of every old photograph I can find." She
leaned over the table and smoothed the large piece of tag board,
the surface already a third covered. Luis Rubay's pleasant face,
dominated in more recent photos by his heavy Fu Manchu mus-
tache and stubbly brush cut, gazed up at them in dozens of versions.

"When I'm all done, I'm going to have copies made for the
family," she said. "Nice idea, yes?"

"Yes, it is," Estelle said. She glanced at the pile of photo-
graphic rubble to the left. "He was quite a fisherman, wasn't
he?"

"Yes, and I'm hacking out all the damn fish," Maria said.
"A trout is a trout. Maybe I'll save one or two, just to make
him happy."

"It looks like he was a happy man, Maria." And true enough,
Luis Rubay's engaging smile was missing only in one or two
candid snaps.

"He was." She straightened up and took a deep breath. "But
you didn't come to talk about this, I'm sure." She cast a with-
ering glance at the sheriff. "Although a little visit by Miss Gayle
and his nibs here might be a nice thing, once in a while."

"Actually, Maria, we're interested in what you may have seen
or heard earlier this evening. Right around eight o'clock."

"Ah," Maria said. "When the president was talking."

"I missed that," Estelle said.

"No, you didn't," Maria said. "Yakketty-yak-yak, my fellow
Americans." She waved a hand in dismissal. "Didn't miss a
thing." She smoothed the tag board collage again gently. "This
is about all the racing going on outside?"

"We'd be interested in whatever you heard, Maria." She
withdrew the small microcassette recorder from her pocket, and
Maria nodded.

"Long, dull evening," she replied. "I went out to empty the

garbage just before the prez came on, and saw the village cops careening around after a kid on a motorcycle. That's the sum and substance of my evening. I assume there's been an accident, and that somebody's been hurt? Otherwise you wouldn't be here."

"We'd like to know what you saw, Maria," Estelle said, and Maria smiled at her.

"A fountain of information you are," she said with a chuckle. "Okay. I went outside, just before eight…that's when the prez was supposed to start his spiel. I put the trash in the can. There's a board fence right there, between me and Highland Court, as I'm sure you already know. And it continues around the front corner, too. I heard them first, you know. Before I saw them. Sound like that travels."

"What did you hear?"

"The two of them. I guess I didn't notice until I actually saw the headlights and all, coming right down Highland Court toward me. They were both just ripping along." She beckoned at the two officers. "Step outside. I'll show you exactly where I was." Estelle's heart felt like a large chunk of inert lead sinking down through her innards. She realized that she had been hanging on to a slender hope that she was somehow mistaken, that Maria Rubay would tell them that Perry Kenderman had been stopped on the street, after all, had seen the speeding bike, and taken off in hot pursuit.

"Come, come," Maria said, and took Estelle by the elbow. With Sheriff Torrez following, they walked across the kitchen, out the back door, and stood on the concrete stoop. "There's *los botes*." She nodded at the twin garbage cans. "And this is the fence. That's Highland Court." She stepped off the stoop and walked the eight short strides to the cedar fence and rested both hands on it, then pointed to the east, toward the intersection. "And that's Twelfth." She walked to the two trash cans. "Now, when I'm standing here," and she planted herself in front of one of the cans, "I can see right through the gaps in this old fence. And what am I looking at?" She pointed east. "Right across Twelfth and on down Highland."

"And where were the bike and the police car?"

"Like I said, coming right at me. Coming right down Highland Court, headlights bobbing, motors roaring." She turned and raised her eyebrows at Estelle.

"So it appeared to you that the police car was in pursuit of the motorcycle?"

"Certainly was. Flyin' low, both of them."

"And you're absolutely certain that the police car was following the bike on Highland, westbound?" When Maria Rubay looked puzzled, Estelle quickly added, "You're certain that the police car didn't appear out of some other street to cut off the bike. The officer wasn't on Highland Court on this side of the intersection, for example?"

"No," Maria said patiently. "Most certainly not. One behind the other. Vaaarrooom. Vaaarrooom. If either of the drivers had lost control, they'd have crashed right into my house."

"And what then? After you saw them race through the intersection and turn southbound on Twelfth, what did you do?"

"Then I went into the house to listen to the prez." She rubbed her arms. "And this is a chilly breeze."

"Did you put the garbage in the cans before or after you saw the chase?"

"Before. I crammed on the lid, put the board on top to keep the skunks out, and was about to turn to go back in the house when here they come." She clasped her hands together. "Like I said, I heard them first and naturally enough glanced that way. Swoosh, whoosh, there they all go." She shrugged. "Then I went back in the house."

"Immediately?"

"And that means...what, did I stand around outside? No, I went right back in the house." She grimaced and reached for the back door. "I heard the sirens later." She held the door for Estelle and Torrez. "Just minutes later. And then a bit ago, I heard voices outside, snuck a peek, and saw the convocation. I should have left the porch light on for you, but it's on a timer, and I didn't even think. I heard the doorbell, but by then I was back to my project, and just ignored it."

"That's all right."

"Nobody ignores the darn telephone, though, right?" Maria smiled conspiratorially.

"Usually not, no."

Back inside the brightness of the kitchen, Maria looked sympathetic. "I'm not sure I told you what you want to hear, but that's the way it happened. At least as far as I'm concerned."

Estelle held the small tape recorder to her lips, forehead furrowed in thought. "Did you hear any other vehicles?"

"Around that same time? None that I noticed. There might have been another one on Highland, way on down the street. It seems to me that I saw some lights. But I don't know. Maybe just someone backing out of a driveway, you know. I didn't pay attention."

The undersheriff switched off the recorder and slipped it into her pocket.

"You guys want a snack of some sort?"

Torrez shook his head. "Many thanks, Maria. A deputy may be coming around with a deposition for you to sign in a day or two."

"Just whatever," she said cheerfully. "Bring Miss Gayle over."

"We'll do that."

Leaving Maria Rubay to her welter of photos and cropping, Estelle followed Robert Torrez down the long sidewalk to Twelfth Street. With hardly a glance up or down the street, Torrez crossed and then waited at Estelle's unmarked car as she ambled toward him, head down and lost in thought.

"Score one for you," he said when she reached the car. "And you were right about something else, too."

"What's that?"

"Maria called the bike rider 'he,' just like you said."

"Whoopee," Estelle said. She let out a sigh. "I'd just as soon be wrong about the whole mess, Bobby." Torrez made no reply. Estelle turned and gazed across the intersection. "Your cousin sounded sure of herself."

"Maria *is* sure of herself. Always has been. Even when she's wrong."

"I don't think she is, this time. But if we talk to ten witnesses, we'll hear ten versions," Estelle said. "I'd like to talk to…what did you say her name was? Mrs. Corning?"

"Yep."

"She's not a relative?" Estelle managed a smile.

"Nope. And actually, it's Miss Corning. She was my second-grade teacher."

"Ah," Estelle said. "Second grade. She's something of an institution, then."

Torrez hunched his shoulders. "I guess. Second grade was my three favorite years."

"Then Miss Corning is something of a saint, too," Estelle said, and glanced at her watch. "She's awake, so let's see if she answers her door. Then we can hear version number three."

The sheriff's broad face was impassive, but Estelle saw a little tick of his eyebrows and found herself wishing that she could read Robert Torrez's mind.

"What?" she asked.

"I was just wondering how all this would have turned out if you hadn't stopped at the dry cleaners."

"Scary thought."

SIX

SOMEWHERE IN the house, something ticked—a single, quiet little *snick* that might have been the thermostat trying to light the wall furnace, or the cooling coffeepot in the kitchen, or maybe even little Carlos, briefly awake and confirming that he could still snap his fingers the way his older brother had taught him.

Estelle lay flat on her back and stared up into the darkness. The luminous dial of the clock on the nightstand soundlessly flashed 2:52. An hour's sleep, maybe two and then her mind had churned the rest of her system awake.

"You want to get up and jog around the block?" Her husband's voice was hardly more than the softest exhalation, gentle and warm against her left ear. He was lying on his right side, and she wasn't sure when he had awakened.

"I'd be too tired to find my way back home," she whispered. She felt a finger trace the outer margin of her ear. "What time did *Padrino* finally leave?"

"He played one more game after you called. A little after nine, maybe."

She sighed. "I wanted to see his face when he opened the gifts from *los hijos*. I'm sorry I missed that."

A brief chuckle popped warm air against her ear. "He deserved an Academy Award." Estelle smiled at the thought. Bill Gastner, the retired lawman, had been given a western video sometime in the distant past by one of his own children, no doubt with the thought that the video would prompt the start of a collection. As far as she knew, the video had been gathering dust alone, sitting on top of a VCR whose guts, she was sure, showed no sign of wear.

Undaunted, her eldest son Francisco had been adamant in his choice of a birthday gift for *Padrino*. Francisco's agile little mind was convinced that everyone needed to own a personal copy of the same wonderful video that so enchanted him.

Estelle tried to picture Bill Gastner sitting through the loud, flashy attacks by the various dinosaurs that somehow had evolved a sophisticated yearning for bloody revenge on mankind. She knew that by the time the third whatever-saurus had galloped across the screen in full digital wonder, the old man's eyes would start to droop. Francisco remained convinced that *Padrino* would watch the dinosaur tape until he knew it by heart.

"It was only by incredible diplomacy on Bill's part that we didn't all end up watching the damn thing right then and there." Francis shifted position slightly so that the side of his face rested comfortably against his wife's shoulder. "Fortunately, he opened the present from Carlos first. I think Bill was intrigued with the concept of using modeling clay to hold the wrapping paper in place. He liked the knife, though."

"He already has about six of those utility tool things," Estelle said.

"Eight. He told Carlos that he has one lost in every room of his house. Anyway, he was able to use one of the thirty-nine blades to open the other packages, and Carlos liked that." He shifted a leg. "Your feet are like ice, *querida*."

"All the blood's in my head. My brain's going around in circles."

Francis puffed another hot breath against her shoulder. "Maybe if you tell me about it, it'll put us both to sleep."

"Ay," Estelle murmured. She wondered if Perry Kenderman was lying in bed too, eyes bloodshot, staring upward at the invisible barrier of his bedroom ceiling. "I've had better days, *Oso*."

"Nasty crash?"

"Very."

Francis made no response, and she reached across with her right hand and gathered a fistful of hair, tugging it just enough to rock his head gently. "One of the village cops made a bad mistake, *querido*."

Francis switched to Spanish, the words soft and graceful. *"Me puedes decir el cómo y el porqué?"* Estelle smiled. *Can you tell me the how and the why of it?* She had heard her mother, Teresa Reyes, say the same thing countless times to one or the other of the children during moments when something in their universe tangled.

"The only thing we know right now is *el qué, querido.* We know what happened. I was coming out of Kealey's and heard what I thought was a high-speed chase between a car and a motorcycle. Then I saw a motorcycle crash at the intersection of Bustos and Twelfth. A village police car entered the intersection at almost the same instant, for all intents and purposes in hot pursuit."

"What's the mistake?"

"Officer Kenderman says that's not the way it happened. Except for one little aspect, though, that's *exactly* what happened."

Francis puffed hot air against her shoulder, then said, "I'm lost."

"Kenderman's version doesn't match what happened, *Oso.* I know what I heard, and I know what I saw. He says he only started the chase a couple of blocks north of where the bike crashed. I know that's not true."

"You have other witnesses?"

"Yes. We talked to two ladies who live right at the intersection of Twelfth and Highland Court. They saw exactly what I heard. Maria Rubay was outside emptying the garbage and saw the whole thing. Ethel Corning lives on the other side of Highland and happened to glance out her window. She said she heard the garbage can lid, saw Maria, and then saw the rest."

"Ethel Corning?"

"Bobby's second-grade teacher."

"She of the cancerous pancreas."

"I'm sorry to hear that," Estelle whispered. "Bobby and I talked to her. She seemed so frail and wasted, but she never mentioned that she was ill."

"That she is. Don't linger in getting a signed deposition from her."

"A sharp mind, still. She described the incident exactly the way Maria Rubay did."

"And despite all this, Kenderman still maintains that he *wasn't* chasing the bike all over town? I guess I'm not surprised. He's trying to save his sorry ass. He doesn't know that you heard the whole thing?"

"No."

"I mean, you didn't tell him?"

"Nope. And for another thing, Kenderman lied to me about knowing who the victim was. The normal thing to do would be to rush to her side to see if he could administer some kind of first aid. He didn't do that. He *knew* who the victim was, and he panicked."

"That's even more support that the three witnesses are right," Francis said. "The cop and the kid on the bike are having a fun time drag racing, and now the cop knows he's in deep, deep *caca*."

"It wasn't fun they were having," Estelle said. "The girl's mother says that Kenderman and her daughter were arguing earlier in the evening."

"Huh." His hand moved down so that his index finger tapped the center of her chest. "So was he chasing after her just to talk to her again, and she's doing her best to ignore him, or," and he tapped a second finger, "was she *running* from him, out of fear?" He tapped with his ring finger. "Or, it could have just been a normal chase. Some traffic infraction, and she refuses to stop when he turns on the lights. Off they go."

"There's no such thing as a normal chase, *Oso*. You chase a bike, especially a kid, and someone's going to get hurt. We don't do it, and Chief Mitchell doesn't allow it. Nor did Chief Martínez before him. Kenderman would know that. Besides, he never turned on his red lights."

"He may have just forgotten them."

"Not likely, *querido*." She fell silent. She could tell that Francis was patiently waiting. "He followed her into the intersection so closely, you can't believe it," she said finally. "Right on her tail. It was almost as if he was trying to *force* her into a crash. Or even hit her."

"Maybe he was."

"And he lied to me besides."

"Well," Francis said and fell silent. His fingers resumed their gentle tapping. "Then you need to pick through the pieces until you find one that fits, as *Padrino* is fond of saying." His fingers slid upward and traced the line of her lower jaw. "And you're sure it was his car all the time."

"Reasonably. It was a start-to-finish thing. I didn't hear one car chasing, then that one leave off to be replaced by another."

"Is that possible, though?"

When she didn't respond, he stroked her cheek. "You asleep yet?"

"Uh uh." She squeezed his hand and pushed herself to a sitting position.

"What's Kenderman likely to do when he knows he's caught up in a lie?"

Estelle sighed and swung her legs off the side of the bed. "I don't know, *querido*. First I need to make sure I'm right about what happened. Then..." She stood up and flipped the bedding back up to cover the warm spot where she'd been lying. She bent over, found her husband's face in the dark, and kissed him hard. "Then I can start on the *porqué*."

SEVEN

BUSTOS AVENUE was a flat, lonely macadam desert. For the second time in six hours, Estelle Reyes-Guzman stood by her unmarked car in front of Kealey's Kleaners. The gas station across the street was dark. In the distance, she could hear the bass mutter of a tractor-trailer on the interstate. Above her head, the streetlight transformer fizzed and hummed.

She waited, leaning against the open door of her car, cell phone in hand.

"Okay, I'm here," Deputy Jackie Taber's soft voice announced. "The Parkers' house is just across the street." The deputy was driving Kenderman's patrol car. Eight blocks and the triangular wedge of Pershing Park separated Taber from the spot where Estelle's unit was parked in front of Kealey's—six tenths of a mile on the odometer. More than three thousand feet—ten football fields. Estelle closed her eyes, listening.

Two miles to the south, another tractor-trailer rode its Jake brake down the interstate exit ramp, a deep, guttural flutter of compressed exhaust that carried effortlessly on the still air.

"Wait a second," Estelle said. She listened until the sound of the truck faded. "Okay. Keep the phone open. The street's clear."

"Yep. See you in a bit."

Estelle slipped the phone into her jacket pocket and turned so that she was facing west, looking down the tunnel of widely spaced streetlights that was Bustos Avenue. She pictured the amber taillights of Maggie Archer's Volvo, ambling away from her down the street. Off to the north, she heard the faint chirp of tires and a muffled, almost strangled engine note that grew until the deputy backed off for the first corner.

The undersheriff found herself exhaling an imitation of the high, keening alto of the two-stroke motorcycle, pacing the speeding police car. At the same time, she watched Mrs. Archer's phantom Volvo make its way down the street. For a second, no sound carried at all as Taber flogged the car through the neighborhood most distant from Estelle's position, but then she heard the car turn south toward the bridge. Suddenly, even as Estelle's eyes fixed on the intersection six blocks away, the village car appeared, flashing into the intersection nose down as Jackie Taber braked hard, stopping in the middle of Twelfth Street on the south side of Bustos.

Estelle realized that she had been holding her breath. She pulled the phone out of her pocket. "That's it."

"Do you want me to put the car back in impound?" Deputy Taber asked. Estelle watched as the village car backed out into Bustos and then drove toward her.

"Yes. I'll meet you there."

A few minutes later, after parking the patrol car in the locked bay of the county maintenance barn, Jackie Taber slid into the passenger seat of the undersheriff's car. A faint wave of lavender accompanied her. A stout young woman, long enough in the military to have adopted a precise, economical habit of movement, she spun the key ring on her index finger.

"So," she said.

"So. What a mess."

"Tommy tells me that there are some holes in Perry Kenderman's story."

"Caverns is more like it. Kenderman is lying. It's that simple. Colette Parker was running from him."

"It could be that," Jackie said.

"Statistics say it is," Estelle replied, and the deputy grinned. "Colette's mother said that Perry stopped by the house earlier and had an argument with Colette." She held up an index finger. "Just a bit later, he chases her half way across town, drives her so hard that she makes a mistake and breaks her neck against the base of a utility pole. He's so shook that he can't bring himself to take a step toward her.'' She held up a second finger, then bound the two together with her left hand. ''I thought maybe there was a chance that it happened some other way.'' She shook her head. ''Hearing the patrol car again convinced me. I heard it right.''

''What do you want me to check tonight?''

''Nothing. Colette's two little kids are with their grandmother. You might keep a close watch on their place. That and Kenderman's apartment. Chief Mitchell said that he's going to do the same. We want to make sure Perry stays put until we have time to sort all this out.''

Taber nodded. ''You look beat.''

''I am. And irritated. I missed a birthday party for *Padrino*, for one thing. I have grand jury later this morning, and George Enriquez has gone missing just after he tells the district attorney that he's got something on me that he'll trade for immunity.''

Jackie leaned forward toward Estelle in astonishment. ''No shit?''

''*Verdad*, no shit.''

''Mr. Enriquez has an active imagination,'' Jackie said. ''What's the 'gone missing' part?''

''I don't know. His wife hasn't seen him since early Monday morning, when he said that he was going down to his office. I was going to swing by the house and talk to her on my way home.''

''You want some advice?''

''Sure.''

''Don't swing by. Just go home. Get some rest. There's nothing you can do about him at three o'clock in the morning. Don't worry about him now. Nail him later in grand jury.'' She unlatched the door and swung herself out of the car. ''He's desperate, Estelle. That's all.''

''That's what's kind of scary, Jackie. He's not the kind of guy who has a whole lot of practice being desperate. The same thing goes for Perry Kenderman. We've got two of a kind, Jackie.''

''At least that's what we *think*,'' the deputy said. She touched the brim of her Stetson and started to close the door.

''And thanks for the demo,'' Estelle said.

"Any time," Jackie grinned. "Tommy Pasquale is going to be irritated if he doesn't get the opportunity to shave some time off my record."

Estelle laughed. "He crashed a village car at the bridge once before. I'd hate to have to explain a repeat performance to Chief Mitchell."

Despite Jackie Taber's suggestion, Estelle did drive through the quiet neighborhoods of Posadas until she paused in front of 419 Mimbres Drive. The well-kept house was dark, with both garage doors down, handles locked horizontal. A single porch light burned above the front door, and Estelle grimaced. She knew that inside the house, Connie Enriquez was probably lying in bed, staring at the ceiling, wondering what had happened to her husband and her world—and hoping that come the wee hours of the morning, George Enriquez would show up under the porch light with nothing worse than the smell of alcohol on his breath.

EIGHT

IN 1952, AFTER POURING an eight-block series of concrete slabs along North Third Street as the start of a housing development for copper miners' families, the developer—in an uncharacteristic gesture of generosity—had planted a row of elm trees along the new curb. Somehow, the tree roots had burrowed their way down to adequate water, and while the houses along Third remained scrubby and minimal, the elms flourished.

The lot at 709 Third Street was blessed with two gigantic trees that straddled the tiny, square residence.

Estelle stopped the unmarked county car and looked up the short gravel driveway. A dilapidated blue Ford Courier pickup truck was parked behind a tiny imported sedan whose make Estelle didn't immediately recognize.

She reached for the mike, then changed her mind, digging out the small cellular phone instead. Brent Sutherland, the dispatcher at the sheriff's office, answered as if his hand had been poised over the receiver, waiting for the first call since the sun had cracked the horizon.

"Good morning. Posadas County Sheriff's Department. Sutherland."

"You sound cheerful this morning," Estelle said.

"Yes, ma'am," Sutherland replied brightly and then, as if reading out of one of his beloved self-motivational books, added, "After all, this is the first day of the rest of our lives."

And I wonder if that sunny thought crossed Perry Kenderman's mind when he got up today, Estelle thought. "Yes, it is. Do you have time to run a couple of plates for me?"

"You bet," Sutherland said. "Fire away."

"The first one is New Mexico Eight Two Seven Kiló Thomas Lincoln." While Sutherland repeated the number, Estelle idled the car ahead a few feet so that she could see the license on the little import. "The second is New Mexico One Eight One Thomas Edward Mike."

"Ten four. It'll be just a minute."

She settled back in the seat, phone resting lightly on her shoulder. The pickup lacked a tailgate, the left taillight assembly, and the back bumper. What looked like an aluminum ramp lay in the back, the sort of thing a bike owner would use to load a motorcycle up into the truck's sagging bed. The little truck's right rear tire was soft, adding to the derelict tilt of the aging suspension.

In less than a minute, Sutherland's smooth, efficient voice was back on the phone. "Ma'am, are you still there?"

"Yes."

"All right. Eight Two Seven Kilo Thomas Lincoln should appear on a blue nineteen seventy-seven Ford Courier pickup truck registered to a Richard Charles Kenderman, two four four De La Mar, Las Cruces. Negative twenty-nine."

Estelle frowned. *Richard Charles,* she thought. "Do you know him?"

"Sure don't," Brent said. "But he's got to be related to Perry. Not that many Kendermans around these parts."

"See what you can track down, will you? What's the other tag?"

"One Eight One Thomas Edward Mike should appear on a white nineteen ninety-four Nissan registered to a Barbara Cole Parker, seven oh nine Third Street, Posadas. No wants or warrants."

"Thanks. I'll be out of the car for a while at that address, Brent."

"Okay. And before you go, I have a note here from the sheriff to remind you of your appointment at zero nine hundred."

Estelle glanced at the dash clock. In two hours and three minutes, the Posadas County Grand Jury would convene to decide the fate of insurance agent George Enriquez—on the first day of the rest of *his* life.

"I'll be there. Thanks, Brent." Across the street, a truck started up with a plume of blue smoke, then backed out of a driveway and headed south. From the first house north of the Parkers', a small, ratty dog trotted out to stand in the street, watching the truck depart. After a moment, the animal turned, glanced at Estelle's car, and sauntered back onto the brick path that connected house to sidewalk.

When the undersheriff got out of her car, the dog stopped and regarded her, tail a motionless flag at half-mast. Then the ears dropped, the tail flicked, and the dog approached, nose close to the ground.

Estelle stopped on the sidewalk and let the little animal sniff the cuffs of her slacks.

"You know exactly what happened last night, don't you," Estelle said. The little dog jumped sideways at the sound of her voice, ears pricked and tail wagging. With no head-scratch forthcoming, the animal turned to pursue interests elsewhere.

Estelle walked up beside the pickup. It was unlocked, the keys in the ignition. The ashtray yawned open, full to overflowing with cigarette butts. A light film of dust coated the dashboard, the perfect canvas for a welter of finger- and handprints and smudges. A hole gaped in the narrow dashboard where the radio had been.

The driver's door was only partially closed, and Estelle lifted the latch. The rich, cloying fragrance of burned hemp wafted out. "Party time," Estelle murmured and nudged the door shut. She walked forward past the truck and glanced at the sedan. Other than a cardboard carton that had once held canning jars and now might be home to any number of things, the inside of the Nissan was clean.

As she stepped to the front door of the house, Estelle paused to survey the neighborhood. Little boxy houses nested in small yards with occasional chain-link fences and shaggy, unkempt elms as yet untouched by breezes. At 6:57 that morning, the neighborhood was quiet. Inside the Parker house, she heard a child's voice, then an adult's, low-pitched and gentle.

Barbara Parker might have drifted off to sleep after the brutal evening the day before, after cops had left and well-meaning neighbors had gone home, after the children were settled. Perhaps she'd jarred awake at dawn, then forced herself to slip into her daughter's bedroom to see if the girl was still lying there innocently asleep, the whole incident nothing more than the mother's personal nightmare.

Taking a deep breath, Estelle rapped on the door.

"Just a minute!" a voice called, and Estelle heard the conversation continuing as footsteps approached the front door. It opened, but the woman's back was turned momentarily as she said, "Make sure you put the top on Mindi's," and then she turned her attention to the visitor. "Hello," she said. Maybe thirty-eight, maybe fifty-five, it was impossible to tell. The woman's eyes were bloodshot, the black circles under them accentuated by the prematurely wrinkled skin of a heavy smoker. An inch or so shorter than Estelle's five feet seven inches, she was fine-boned and so thin that her faded jeans molded over the projections of her hip bones.

"Good morning," Estelle said. "Mrs. Parker?"

"Yes." The woman's tone was neutral, carrying no particular greeting or curiosity.

"I'm Estelle Guzman with the sheriff's department. I'm sorry to bother you so early."

The corner of the woman's mouth twitched. "With two little kids, this is just about mid-morning. What did you need?"

"I need to talk with you for a few minutes, Mrs. Parker."

"I think I know you, don't I? You're a social worker or something with the department."

"I'm Undersheriff Guzman. I'm investigating your daughter's death, Mrs. Parker."

"I talked to the officers last night." She said it without petulance and opened the door. She beckoned Estelle inside. "You don't look like you got much more sleep than I did." She nodded toward the kitchen. "The kiddos are having some breakfast, so you'll have to put up with that."

Estelle smiled. "I'm used to it. I have two of my own."

Barbara Parker shot a quick glance at Estelle as she walked toward the kitchen. "I tell you, without these two little poppets,

I don't think the sun would have bothered to come up this morning.''

A little boy with wheat-colored hair that had been buzzed uniformly close to his skull was kneeling precariously on his chair, holding a quart milk carton with both hands, and using the milk carton for balance. In a high-chair with its back to the kitchen sink sat a sober little girl. She looked at her grandmother, then at Estelle, then at the bright blue plastic cup between her tiny hands.

"This is Ryan," Barbara Parker said, watching the boy's maneuvers with the carton. She snapped the cover on the little girl's plastic cup and then took the carton of milk from Ryan and set it on the table. Freed of the challenge of the milk carton, Ryan scrambled down out of his chair. "He's four. And this is Mindi. She was two in August, weren't you, sweetheart." Ryan approached Estelle, his broad face puckered into a frown. Estelle sank to one knee so the two of them were eye to eye. She held out a hand. As she did so, her jacket drew away enough that the boy saw the gold badge clipped to her belt.

"How come you got that?" he asked. He allowed Estelle to take his hand.

"Because I'm a police officer," she said.

"Oh."

"My name's Estelle, Ryan."

"Okay." He nodded, and Estelle released his hand. He didn't move away but reached out and smoothed a wrinkled picture that had been magnet-tacked to the refrigerator door. The crayon sketch showed a huge, glowering sun. The four letters of Ryan's name stretched across the blue yard in front of a red house. "There was two policemans here." He reached up and placed a hand against the side of his face. "The lady looked funny."

"She had an accident a long time ago, Ryan."

"Like mommy?"

Estelle nodded. "Sort of like that."

"Mommy died."

"Yes."

"Did that lady?"

"No, she didn't die." She glanced up to see Barbara Parker

gathering Mindi out of the high-chair. Ryan reached out and touched the dark arc of Estelle's right eyebrow, the light tentative touch of the artist trying to fix a shape, a texture, a color in his mind.

"You got funny eyebrows," he said.

"I think so, too," Estelle agreed.

"He's a young man who says exactly what's on his mind," the boy's grandmother said.

"I'm familiar with that," Estelle said, and pushed herself to her feet. Ryan backed off, scrubbing his back along the smooth surface of the refrigerator door.

"Let's sit," Barbara said. She edged one of the kitchen chairs out with her toe, then sat down with Mindi in her lap. The child seemed content with her plastic, lidded cup. Ryan walked a wide circle around Estelle and clambered back into his chair.

"I got this," he said and hoisted the cereal box.

"Just keep 'em in the bowl, sport," Barbara Parker said.

"I understand that you're a counselor at the schools?"

Barbara nodded. "Of a sort. I'm the district's occupational therapist. I work with kids all day long, all ages, all makes and models," she said. "But I'm lost right now, I can tell you."

"It's not easy," Estelle said.

The woman shook her head and tears welled to the surface once again. "Oh, boy," she said and reached behind her to the box of tissues on the kitchen counter. Mindi rested her head back against her grandmother's shoulder and regarded Estelle solemnly. Both hands remained locked on the plastic cup. Estelle smiled at the child but saw no response behind the brown eyes. Ryan picked up a spoon and began a methodical thumping on the edge of his plastic cereal bowl. Sugar-coated cereal pellets about the size and shape of rabbit droppings scattered across the table. He seemed in no hurry to drench the mound with milk.

"Mrs. Parker, who is Richard Kenderman?" Estelle asked.

"That's my dad," Ryan said loudly, spoon heaped with cereal. He shoved the sugar bombs into his mouth. More scattered on the table. Estelle watched him with interest. Barbara Parker dabbed her eyes, then reached across the small table, opened the milk carton again, and poured a flood over Ryan's cereal. "Rick

and Colette lived together for a few months some time ago,"
she said, and shrugged helplessly.

"He's Perry's brother?"

She nodded. "Rick's the younger of the two. And they're as
different as night and day, let me tell you," Barbara Parker said.
"Come on," she said to Ryan. "Don't make such a mess.
You're showing off."

The boy made a face and tossed the spoon on the table. One
of the cereal droppings flicked across the table onto Estelle's lap.
Ryan watched it go, then slipped down out of his chair.

"You want to see my new car?"

"Sure."

"Ryan, you go drive it into the living room, and we'll be right
in," his grandmother said. "One of those remote things," she
added as Ryan scampered off. She sighed. "We've got about
thirty seconds of peace and quiet now."

Estelle smiled in sympathy. "Tell me about Richard Kenderman."

"He's a heller, and I just hate it when he shows up, Sheriff,"
Barbara said. "He and Colette lived together up until she started
to show with Mindi. Then we didn't see much of him for quite
a while—a couple years or so. And then, a few weeks ago, he
started coming by again." She nuzzled the side of the little girl's
head. The child didn't respond. "She's got more than her share
of developmental troubles, too." Estelle saw that Mindi's facial
expression was more slack than uninterested.

"And Ryan is…"

"Ryan is from their first go-around, when C…Colette was
still in high school." She grimaced and glanced at Estelle, a flush
rising on her cheeks. "I think."

"And Perry?"

"Perry has a heart of gold, Sheriff. He and his brother don't
see eye to eye on much of anything, but Perry's got a soft spot
for Colette. Nothing pushy…just tries to be around when there's
trouble. And…" she shuddered a deep sigh. "Lord, I hate to
say it, but Colette treats him like dirt. Borrows money from him,
doesn't pay it back, gets him to sit the kids…oh, you name it."
She leaned forward toward Estelle. "He's just a decent, good

guy. And you know…'' she hesitated and dabbed her eyes again. ''There isn't anything he wouldn't do for Ryan and Mindi. I think he loves 'em like they were his own. That's more than I can say for their father.''

''What happened last night, Mrs. Parker?''

The woman didn't reply immediately. She helped Mindi manage the cup, and the child's eyes closed as she sucked on the plastic rim. ''For the past six months or so…'' and Barbara stopped. She shook her head, refusing to meet Estelle's gaze. ''Colette was doing so well. She'd moved in here, getting herself out of that little hole-in-the-wall apartment she had over behind the school. I didn't mind.'' She shrugged. ''I was happy for the company.'' Mindi's face wrinkled up, and her grandmother removed the cup. ''She started working at the deli, regular hours. The kids are even enjoying day care.''

''Which one?''

''Tiny Tots, over on Grande.''

''And then what happened?'' Estelle asked.

''And then…and then I guess you could say that *Rick* happened again. He wants Colette to move to Las Cruces to live with him. Last time he was here, I heard them talking about that.''

''Colette didn't want to go?''

Barbara Parker sighed. ''*I* certainly didn't want her to go. Uproot the kids and all. But *she* wanted to, depending on which day you asked her. You know how kids are, Sheriff. And Rick's a charmer. There's no doubt about that. He walks into the room, and Colette just melts. I don't know what it is. Ryan thinks he's Mister Wonderful, too.''

''Chemistry,'' Estelle said.

''I suppose. *I* don't see it. And Perry doesn't see it, either. He knows what kind of thug Rick is. He knew what would happen if Colette went back to Cruces with his brother.''

''What do you think was going to happen?''

Barbara leaned her head to the left until her hair just touched Mindi's. ''Do you know what FAS is, Sheriff?''

''Fetal alcohol syndrome? Yes, I do, Mrs. Parker.''

''Well, as far as I'm concerned, that's Rick Kenderman's gift to Mindi. I know, I know. Nobody held the bottle to Colette's lips and forced her to drink while she was pregnant, but you know what I mean." She shook her head helplessly. "She was doing so *well*, Sheriff. And now all of a sudden he's back into her life."

"That's what the argument between Perry and Colette was about last night?"

Barbara nodded. "Perfect timing, I suppose. Colette's been at the deli now for almost six months. The newness has worn off. She's looking for something, although what I don't know. The kids are doing well, but I guess that's not enough for Colette. Rick comes back into her life, and off she goes. She's supposed to pack everything in that awful little truck he brought up. Rick took her old Chevy back over to Las Cruces. It needs all kinds of work that he promises to do…and never will."

"Perry tried to talk her out of going?"

"Yes. He came over, still on duty, I guess. They were arguing out in the front yard, putting on a good show for the neighbors. Something about the truck set him off—I haven't seen him so angry in a long time. I don't think I've ever heard him raise his voice until last night. I tell you, *long suffering* is the term invented especially for Perry Kenderman. But he got angry this time, and I think it was the sight of his worthless brother's truck. Then *she* got angry. You know how it goes. She got on her bike, with Perry trying to talk some reason. She *kicked* him, actually kicked him. I was watching from the window. Then she slammed her boot into the taillight of his patrol car. Oh, boy."

"And then they took off?"

"Yes." She reached over and stroked a strand of hair from Mindi's eyes. "It was just one thing leading to another," she said. "Just so stupid." She ran a finger lightly down Mindi's cheek. "And I just know that if they hadn't had a fight, you know what Perry would have done? Eventually, I mean? Colette would have talked him into helping her pack that stupid truck. And he would have done it."

"When was Rick here, Mrs. Parker? The last time."

"Friday night. He brought the truck up Friday night."

"Did you talk with him at that time? Did he say what his intentions were?"

"No. And if I never talk to him again, it's too soon. I'm sure he'll figure out a way to come over and get his truck." She wrapped her arms around Mindi. "That's *all* he's going to get, Sheriff. I'm fifty-one years old. However many good years I'm blessed with are going to these two. I don't care what it takes."

Estelle drew a business card out of her pocket and slid it across the table. "Will you call me, Mrs. Parker?"

"I don't know what you can do."

"Sometimes it's nice to have another voice when you're dealing with custody issues."

"Richard Kenderman has no custody, Sheriff. Let me tell you that right now."

"If he's the father, yes he does, ma'am. Because there was no formal marriage involved, and Richard wasn't actually living here, the court might order paternity testing…if he's the father, he has a legitimate claim of custody, whether he lives here or not. That's something that you're going to have to deal with, I think. In the meantime, our concern is with his brother, Mrs. Parker. There's one more thing I need to ask you. Last night, you told Sergeant Mears that Perry and Colette had been 'going together' for six months. That's not really the case, is it?"

"From Perry Kenderman's view, it might be," Barbara Parker said.

"And you told the sergeant that you didn't hear what the argument was about?"

Barbara flushed. "I was trying to keep things simple for a few minutes, Sheriff. I wanted time to think. I know how stupid that sounds, but it's the truth. And I really *didn't* hear them…I'm *assuming* that they were arguing about Colette's wanting to go to Cruces. Perry will tell you."

Estelle nodded. She pointed at the card. "Use that, Mrs. Parker." She got up and pushed the chair back in place. "I promised to look at Ryan's car."

"Oh, you don't have to waste time on that," Barbara Parker said. "He's on to something else by now."

"I don't think it's a waste," Estelle said.

Out in the living room, Ryan Parker had indeed moved on to something else. He was curled up on the sofa, a large red cat stretched on its back across his lap. The cat's front paws were poised like a boxer, waiting for the imminent attack of a tiny stuffed bear advancing over the top of a pillow.

Beyond the battle scene, the front window looked out on the street. Estelle saw an older-model pickup truck parked behind hers. Perry Kenderman, dressed in civilian clothes, was leaning against the front fender of Estelle's county car, obviously waiting.

"Ay," Estelle whispered to herself. She crossed to Ryan, bent down, and stroked the massive cat's belly. The animal squirmed and purred. "What's your friend's name?"

"That's Franklin. He's lazy."

"I see that." She stroked the cat's chin, and the animal closed his eyes, turning up the volume until the purr became a rattle. "Hello, Franklin. You take care of Ryan for me, okay?"

"Are you coming back?"

"Yes, I am." She reached over and ruffled the stubble on Ryan's head, then let her hand rest there motionless for a moment. The boy blinked, and Estelle felt the slight nod.

"That's good," he said.

Estelle straightened up and turned to Barbara Parker. The woman stood by the front door, Mindi in her arms.

"You know who's waiting out front, don't you?" she said.

"Yes," Estelle replied. "I saw him."

"I hope things work out for him. You know, I really like him. And none of this is his fault."

Estelle nodded. "We'll just have to see," she said. "I need to ask you to stay inside with the children." She stopped short of the front door and pulled out her cell phone. "Brent," she said when Sutherland answered, "I'll be talking with Perry Kenderman at the Third Street address. Have a unit circle around that way, code one."

"I hope you're not expecting trouble," Barbara Parker said as Estelle put the phone in her pocket and reached for the door.

"I sincerely hope not, ma'am. But I'm not feeling particularly heroic just now."

NINE

As THE UNDERSHERIFF approached, Perry Kenderman drew himself up so that he wasn't slouching against the car. One hand rested on the fender, the other was thrust into the pocket of his jeans. That pose didn't work, and he crossed his arms over his chest.

Estelle walked up so close she almost stepped on Kenderman's feet. Her face was less than twelve inches from his. He stood a little straighter and tried to meet her gaze, but looked away after a few seconds.

She leaned even closer, and when she spoke it was no more than a husky whisper. "I'm testifying before the grand jury in fifty-five minutes, Perry. That's enough time for you to tell me what happened, don't you think?"

"I..." he started to say and bit it off.

"No, you didn't," Estelle said, finishing his thought for him. "You've lied to me since minute one."

He managed to face her then, so close she could smell his breath.

"I..."

"You and Colette had an argument last night. Right here at the Parkers'. Start from there."

He looked past her toward the house. "You know about my brother?"

"Yes."

"She was going to move back to Las Cruces. To live with him."

"Go on."

"Well, I..."

Estelle remained silent, trying to read through the amber-speckled blue of Perry Kenderman's eyes to the backside of his mind. While they stood there, two vehicles passed, and Estelle heard a third idle to a stop further up the street. She glanced in that direction and saw Deputy Jackie Taber's unit. Kenderman saw it as well, and that seemed to prompt him.

"All I wanted was for the kids to be safe," he said, turning back to Estelle. "That's all I wanted."

"They're safe with their grandmother, Perry."

"No, they're not. Not if he comes back for 'em. You don't know my brother."

"You're right, I don't. Has he threatened them?"

"No. Nothing outright."

Estelle frowned. "It was you who was chasing Colette when she slammed into a utility pole, Perry. Not your brother."

The bluntness of her comment brought a flash of pain that made his eyes blink.

"What was the argument with Colette about?"

He nodded as if the question put him back on ground that he understood. "She was going to give up her job and everything. Move back to Cruces."

"To be with Richard?"

Perry nodded.

"And you didn't want that."

He shook his head.

"So tell me what happened."

He looked down at his boots. "She got mad, said some things. I said some things I shouldn'ta said. I tried to talk some sense into her, tried to make her understand what Rick was doin' to her."

"And what was he doing to her?"

"You been inside?"

"Yes."

"Then you met Mindi."

"And Ryan."

"Yeah, well..." he stopped.

"Did you attempt to physically restrain Colette last night?"

"No. I tried to take her arm once, when she was gettin' all wound up. That was all."

"And then?"

"And then she got on her bike and rode off."

"That's it? Nothing else?"

Kenderman shook his head.

"What about the taillight of your patrol car?"

His eyes snapped back to Estelle's, and then he slumped in resignation. "Yeah, well. She was takin' off on the bike, and kicked the light. It broke the plastic cover."

"Is that why you chased her?"

"Partly, I guess. I chased her because I was angry. Because I wanted to talk some sense into that stupid little head of hers. If she moves them kids down to Las Cruces, there's no way to tell what'll happen. She'll be stoned half the time; they won't have nobody to take care of 'em. That's why I wanted to talk with her."

"So you pushed her in a high-speed chase halfway across town…just to talk with her."

"I…"

"You…what?"

"I didn't see it as me chasin' her. She was runnin', wouldn't listen to sense. I was just tryin' to keep up. I figured that maybe she'd cool down a little. Maybe we could go somewheres and talk it out."

"When she crossed the Twelfth Street bridge, how close were you, Perry?"

He looked up at the sky and closed his eyes. "I hit the bridge just as she went off the south end. I was about a hundred, maybe two hundred feet behind her."

Estelle regarded him for a moment and then stepped back to give him room. "Tell me something, Perry."

"What?"

"If Colette didn't want to live with you, if she wanted to live with your brother, didn't she have the right to do that? That was her choice, wasn't it?"

"I thought that maybe I could talk her around to my way of thinking."

"Were things different between the two of you once upon a time?"

Kenderman grimaced. "A whole lot different."

Estelle shifted position ever so slightly, watching the light play on Perry Kenderman's eyes. The rest of him wasn't much to look at, at least not now, with all the steel taken out of his spine. His eyes, though...

She reached out a hand and rested it on his shoulder. He was taller than her by a good six inches, but slumped half off the curb, his butt resting on the car, the two of them were eye to eye. He started to twist away, and she dug her thumb in just above his right collarbone—not enough to hurt, but enough to weld them together for that brief moment.

"Perry," she said. "I need to know one more thing." She jogged her grip on his shoulder until his eyes met hers.

"Nothing you or me has got to say is going to bring her back," he said.

"No, it's not. But you and I both know there's some unfinished business, or you wouldn't be standing here right now." Perry Kenderman didn't respond, and Estelle released her grip on his shoulder. "Ryan's your son, isn't he."

She watched his throat work, but no sound came out. Up the street, another car backed out from a driveway and drove off. The neighbor's dog had returned and taken up his sentry post under one of the elms, patient and watchful.

"I think so," Perry said finally.

"You *think* so?"

"That's right."

"You of all people should know how simple it would be to establish paternity, Perry."

"I just..." and he shrugged helplessly.

"Let me lay it out for you in a nutshell, Perry," Estelle said. "If you are Ryan's father, that gives you some rights in this whole mess. Not to mention a few minor responsibilities." He heard the acid in her tone and met her gaze. "That's important," she continued. She held out her hands. "Just as your brother's paternity of Mindi gives *him* some legal leverage. Unless both of you agree to leave Ryan and Mindi with their grandmother, the courts are going to have to decide who gets custody of whom."

"I don't even know where to start."

"That's the simple part," Estelle said. "The kids are fine with their grandmother. They stay with her until you have time to unsnarl the rest of the knot. There's a possibility that your brother isn't the least bit interested in the kids."

The young man looked pained.

"And we don't know what Perry Kenderman wants to do either, do we?" she added. He didn't reply. "What I want you to do right now is go home. Go about your business. Hash things out in your mind so you know where you stand...so you know what you want to do."

"I want what's best for those two kids."

For an instant, a half smile of sympathy softened Estelle's face. "That's easily said, Perry. It's the *doing* of it that's the hard part." She reached out again and lightly punched his arm. "You decide what *you* want to do. And work up a plan for how you're going to do it. Judge Hobart will want answers, Perry. It would be a good idea to find yourself a lawyer."

"I can't afford that."

"You don't have much choice, Perry."

"What about last night?"

"I don't know," Estelle said. "I'm going to talk with the sheriff, and I'll be seeing the district attorney in about..." She glanced at her watch. ". . . thirty minutes. He was there last night, too. We'll have a chat and see what he wants to do. And I'll almost guarantee, from the way they were talking last night, that your lawyer's going to be doing double duty. You made some mistakes, Perry. It's that simple. That's the fairest answer I can give you."

"If it was up to you..."

Estelle could see the agony in Perry Kenderman's eyes. "Just hang in there, Perry," she said. "I'm not promising anything. You made some mistakes, and there's no way to brush them under the rug. Right now, go home, get yourself together, and be thankful for grandmothers."

TEN

THE DISTRICT ATTORNEY hesitated in mid-sentence, one hand poised in the air as if his orchestra was locked in a pause before the next movement. His other hand shuffled the notes on the lectern. Estelle Reyes-Guzman waited, aware that District Attorney Daniel R. Schroeder knew exactly what he wanted to ask, that the notes he wanted were right there on top of the heap. The grand jurors sat silent and watchful, eager to hear secret testimony that was better than the juiciest gossip.

Schroeder finally looked up, his hand still raised. He looked at the jurors as if surprised to find them still in attendance, grimaced, and dropped his hand.

"Undersheriff Guzman, when did your department commence its investigation into the affairs of Mr. George Enriquez?"

"In early February of this year, sir."

"Would you explain for the jury what it was that prompted that investigation?"

"We were in the process of investigating the circumstances of a fatal fire that destroyed the home of Eleanor Pope. Mrs. Pope's son, Denton, died in that fire."

"And in that case," Schroeder interrupted, "you had reason to believe that Denton Pope might have tried to set that house on fire so that he could collect on the home-owner's policy held by his mother. Is that correct?"

"Yes, sir."

"Would you describe how the fire occurred."

Estelle took a deep breath and looked at the jury. A heavy-set, elderly woman in front was either jotting notes or writing a letter to a relative. When the courtroom fell silent, the woman looked up. "It appeared that Denton Pope punched a small hole in the propane line to the wall furnace," Estelle said. "That caused a massive leak of propane fumes into the house. He also placed a pan of gasoline under the stove, apparently to act as an accelerant. When the thermostat was turned up and triggered the furnace igniter, the whole thing blew up."

"The plan being that his mother—or someone—would come home and turn up the thermostat in the chilly house, and the furnace would explode."

"It appears so, sir."

"And there is some evidence that the *late* Mr. Denton Pope actually turned up the thermostat himself. Is that correct?"

"Yes, sir."

"Why would he do that?"

"It appears to have been a mistake, sir."

Schroeder looked at the jury, the crow's-feet around his eyes deepening. "So he blew himself up. But that wasn't his intention, was it." The question was phrased as an aside, and Estelle didn't respond. There was no need for the grand jury to indict a dead man. The district attorney shifted his papers again. "Eleanor Pope subsequently died from stroke complications. Is that correct?"

"Yes, sir."

"Not from fire-related injuries?"

"No, sir. She wasn't home at the time."

"Were you at any time able to interview Mrs. Pope after the fire that killed her son?"

"No, sir."

"Why is that?"

"She suffered a stroke that night, shortly after receiving news of the fire. She slipped into a coma and never recovered."

"During the routine investigation that followed the fatal fire…" and Schroeder paused again. Estelle wondered if he was reflecting on the word *routine,* since nothing about the Pope case had been "routine."

"Would you tell the grand jury what you discovered after the fire relative to the Popes' home-owner's insurance."

"We could find no record of a home-owner's policy, sir."

"No written record at all?"

"No, sir."

"So such a policy did not exist. Is that correct?"

"We did not find one, sir."

The half smile again touched Schroeder's face. "It's possible that the paperwork burned in the fire?"

"Yes, sir."

"Did you make enquiries with various insurance agents to that effect?"

"Yes, sir."

"And no policy was ever issued, as far as these various agents were concerned?"

"That's correct."

"Was one of the agents whom you queried Mr. George Enriquez?"

"Yes, sir."

"And he told you that no such policy existed?"

"Yes, sir. The Popes had no home-owner's policy with his firm."

"Did Mrs. Pope have any insurance at all with Mr. Enriquez's agency?"

"Yes, sir. She had auto insurance."

Schroeder stopped and thrust out his lower lip, regarding the papers in front of him. He patted the lectern and turned to the jury. Estelle glanced at the eight faces and saw the keen interest of a jury that was listening to the first witness in a case destined to be a long one. By the twenty-fifth witness, the open-eyed coma would have set in, and the difficulty of Schroeder's job would escalate.

"Did there come a time," Schroeder said carefully, still looking at the jurors, "when you found evidence suggesting that Mrs. Eleanor Pope in fact had been making payments for home-owner's insurance?"

"We were able to establish that Eleanor Pope had written checks on a monthly basis to George Enriquez."

"And you were led to believe that those payments were for home-owner's insurance?"

"Yes, sir."

"What led you to that conclusion?"

"On several of the checks, Mrs. Pope had made the notation 'house insurance.'" One of the jurors chuckled.

Schroeder lifted a clear plastic folder from the lectern and walked across to the witness stand. He handed the folder to Estelle.

"Do you recognize these, Undersheriff Guzman?"

"Yes, sir."

"Would you identify them for the jury."

"They're several of the checks written by Eleanor Pope to George Enriquez."

Schroeder nodded, took the exhibit, and handed it to the jury. "Where were they found?"

"In a desk drawer in the burned trailer."

"A metal desk?"

"Yes, sir."

"And despite the protection of the metal drawer, we can still see scorching and water stains. But they're quite readable, aren't they."

"Yes, sir."

"Undersheriff, are those checks written to Mr. Enriquez's insurance agency?"

"No, sir."

"To whom are they written?"

"They're written to Mr. Enriquez personally, sir."

"Is that a usual procedure, to write checks to an agent rather than an *agency?*"

"I don't know what the usual procedure is for an insurance agent, sir."

Schroeder smiled and ducked his head, then grinned at the jury. "What is *your* practice when you write checks for your own home-owner's insurance, Undersheriff Guzman?"

"I write them to the home office of the insurance company, sir."

"And so do I." He patted the railing of the jury box enclosure. "And so do most of you folks, I'm sure." Still standing in front of the jurors, he turned to look at Estelle. "During the course of your investigation, you found no insurance policy at all. Is that correct?"

"We found no policy. That's correct."

"So it appears that Mrs. Pope was writing monthly premium checks…each one for…" and he leaned over the jury box rail, twisting his head so that he could see the checks being scrutinized at that moment by Mark Harrell, a retired cabinet maker. "…eighty-seven dollars and fifty-seven cents, without any policy in hand. Something over a thousand dollars a year."

Schroeder returned to the lectern and thrust his hands in his suit coat pockets. "Undersheriff, did you have reason to believe that Mrs. Pope *thought* that she had home-owner's insurance?"

"Yes, sir."

"What led you to that conclusion?"

"One of the sheriff's department employees had a conversation with Mrs. Pope some time before the fire—a casual conversation in passing. The subject of house insurance came up."

"What prompted the suspicion that Mrs. Pope might not have actually *had* a policy?"

"During the initial stages of the fire investigation, a member of our own department volunteered information to us that he had been making monthly payments to Mr. George Enriquez as well, in his case for coverage on a motorcycle."

"And this officer told you at that time that he didn't have an actual insurance policy in hand?"

"That's correct."

"Did he have a proof-of-insurance card so that he could register the motorcycle?"

"He told us that George Enriquez's secretary typed out a proof-of-insurance card right there in the office, while he waited."

"And that's the usual procedure, is it not?"

"I believe so, sir."

Schroeder sighed with feigned weariness and nodded at the jury. "We'll be hearing from the deputy later today for the exact details on all of this, but suffice to say right now, it's your understanding, Undersheriff Guzman, that a member of your department was making monthly payments for motorcycle insurance to Mr. George Enriquez, payments *directly* to Mr. Enriquez, not the parent insurance company. Is that correct?"

"Yes, sir."

"And when you contacted the insurance company's national office, it turned out that the deputy had *no* motorcycle policy with that company."

"That's correct."

Schroeder nodded with an exaggerated backward tilt of his head as if all the details had suddenly fallen into place that very moment, rather than during the tedious months of investigation that he had personally directed through the Posadas County Sheriff's Office and the state insurance commission.

"Or any other company."

"That's correct."

"During the period when the deputy was making those payments, did he ever file a claim on his motorcycle insurance?"

"Yes, he did."

"And was it paid?"

"Yes, it was."

Schroeder's eyebrows shot up again as if he were genuinely surprised at the answer. The jury certainly was, since eight heads swiveled to face Estelle.

"It *was* paid?" Schroeder asked.

"Yes, sir."

"By the insurance company's home office?"

"No, sir."

"Who made the payment?"

"Mr. Enriquez made the payment with a personal check."

"So the deputy made a damage claim, and the agent paid the claim out of his own pocket." Schroeder eyed the jury, his eyebrows arched quizzically. He held out his hand and bent one index finger down with the other. "One of the sheriff's deputies *thought* that he had a policy…and didn't. He made a claim, and it was quickly paid, no questions asked, by the agent's own personal check."

He turned to Estelle. "Did the deputy make a copy of that personal check for his records, Undersheriff Guzman?"

"No, sir."

"But the bank has records, as we'll see in a bit," Schroeder said. He turned to face the jury again. "Eleanor Pope thought she had insurance, and made monthly payments. She would have been able to make a hefty insurance claim, had she survived the night." He paused. "Now, sadly enough, it's only her *estate* that has a claim." He took a deep breath. "Any questions for the undersheriff at this point?"

A hand drifted up in the back row. Dr. Silvia Todd didn't look husky enough to be a chiropractor. Estelle hadn't seen her use the notepad provided by the court, but she had listened attentively. She shifted in her chair, leaning forward. "Are you saying that what's his name...Denton Pope? Is that the son?"

Schroeder nodded. "Eleanor Pope's son, yes."

"Are you saying that Denton Pope planned to murder his mother and burn down the family home so that he could claim the insurance?"

The district attorney gently pushed his podium microphone a fraction of an inch further way. "That's a good question, but actually, that's not the task facing this particular grand jury," he said. "Obviously, had Denton Pope *not* been killed in the explosion, it would be a different story."

"But I mean, that's what he did?" Dr. Todd pursued.

"It appears so, yes."

"So let me get this straight," Dr. Todd said, with the same sort of eager enthusiasm she might show while regarding a crooked spine. "Denton Pope *thought* that he had home-owner's insurance...or he thought that his mother did."

"That's correct. That's what we think," Schroeder said.

"But he...they...didn't."

"That's correct."

"Oh." Silvia Todd settled back in the padded swivel chair, shaking her head. "I don't suppose we can indict somebody on the other side of the grave, huh."

Schroeder laughed gently, resting his hand over the microphone. "Any other questions right now for Undersheriff Guzman?"

Various heads shook in the jury, and Schroeder nodded at

Estelle. "Undersheriff, how long did you investigate the insurance dealings of George Enriquez?"

"Over the course of approximately four months, sir."

"And during that investigation, did you discover that other people had been writing checks or giving cash to Mr. Enriquez, thinking that they were making insurance premium payments?"

"Yes, sir."

"In some of those cases, is it true that no insurance policy had actually been issued?"

"Yes, sir."

"In how many instances?"

"We have established thirty-seven separate cases so far where premiums were allegedly paid but no policy was issued."

The courtroom fell silent as Schroeder gave the jury time to digest the number, and then he said, "Thirty-seven people were paying George Enriquez for insurance policies that did not exist. Is that correct?"

"Yes, sir."

The district attorney rested both elbows on the podium, his hands clasped together under his chin. "Did any one of these thirty-seven people ever file a complaint that they had been denied payment of an insurance claim by Mr. Enriquez or his agency?"

"No, sir."

"Not one?"

"No, sir. Not one of the thirty-seven people that we interviewed."

"Were any claims actually settled or paid out during that period to any of those thirty-seven people?" He waved a hand in dismissal. "Other than the one to the sheriff's deputy that you've already mentioned."

"Yes, sir."

"What claims were paid?"

"We found a total of nineteen claims that were paid by personal checks written by Mr. Enriquez."

"Over how long a period?"

"Approximately four years."

"Did you compute an average amount for the claims?"

"Yes, sir. The average for the nineteen claims was two hundred twelve dollars and nineteen cents."

Schroeder once more looked up at the ceiling, as if the figures were on the acoustical tile rather than in bold red ink in his notes. "Nineteen claims averaging a little over two hundred dollars. Some more, some less. Added together, Mr. Enriquez paid out a total of about four thousand dollars in claims. Is that correct?"

"Four thousand thirty-one dollars and sixty-one cents."

Schroeder pursed his lips. "So four thousand bucks over four years. Out of his own pocket." He shrugged. "Acting as his own small insurance pool, so to speak. Do you happen to know the average payment made by those thirty-seven customers to Mr. Enriquez?"

Estelle glanced down at her small notebook. "The average monthly payment was seventy-two dollars and thirteen cents."

"Math isn't my strong suit, but let's see if we can make this simple. You've got an average payment of seventy-two bucks a month. So that's something like eight hundred a year."

"Eight hundred and sixty-five dollars and fifty-six cents," Estelle said.

"Per person."

"Yes, sir."

"So thirty-seven times that eight hundred dollars."

"Yes, sir. Thirty-two thousand twenty-five dollars and seventy-two cents."

Schroeder turned in wonder to the jury. "Thirty-two grand a *year,* for four years."

"Yes, sir."

He glanced at his notes. "My math tells me that's a hundred and twenty-eight thousand dollars."

"Yes, sir."

"Four thousand out, a hundred and twenty-eight thousand in."

"Yes, sir."

For a long moment, Schroeder stood quietly, gazing at his notes. "Undersheriff, during your investigations of these activities, did you come to believe that there was any certain type of person that Mr. George Enriquez favored with his insurance 'deals'?"

"A certain type of person, sir?"

A flash of impatience shot across the district attorney's face. "Did any of the thirty-seven people share common characteristics...or to put it another way, was there anything about their *circumstances* that they had in common?"

"It appeared in each instance that the person either had difficulty obtaining insurance through normal channels or had an insurance history such that their rates would be higher than they were able to afford," Estelle said.

"So each one was a tough case. Is that what you're saying?"

"Yes, sir."

"In Mrs. Pope's case, why would home-owner's insurance through normal channels have been difficult...or expensive?"

"They were heating with a defective, out-of-date wall unit as well as a wood stove elsewhere in the trailer that had not been installed according to code. They had also run a number of extension cords out to livestock pens in lieu of appropriate wiring. The mobile home itself was an older model that had been extensively altered by the home owners over the years."

"You understood this after conversations with fire department investigators?"

"Yes, sir."

"Had you been an insurance agent visiting the Popes' property, would you have issued a policy based on what you saw?"

"I'm not an insurance agent, sir. I couldn't say."

"But George Enriquez issued the policy, didn't he?"

"As far as we can tell, there was *no* policy issued, sir."

"I stand corrected." Schroeder grinned at the jury. "Mrs. Pope *thought* that she had an insurance policy and was no doubt grateful to Mr. Enriquez for providing some form of protection against loss. It appears that she was making monthly payments on that fictitious policy. Is that correct?"

"Yes, sir."

He was about to say something else when the door beside the vacant judge's bench opened. Howard Bell, the court bailiff, stepped into the courtroom, closing the door behind him with exaggerated care. "Excuse me a minute," the district attorney said to the jury, and walked across the courtroom toward Bell.

The two men conferred briefly, and then Schroeder nodded and strode back toward the witness stand.

As he bent close, he pushed the microphone boom far to one side. "You've got a phone call that you need to take, Undersheriff Guzman," he said. "Use the phone in the judge's chambers." He turned to the jury. "Ladies and gentlemen, we're going to take a short break. Please remain in the courtroom. If it's going to be more than five or ten minutes, I'll let you know."

Estelle's pulse kicked as she hurried out of the courtroom, glancing at the wall clock as she passed the door to the court clerk's office. She'd been in court for less than thirty minutes—a little more than an hour since she had left Perry Kenderman with instructions to go home and behave himself.

ELEVEN

ESTELLE SETTLED the telephone receiver back in its cradle. Another button flashed on the phone console, a message just as quickly routed somewhere else in the county building as business carried on as usual. She pushed the chair back in and skirted around Judge Lester Hobart's tidy walnut desk.

Back in the courtroom, most of the jurors lounged in and around the jury box. One walked the perimeter of the room, swinging her arms to encourage a return of blood to her extremities. The jurors looked toward Estelle with interest as she reentered. Dan Schroeder leaned on the broad table used by the prosecution during regular trials, his hands planted among a sea of papers. He glanced up as Estelle approached. She leaned over the table, her back to the jurors.

"Sir, we have a problem," Estelle whispered.

Schroeder straightened up.

"George Enriquez's secretary found his body a few minutes ago."

The district attorney looked hard at Estelle, the hand holding the papers sagging back toward the table. He drew a slow, deep breath. "Where?"

"In his office, sir."

Schroeder slumped against the table and dropped the papers. "Christ," he muttered. "Natural causes?"

"No, sir. The sheriff asked that I break loose here, if that's possible."

"Of course it's possible." He shook his head in frustration. "Keep me in the loop, all right?"

Estelle nodded.

"I'll get these folks out of here in the next few minutes." He flashed a humorless grin and rapped on the table with his knuckle. "I guess we'll find out what the grand juror's oath of secrecy is really worth."

As Estelle turned away, he stepped around the table and touched her elbow, whispering directly into her right ear. "And we need to talk about Officer Kenderman, too. Today sometime, if you can fit it in. I'll be in Posadas at least until tomorrow morning, so…" He released her elbow. The jurors, sensing that something important had happened, had taken their seats, including the power-walking woman. Estelle nodded at them and left the court.

The sheriff's office was no more than a hundred steps away, across the small enclosed courtyard. Gayle Torrez, the sheriff's wife, administrative assistant, and head dispatcher, glanced up as Estelle hurried in.

She made a face of frustration and opened the glass door to the dispatch room. "Bobby just took off," Gayle said. "Dennis took the first call. Howard's over there, too."

"Right at the insurance office?" Estelle asked.

Gayle nodded. "And I called Linda. She's on her way."

"Good."

As soon as Estelle pulled her unmarked car out of the county parking lot, she looked down East Bustos toward the oval sign that announced GEORGE ENRIQUEZ, AGENT—LU, AUTO, LIFE INSURANCE. The long, low stucco building was tucked in the lot immediately adjacent to Chavez Chevrolet-Olds, the two businesses separated by a low chain-link fence.

A county patrol unit was parked straddling the street's center line, facing westbound and nose to nose with one of the village cars. Nate Olguin, a part-time officer with the village, touched his cap when he recognized Estelle, and waved her through. The sheriff's battered pickup was parked along the curb at the west end of the auto dealer's lot. The ambulance hadn't arrived, but Dr. Alan Perrone had, his dark green BMW so close to Collins's Expedition that their bumpers appeared to be touching.

As Estelle drove past and prepared to swing a U-turn, she saw two other vehicles in the lot beyond Torrez's truck. Several people were standing in the parking lot of the car dealership, leaning against the new cars and waiting to see something interesting. As she pulled the car to a halt, Estelle heard the distant wail of a siren from the direction of the hospital.

A yellow crime-scene ribbon stretched from the corner of the car dealer's fence across the sidewalk to a street sign, then across the westbound lane to Collins's unit, finally angling back across the street to the corner of a small abandoned building west of the insurance agency that at one time had been a hairdresser's salon. Deputy Dennis Collins was standing at the front door of the agency, head swiveling this way and that as he watched street and sidewalk. As Estelle ducked under the ribbon and approached, he stepped away from the building.

"They're all inside," he said.

Estelle nodded and refrained from smiling at the young deputy's earnest statement of the obvious. She stepped to the edge of the sidewalk. "Whose vehicles are those?"

Collins turned to glance at the parking lot. "The Subaru belongs to Kiki Tafoya...she's one of the office staff. And she's the one who reported finding the body."

"The SUV is George's?"

"Yes, ma'am. I believe so."

Estelle walked the few steps to the corner of the building. The rest of the parking lot was empty. A second yellow ribbon stretched across the alley, looped around a scrubby saltbush, and then disappeared behind the building. "Is someone at the back door?"

"Sergeant Bishop was back there, ma'am. He was kinda scouting the alley."

"Any signs of forced entry?"

"No, ma'am." Collins looked puzzled. "He shot himself. That's what they were saying."

"Ah." Estelle nodded, feeling a twinge of genuine sadness. Despite his penchant for fictitious insurance policies, George Enriquez had been a likable fellow—part of his secret as a successful salesman. Estelle realized that the looming threat of a grand jury investigation, with its promise that someone's life was going to be forever changed, could be cause enough for depression, especially when, in George's view, he'd done nothing to harm anyone.

The undersheriff snapped on a pair of rubber surgical gloves and then paused with her finger hovering near the door handle. A computer-printed sign was taped to the inside of the window: OUR OFFICES WILL BE CLOSED THIS WEEK DUE TO FAMILY ILLNESS. Two emergency numbers were listed, and Estelle recognized Enriquez's home number as well as National Mutual's toll-free number.

"Family illness," she said aloud.

"Well, in a way," Collins said cheerfully.

Estelle pulled the outer door open, keeping a single finger on the underside of the latch. The vestibule was no more than six feet square, just enough buffer to keep the sand from blowing into the office when customers opened the door to the street. The ornately carved inner door rested ajar, a rubber stop placed between it and the jamb. A plastic bag enclosed the brass door lever. Estelle nudged the door open with her elbow.

Kiki Tafoya sat in the swivel chair behind her desk, doubled over with her elbows on her knees and her face buried in her hands. Posadas Police Chief Eddie Mitchell knelt beside her, balanced on one knee so that his face was close to the girl's, one large arm resting on the corner of her desk for balance. He glanced up as Estelle entered. Kiki nodded at something the chief said, and he patted her shoulder as he pushed himself to his feet.

"Not pretty in there," he murmured to Estelle as he stepped close. Estelle's eyes roamed the small office. Enriquez had three employees, the other two working in cubicles whose boundaries were marked by six-foot partitions covered in soft yellow fabric. Behind Kiki Tafoya's desk, the solid wall of wood paneling angled off to meet a section of tinted glass above three-foot paneled wainscoting. A heavy glass door marked George Enriquez's private domain.

She saw Sheriff Robert Torrez back partially out of the office doorway, his hands in his back pockets. He shook his head at something someone in the office said, then turned and saw Estelle. He nodded toward the interior of the office.

Estelle stepped around Kiki's desk. The girl didn't look up, and Estelle could see her slender shoulders shaking. Kneeling down as the chief had done, she slid her arm across Kiki's shoulders. The girl was strung as tight as a guy wire, her entire body quivering in shock.

"Try to breathe slowly," Estelle whispered. The girl uttered a little *ummm* of distress, refusing to lift her face from her hands.

"Perrone gave her a sedative," Mitchell said. "Her husband is coming down to pick her up in a few minutes." Even as he said that, the ambulance arrived outside, its siren dying in a truncated yowl.

"Okay." She looked up at Mitchell, questioning.

The chief shook his head. "She told Collins that she came in to the office this morning to pick up a jacket that she'd left here yesterday morning, when she was here for a few minutes, catching up on some paperwork. She said that she noticed that the light was on in the boss's office this morning, and she looked in and saw him." He shrugged. "That's what we've got so far, anyway."

Another spasm shook Kiki's shoulders, and Estelle waited silently, arm around the girl, until one of the EMTs appeared at the door. "We need a blanket," she said. In another moment, Kiki Tafoya was wrapped snugly, and Estelle backed off, giving the EMT room to work.

"Let's take a look," she said. Bob Torrez had turned sideways in the office door, hands still in his pockets. Dr. Alan Perrone was writing quickly on a small aluminum clipboard, talking just as rapidly. Behind them, seated at his desk, was George Enriquez.

"Single, large caliber gunshot wound to the head," Perrone said without looking up from his writing. "My best ballpark guess is sometime yesterday. I'll be able to narrow that down some for you, Estelle. For the moment, I'm finished here." He tapped a period with his gold ballpoint and sighed. "I don't think the young lady who found him is going to be in any shape to tell you much. At least not for a few hours."

"We'll talk to her when we can," Estelle said. Without stepping closer to the ornate wooden desk, she regarded Enriquez. The man was slumped back in his chair as if napping, head lolled to the right. The top of the chair back cushioned his head at the junction of spine and skull. His jaw hung slack.

The single bullet had crashed into his skull through the thick, silver hair of his left sideburn, leaving a large corona of powder dappling that extended to the corner of his left eye.

"The bullet is in the wall over there," Torrez said. He extended an arm past Estelle's shoulder, pointing. "It hit the edge of the bookcase, punched through the side support, and then smacked into the wall. It didn't go through."

Estelle nodded and moved around the desk.

"A thorough job," the sheriff observed. The single bullet had passed obliquely through the victim's skull, exiting along with a large chunk of skull from behind the right ear. "The weapon is under his chair."

Enriquez's body rested like a sandbag in the modern fabric-and-fiberglass swivel chair. His left arm hung straight down, index finger extended as if he'd been pointing at the large revolver that lay between two of the swivel chair's five black legs. His left shoe rested flat on the clear plastic carpet protector under the chair, and his right leg was extended under the desk.

"It's supposed to be a pretty standard picture," Torrez said, and Estelle looked up at him quickly. He didn't elaborate but let the remark pass with a shrug.

Kneeling carefully on the carpet an arm's length from the corpse, Estelle looked at the revolver. Its satin stainless-steel finish was flecked here and there with gore, but she could easily read the legend on the right side of the barrel.

"What do we know about this?" Estelle asked, not because anyone had had the time to run the weapon through NCIC or put it under the microscope but because Bob Torrez's consuming personal interest in firearms made it likely that the sheriff had already reached some conclusions.

"Smith and Wesson Model 657," he said. "Stainless, forty-one mag, and the grips probably didn't come with the gun." Estelle looked at the grips and frowned. "The stainless usually comes with soft, black rubber grips," Torrez said. "Those wood ones are the standard issue on older models of blued guns. Some folks like the looks better, with the fancy grain and all. The wood is goncalvo alves, I think.''

Using her pen, Estelle reached out and moved Enriquez's hand slightly, looking at the palm for a long moment.

"I didn't see any, either," Torrez said. "Neither did doc."

George Enriquez's hands were soft and well manicured, not the work-hardened, calloused hands of a laborer. The under-sheriff looked back and forth, from hand to revolver. Estelle could imagine that the big magnum was a challenge to fire one-handed in any case, requiring a firm grip. Someone about to unleash that tremendous, shattering power against his own skull would have held the gun so hard his knuckles would have been white and trembling. The resultant recoil would have pounded the sharp checkering of the hardwood grips into the palm of the victim's hand, leaving characteristic marks.

"That's a puzzle," Estelle murmured. She stood up and stepped back from Enriquez's chair. "I'm surprised that the re-volver would land there."

"You ain't the only one," Torrez said. "Recoil's going to bust it back. If he had a death grip on it, maybe it stayed in his hand and then just kind of fell on the floor under the chair, there." He grimaced. "Not likely." He knelt, balancing on the balls of his feet. "If he had a death grip on it, then relaxed..." he glanced back up at Estelle, "I'd expect to see the weapon directly under his fingers, wouldn't you?"

"Probably."

"But it's not under his fingers. It's a good foot away from his hand, in a direction that would have taken some effort to accomplish." He stood back up with a creak of leather.

"No signs of forced entry, though?"

"None."

"And no struggle."

"Nothing that's turned up yet."

"And he had plenty of reason," Estelle said.

"Maybe. Maybe not. If he was the suicidal type, I'd say yes. But we don't know that he was. Folks face a grand jury probe all the time without offing themselves."

"Did you already send someone over to notify Connie?"

Torrez nodded. "Taber picked up Father Anselmo and swung by. Nobody's interviewed the woman yet." He looked expectantly at Estelle.

"I'll break away from here in a few minutes and see what she has to say."

"Best of luck," the sheriff said, then followed her gaze to the far wall where the small bullet hole pocked the textured plaster. "You're thinking that you'd like to make sure the bullet we dig out of that wall comes close to matching this revolver?"

Estelle shrugged and smiled at the sheriff. "It's just a small detail."

Torrez grinned. "Oh, *sí.*"

TWELVE

IN ANOTHER HOUR, Estelle was convinced that George Enriquez's office was not going to offer any easy answers. Photographed, scrutinized, measured and probed, the insurance agent's body was finally released to the EMTs. Dr. Alan Perrone nodded curtly as the gurney was wheeled out the door.

"I'll let you know," the medical examiner said. "There are some interesting questions here." He glanced back at the gore-draped chair, empty behind the spattered desk, as if he'd forgotten something. For a moment he watched as Linda Real maneuvered for a close-up series of the blood and gore spatters across the top of the chair, then turned to watch preparations for the excavation of the bullet lodged in the wall. "Let me know about that, too," he said. He nodded once again at Estelle and left, black bag in hand.

Working meticulously under the watchful eye of Linda Real's videotape camera, Sheriff Robert Torrez and Chief Eddie Mitchell spent twenty minutes extracting the mushroomed revolver slug, first carving an impressive hole in the plaster and Sheetrock to give them room to work.

"If we're lucky, we won't end up out in the alley," Mitchell muttered as he nudged the chards of Sheetrock into a neat pile near the baseboard.

"Nah," Torrez said. "It's right here." The victim's skull had slowed the bullet sufficiently that the wall stud and a section of electrical wiring had finished the job. With the tip of his heavy pocket knife's blade, Torrez worked around the wiring, removing splinters of the wall stud until the deformed bullet could be nudged gently from its resting place without further damaging the soft lead. As Torrez dropped the slug into an evidence bag, he mouthed something that Estelle couldn't hear.

The undersheriff raised an eyebrow. "No surprises?"

"I don't think so," Torrez replied. "Half-jacketed lead bullet...same general kind that's loaded in factory ammo." He held the bag up to the light. "And it's forty-one."

"Old micrometer eyes," Mitchell said dryly, but he didn't challenge Torrez's assessment.

"That's not the most common cartridge in the world," Estelle said.

"Far from it," the sheriff said. "This one's clean enough that we can do a comparison *inmediamente.*" He slipped the evidence bag into his briefcase and paused for a moment, regarding the bagged and labeled weapon. "We want to know whose forty-one that is," he said. "Connie might know something about it. At least that's a place to start. I'll get Mears on the weapon right away. We'll see what he comes up with."

Estelle caught motion in the corner of her eye and turned to see Daniel Schroeder standing in the office doorway. He regarded the chair and desk, his nose wrinkling from the mingled smells. "Wonderful," the district attorney muttered. "What a goddamn stupid thing to do." He looked at Estelle. "Frank Dayan is waiting outside when you get a chance, by the way."

"He'll be happy that this is a Tuesday," Chief Mitchell said.

"Hold the presses," Linda quipped.

"He needs to talk with the sheriff," Estelle said, knowing full well what Bob Torrez's reaction would be.

"No, he doesn't," Torrez said promptly. "He asked for you 'cause he knows better."

As Estelle made her way around the desk and toward the door, the district attorney reached out a hand to touch her on the elbow. "I need to talk with you for a few minutes before you take off." He smiled. "Go ahead and talk to Frank while these guys bring me up to speed on what happened here. I'll catch up outside."

The newspaper publisher was leaning against the fender of Dennis Collins's patrol unit, his hip pushing against the yellow tape. A black Posadas State Bank baseball cap was pulled low to keep the sun out of his eyes. An impressive digital camera hung from his left shoulder, a constant companion whether he was roaming about town selling advertising, attending a Rotary Club meeting, or as now, doing the leg work that his plump, lethargic editor should have been doing.

Estelle knew that the camera amused Linda Real. *Now if only Frank would learn how to use it,* she was apt to say. Since Linda had left the newspaper four years before, the photos in the *Posadas Register* tended toward fuzzy on the best of days, and the switch to digital cameras hadn't helped. But, as Dayan himself had once happily observed, "Our photos may be bad, but at least there are a *lot* of them."

"Hello, Frank," Estelle said. Deputy Collins pushed himself away from his comfortable spot against the wall and touched his Stetson just a shade lower toward the bridge of his nose. Across the street, several "lookie-louies" had gathered, hoping for a glimpse of the corpse.

"Estelle, what in heck is going on?" Dayan stepped away from the deputy's car and extended his hand. He pumped Estelle's with a quick, excited shake, then jerked his head toward Deputy Collins. "This one here is just as tight-lipped as the big guy." Being compared with Sheriff Torrez put another steel support in the young deputy's spine.

"We have an unattended death, Frank. That's all I can tell you."

The newspaper publisher glanced up at the hanging sign over his head as if the name on it might have somehow changed since he last looked. "George?"

Estelle nodded.

"My God. What, this morning sometime?"

"We don't know."

"Grand jury was supposed to convene this morning, wasn't it?"

Estelle let a nod suffice.

"He had a heart attack, or what? Is this related to the jury thing, do you think?"

Estelle hesitated just long enough for the newspaper publisher to notice. "This is one of those times when 'investigation is continuing' works pretty well, Frank."

"Oh, please," Dayan protested with a roll of his eyes. "Now you sound like Bill Gastner."

"Cheer up. It's only Tuesday." He looked pained, but the expression on Estelle's dark, sober face held no hint of sarcasm. The undersheriff knew that the *Register*'s inexorable decline from a prospering daily during the heyday of the copper mines to a biweekly and then finally to a single edition on Thursday was a sore point with Dayan. He answered to out-of-state owners who had been trying to sell the newspaper since the previous spring.

"You gotta give me a little more than that. Give me something to work with."

"How about everything I know at the moment," Estelle said.

"I'll settle for that."

"It appears that George, spelled the usual way, Enriquez, spelled with a 'z,' sustained a single gunshot wound to the head." She stopped and regarded Dayan patiently.

"That's it? You mean he shot himself?"

"He sustained a single gunshot wound to the head."

"Come on. Was it suicide, or what?"

"We don't know."

"And you said 'sustained,'" Dayan added. "Is the gunshot what killed him?"

"We don't know yet."

"Did he pull the trigger?"

"We don't know yet."

"They're going to put that on your tombstone," Dayan said, and Deputy Collins laughed. "Was the weapon his?" Dayan persisted, then saw the hint of a smile cross Estelle's face. He held up a hand to fend off the inevitable. "All right. You don't need to say it."

Daniel Schroeder appeared at Estelle's elbow. "Got a few minutes?"

"Yes, sir," she said and smiled sympathetically at Frank Dayan. "Excuse me," she said. "I'll have more for you later in the day."

"I'll give you a call this evening," Dayan countered quickly. "Or maybe first thing in the morning." He switched his attention to the district attorney. "Today was the first day of grand jury, was it not?" he asked.

"Sure enough, Frank," Schroeder replied.

"Those proceedings will be interrupted now?"

"Uh, yes," Schroeder said, frowning as if to add *and that's a really stupid question.*

Dayan nodded and turned back to Estelle. "I understand that no charges have been filed yet against Perry Kenderman, by the way. Is that correct?"

"That's correct."

"Are they going to be?" He looked at Schroeder, but the district attorney was content to let Estelle field the question.

"I'll let you know, Frank. Give us a chance to sort things out."

"Does that mean they *might* be? Dan, is your office considering filing charges? I talked with Maggie Archer this morning, and she said that Kenderman's patrol car was right on top of the bike, practically. No lights, no siren, no nothing."

Dan Schroeder smiled pleasantly. "Before you run with that, Frank, remember what screwy versions of events we sometimes have to work with when we talk to witnesses."

"Mrs. Archer is wrong?" Dayan asked, and Estelle saw a flash of irritation on the district attorney's face.

"We'd appreciate it if you'd wait a bit until we get things straightened out," he said.

"You go to press tomorrow afternoon, right?" Estelle asked, and Dayan nodded. "I'll keep you posted," she added.

"That's a deal. Can I go inside, or…"

"No, sir, you can't. But if you wait here, you'll catch the sheriff when he comes out."

"Oh, that's a help," Dayan said.

Dan Schroeder fell in step with Estelle as she walked back toward her car. When they were well beyond Frank Dayan's earshot, the district attorney said quietly, "I'm going to file against Kenderman, by the way."

"I guess I'm not surprised," Estelle said. She reached the car and paused with her hand on the door. Schroeder's late-model SUV was parked directly in front of hers.

"I talked with both Bobby and the chief last night, and they haven't changed their minds this morning. I'd be interested in your thoughts," he said.

Estelle regarded the juncture of car door and roof, running her finger along the seam. "We have no way of ever knowing if Colette Parker would have crashed at that corner if Kenderman hadn't been in pursuit," she said finally.

"That's not the issue," Schroeder said. "He *was* in pursuit. That's an established fact. And with no lights, no siren—hell, it was just a drag race. You heard the whole sorry episode."

"Yes, sir, I did."

"I can't think of a better definition of *reckless endangerment*," Schroeder said.

Estelle's gaze drifted off to the car dealer's parking lot next door. The bright sea of metal and plastic and the gaggle of curious faces didn't register. Instead, she saw Colette Parker's small, delicate face framed by the scarred motorcycle helmet. "Charges of reckless endangerment and vehicular homicide would be appropriate," she said finally.

Schroeder nodded with satisfaction. "In a way, I feel sorry for the guy," he said. "I don't know what he thought he'd accomplish, but whatever it was, it sure went to shit."

"I feel a little uneasy about his state of mind right now," Estelle said.

"That's interesting." Schroeder's eyes narrowed. "Because he's not in custody yet, is he."

"No, sir."

"You have plenty to hold him on, you know," Schroeder said. "You don't have to wait for me."

"I understand that, sir. We're a little bit tied up just now. He's not going anywhere." She glanced again toward the car dealer's lot. Each of those faces represented a pending interview in the search to find someone who had heard or seen something related to Enriquez's death.

"I can understand you giving him the benefit of the doubt, I suppose. But there's not much doubt anymore, is there."

"No, sir."

"You said you felt 'uneasy' about him. You saw him this morning?"

"Yes, sir."

"He's got to know that charges are pending. He's no rocket scientist, but the formula here is pretty simple. Don't let it go too long before you guys move on it."

"I'm sure he knows. He's a cop, after all."

Schroeder coughed. "*Was* a cop."

"He's worried about the two kids. Colette's two."

"Now, he's worried. That's nice. Would that that concern had surfaced before he decided to run their mother off the road." Estelle remained silent, and Schroeder sighed and shook his head. "How old are they?"

"The little girl is two. The boy is four. I think Perry may be the boy's father."

"Ah," Schroeder said. "The kids' father."

"Just Ryan's. The boy."

"Really?" The district attorney's eyebrows arched. "She got around some, then. Who's father of the girl? She's the youngest, right?"

Estelle nodded. "I think the little girl's father is Perry's younger brother, Rick."

"You're kidding."

"No, sir. He lives down in Las Cruces."

"What a mess," Schroeder said, and this time, some sympathy crept into his tone.

"Yes, sir. The grandmother is taking care of the two kids for a while."

"No marriage licenses in all this, though?"

"No, sir."

"Our lives should be so simple," Schroeder said.

"I can't argue that, sir," Estelle said. "You're filing this morning?"

"Unless you can convince me otherwise." He looked hard at Estelle. "I wanted to give you folks some time to clean up this mess first. But don't wait too long. Perry doesn't need to have a long leash."

Estelle smiled wryly. Evidently Bobby Torrez hadn't shared

his concerns about Enriquez's death with the district attorney. "Thanks, sir."

"I'll ask Judge Hobart to schedule a preliminary hearing for this afternoon. You'll certainly have Perry in custody by then, right? I don't see any point in dragging our feet."

"No, sir. We're keeping an eye on him," Estelle said. "I don't know what's going on between him and his brother. All we know is that Rick isn't in town."

"Then let's hope it stays that way," Schroeder said.

THIRTEEN

ESTELLE GLANCED AT her watch, then hesitated before pulling the county car into gear. Bob Torrez was right…George Enriquez's death included too many inconsistencies to be written off as a suicide. There might be a simple explanation for the heavy revolver's position under the chair, a simple explanation for the absence of checkering marks that should have been left by the revolver's grips against Enriquez's palms. But those simple explanations were eluding them.

Dan Schroeder hadn't voiced his thoughts, but Estelle knew what they had to be. The coincidence of George Enriquez's promised *"I can give you Guzman"* followed by his convenient death before he could make an explanation was enough to make anyone curious.

Alan Perrone would perform the preliminary NAA test on Enriquez's corpse to determine if the insurance agent had fired the revolver…or at least had had it in hand when it was fired. But the odds were good that none of the lab tests, or the preliminary autopsy, would be completed before late afternoon.

Estelle had tried unsuccessfully to conjure up some recollection of Constance Enriquez, to remember a face to go with the name. Mrs. Enriquez hadn't attended the preliminary hearing months ago when Judge Lester Hobart had released her husband on his own recognizance pending grand jury action. Estelle could see George's round, pleasant face with the quick, flashing smile of the professional salesman. In court, George had seemed more confident and cheerful than his attorney had been, as if he were appearing to settle a simple traffic ticket.

But Connie? How had she survived through all this mess that her husband had heaped upon them?

Mimbres Drive was a short cul-de-sac, gracefully curved not because of the natural terrain but simply because that's the way the developer had chosen to steer the bulldozer twenty years before when he turned the old Gallegos ranch into a subdivision. The dozen houses in the development were brick with wood trim.

The residence at 419 Mimbres was no surprise, showing those touches that the profits from a successful career could buy. A semicircular concrete driveway arced across the front yard, passing through decorative beds of tamed desert plants. A large self-contained camper was parked in the driveway, flanked by a late-model Cadillac. Behind the camper sat a new van, the temporary tag still taped in the tinted back window.

Estelle got out of the car and glanced at the other vehicles parked on both sides of Mimbres Drive. Several bore Texas plates. She paused behind the van long enough to read the temporary tag. The new owner, Owen Frieberg, was a partner at Salazar and Sons Funeral Home. He either was a friend of the family's or wasn't wasting any time drumming up business. Mr. Frieberg hadn't shopped locally for his new van, despite the oft-published pleas of his own chamber of commerce. The expensive unit had been purchased two weeks before, in Albuquerque.

A rotund woman poured into a pair of blue jeans with a western-style blouse answered Estelle's ring. Her eyes flicked the undersheriff from top to bottom, and she almost immediately began to shut the door.

"We're really not interested," she said. "There's been a death in the family, but thanks for stopping by." Her voice carried the nasal twang of west Texas.

"Ma'am," Estelle said and held her badge case up briefly. "I'm Undersheriff Estelle Guzman. I need to speak with Mrs. Enriquez."

"Oh," the woman said. Her penciled eyebrows went up and stayed there. "Just a minute, then." She closed the door. Estelle could hear voices inside the house, and after a moment the door opened again. Estelle smiled at the odd face that peered out at her.

"Is that who I think it is?" Father Bertrand Anselmo chortled. His bottle-bottom glasses couldn't hide the twinkle in his eyes. Anselmo was bald except for a gray fringe around his head at ear level that looked as if a house cat had draped itself around his skull. He beamed at Estelle, showing a collection of fillings, crowns, and gaps all generated by the low-bidding dentist of the moment.

The priest held the door wide open. He gripped it tightly with one hand as if the excitement of the moment might slam it shut. "It *is* who I think it is. Look at this." He released the door and advanced, both arms held wide. "Blessed saints, but it's good to see you."

"Father," Estelle said, and patted him on the back until he released her. His black shirt smelled musty.

"Oh, my goodness, look at you," he said, and for a moment it appeared as if he was going to launch into the ritual how's-the-family grilling. But the ebullient expression faded, replaced by an awareness of the sad day in the home behind him. "There's quite a mob scene in here," he said, lowering his voice to a whisper.

"I would think so," Estelle said. *Brunch with the widow.*

"Do you have any news for us?" the priest asked, and for a moment he sounded as if he were more from Dublin than Deming.

Estelle shook her head. "Actually, Father, I need to talk with Mrs. Enriquez. Is she home?"

"Surely, surely," he said. "Won't you come in?"

Estelle stepped inside and stopped on the tiled foyer. Off to the left was what appeared to be a well-appointed game room where at least fifteen people milled about, all talking at once. Another mob had taken over the kitchen. Through an archway to the right, Estelle saw three elderly women in the living room, coffee cups in hand, deep in conversation.

"Ay," Estelle whispered to herself, and despite Father Anselmo's hand on her elbow, she remained firmly rooted in place, fascinated by the spectacle. One way to take the widow's mind off the deceased husband was to make her life miserable in every other way. After a day or two, that would wear off. The people would leave, and the house would become a big, silent mausoleum.

"Father," Estelle said quietly, "I can't talk with her here."

Anselmo's face hardened a bit with resolve, his shaggy eyebrows lowering until they rested on the rims of his glasses. "What do you need? You just tell me, and I'll see to it."

Estelle drew a card from her badge case and handed it to the priest. "Maybe…" she started to say, when one of the most enormous women she had ever seen appeared in the doorway to the kitchen.

"Ah, Connie," the priest said, and held out a hand. "You know the undersheriff?"

"No, I don't. Heard of you. We've never met," Constance Enriquez said. She didn't take the priest's hand. Two inches shorter than Estelle's five foot seven inches, the woman's massive weight ballooned from a frame that, judging from the fine hand she extended to accept the business card, could barely cope. She walked with a slight roll, as if having to hitch each step along with protesting hips.

Plump cheeks, wet from recent tears, crowded her eyes in a broad face. Thinning hair had been chopped into a sort of modified pageboy, keeping it from being buried in the folds of fat at the back of her neck. She regarded the business card for a long moment, and when her glacial eyes flicked back up to Estelle's, they were hard and unwelcoming.

"What can I do for you?" she said. She extended the card back toward Estelle.

"Mrs. Enriquez, I need to talk with you at some length. That's going to be very difficult to do here. I wonder if there's someplace that we might…"

The woman waved a hand, the curtains of fat that hung from her upper arms undulating. "We'll use his room. That's easiest." She turned away. "Come on," she said, and Estelle followed, Father Bertrand Anselmo trailing behind. Connie Enriquez ignored the glances and murmurs as they navigated past the kitchen. At the end of the long hallway, Connie Enriquez pushed open a set of double doors, revealing a spacious den.

"This'll do," she said.

"Father, excuse us," Estelle said when Anselmo started to enter.

"Oh, certainly. Connie, if you need anything…" he said.

"What I need is for the circus to be over," she muttered and reached past Estelle to latch one side of the doors. "You gotta hook this, or they'll drift open," she said, stretching up to push the small brass bolt into the jamb. She forcefully pushed the other side shut. "There." She beckoned toward a leather-covered chair near a bookcase. "Sit yourself."

She chose a stout, straight-backed chair that looked up to the challenge, reached over to the large walnut desk, and pulled the box of tissues closer. She extracted one and wadded it into a ball, dropping her hands to her lap.

"So," she said. "You're a very attractive young woman. How'd you happen to fall into such an awful job?"

"Thank you. And that's a very long story, Mrs. Enriquez."

"Call me Connie."

"Connie. I know this is going to be painful for you, but there are some things I need to know concerning your husband and the circumstances of his death. You may be able to help us."

"Is this all standard procedure? I mean, is this what you normally *do*, with things like this?"

"Yes, ma'am."

"All right." She shifted her bulk on the chair.

Estelle pulled the microrecorder from her jacket pocket and held it up. "I need to use this. Do you mind?"

"Of course not."

The undersheriff pushed the Record button and gently rested the gadget on the corner of the desk. "Mrs. Enriquez, in the past few days, did your husband discuss his difficulties with you?"

For the first time, something akin to a smile ghosted across the woman's face, not enough to show teeth, but enough to touch the creases.

"Undersheriff," the woman said. "That's an interesting title."

Her hands folded around the tissue. "Do I call you that? Or is it *officer,* or what?"

"Estelle would be fine."

"Estelle. Doesn't that mean *star* or something like that in Spanish?"

Estelle smiled. "No, ma'am. You may be thinking of *estrella,* with an 'r.'"

Connie nodded and pursed her lips. The half smile reappeared. "Let me tell you how I first learned of my husband's antics, Estelle," she said. "A neighbor across the way met me out in the driveway with the local paper in hand." As she talked, Connie Enriquez's hands remained motionless. "Nice little front-page story about my husband's arraignment." She paused for a moment. "Now isn't that wonderful? A thoughtful neighbor shows me a front-page newspaper story."

Estelle didn't respond, and Connie continued, "Tell me how that could have happened without my knowing about it, Mrs. Undersheriff." She took a deep, shuddering breath. "My husband's business was investigated, charges were brought against him by your office and the state insurance board, and he was arraigned before the local judge. And when did I hear about it? When it's splashed on the front page of the local newspaper." Her mouth twisted in a tight-lipped smile.

"I'm not complaining, mind you," she said. "Not knowing probably spared me some moments with George that we both would have regretted. You asked me if my husband discussed his business life with me? He didn't. In spades." She dabbed at her left eye. "How well do you know your husband, Estelle?"

When the undersheriff didn't answer, Connie Enriquez leaned forward just a bit, the tissue still grubbing into her left eye. "Someone out in the kitchen is a cat lover," she said. "Damn things drive me crazy. The dander's all over my clothes now." She shook her head and examined the wad of tissue. "Your husband's the one who opened the new clinic with Alan Perrone, right? The coroner? Alan's the dapper little guy; Dr. Guzman's the big hunk, am I right? Great big guy with a nicely trimmed beard?"

Estelle nodded.

"If I asked you to sit down and tell me what the good doctor does all day long—and I mean in detail—I don't think you could tell me. Am I right? And he couldn't tell me what *you* do. Now maybe the two of you discuss your days with each other when you get home." Her eyes narrowed until they almost disappeared when Estelle didn't offer an answer. "Maybe you do. *I* certainly wouldn't know. George and I didn't discuss his days, Estelle. Or mine. Never. Ever."

"Mrs. Enriquez, to the best of your knowledge, did your husband own any firearms?"

"No," she said quickly. "I won't have them in the house. And now you know why."

"I beg your pardon?"

"George was no handyman, Estelle. He was one of those unfortunate guys who stabs himself with a screwdriver when he reaches into the toolbox to pick up a wrench. He once tried to change the oil on the Jeep, I think just to prove that he could. He dropped the thingie that plugs up the drain hole and then never could find it. He had to buy another one, which the dealer had to special-order, by the way, since no one else loses that sort of thing. That's George and mechanical things." She wadded the tissue and pressed it against her left eye. "If he had a gun, I could picture him trying to clean the damn thing and blowing his head off. Just like what you read about in the papers."

"So to the best of your knowledge, your husband did not own a handgun. For that matter, a gun of any kind?"

"Not as far as I know." She regarded the tissue, lips pursed. "I know for a while he was talking about going elk hunting, if you can imagine that. I saw one of those what do you call 'ems...game proclamations. And then I heard him talking on the phone about a hunt. Most ridiculous thing I ever heard. It would be just like George to huff and puff his way up a mountain and then drop dead from a heart attack. And *elk?* What would we do with one of those monstrous things?"

"He would need a rifle for that hunt."

"I suppose. Maybe he was going to borrow one. Or buy one. I don't know. As long as I don't have to look at it in this house."

She heaved a heavy breath.

"Do you know who he discussed the hunt with? Or whether he actually had firmed up plans about when to go?"

"No idea. You could ask Joe Tones. He'd probably know. You know Joe?"

Estelle nodded. "Yes, ma'am."

"They work together with the chamber of commerce all the time," Connie said. "I think the hunt was Joe's idea. Or Owen's. Owen Frieberg? He was here a bit ago. Who knows? Maybe he still is. I really don't know whose idea the whole crazy thing was, but I would guess Joe. He's the one who got my husband excited about Mexico, too—one of George's other daring escapades."

"Mexico?"

Connie raised a hand in mock surrender. "That sister-village thing?"

"Through the chamber, you mean?"

She tipped her head ever so slightly in agreement. "What's the name of the place across the border? *Aca* something."

"Acámbaro?"

"That's it." Her eyes narrowed slightly. "It sounds so pretty when you say it. Why another town would want a place as pathetic as Posadas as a sister village is beyond me. Sisters in misery, I guess. Anyway, the chamber goes there a couple times a year. Christmas for the kids is one time, I know. A group of students from the school goes down with 'em. That's Tones's big deal. Him and George. They liked working with the schools. I know that. Joe didn't go on the trip with them last year. I don't remember just what the reason was."

"Do you recall anyone else associated with the hunting trip idea?"

"Some guy called here a few nights ago, but I don't remember his name. It wasn't Tones or Owen."

"But several of them were going together? It wasn't just Tones, Frieberg, and your husband?"

Connie nodded. "George was going to take the RV to use as a base camp. I heard him say that. And I think it was on one of those game ranches up north. A 'boys night out' sort of thing."

She tossed the tissue into a small brass trash can with unerring aim and pulled a fresh one from the box. "And wives weren't invited, by the way, not that I would have gone anyway. I had visions of him getting drunk and then tripping over a fence while trying to carry a loaded rifle like in one of those hunter training films we used to see in school, or maybe one of his buddies would mistake him for an elk." She grunted with amusement. "I'd end up having *his* head mounted on the wall."

"Mrs. Enriquez, do you know why your husband was at his office downtown on the day of his death?"

"*Why?* No idea whatsoever, other than the obvious. That's where he goes."

"But he'd closed the office for the week, had he not?"

"I think so. But who knows."

"When was the last time you saw him?"

"When he left the house yesterday morning. Monday morning."

"Did he say anything when he left?"

"If he did, he was talking to himself. I was still asleep." She regarded Estelle for a moment as if waiting for a comment. "We sleep in separate bedrooms. I snore, apparently," she said finally, and then frowned. "So actually, no...I didn't *see* him Monday morning. I *heard* him. I remember hearing his electric razor, and then I heard the front door when he went out."

"Did he call you at any time during the day? Either late yesterday or early this morning?"

"No."

"Did anyone else call?"

"Other than friends of mine, no."

"Are you aware of any arguments that your husband might have had in the past few days with anyone?"

Connie Enriquez frowned and turned her head slightly sideways, skeptical. "*Argue* is a word that I wouldn't have associated with my husband, Undersheriff. Once in a while I tried to bait him just a bit, to see if he knew I was still on the planet. That didn't do much good. He'd give that cute little shrug of his and just walk off. But that's with me. After hearing about the grand jury investigation, I guess it wouldn't surprise me if he had arguments with half the planet. *I* didn't know anything about them. That's what I'm saying." She pushed at the inside of her cheek with her tongue, thoughtfully. "Are you saying that my husband's death wasn't an accident?"

"We're still investigating," Estelle said quietly.

"I *can* picture my husband trying to struggle out of that Jeep and accidentally shooting himself, Undersheriff. That's *exactly* the sort of thing that he'd do. I *can't* imagine someone else wanting to shoot George, and I *can't* imagine him trying to commit suicide. That's *my* bailiwick, more likely."

"Mrs. Enriquez…" Estelle started to say gently, but the woman waved a hand in dismissal.

"Not anymore. I went through a stage for a while until I just said *to hell with it.* Life goes on. And now…" she shrugged. "Now I'll play the black veil bit for a little while, make all the friends feel better, and then we'll see."

"What will you do?"

After a moment's hesitation, Connie said, "Promise not to laugh?" With a forward lunge, she pushed away from the chair, using a steadying hand on the corner of the desk. She waddled around to one of the bookshelves, one that wasn't crowded with bowling trophies, various small awards and commendations, and a handful of books, mostly insurance references. From a sea of photos, she selected one in a gold frame that was no more than three inches square.

Estelle rose and met her at the corner of the desk, taking the picture. In it, a young couple stood hand in hand, up to their ankles in surf with pure white sand behind them, lava cliffs off to the right. She recognized George Enriquez, dressed in sunglasses and skimpy bathing suit. Only twenty years old or so, he was already beginning to show sleekness around the torso. With her free hand, the girl held a sun bonnet on her head. She wore a one-piece bathing suit the same color as the surf. Soaking wet, she might have tipped the scales at ninety pounds.

"I really loved him then," Connie Enriquez said.

"The two of you on your honeymoon?" Estelle asked.

Connie nodded. "Would you believe it?"

"It's a beautiful spot."

Connie laughed. "You're such a diplomat," she said. "I'm going back there, you know. I'm serious. By the time those Mexican doctors are through with me, I'm going to look like that again." Her nod was slow and determined. "And *then* we'll see."

Estelle handed her the picture.

"Mrs. Enriquez, during the next few days you may remember something about your husband's activities. I need to know who he was associating with, basically what he was doing up until the time of his death. Anything you can remember would be a help." She withdrew the business card again, made sure that Connie Enriquez saw it, and placed it on the corner of the desk.

"George was well insured, you know," Connie said.

Estelle raised an eyebrow in question but said nothing.

"If they think it was suicide—and it wasn't, believe me—the insurance is void. No question about that. If someone murdered my husband, odds are that the insurance company will force me to sue somebody to hell and gone to collect a penny. If it was an accident, insurance will pay. I know that sounds cold-blooded, but that's the way it is." With her hands still on the desk for support, she moved closer to Estelle and lowered her voice. "Obviously, that's not a topic of conversation for out in the kitchen. But you and I know how things go. You'll do what you have to do."

"May I have permission to look through George's papers here?" Estelle asked. "I'll get a court order if you prefer."

Connie Enriquez pushed herself upright. "You go right ahead and look to your heart's content, Estelle Guzman. I'd be surprised if you found anything of any value. But we never know, do we? And before you ask...I don't know if George had any safe deposit boxes. But I'm sure you'll find out." The woman waddled toward the double doors. "I'll leave you to it. If you need me again for anything, just holler. I'll be out there dealing with cat dander." She smiled this time, showing a set of perfectly even, fine white teeth.

The door closed behind her, leaving Estelle alone in George Enriquez's study. She sat down in the large, padded swivel chair and gazed around the room, letting her eyes drift from object to

object, taking her time. The trophy clock on the desk said that
in ten minutes, Francis might be free for lunch. She found herself
yearning to see his face, to feel the brush of his beard, to hear
the sound of his voice.

FOURTEEN

CONSTANCE ENRIQUEZ had never sat in her husband's swivel chair behind the big walnut desk. For one thing, her hips wouldn't have wedged into the space between the chair's padded arms. That problem aside, had she spent time foraging in her husband's desk…had she cared enough about his activities to do so…her curiosities might have been stirred.

Estelle snapped on a thin pair of latex gloves. She started with the wide center drawer and found the usual potpourri of junk that cluttered most desks. Lying amid the paper clips and roller-ball pens in the forward tray was a rubber stamp bearing the legend of the Posadas Old Timers' Club, for deposit only, and the service club's bank account number. Estelle flipped her own small notebook to a blank page and pressed the stamp gently. The ink was fresh enough to leave a clear imprint.

She put the stamp back and ran her hand far into the drawer, feeling along the sides, into the corners, and under the desk's polished top. In the far back right-hand corner, so far that she had to scoot the chair back against the trophy case to gain clearance, she felt a small, hard object that rolled away at her touch. Her fingers chased it, already recognizing the shape.

Holding the cartridge by the rim between the fingernails of her thumb and index finger, Estelle frowned at the head stamp as she snapped on the desk light to read the small print: R-P across the top arc, .41 MAGNUM across the bottom. The bright brass casing would present fingerprints beautifully.

"Okay," she said to herself. "Just one of you?" Holding the cartridge over the desk, she rummaged a small plastic evidence bag out of her briefcase and dropped the shell inside. For a moment, she sat quietly, regarding the drawer and its contents. Then, grasping the drawer with both hands, she eased it out further, ducking her head to see into the shadows before pushing it back into place.

The top drawer on the right-hand side of the desk yielded stationery, both for Enriquez's insurance agency and the Old Timers' service club, a half ream of expensive onion-skin paper, envelopes, and an unopened package of correction ribbons for an electric typewriter.

Estelle slid that drawer shut and heaved the large bottom file drawer open, raising an eyebrow at the neat rows of manila folders, each labeled across the top. She sat back in the chair. State insurance investigators hadn't found paperwork in Enriquez's office for any of the out-of-pocket deals he'd worked with customers like Deputy Thomas Pasquale or Eleanor Pope, each one eager to save a little cash.

The case against Enriquez had been built almost entirely through the testimony of those people who thought they had legitimate policies...their embarrassed testimony, for the most part, and their cancelled checks as proof of payment. Pursuing Enriquez hadn't been a monumental priority for the district attorney's office—not enough to bother with a search warrant for the man's home.

That search wouldn't have turned up much in this collection of files, Estelle saw. She pulled out the first folder, marked '95 HEATING AND COOLING. Stubs of bills, with the corresponding cancelled checks, were ranked neatly, from January through December. Similar folders for seven more years marched back through the drawer, followed by records for telephone, automotive, health care, and more.

If he had kept files on his private insurance dealings, he hadn't cluttered his private life with them, or he'd gotten rid of them at the first whiff of interest from the D.A. and the insurance board...unless he'd used one of those little black books favored by Hollywood gangsters, so filled with convenient answers.

Estelle worked her way toward the back of the drawer, fingering each folder in turn. Then, leaning forward, she frowned with curiosity. With the drawer pulled out to the stops, she was just able to slide a walnut box up past the folders, feeling its weight and elegant, smooth finish. She sat back in the chair, the box on her lap. "Well," she said aloud and ran her fingers over the embossed logo on the lid.

She released the simple catch and opened the box. The blue velvet lining of the box was formed to fit around a large revolver, the fabric crushed smooth in places from the weight of the gun. After a moment, Estelle realized that she was holding her breath, and exhaled in a long, audible sigh.

A yellow sales ticket was tucked into the lid, and Estelle unfolded it carefully. George Enriquez was listed as the buyer, paying the Posadas Sportsmen's Emporium $359.95 plus tax for a .41-magnum Smith & Wesson Model 657. Estelle recognized old George Payton's meticulous handwriting on the invoice, including the parenthetical notation, *nonoriginal case included.* Dated September 26, 1998, the sale had been made two years before Payton had sold the Emporium.

Estelle leaned back, the open box on her lap. Just six months before, she had investigated Payton's death. The old gun dealer had had troubles of his own. What had the two Georges talked about on that September day four years before? Had the insurance salesman just fallen in love with the heft and balance of the weapon, with no intention of ever using it? Had he wanted something to carry in his car when he traveled?

She looked down at the single cartridge in its plastic bag. One orphan stayed home, perhaps forgotten as it rolled toward the back of the drawer. Estelle closed the wooden case and transferred it to another, large evidence bag. Laying the case on the desk's blotter pad, she searched the left-hand drawers, finding nothing of particular interest.

Satisfied, she got down on her hands and knees and surveyed the underside of the desk. The housekeeper whose payments were documented in the folder marked CLEANING LADY had done a meticulous job, discouraging all but one spider, whose tiny web clung to one desk leg.

The shelving that surrounded the room was equally tidy, with the flood of mementos and awards dusted and neatly arranged in echelons. George Enriquez had spent thirty years in Posadas

as a member of virtually every service club that existed, holding
offices in all of them, credited by all of them with continuing
generosity. From 1985 through 1991, he had served on the Posadas Board of Education, acting as president in 1990. He had
been cited by his own parent insurance company every year since
1978, including a shiny new Nambé tray dated less than two
months before.

What George Enriquez apparently spent very little time doing
was reading. The array of books was limited to a single shelf,
mostly insurance manuals and five years' worth of Posadas telephone directories. Estelle cocked her head, reading the title of
each volume as she moved down the shelf, stopping with a raised
eyebrow at two large volumes, *Spurgeon's Home Health Ency-
clopedia* and the *Physician's Pharmaceutical Guide* for 2001.

A bent ear of a yellow Post-it sticking out of the fat *Pharmaceutical Guide*'s pages caught her eye. The text was so fat
and bulky that she used both hands to grasp the spine when she
pulled it off the shelf. Lugging it to the desk, she thudded it
down beside the walnut revolver case and flipped it open to the
marker.

The Post-it marked one of the glossy pages of photographs of
prescription drugs, arranged by manufacturer. On the tag were
written a column of eight three-digit numbers, beginning with
311 and ranging up to 341. The obvious starting place was to
assume that the numbers referred to pages, and sure enough,
Estelle saw that the entire thirty-page series of numbers on the
Post-it was included by the gray section of the drug identification
guide.

She turned to page 311. Columns of little pills marched up
and down the page, with a sprinkling of bottles, inserts, and
inhaler systems. Nothing was checked and nothing was marked.
Page 315 was a repeat, with no marks, no dog-ears. In each case,
the number on the Post-it corresponded to a page of the photo-
graphic drug identification guide, with no additional marks. She
frowned and fanned the rest of the pages, finding nothing. She
closed the book, making sure the Post-it remained in place, and
slid the bulky text into an evidence bag.

For another hour, Estelle poked into every nook and corner

112 A DISCOUNT FOR DEATH

of George Enriquez's den. Finally convinced that she had missed no hidden shelves, no floor safes, no locked cabinets, she repacked her briefcase. For a moment she stood by the desk, gazing around the room. George Enriquez had been a tidy man. For someone who worked with paper all day, he showed no inclination to allow the flood of paperwork from his office to assault his home.

Indeed, he kept so few papers that the single drawer of files in the desk evidently sufficed for all his needs; there was no other filing cabinet.

Estelle moved to the door and opened it. The same woman who had greeted her at the front door was just leaving the bathroom, and Estelle smiled warmly at her. "Would you do me a favor?" she asked.

The woman halted, uneasy.

"Would you see if Connie can break away for a few minutes?"

"I'll see."

"Thank you."

Estelle retreated back inside the office and pushed the door closed without latching it. She walked back to the desk, popped a fresh cassette into the recorder, and placed the little unit conspicuously on her briefcase after making sure the reels were spinning.

FIFTEEN

WHEN CONNIE ENRIQUEZ opened the door of her husband's office, Estelle could see that either one of the guests had managed to say just the right thing, or the cat dander had been flying again. The woman's eyes were puffy and red, and she was in the process of loudly blowing her nose.

She took a moment to organize the wad of tissue, then closed the door behind her.

"Here I am," she said. "For better or worse."

"Mrs. Enriquez, is the condition of this room pretty much the way your husband usually kept it?"

"Nobody's been in here."

"That's not what I meant. I was impressed with how neat and uncluttered his personal papers were. I wish I could be so organized."

"A place for everything, and everything in its place," Connie said. "That was George. He hated 'visual clutter.' That's what he called it. He could hold more stuff in his head than most people could fit in a dozen filing cabinets." She glanced quickly around the room without much interest. "You know," and she moved to the straight-backed chair, standing beside it for a moment before sagging down onto the cushion, "there are a lot of things I respected about my husband, and I guess I admired that talent."

She fell silent, eyes focused somewhere off in the distance. "There was that, at least," she said finally.

"He was an interesting man, Connie."

The large woman heaved what might have been a sigh or a short chuckle. "*Interesting* is a nice word, isn't it. Covers a multitude of things. Maybe I'm interesting, too." She looked at Estelle and shook her head slowly. "*Interesting*. That's the word. I guess this is about the time I'm supposed to profess that despite our *interesting* habits, we loved each other just the same." She paused, and Estelle remained silent. "I don't think we've loved each other for twenty years, Undersheriff. Maybe longer than that. Most of the time, I didn't even *like* him very much, you know?" She looked at Estelle. "I'm sure there wasn't a whole lot to like about me, either. Funny how that goes sometimes, isn't it."

"Have you talked with the children?"

"The children," Connie repeated, as if she had forgotten that she had three of them. "The children have their own lives to lead. But, yes...I called two of them last night. I don't know where the third one is, and she probably doesn't want me to know. The others will get a hold of her." She squinted across the room, looking at the shelf of photographs. "There's a picture of them up there, the last time we were all together."

"I saw that. It's a nice looking family."

"Bart's the oldest. He wasn't home when I called, but his wife said she'd give him the message when she saw him. She wasn't sure when that would be."

The woman's gaze drifted off again, and Estelle waited patiently. "Debbie's teaching school in Houston," Connie said and shrugged. "She may come down on the weekend. I don't know." Her eyes found Estelle's. "And I don't know about Virginia. The last time we spoke, she was selling real estate somewhere in North Carolina. But she's moved since then. We don't see eye to eye on much of anything."

She fell silent for a moment, then added, "Now tell me how that happens over the years. A family drifts apart so much that when the father dies, children don't care enough to take time off from work to come to a funeral. That tells you something, doesn't it."

"I'm sorry, Connie."

"*You're* sorry." She shook with one jolt that could have been a laugh or a sob. "Anyway, you didn't want to hear me blather on about all that." Her wide face softened. "You're easy to talk to, my dear. I'm not just sure why that is. I suppose that's what makes you good at what you do.'' She heaved a huge sigh. ''Now, what did you need?''

Estelle hesitated. ''I'd like to take a couple of items with me, Mrs. Enriquez. I'll write a receipt for them, and you'll have them back fairly promptly.''

''Take anything you like.''

''I'd like to take this book,'' she said, placing her hand on the prescription drug guide. ''Do you happen to know why your husband had it?''

''I have no idea. But nothing would surprise me at this point.''

''Was he taking medication for anything?''

''I know that he had a prescription for Somdex. I saw the bottle in the bathroom. He had a bad back for a while. I don't know if that's what it was for or not.''

''That's all?''

''He could have been taking the entire drugstore, for all I know.''

''Had you noticed any changes in his behavior recently?''

''No.'' Connie managed a tight smile, a thinning of the lips. ''Undersheriff—that really does sound silly, doesn't it? *Estelle,*'' and she paused, looking down at the floor's polished parquet. ''Let me put it this way. George and I shared this house. We slept in separate bedrooms. We went our own way. On rare occasions, we managed to eat a meal at the same time, at the same table. Our relationship was like two strangers who give each other a pleasant nod when they pass on the street.'' She cocked her head expectantly. When Estelle didn't respond, she added, ''Make of that what you will.'' She pushed herself out of the chair.

''The obvious question that you're too polite to ask,'' she said, ''is why in holy hell we didn't just go our separate ways. Get a separation, a divorce...something.'' She smiled, showing her fine teeth once more. ''And if you asked, I wouldn't know how to answer. Hell, even *murdering* each other would have taken more initiative than both of us had put together. That's an awful thing to say, I suppose.''

''Mrs. Enriquez...''

The woman interrupted her. "*You* obviously think that some-one killed George, am I right? I mean, otherwise you wouldn't be going to all this trouble."

"Whenever there are unanswered questions, Mrs. Enriquez."

"I'm not sure I'm even curious enough anymore to hear the answers, my dear."

Estelle reached across the desk and picked up the walnut box. "This was in your husband's desk." She turned the box toward Connie and opened the lid. She saw the woman's head jerk back a fraction.

"Oh, for heaven's sakes," she said with disgust, as if the empty case still carried the effluvium of the weapon that nor-mally lay on the velvet.

"That and a single cartridge," Estelle said, holding up the plastic evidence bag containing the shell.

"You're kidding." Connie leaned forward a bit, like someone fascinated by a snake. "Do you suppose someone gave this to him?"

"There's a receipt inside indicating that George purchased the revolver four years ago from a dealer here in town. Maybe it just struck his fancy at the time."

Connie's eyes shifted to the bagged cartridge. "Is this the old 'save the last bullet for yourself' story?" she said, and Estelle was surprised at the venom in her voice. She didn't give the undersheriff time to answer. "And it was in his desk?"

"In the center drawer, rolled to the back."

"And the gun that was in the case? That's down at his of-fice?"

"I think so."

"Secrets, secrets," Connie said. She waved a hand in regal dismissal. "Take the damn thing, please. And don't return it. Add it to the sheriff department's museum. Or, hell, bury it with George." She rose and straightened the enormous salmon-colored muumuu that tented over her vast body. For just a mo-ment, her shoulders slumped, and she reached out for the corner of the desk.

"I sound terrible, I know, Estelle." She turned and looked at the undersheriff, and Estelle could see the misery in the woman's eyes. "I *would* like to know what happened to George. Will you keep me posted?"

"Yes, I will." Estelle extended the receipt toward her, with her business card on top.

"Maybe when all the circus is over, you'd like to come over and we could have a chat. You're from Mexico?"

"Yes, ma'am."

"How old were you when you came to this country?"

"Sixteen."

"For heaven's sakes. Is Dr. Guzman an import, too?"

Estelle smiled. "Actually, he was born in Flagstaff. But he has family in Mexico."

"Well, then, maybe you can give me the inside scoop on where to go and who to see."

"I'll mention it to Francis," Estelle said.

"Be kind," Connie Enriquez said, and when she saw the puzzled look cross Estelle's face, she added hastily, "I didn't need to say that. I'm sorry." She extended her hand for the receipt and the card, then took Estelle's hand in hers. "Thanks." She smiled, and this time Estelle saw tears well up. "I'm glad it was you that came over to talk to me."

"I'll be in touch," Estelle said.

"And you will be, too, won't you. You're not the kind who makes promises that she doesn't keep," Connie said. She held the office door for Estelle and then waved a hand at one of the faces in the kitchen. "Get the front door for the undersheriff, please," she called.

With briefcase in one hand and the tome and revolver case tucked under the other arm, Estelle nodded her thanks as Father Bertrand Anselmo scuttled to open the front door for her.

"Why don't you let me take some of that," he said.

"Thanks, Father. I've got it all."

"Don't be such a stranger," he said, and she knew exactly what he meant.

SIXTEEN

"THE PAPERWORK IS the easy part," Estelle said. She looked again at the arrest warrant for Perry Lawrence Kenderman before tucking it into her briefcase.

Sheriff Robert Torrez shrugged. "I don't think he'll give us any trouble."

"I wasn't thinking about that," she said. As she expected, he didn't ask her to elaborate. That was fine with Estelle, since her own mind was a mish-mash of mixed emotions.

Two minutes took them from the county building to Perry Kenderman's apartment on Sylvester Street, behind the high school's football field and track complex. Posadas HomeStyle Apartments included eight units, nothing more than rooms in what had once been a '50s-era cinder-block motel before the interstate had eclipsed the business and the rooms were lumped together with minimal remodeling.

"Nice place," Torrez said.

"Oh, yes," Estelle said. No response followed their knock on the door to unit three, and when Estelle glanced through the window of the first apartment, the one with MANAGER written in black marker on the turquoise door, she saw that the room was vacant. "Absentee landlord, I guess," she said. "And I don't see Perry's truck."

"At the Parker's, maybe?" Torrez asked, already heading back toward the county car.

Estelle nodded.

"He might be halfway to Wichita Falls by now," Torrez said and slammed the door of the Expedition so hard the vehicle rocked.

"Or Mexico City," Estelle said.

"His relatives are in Wichita Falls," the sheriff said. "Mother, an aunt and uncle, one sister."

"And brother Richard in Las Cruces," Estelle said. Torrez turned the vehicle onto Bustos and then headed one block west to loop around Pershing Park. A quarter block later, they turned onto Third Street. Parked directly in front of 709 was an older-model Ford Mustang, jacked up on enormous back tires so wide that part of the fender wells had been hacked away for clearance. As they coasted up behind it, they both saw the Doña Ana County sticker on the license plate.

"Except Brother Richard is now in Posadas," Estelle said. "This could be really interesting." She picked up the cell phone, pressed two buttons, and waited. "Gayle," she said when the sheriff's wife answered the phone in Dispatch, "have Collins swing around to seven oh nine Third Street."

"He's serving a set of papers in Regál at the moment," Gayle said. "He just left about ten minutes ago, so he's a fair ways out. Jackie's sitting here doing some paperwork. Can I ask her to go?"

"Even better," Estelle said. "Bobby and I will be at that address. And run a plate for me, please. Ida Mike Baker Alpha Delta."

"That's cute."

"Uh huh. I can't wait."

"Just a sec."

Estelle let the phone drop against her shoulder and looked across at Torrez. "What do you think?"

"No bets." He unlatched the door and stepped down.

She nodded at the two vehicles parked in the driveway. "The little truck is Richard's. The car belongs to Barbara Parker. That means the kids are home. I don't want them caught in the middle of something." Despite a deep respect for Robert Torrez, she was also keenly aware of his preference for direct frontal assaults.

"Huh," Torrez said. He closed the door, turned, and leaned both forearms on the Expedition's roof, regarded the house. The front door stirred, opened partially, and then closed again. In another moment, a young man stepped outside, frowning at them.

Although Estelle had never met Richard Kenderman, she saw the family resemblance with all the bumps and blemishes smoothed out. Rick Kenderman was a couple of inches under six feet, buff where his older brother was gangly, sure-footed and catlike where Perry tended to shuffle. The young man wore faded jeans and a white T-shirt. He was barefoot.

Gayle Torrez came back on the line. "Estelle, I'M BAD is registered to Richard Kenderman, Las Cruces. It should appear on a '68 Mustang, no outstanding."

"Thanks, Gayle." She switched off the phone and slid it back on her belt. Kenderman walked down the sidewalk and stopped when he reached the back bumper of his car. He looked Torrez up and down with casual bravado as if to dismiss someone of the sheriff's size. He glanced in Estelle's direction as she slipped out of the county vehicle.

"Where's Perry?" he said to Torrez without preamble.

"We don't know," Estelle replied quickly. "I thought maybe you could tell us."

Rick Kenderman sat down on the back fender of his car and ran a hand through his carefully mussed hair—the style favored by a generation of movie stars for the "slept in" look. He then folded his arms across his chest and regarded Estelle with amusement, eyes lingering here and there.

"I don't know where he is, lady. If I knew, I'd serve him up to the sheriff here in a fucking garbage bag." He picked something off his lower lip and then wiped his hands on his jeans. "Maybe he's still driving around in his squad car, chasing people."

"I can guarantee he's not doing that."

"I can guarantee," the young man mimicked and then shook his head in disgust. He pushed himself away from the Mustang and turned toward the house.

He glanced up the street and saw Jackie Taber's Bronco just as she turned onto Third. "What do you guys want, anyway?" he snapped.

"We're looking for your brother," Estelle said.

"Well, good luck. I got things to do." He walked quickly back toward the front door. Estelle caught sight of Barbara Parker inside, and she followed Kenderman up the walk. He stopped half in the doorway and held out a hand. "I didn't invite you in here, lady."

"No, but this isn't your house, either, Mr. Kenderman." As Estelle moved forward, the young man had the choice of retreating inside or hugging her. He quickly stepped away.

"Don't be such an idiot, Rick," Barbara Parker said. "These people are here to help."

"Oh, absolutely that," he said. Little Ryan appeared in the hallway, and Rick Kenderman scooted him back with a gentle push on the back of the head. "Come on, guys. We got packin' to do."

"What's going on?" Torrez asked, turning to the children's grandmother.

"Rick was going to take the kids down to Las Cruces until things settled down," Mrs. Parker said, and Estelle's stomach clenched at the hopeless tone in the woman's voice.

"You were just going to let him do that?" Torrez said in wonder.

Estelle stepped close to Barbara Parker and lowered her voice to a husky whisper. "I told you to call me."

"Well," the woman said, and her explanation drifted off into nothing.

"Mrs. Parker," Estelle snapped, and lowered her voice another notch, "we had two choices after Colette's death. We could have placed both children with protective services for forty-eight hours without a court order. But at the time, it made more sense to leave them with their grandmother. In your care. You led me to believe that's what you wanted."

"I do, but…"

"There are no *buts* here, Mrs. Parker." She glared at the woman. "Richard Kenderman is not taking those children to Las Cruces. It's that simple."

Something that might have been hope sprang into Barbara Parker's eyes. "Well, you better tell him that, then," she said.

"With pleasure," Estelle muttered. Rick Kenderman had disappeared down the narrow hall, and Estelle followed, aware of the heavy footsteps of Robert Torrez behind her. The young man confronted her at the door of Ryan's room, a tiny bedroom with toys covering every flat surface. Franklin the cat lay on the pillow, undisturbed.

"Mr. Kenderman, we have placed the children in their grandmother's custody until a determination for permanent custody has been made."

Rick raised an eyebrow. "Oh, sure."

"That's the way it's going to be."

The young man grinned and shook his head. "You guys are something else. Who appointed you God? They're my kids, and they're going with me. End of story."

"I don't think so," Torrez said, and Estelle saw his weight shift. She stepped forward quickly to buy some time.

"The last thing these two children need is to be yanked up by the roots, Richard. They just lost their mother. They belong here until all this can be sorted out."

"There's nothing to sort out," he said.

"Paternity, for one thing," Estelle said.

"What's that supposed to mean?"

"Just what I said. There's a question of paternity. Right now, it's your word that one or both of these children might be yours. Maybe, maybe not."

"Who's been feeding you this horseshit?"

Estelle smiled. Richard Kenderman's eyes were a shade darker than Perry's, without the amber flecks. He held her gaze, waiting.

"It's this simple, Richard. The law says that the children *will* stay here. Not that they might stay here if it's okay with you. They *will* stay here. And if you can't cooperate with that, then that's something we'll have to deal with."

"Oh, yeah?" He regarded Estelle calmly, assessing.

"You're a bright young man, Richard. You think on it." She looked across the room at Ryan, who'd taken up a position near the head of the bed, one hand clawed into the soft fur of Franklin's hip. A flicker of something crossed his face, whether relief or hope, Estelle wasn't sure. "You're going to stay with Grandma for a while, Ryan. Okay?"

He nodded. Heavy footfalls thumped in the hallway, and Jackie Taber's stout figure appeared behind the sheriff. Rick Kenderman saw the deputy, and Estelle watched the calculation registering in his eyes. After a couple of heartbeats spent weighing the odds, he muttered an obscenity and pushed past Estelle. Robert Torrez was standing squarely in the doorway, and Kenderman came to an abrupt halt. "What the hell do you want, Igor?" he snapped.

Estelle turned to see the explosion. But a slow grin broke the sheriff's face. "What I want is for you to slow down, buddy."

"I'm not..." Kenderman started to say, then bit it off.

"You take some time to think, and odds are we'll all get through this in one piece," Torrez added.

Kenderman turned toward Estelle. "You want to tell your retard deputy to move?"

"I don't tell the sheriff what to do," Estelle said. "And by the way, Kenderman," she added, and her voice took on an edge. "We'll be processing that little truck that's sitting out in the yard. There's enough odor of marijuana in that cab to justify a strip search. And since you're the owner, maybe that search should move on to that nifty bad Mustang parked out there."

He started to snap back but settled for a disgusted shake of the head. "Can I go now, missy?"

"You bet."

Sheriff Torrez stepped to one side and allowed Kenderman to pass.

"I'll be talkin' to you later," the young man said to Barbara Parker as he passed.

"Actually, you won't," Estelle said as she followed Kenderman outside. "If Mrs. Parker needs to talk to you, she'll call you. Otherwise, relax and have a good time in Las Cruces. When it's time for the court-ordered paternity tests, you'll hear from the Las Cruces P.D. And then on the basis of that, the courts will decide who pays child support and how much."

Kenderman's eyes narrowed. "This is a bunch of bullshit, and you know it. You think you can just..." he finished the thought with a disgusted shrug.

"You don't know what I'm thinking, Mr. Kenderman," Estelle said. "And there's a good possibility you don't want to know. I'm telling you the way things are going to be. So there's no misunderstanding."

"You guys should be spending your time trying to find my brother," Rick Kenderman said. "I'm not going to do anything to hurt those two kids."

"I'm glad to hear that," Estelle said. "We'll let you know when we need to talk to you again." She glanced at the little pickup truck. "The truck will be in the impound yard. There's a good chance you'll be hearing from us about that."

Kenderman's eyes narrowed.

"Then again, we may not even have time to get to it," Estelle said easily. She shrugged and gave Kenderman a pleasant smile. "Sometimes we get busy."

As she watched the young man climb into the Mustang, she sensed Jackie Taber at her elbow.

"Fun times?" the deputy said. Her level gaze followed the Mustang as Kenderman accelerated down the street, hard enough to make his point, not hard enough to break the law.

"Oh sure. Do me a favor? Escort him down to the interstate and make sure he gets headed in the right direction, all right?"

"Yes, ma'am." She strode across the street toward the Bronco and paused at the door. "I heard there's a want out for Perry. Is that right?"

"Yes. If anyone sees him, give me a call first. I want to be there when he's taken in."

Jackie nodded, and Estelle stepped back on the curb.

Bob Torrez waited patiently by the Expedition. As Estelle approached, she grinned at him. "So it's *Igor* now. I half expected young Mr. Kenderman to end up with a Sheetrock face."

Torrez's smile actually revealed teeth, a rare expression for him. "It's got a nice ring to it, missy," he said. "Were you serious about the marijuana bit?" He glanced across at the pickup. "If that's the case, why didn't we just arrest the punk and settle his ass in jail?"

"I wanted him out of town, *Roberto*. He'd just be out of jail in ten minutes on five hundred bucks bail, and we'd be right back where we started. This way, he's out of town...and he doesn't know for sure what we'll do."

"Do we know?" Torrez said.

"At the moment, all I know is that one Kenderman is headed out of town, and that his brother can't hide forever. I'll go with that for the time being."

SEVENTEEN

CARLOS GUZMAN'S FACE appeared in front of Estelle's as if he'd coalesced out of smoke. She shifted her head slightly so the pillow didn't block her view but otherwise didn't stir. His enormous eyes, about the color of semisweet chocolate, regarded her from out of a small round face that was just beginning to lose the indistinct lines of infancy.

"Teléfono, Mamá." He whispered the two words and leaned his chin on the edge of the bed.

She lifted her head, loath to move more than that. The hours had finally caught up with her, and she'd almost fallen asleep during an early dinner. She'd stretched out, intending to catnap for half an hour or so—three and a half hours ago.

"Grandmamá said you're supposed to talk on the telephone," Carlos said when he got no response, and Estelle shifted so she could see the phone on the nightstand. She had never heard it ring.

"Thanks, *hijo*," she murmured and reached for the receiver. The little boy remained motionless, watching. "Guzman," she said, tucking the phone between her ear and the pillow.

"Estelle, Eddie. Catch you at a bad time?"

She captured her son's spider-leg finger. With index hooked in index, she was surprised at the strength in that three-year-old finger. "No, it's just fine," she said into the phone. And if it weren't, what difference would it make, she thought. The Posadas chief of police didn't call to touch bases or engage in idle chitchat.

"We found Perry Kenderman's truck," Mitchell said. "I thought you'd want to know."

"Found it where, Chief?"

"It's parked in the student parking lot at the high school." She frowned and unhooked her finger from her son's, and he took a step back as she pushed herself upright. "You still there?"

"I'm here," she said. "That's an odd place."

"Maybe so," Mitchell said. "Or maybe not. He lives right across the way, there, and knows we'd be watching his apartment. Mix in with all the student vehicles and he might gain himself an hour or two. Maybe he thought we wouldn't check." He paused for a heartbeat. "And sure enough, we didn't. Tom Pasquale found it."

She glanced at the clock and saw that it was almost eight. "There shouldn't be many vehicles there this time of day," she said.

"Nope. But a few. Some kids still in the weight room, a few working in the science lab. There's always something going on."

"Any sign of him?"

"Nothing yet. If he left town, he didn't take his truck. As far as I know, that's the only vehicle he owns."

Estelle ran her fingers through her hair. Carlos waved a silent good-bye and thumped out of the room. "Who's working tonight for you, Eddie?"

"Me. I'd call my part-timer in, but he's done something to his knee. I'll be out and about. But I just thought you should know."

"Thanks, Chief. I wouldn't be surprised if he just walks into the office in another couple of hours. Give him long enough to think about it. He doesn't have many options."

"If he's smart, that's what he'll do," Mitchell said. "But he doesn't have much of a batting average for smarts so far. Maybe he's wrapped himself around a bottle somewhere."

"He never impressed me as the drinking type," Estelle said, and that prompted a short, barking laugh from the chief.

"What type's that?" he said. "Anyway, in a town this small, he's not going to hide for long. He's done good just keeping out of sight for a few hours. I wanted to let you know about the truck."

"Thanks."

She hung up the receiver and sat on the edge of the bed for a moment with her eyes closed. Perry Kenderman was a puzzle, an unpredictable enigma. He'd chased Colette Parker, behaving like a hotheaded teenager. What had he planned to accomplish by that? He supposedly harbored a deep affection for the two children, yet he'd been unable to admit, let alone assert, his paternity. And what was he doing now? Sitting in the darkened corner of a bar somewhere, nursing his confusion and frustration? Hitchhiking to Wichita Falls? At the time, it had seemed reasonable to give Kenderman the benefit of the doubt, allowing him to remain free on his own recognizance during the initial investigation.

Estelle sighed, arose, and shook the wrinkles out of her blouse and slacks. Her mother sat at the kitchen table, walker at hand. She was frowning over a crossword puzzle in the newspaper but looked up when Estelle appeared.

"You slept quite a while, *hija*," she said in Spanish. "This is a funny business. For weeks and weeks, the only excitement we hear about is the county budget. Now there aren't enough hours in the day."

"That's true, *Mamá*," Estelle said. "Ninety-nine point nine nine nine percent of the time, the county could make do with one deputy. That's just the nature of things."

"Well, you work too hard, *hija*. Buena es culantro…"

"…*pero no tanto*." Estelle finished the proverb for her, and Teresa nodded with approval.

"You remember that," she said. "Too much of a good thing is no good," she repeated.

"I do remember, *Mamá*, but sometimes I have no choice in the matter."

"It's almost bedtime, anyway. *Los Dos* are with their father, by the way."

What had been a one-car garage off the living room had been converted into an office, sunken half a foot below the floor level of the rest of the house. The plastered walls could be glimpsed here and there through the vast sea of books and magazines. A pool table dominated the center of the room, but the cover hadn't been off the velvet for months and was now weighted down with its own sea of books, magazines, and an odd assortment of children's toys.

Dr. Francis Guzman sat at the computer with Carlos on his lap and five-year-old Francisco standing at one corner of the keyboard. Estelle could see that the computer's huge, hi-tech screen was filled with a single photograph of herself—the same photo that Linda Real had taken for the department's calendar, a Christmas gift to the dozen employees that each month featured a different employee caught in an appropriate moment of unawareness.

Estelle moved closer, her footsteps muffled by the carpet. The original photo had been striking, catching Estelle as she crawled out from under the sagging chassis of the Popes' burned-out mobile home, her own camera slung around her neck. The photo didn't show how disheveled and filthy she'd really been at the time. A single theatrical smudge adorned one side of her face as if applied by a Hollywood makeup artist.

She had just enough time to see that the photo was being morphed into something unrecognizable before Francisco, her oldest son, turned and saw her. He screeched and tried to cover the screen with both of his small hands. His father was quicker, hitting the closure X and sending the photo off into the ether.

"You can't see," Francisco said, allowing his father to pry his hands off the screen.

The physician pushed the chair back a bit and turned away from the computer. "Top secret project," he said. He turned Carlos upside down and lowered him to the floor between his knees until the boy's head touched the carpet before letting him go to complete the somersault by himself. "And time for bed for you guys," he added and glanced up at Estelle. "Who was the call?"

"Chief Mitchell. They found Kenderman's truck over in the high school student parking lot."

"But he wasn't in it?"

"Nope."

"Don't mess with that now, geek," he said to Francisco, who was having a hard time tearing himself away from the keyboard. "We'll work on it tomorrow." He stood up and pushed the chair under the table. "You have to go out?"

"No. The chief just wanted me to know that they found the truck. That was all."

"So what's that mean?"

She bent down and stroked the top of Carlos's head. "I'm not sure," she said, but she saw that Francis had heard the hesitation in her reply.

"You don't know what he's going to do, do you."

"What who's going to do, *Mamá?*" Francisco asked.

"Bed time, *hijos,*" she said and ushered Carlos toward the door.

"You read to us?"

"Por supuesto, querido," she said. Francis leaned against the pool table, arms folded across his chest, and watched the two children race through the living room and vanish down the hall-way.

"Alan said you had a puzzler with Enriquez."

Estelle grimaced. "No puzzler. Someone shot him while he sat behind his desk in his office. We were supposed to think it was suicide."

"I think he meant *los porqués, querida.*"

"We have lots of 'whys' still. We're doing pretty well with the 'whats.'"

She turned at the thumping of her mother's walker. Teresa Reyes stopped halfway across the living room. "You want me to answer the door, or are you going to?"

Estelle looked puzzled. She stepped quickly into the living room. "I didn't hear it, *Mamá.*"

"I mean the back door," Teresa said. Estelle stopped in her tracks. The Guzmans' back door opened to the yard, a yard made secure for the two boys by a four-foot chain-link fence. Because the fence was essentially the property boundary, and because the renovated garage-studio blocked the driveway's route to the back of their lot, the backyard fence had no gates; entry to the yard was gained through the house.

"You heard someone at the back door, *Mamá?*" Her hand drifted down to her belt, where her cellular phone should have been.

Teresa nodded. "That's what I just said."

"Stay here," Estelle said to her mother. In three strides, she reached the phone extension on the small table by the sofa. By the time she had stepped into the kitchen, the swing-shift dispatcher, Ernie Wheeler, had answered. "Ernie, this is Estelle. Hang on a minute."

With a quick sweep of her hand, she turned off the kitchen lights and flicked on the switch for the outside light over the back door. Nothing happened, but this time she heard the knocking herself, four quick raps, just the way a neighbor might knock on an errand to borrow a cup of sugar.

"Who is it?" she said, just loud enough that she knew she'd be heard.

"I need to talk to you."

Estelle froze, the only movement the telephone receiver as she brought it so close that the mouthpiece touched her lips. "Send a car to my house, Ernie. Kenderman's here."

EIGHTEEN

THE DOOR TO the backyard was closed and dead bolted. The small double Thermo Pane window panel had proved resistant to baseballs, rocks, or elbows. Although Estelle's first thought was to jerk open the door, grab Kenderman by the neck, and slam him up against the house as she snapped cuffs on him, she knew that to open the door was inviting disaster. Kenderman was no lightweight adolescent. He could as easily be armed as not.

For the moment, her family was safe inside. Kenderman was locked outside and could stay there until burly assistance arrived. Deputy Tom Pasquale was on alone during the swing shift, and if he wasn't at the far end of the county, he could be at the Twelfth Street address in a few minutes. Chief Mitchell was roaming the village, only seconds away.

Estelle backed away from the door and jumped with a start as she stepped on her husband's foot. He held one of the sheriff's department's enormous flashlights.

"I need that," Estelle said and nodded down the hall. "Stay out of the kitchen, and stay with the boys and *Mamá* in our bedroom." Before he had a chance to reply, she darted ahead of him into the master bedroom and touched the code into the gun safe's door release. The door sprang open and she pulled out the loaded automatic.

In the hallway, her husband loomed enormous in the dim aura of the night light. "How dare he come to my house," Estelle hissed and pushed past Francis. Back in the kitchen, she stopped by the divider into the dining area. "Perry, are you still there?" she called.

"Look," he said, and she could tell he was standing immediately in front of the door, "I need to talk to you."

"Not here, you don't. You want to talk to me, you come down to the sheriff's office."

"They'll arrest me if I do that."

"And I'll arrest you here," Estelle snapped. She took a deep breath and glanced behind her. Everyone in the house was safe. Francis hadn't argued with her. Despite his size, agility, and tremendous strength, there was nothing to gain by changing the balance, nothing to be gained by some grandstand play that could as easily turn disastrous as not. If Kenderman forced his way through the door, he was dead. It was that simple. No negotiations, no heroics, no struggles.

The Beretta was heavy in her hand, one cartridge in the chamber and fourteen in the magazine. She snapped the safety off.

"You gotta tell 'em," Kenderman said, and for the first time Estelle could hear the slur of alcohol in his speech.

"Back away, Perry."

"You gotta tell 'em that what happened to Colette wasn't my fault."

It was your fault, she almost said. "There'll be plenty of time for everyone to tell their versions, Perry," she said. A car drove by on the street, and she turned. It went by without slowing. "Come on, Thomas," she breathed.

"You gotta tell 'em you were mistaken about hearin' me chasin' Colette."

"I can't do that, Perry. Now back away."

A fist rattled the back door, and Estelle flinched backward. Her grip on the Beretta tightened.

"You're the only one," he said, and she could hear the tension in his voice. "They'll do what you say."

"This is just going to make things worse for you, Perry. Use your head."

"You gotta listen to me." His voice sounded closer, as if he'd thrust his face close to the crack between door and jamb. "If you go tellin' 'em that I was chasin' her, they'll lock me up and throw away the key."

Which might not be a bad thing. "Back away from the door, Perry."

For a moment, she heard nothing outside. "How long have you been out there, Perry?"

He said something unintelligible and struck the door again, the blow sounding like the flat of his hand, then silence. Almost simultaneously, two vehicles pulled up in front of the house from opposite directions.

"Perry, are you there?" She heard no response. In slow motion, she pushed the window curtain to one side with the body of the flashlight, pressed the lens against the glass to cut reflection, and turned it on. The beam lanced out across the yard. Perry Kenderman was gone. She swung the flashlight beam to each side.

At the front door, a familiar set of knuckles rapped a quick drum roll that she'd heard a thousand times. She crossed quickly to the door but hesitated.

"Padrino?" she said.

"You okay?" Bill Gastner's voice was gruff, muffled by the heavy front door. She pulled it open. He frowned when he saw the Beretta. "He still out there?"

"No, he's gone."

"Well, give 'em a minute." He stepped inside and shut the door behind him. "And put that away. You make me nervous."

"I *am* nervous, sir."

He grinned and spoke into a small handheld radio. "Chief, she says he's gone. Give it a good look." The radio barked twice by way of reply. "Tom's going around on one side, Eddie's on the other. If Kenderman's still there, they should all meet in the middle." He reached out and tapped the flashlight. "You got lights in this place?"

"I'm not in any hurry," Estelle said.

"Just as well, I suppose. Wait until they give the all clear."

"He sounded like he's half looped," Estelle said. She breathed a deep, shuddering sigh and glanced down at the automatic. "I can't believe he came to my house."

"Makes sense to me," Gastner said. "You hold the keys to

his cell, sweetheart. The chief and I were trying out some of Ernie's coffee when you called. Scared the shit out of me."

"Sorry, sir."

"I rode over here with him. Old Parnelli Pasquale was all the way south on Grande, just past the Interstate. He damn near beat us here."

The radio crackled. "Estelle, you want to open the back door?"

Once again she drew the curtain, and this time saw the chief's blocky figure on the back stoop. Another flashlight cut this way and that toward the back of the yard. She twisted the dead bolt and opened the door.

"Where was he?" Mitchell asked.

"Right where you're standing. He sounded like he'd been drinking."

"Why doesn't that surprise me," the chief said. He thumped the solid door with the heel of his hand and nodded. He saw the automatic in Estelle's hand. "Good thing he didn't press the point."

"Hey," Pasquale said from across the yard. "Did you guys have a beer party?"

"Not likely," Gastner replied before Estelle had a chance. He and Estelle stepped outside just as Francis Guzman's tall, broad figure appeared in the kitchen.

"Stay here just a bit, Doc," Mitchell said to him.

Toward the back of the lawn, just to one side of the old-fashioned swing set, were two wooden Adirondack chairs. On the gravel beside one were five beer cans, each one crumpled into a small ball.

"Jesus," Mitchell said. He reached out and laid his hand on the chair's slats. "He sat here a while," he added. "Sat here and watched the house."

"The guy's gone fruitcake on us," Pasquale said.

"He can't get far," Mitchell said, and turned to Estelle. "Best guess?"

"He must have walked over here from the school," Pasquale said. "He left his truck there, thinking maybe it was a clever place to hide it. My bet is that's where he's headed. He's got to have wheels.''

"What is that, nine blocks?''

"I'll go around Bustos and down Pershing,'' Pasquale said. "Cut around to the south, and we'll have him in the middle.'' Mitchell nodded. "You okay?''

"Sure,'' Estelle said.

"You got any lights in this place?'' Gastner had walked back to the kitchen door and stood with it half open.

She smiled. "Dark's safer,'' she said.

"Bill, you want to come with me, or…'' Mitchell asked.

"I'm fine,'' Gastner said. "They might have some decent coffee here.'' The kitchen light came on behind them.

"One last check,'' Pasquale said and headed for the fence. "I'll pick up the cans on the way back.'' He scissor-jumped it effortlessly and disappeared into the shadows beside the house.

Eddie Mitchell followed them into the kitchen and shook hands with Francis. "Sorry for the disturbance,'' the chief said.

"It just sounded like he wanted to talk,'' the physician said.

Mitchell shook his head slowly. "When a guy sits in a lawn chair in somebody's backyard and watches 'em all evening…there's a screw loose somewhere, Doc.'' He turned to Estelle. "I'll keep you posted.'' He walked through the house, and as he opened the front door, an aging pickup truck pulled onto Twelfth Street. "Here's the sheriff.'' He flashed a grin at Estelle. "Old Perry's getting the attention he wanted.''

"Maybe so,'' Estelle said. She followed the chief down the front sidewalk as Sheriff Torrez swung the truck in a U-turn and pulled to a stop, tires scrubbing the curb.

"You guys all okay?''

"Fine…I guess.''

"You guess?''

Estelle took a deep breath. "He came to the back door, Bobby. He asked me not to testify against him.''

"Not testify? That's likely.''

"He hit the door a couple of times. I don't think he was trying to get in. Just an anger thing. The scary part is that earlier, while

I was taking a nap, it looks like he was sitting out in one of our lawn chairs, just watching the house.''

"You're kidding.''

"I wish I were. That's not the Perry Kenderman I know.''

"Evening, sir,'' Torrez said, and Estelle turned to see Gastner's rotund figure ambling down the sidewalk toward them from the house. The sheriff turned back to Estelle. "And he's never been in a mess like this one, either.''

"Tom's bagging the cans,'' Gastner said.

"What cans are those?'' Torrez asked.

"Perry's party,'' Gastner said. Torrez frowned, puzzled, and the older man shrugged. "What can I say.''

"Bobby, can we use your truck?'' Estelle asked, and the question took the sheriff by surprise.

"Sure. For what?''

"I think I know where Perry's going to go.''

NINETEEN

THE CAB OF Robert Torrez's Chevy pickup was a tight squeeze. Estelle sat in the middle, scrunched sideways toward Bill Gastner so Torrez had room to shift. The truck smelled its twenty-eight years, a potpourri of motor oil, chewing tobacco, and dog. The cab was more than a convenient spot for the driver to sit. It was a vast depository for things both needed and forgotten.

Gastner hitched his bulk toward the door another millimeter. "Nice rig, eh?" he said, and patted the dash, leaving fingerprints in the ancient greasy dust.

"Spectacular," Estelle replied. "But Kenderman is thinking police cruisers right about now. This might give us an edge."

"A new low in undercover," Gastner chuckled. Torrez remained studiously silent. They rolled through the stop sign at Twelfth and Bustos, pausing just long enough to allow an eastbound livestock tractor trailer to pass through.

"Can you follow him?" Estelle asked, pointing at the semi.

"Sure," Torrez said, and the pickup accelerated with respectable speed, a minor vibration from the drive train, and the smell of hot oil.

Estelle looked out over the broad, weather-beaten hood at the towering rear end of the stock trailer ahead of them. In another couple of seconds, they would reach Pershing Park, the historical marker that graced the two-block "downtown" area. Just north of the park a handful of blocks nestled the little cinder-block house owned by Barbara Parker.

She tried to imagine what route Perry Kenderman would take through the neighborhoods that lay between her own home and the Parkers' as he jogged along, his mind fuzzed with overcharges of emotion and alcohol. The village of Posadas was no metropolis, but if he was on foot, Kenderman had a dozen blocks to cover, skirting dogs, fences, and ducking out of sight when the odd car cruised by. He might have sprinted up the alleyway behind the Guzmans', coming out on Bustos near the Don Juan restaurant. Once into the neighborhoods north and east of the Twelfth Street-Bustos Avenue intersection, he could meander his way to Third Street, keeping to the shadows.

"You're sure he's on foot?" Gastner asked.

"No. I'm guessing that he is...he might have borrowed a car from a friend, but we impounded his brother's little pickup, so that's out."

"Does he know we've got his truck nailed down?" Torrez asked. "He might be headed back that way."

"And if he does, Pasquale's right there," Estelle said.

"We'll cut through the back," Torrez said. He turned the truck onto Second Street, immediately behind Salazar and Sons Funeral Home, and a few minutes later eased to a stop along the curb. Estelle leaned forward and looked past him. She could see the two enormous elms on the other side of the block, their thin crowns illuminated by the streetlight.

"What do you want me to do?" Gastner asked.

"We can cut through right here," Estelle replied. "If he's on foot, we should be way ahead of him. If not..." Torrez opened the door of the truck. "We'll go around front. If you'd cover the back..."

"Let's do it," Gastner said. "Roberto, how do I get out of this thing?"

"Just buck it with your shoulder," Torrez said. "It's kinda bent." Estelle saw that he had the small handheld radio in hand. "PD, three oh eight." The volume was turned so low Estelle had difficulty hearing the reply.

"Turn anything?" Torrez asked.

"Negative." Chief Mitchell managed to sound disappointed. "We're at the Third Street address. We'll be checkin' there."

"We'll head on up that way."

"Hang south of Bustos for a while," Torrez said. "If he's headed up here, I don't want him spooked."

"Ten four."

"Three oh six, you copy that?"

"Three oh six copies. I'm at the school right now. No sign of him."

Torrez slid the radio back in the pocket of his jacket. "Let's go see."

As they crept through the darkness, Estelle waited for the neighbor's dog to sense their presence, but either he was inside or didn't care. The Parkers' house loomed dark against the halo of the streetlight. The backyard was small and unfenced. Torrez led, keeping close to a hedge of runty, water-starved lilac bushes. Gastner touched Estelle's arm and pointed off to the right, toward the back door. She nodded and he drifted that way, walking so slowly that she knew he was searching for level footing, hoping to feel the hidden tricycle or sandbox before he tripped over it.

Estelle could see no lights on in the back of the house, none from the bedroom where Ryan hopefully snuggled, wrapped around Franklin the cat. They had reached the high, frosted window of the bathroom when Estelle heard the voices. Torrez stopped instantly, listening. "Damn television," he whispered.

"No, I don't think so." She held her breath and moved closer to the bathroom window. This time, she heard footsteps. She closed her eyes, recreating the floor plan of the small house in her mind.

"I just don't think this is a good idea, Perry," Barbara Parker said, and the words were so clear she must have been standing near the bathroom door. "The children are both asleep now. Maybe we should…"

"Shit," Torrez muttered, not waiting to hear the rest of the conversation. He sprinted toward the front of the house, moving with surprising speed for a man so large. Ducking around the left front fender of Barbara Parker's little sedan, he reached the front door, breathing hard. He held up a hand as he sensed Estelle beside him. With the other, he reached out and gently turned the knob.

The door swung open noiselessly. In the living room, the television was on, its volume muted. Barbara Parker stood in the hallway, her hands clasped together as if she were praying. Estelle saw her turn, perhaps feeling the change in air pressure or the soft night sounds floating in through the open door. She saw the two officers, and one hand went to her mouth in surprise.

"Perry," she said, and shrank back as Torrez bore down on her. The sheriff stopped in the bedroom doorway. Looking past his shoulder, Estelle could see Perry Kenderman on the far side of the little single bed, Ryan Parker gathered in his arms. She pushed past Torrez, snapping on the bedroom light as she did so. With his free hand, Kenderman was trying to wrap a small blanket around the boy. Ryan's face crumpled into a loud wail.

"Put him down," Estelle barked. Kenderman clutched the boy to him, backing up until his back was against the wall. His left arm slid up until his forearm was across the boy's upper chest, under the chin. Estelle interpreted his movement as protective of the boy, rather than threatening.

"You have to tell 'em it wasn't my fault," Kenderman said helplessly.

"Put the boy down," Estelle repeated, and when she felt Torrez shift behind her, she turned and pushed a hand against his chest, advancing on Kenderman at the same time. She could smell the alcohol on his breath, but saw no weapons. Still, he could snap Ryan's neck like a toothpick. She stopped at the foot of the bed. "Perry, what's this going to accomplish?"

He frowned, and it looked as if he was chewing on his tongue, trying to put words together.

"Perry, listen to me," Estelle said. "The children are safe here. I talked to your brother this afternoon. He's not taking them to Las Cruces. Barbara has custody until this is all straightened out. They're safe with their grandmother, Perry."

Kenderman shifted his hold on Ryan, turning him so that the little boy's face was cradled against his shoulder.

"You know the law as well as I do, Perry," she said. "You can't just take the children away from their guardian. We won't let you do that." For the first time, Perry Kenderman's eyes seemed to focus on Robert Torrez, who stood easy, blocking the doorway, hands at his sides.

"Let him go, Perry," Estelle whispered. Kenderman closed

his eyes and his arms relaxed, letting Ryan slide down to the bed. Estelle held out a hand and Ryan crabbed across the bedding, his hands hot and sweaty in Estelle's as she drew the little boy to her. Torrez moved around her quickly, but Kenderman had already sagged down the wall, ending up on his rump, arms across his knees.

The sheriff grabbed Kenderman's arms and hoisted him to his feet, as if he weighed no more than Ryan, and spun him around face first against the wall. The metallic ratchet of handcuffs was loud in the room, and Torrez wasted no time. He whisked Perry Kenderman out of the house without comment or glance at Barbara Parker.

Still holding Ryan in her arms, Estelle turned away from the bed.

"I just got so flustered," Barbara Parker said. She reached out for Ryan, then looked puzzled as Estelle made no move to release the child.

"Mrs. Parker, do you understand what's going on?"

"Why...I don't...what do you mean?"

"Do you understand that you have *legal* custody of these children?" She glanced across the hall toward the small bedroom where Mindi slept peacefully.

"I...yes, I do."

Estelle moved a step closer, so close she could smell the cigarette smoke on Barbara Parker's breath. "Do you understand what that means, Mrs. Parker?"

The woman bristled a bit as some of her backbone returned. "Now, I'm not stupid, Sheriff."

"Mrs. Parker, we argued Richard out of taking the children earlier. Just now, you allowed Perry Kenderman to walk into your house and apparently it was just fine with you that he take your grandson. I don't understand you."

"I..." The woman looked around the room as if the answer was hiding from her.

"You didn't even call nine one one, Mrs. Parker. Perry had no car. What were you going to do, let him take yours? Or maybe just walk off into the night, the two of them?"

"No, I didn't know he didn't have a car. I let him in, and he seemed so…I don't know, so…frantic about the children. I tried to explain to him, but he just went right to the bedroom. Went right in to fetch Ryan. I tried to talk him out of it.''

Ryan's weight seemed to solidify against her chest and arm, and Estelle bent at the knees until his feet found the floor. ''Good boy,'' she whispered in his ear. He didn't release her hand.

''Mrs. Parker, Perry Kenderman has been formally charged in the death of your daughter. I don't think you'll have to worry about him. Richard Kenderman understands that he's not to be on your property, or not to attempt to contact the children until the court says otherwise.'' She saw the tears in the woman's eyes. ''I know it's hard,'' she added, and her voice softened. ''They're remarkable children for so many people to want them. I think you must be very proud of your daughter.''

Mrs. Parker nodded. ''I am, you know. I really am.''

''Keep them safe,'' Estelle said. She ushered Ryan toward his grandmother, and at the same time smiled at the woman. ''And next time don't take so long to call us. Three little numbers. Nine, one, one. That's your responsibility.'' Heavy footsteps pounded on the rug, and Deputy Thomas Pasquale appeared in the hallway.

''You all right, ma'am?'' His eyes took in Estelle, Barbara Parker, and the small blanket-wrapped boy.

''We're fine,'' Estelle said.

''Kenderman's in the car,'' Pasquale said. ''And the sheriff wants to talk to you when you're done.''

''I'll be there in a minute,'' Estelle said, and turned to Mrs. Parker. ''I'll be in touch, all right?''

The woman nodded. ''Thank you so much. I was stupid, I know.''

''It's hard sometimes,'' Estelle said. ''It's hard to know just what to do.''

She reached over and ruffled Ryan's hair and earned a small smile. ''You take care of Mindi, now,'' she said.

''She's asleep,'' Ryan said.

''That's good. You should be, too.''

She turned and made her way down the hall. Pasquale held

the front door for her, and she puffed her cheeks and looked heavenward as she stepped past him.

"Nice night, huh," he said.

"Wonderful, *Tomás*."

Out at the curb, Robert Torrez leaned against Pasquale's Expedition, one leg crossed over the other, hands in his pockets. Bill Gastner leaned on the hood and appeared to be drawing pictures in the dust while Chief Eddie Mitchell looked on. The three of them looked like ranchers discussing the possibility of rain. She took a deep breath to stop her stomach from churning and walked across the yard toward them. The neighbor's dog had taken up his position by one of the elms, watching.

"You know, the reason I was coming over to your house in the first place," Torrez said as she approached, "was just to tell you that Tom Mears found some interesting prints on the revolver. But we kinda got sidetracked for a bit."

"Just for a bit," Estelle said. She reached out a hand and touched Gastner on the left arm and nodded at Mitchell. "Thanks."

"Hell, no one ever dives out the back door," Gastner said. "I had the easy part."

Estelle glanced in the back of the unit. Perry Kenderman's head was back against the top of the seat, his eyes closed, and his mouth open. "Is he all right?"

"Just stoned," Torrez said.

"So what about the gun?"

"A couple of prints that belonged to George Enriquez on the fired cartridge."

"Well, that's expected, I guess. You weren't driving over to my house just to tell me that."

Torrez shrugged and pushed himself away from the truck as Deputy Pasquale approached. He hitched up his belt. "But none on the gun. None. Zero. *Nada*."

Estelle regarded the sheriff silently.

"Somebody made a dumb mistake," the sheriff said. "Maybe the shooter made some others, too." He glanced at his watch. "It's late. First thing in the morning, let's take a look. That'll give Mears time to finish processing everything anyway. And Alan might have something for us.''

Estelle nodded.

"I'll give you a lift back home.''

Estelle took a deep breath. "Actually, Bobby, I'd like to walk.''

"Walk?'' Torrez sounded as if the idea were preposterous.

She nodded. "A little stroll would suit my nerves just fine.'' She turned to Gastner. "Are you up for that, sir?''

"Oh, certainly,'' the older man said without hesitation. "I'm a great hiker. We all know that.''

A few minutes later, as they watched Pasquale's unit pull away followed by the village car, Estelle breathed a loud sigh of relief. "You just never know,'' she said. Torrez had vanished in the darkness, finding his way through the backyard to his truck. She fished the small cell phone out of her pocket, and as they passed under the next streetlight, she dialed. Francis Guzman answered on the first ring.

TWENTY

FOR THE FIRST BLOCK or so, they walked in companionable silence. Estelle linked her arm through Gastner's and slowed her pace to match his amble. His head bobbed as he worked to keep the shadow of the sidewalk in focus through his bifocals. As they moved out of the aura of each streetlight, his steps became more deliberate, as if he were sinking his feet through murky water, trying to find the bottom of the river crossing.

Their route through the neighborhoods north of Bustos Avenue paralleled that main drag. Each house was marked with the glow of a television, and occasionally Estelle heard indistinct voices through an open window. The symphony of dogs moved with them, a new one taking up the barking as they walked out of range of the last.

"You did a good job with Kenderman," Gastner said as they stepped off the Fifth Street curb.

"I don't remember what I said," Estelle replied. "All I remember is that I was furious when he came to my house and I was still furious with him when I saw him standing in the corner of that bedroom, holding Ryan."

"Hmm," Gastner murmured, sounding amused. "You met the other brother, too, I understand."

"I don't think I like him too much. He's a young man who's really full of himself, as my mother would say."

"I would imagine there are several folks in Posadas who are pleased that Richard decided to move to Las Cruces," Gastner said.

"He needs to stay there, too."

Gastner chuckled. "All kinds," he said. "All kinds." He

sighed heavily. "I knew George Enriquez pretty well," he said,
"speaking of all kinds. He never seemed like the suicidal type,
whatever type that is."

"It wasn't suicide, sir."

"That's what the chief tells me. Pretty clumsy attempt to mis-
lead the cops, then."

"That's not unusual, sir."

"No indeed."

"Tell me what you know about him."

"About George? He's been selling insurance in Posadas for
more than two decades. He's a fixture." He shrugged and
grunted as they stepped up on a curb. "Was a fixture, anyway.
George is a backbone kind of guy, you know what I mean?"

"No, sir."

"He was the backbone of every service club he joined. Hell,
he'd been after me to join one or another for years. Every fund-
raiser, there's old George. You go to a high-school game, and
there he is in the concession booth that the Knights of whoever
runs. He wasn't into politics as such. I mean, he never ran for
office, except for a turn or two on the school board. Never on
the village board, never a county commissioner. That wasn't his
style. But now…" and hesitated while they navigated around a
camper that was blocking the sidewalk, "he just about owned
the chamber of commerce. That was his kingdom."

"He's talked to Francis about that," Estelle said. "Francis
and Alan hadn't even opened the clinic for their first patient
when an entourage from the chamber were on their doorstep."

"And I imagine Georgie was in the lead."

"Yes, he was. He recruited Louis."

"Louis Herrera? Well, that's not surprising. A drugstore is a
pretty important part of a community. And with you guys opening the one at the clinic, that makes two for Posadas. All the
hypochondriacs in town should be in seventh heaven with two
pharmacists to pester."

"Do you remember Enriquez ever having any trouble with
anyone, though?"

"Enemies, you mean? Nah. Well…not more than the average
person who lives in a small town and has to deal with neighbors

and customers. There's always going to be something, you know.''

Estelle fell silent and after a moment Gastner slowed down so he could look at her. "That's what you need to find, sweetheart," he said. "That 'something.' That little 'something' that each one of us has...some more than others, of course."

He looked down the deserted stretch of Eighth Street, pausing on the curb. "With George Enriquez, I wouldn't even hazard a guess about where to start to find that 'something.' As far as I know, he and Connie got along all right—at least no shouting matches out in the street in the wee hours of the morning. They've been married a long time, not that that means anything, either. Georgie had a good business going with the insurance agency, and if a few folks didn't actually have formal policies, well,'' and he shrugged, "that's not the end of the earth. He never shafted anyone out of any money when it came to paying claims.''

"That's one way of looking at it, sir," Estelle said, amused.

"Well,'' Gastner said, shrugging again, "there's the school that says 'no complaint, no crime.' You've heard that one."

"Yes, I have.''

"Now, obviously, given enough time, there *would* have been a complaint, unless George was prepared to cover a whopper of a loss. Maybe he was; I don't know. But I can imagine his rationale. He was working as if he were the parent insurance company. Hell, why pass on all that premium money when he could just go into business for himself? I'm not saying that's right or legal, mind you. I'm just saying I can understand it. And that's the one big chink that I can think of in old Georgie's clean profile. It's a good place to start.''

"I don't think so, sir.''

"Why not?''

"Because whoever murdered George Enriquez did so in desperation. I don't think that the killer had time to really think the whole thing through.''

"They often don't.''

"I know, but this one *really* impresses me as a crime of opportunity. There's the target, sitting in a chair. The door's closed, there's no one watching." She clapped her hands. "Boom."

"Okay. We might wonder how the killer got a hold of George's revolver. What were they doing, playing show and tell?"

"I don't know, *Padrino*. But that kind of rage is more than just astonishment at finding out that you've got a bogus insurance policy, sir. For one thing, if you kill George, you've got no way to recover funds. Kiss the money good-bye. *Mata la gallina de los huevos de oro,* so to speak. You've killed that goose and its golden eggs."

"So to speak. If you ask me, the place to start is with the murder weapon. That's what doesn't make sense to me. I mean, the goddamn thing is a cannon, right? What's George Enriquez doing with a .41 magnum? Fascination? Infatuation?"

"He purchased it legally from George Payton four years ago."

Gastner looked pained at the mention of one of his closest friends. "Would that George Payton could give you some answers, sweetheart. He can't tell us why he sold it, and the other George can't tell us why he bought it. There you go." He held out both hands. "Except."

"Except?"

"Except the old rule. That's what Enriquez had, so that's what he used. Boom."

"That's what we're supposed to think, anyway. I think about that revolver a lot, sir. And I think about what Enriquez told the district attorney."

"And what was that?"

"According to Schroeder, Enriquez called him on Sunday, looking for a last-minute way to hold off the grand jury. He wanted to meet, and when Schroeder asked why, Enriquez said they should meet because he had information about me that would change the complexion of things. According to Schroeder, Enriquez said, *'I can give you Guzman.'* He wouldn't explain what he meant by that."

Gastner stopped abruptly. The streetlight winked off the gold rims of his glasses as he regarded Estelle. "Nobody told me about that."

"Schroeder told me last night when we were at the motorcycle accident. I don't think that he's discussed it with anyone else yet. Bobby doesn't know."

"*I can give you Guzman.*"

"That's what he said."

"Which Guzman? Did he say?"

Estelle found herself tongue-tied, tripped by her own assumption.

"You're thinking that Enriquez meant you?" Gastner asked when she didn't respond.

"Yes, I guess I was," she said. "That's the only thing that makes sense to me."

Gastner nodded slowly. "He could as easily have been referring to Francis, you know. If all he said was *Guzman…*"

"That's something I can't even imagine, sir. Even if he meant *me,* I haven't a clue what he was talking about. He has no dealings with my husband. Never did."

"There has to be a connection," Gastner said, and this time he took Estelle's arm, ushering her south along the Twelfth Street sidewalk toward the bridge two blocks ahead of them. "Nobody says something like that without reason. Maybe Enriquez was just desperate and wanted to stall the grand jury. Everybody makes deals all the time, and maybe he figured that the district attorney would do the same thing. He thought that he could buy himself some time."

"What kind of connection could there be? I don't understand that."

"There doesn't *have* to be one, sweetheart. There only has to be a *perceived* connection in George Enriquez's mind. Something he was dwelling on. Some rumor that he thought might work some magic for him."

"Rumors?"

"The lifeblood of a small town, Estelle. You and your hubby are the perfect target. You know that. Don't be naive."

This time it was Estelle who stopped short. "Tell me."

"Tell you what?"

"What sorts of things have you heard?" He didn't reply, and she added, "Sir, I really need to know."

"Sweetheart, you can't open a wonderful facility like the one built in my backyard without making enemies...or at least jealousies. It's that simple." He thrust his hands in his pockets. "It's along the lines of 'no good deed goes unpunished.' As I'm sure you remember, more than one realtor in Posadas came close to hanging me in effigy when I gave you guys the property behind my house for the clinic. None of them had the opportunity to make a mint off the deal. That's just one angle of the damn thing. We don't even need to talk about what bankers probably thought when your hubby's Aunt Sophia gave him the money to build. And we don't need to talk about what some folks think about poor Mexicans coming across the border, legally or otherwise, so they can receive treatment...treatment that they might pay for...or not."

"That was part of the understanding when Sophia underwrote the idea," Estelle said.

"That doesn't matter, sweetheart. *I* know it was. *You* know it was. But..."

Estelle looked down at the darkened sidewalk, head swimming. "You're saying that maybe George Enriquez had some connection with my husband's clinic. Somehow..."

"It's a place to start, and no, I didn't say that George had any connection. But he might have *thought* there was something there. Maybe something he didn't understand. He heard one of those wonderful rumors and decided to run with it. What you know for sure is that *you* have no connection with George or his business dealings." He laughed gently. "Unless you're a gangster on the side and I don't know about it."

"No," Estelle said. "But Francis isn't either."

"Remember what I said," Gastner said gently.

"I wish I did."

He linked arms with her again. "*Perceived* is the word to keep in mind, sweetheart. *Perceived*. Repeat ten times after me."

"Perceived."

"Right, and that's just once. You've got nine to go. When Georgie Enriquez told our fine district attorney that he could hand over *Guzman*, it's conceivable that he meant Francis...that he was trying to make some hay based on one of the creative rumors that he'd heard. And just as likely that he didn't know what he was talking about.''

"Ay. This makes me sick.''

Gastner squeezed her arm affectionately. "Use it as a place to start, sweetheart. But don't lose sleep over it.''

"That's easy to say," she replied ruefully.

"Exactly. And maybe that's why I'm the world's leading expert on insomnia. I'll worry about it for both of us.'' They crossed the bridge and walked past the broad flanks of the Don Juan de Oñate Restaurant.

"You want to stop for a snack or something?''

"I don't think so, sir. I need to get home. Come have something at the house. We even have some leftover cake from your birthday.''

"Pour some green chile over it, and it's perfect. Have you told Francis, by the way?''

"About?''

"I can give you Guzman.''

"No...I haven't told him. Not yet.''

"Then you should.''

"I know. But he doesn't need anything else to worry about right now.''

"He needs to know, sweetheart. Don't put it off. That's my fatherly advice for the evening.''

"Yes, sir." She grimaced with resignation.

"That wasn't a promise," he said. "That was just an agreement.''

"Yes, *Padrino*.''

TWENTY-ONE

THE REVOLVER LAY on Sheriff Robert Torrez's desk, still enshrouded in plastic. Sgt. Tom Mears sat in the sheriff's swivel chair, head on one fist, writing with a pencil on a yellow legal pad. He reminded Estelle of a kid taking a boring test.

As she walked into the small office, Mears looked up with an economy of movement. The pencil stopped, his eyes shifted, but that was it.

"Long night?" Estelle asked. Mears was one of the "denizens of the night," as Dr. Francis Guzman called them…the deputies who rarely worked day shifts.

"Very," he said. "As if we needed something else, last night was National Domestic Dispute Night." He flashed a tired smile, still not moving his head from its leaning post. "You should see Pasquale negotiate a dispute between a fifteen-year-old pot-head girl and her great aunt, who happens to be the fastest cane in the West."

"Cane?"

"Cane. One of those old, gnarled things made out of briar or whatever." He dropped the pencil and leaned back in the chair, both hands on the sheriff's desk. "She about fractured the kid's skull with it before we got there." He held up index and thumb an eighth of an inch apart. "She came that close to being zapped with the Tazer."

"That might have gotten her attention."

"Yup. Then the kid tried to run auntie down with a pickup truck that she didn't know how to drive, and hit the neighbor's tree instead. Pasquale took the call, and auntie damn near ended up fracturing *his* thumb when he tried to take the cane away from her.''

''It's in the drinking water, I think. Who are they, by the way?''

''You don't want to know.''

Estelle looked quizzically at him.

''Esmirelda Vasquez? Does that ring a bell?''

''Bobby's aunt.''

''Yup. Esmirelda of the cane. And niece Paula. Some such as that.'' He waved a hand in weary dismissal. ''I can't keep track. As Bobby likes to say, 'just arrest 'em all.'''

''Is that where he is now?''

Mears shook his head and glanced over at the wall clock. ''No. He and Chief Mitchell are doing something. I don't know what. He said you'd want to look at this.'' He nudged the revolver with the eraser of his pencil. ''I looked at the case and receipt you found in George's desk at the house.''

''Yes. What did you find out?''

''For one thing, we're reasonably sure that it's the murder weapon. There's blood and tissue on the muzzle.''

''Match?''

''It's O positive, the same as the victim's. We'll be waiting on a DNA profile from the lab. End of the week, if we're lucky.''

''What about the bullet in the wall? Bobby thought it was consistent.''

Mears nodded. ''That's the easy part. No doubt there. One shot, and that was it.'' He opened the left-hand top drawer of the sheriff's desk and drew out a large manila envelope. From it he extracted a smaller plastic pouch and handed it to Estelle. The weight of the single revolver slug nestled in her hand. The brass half jacket was peeled back, but still in place around the lead core. She could see the white traces of Sheetrock imbedded in the lead.

''Ay.''

''Is right. But look here.'' He slid the yellow pad he'd been using across the desk toward Estelle. ''This is what I think is interesting.'' He reached across with the pencil. ''The bullet's path is about like this, Estelle. We really can't tell exactly how he was sitting in his chair…all we know is that the bullet passed through his head from left to right, angling from front to back a little. It hit the edge of the bookcase behind him at enough of an angle that it glanced off and into the wall.'' He drew a lightly dotted line from the drawing of a figure in a chair.

"Two things," he continued, and his pencil paused in midair as he looked up at Estelle. His head still rested on his hand. "For one thing, there's blood and bone fragments along the top of the chair back." He pushed himself up and twisted, resting a hand on top of the sheriff's swivel chair. "Right here. And the residue extends *down* the backside a little bit." He ran his hand over the top of the chair, out of sight.

Estelle straightened up. "He would have had to be leaning backward, then, as if he was resting his head against the chair back."

Mears nodded, and he relaxed in the sheriff's chair, his own head against the leather padding. "His office chair doesn't have a real high back," he said, reaching around with his right hand. "The top of it catches you right at the base of the skull if you're average height. If Enriquez's head was resting against the back of the chair, and the bullet exited above his ear, it's likely that there'd be blood and tissue on the top and back of the chair." He rocked forward and closed his eyes. "That's one thing." He propped his head on his hand again, opened his eyes, and regarded Estelle. "We're kinda eager to see Perrone's preliminary. The sheriff said that Enriquez had what appeared to be a powder burn on his left forearm, just ahead of his elbow." He reached over and patted his own arm.

"How would that happen?"

"I don't know."

Estelle frowned. "But it wouldn't happen if he were holding the gun himself, in his left hand."

"I wouldn't think so," Mears said. "And I think the sheriff told you that the gun didn't have a single print on it. Not one. That's not possible unless George used gloves, which he didn't. There are prints on the cartridges, and every one that I can read worth a damn belongs to George."

"So he loaded it."

"But didn't fire it," Mears said. "The other interesting thing is that there is what appears to be a little hair and some tissue along the *side* of the barrel, just about where the legend is printed. That's an odd place for blow-back debris."

"How is Linda coming with the photos?"

"I know she printed about a jillion. She's got 'em downstairs." He glanced at the clock again. "She finally went home about three-thirty." He grinned and closed one eye conspiratorially. "When she was sure that Tom was going to make it away from Bobby's aunt in one piece."

Estelle's brows furrowed as she looked at the silent revolver, and she slowly sank back against the edge of the desk. "Huh," she said after a minute, and shook her head. "Georgie, Georgie." She looked up at Mears, who waited patiently, arms crossed over his chest. "Connie Enriquez has no idea about this, Tom. As far as she knew, her husband didn't own a single gun. At least she didn't think that he kept it in the house. She was surprised to see the gun case."

"I bet she was. And by the way, the only prints on that case belong to George. The case was nicely cleaned and polished. Very thoughtful of him."

Estelle took a deep breath. "How did Kenderman's arraignment go?"

"Judge Hobart wasn't in an understanding mood either," Mears said with a laugh. "You know how the old man likes being bothered off-hours. Perry's cooling his heels in the lockup."

"Bond?"

"Fifty thousand. Ten percent up."

"Perry's not going to find five thousand any quicker than he'd find fifty," Estelle said. "It'll give him time to think."

She gazed at the heavy revolver and shook her head. "Now we find out the *why,* Tom. Perry Kenderman is simple."

"I'll agree with that," Mears said, and grinned.

"That's not what I meant. I *understand* him. He was infatuated with Colette and the two kids, and got cross-wise with his brother, who evidently had a weak spot for the girl himself. George Enriquez, though…I just find it hard to believe that a guy like him could do anything dark enough that someone would want to kill him.''

"There's the other side of that, Estelle.''

"Yes, there is. Maybe it's not what he did, necessarily, but what he knew. That's a good place to start.''

TWENTY-TWO

ESTELLE TURNED the county car off Grande onto Escondido, and for a few yards, before the intersection with Guadalupe to the right, the neighborhood looked unchanged since the first time she'd seen it two decades before. Bill Gastner's sprawling adobe was just visible through enormous cottonwoods overshadowing the narrow asphalt of Guadalupe.

What had been five acres of scrub, brush, and crowded trees behind Gastner's old adobe was now home to the Posadas Clinic and Pharmacy. Despite the grandiose wishes of the architects, Francis Guzman and Alan Perrone had prevailed. The clinic was low, dark brown adobe with turquoise trim around multipane windows. As many trees as possible had been untouched during construction, and the bulk of the parking lot was behind the building. The result was a new facility that didn't overwhelm the old neighborhood.

Estelle slowed for the driveway and turned into the packed lot. As she idled the car through the lanes, she saw that nearly a third of the license plates were Mexican. Francis would be swamped. Estelle knew that it was wishful thinking to expect that he could break away for lunch.

The west end of the building was a pharmacy, and she entered there, knowing the back door behind the prescription counter would let her skirt the crowded waiting room, entering directly into the hallway leading to the physicians' private offices and the lab.

She saw the top of Louis Herrera's head as the pharmacist concentrated, bowed over his workstation. At the pickup window, one of the girls was explaining something about a medication in Spanish to an elderly woman, and Herrera looked up, interrupting the girl. Even as he talked, he lifted a hand in greeting as Estelle slipped past.

"I think he just got back," the pharmacist said in English to Estelle. He lightly touched the old woman on the back of the hand as if to keep his place in that conversation, stepped across to the door, and swiped a card through the lock. He pulled the door open and held it for Estelle. "I just saw his car drive in."

"Thanks, Lou," she said.

He grinned at the drug reference book as she passed. "You planning to go to work here soon?"

"Not on your life," she laughed. The door closed behind her with a well-insulated thud and the click of the electronic lock.

As if one door had triggered another, she saw her husband step out of his office down the hall. He stopped, hand on the knob as she approached, and then opened the door for her. "Perfect timing, *querida*. I'm headed for the war zone."

"I was going to take you to lunch, *Oso,* but I can see that's not going to happen."

He laughed. "I wish," he said. He followed her into the office and closed the door. Estelle thumped the heavy volume down on his cluttered desk. Before he had a chance to take a step, she wrapped her arms around him in a ferocious hug. "Whoa," he gasped. He put a hand on either side of her head, trying to turn her so that he could look into her eyes. Instead, she drove her face hard into his white lab coat, ignoring the pen that pressed into her cheek. The physician locked his arms around Estelle and held her in an "Oso" hug, both of them silent for several minutes.

"I'm turning cyanotic," Francis said finally.

"Too bad." Estelle's voice was muffled in his coat.

"Good morning, eh?"

"Spectacular," she said. She lifted her head and looked up at him, brushing his lips lightly with hers. "Tell me what you did this morning." She tightened her grip and Francis smiled.

"The really exciting part was getting called out to do an emergency appendectomy."

"On who?"

"Her name's Kittie Wheeler. Ernie's niece."

"She's doing fine?"

"She's doing fine, *querida*." He reached up and moved a stray strand of hair to one side of her forehead.

"Was she at school?"

Francis grinned. "Yes…she was at school. And as the current generation is fond of saying, 'and this is important be-caaaause?'"

"I don't know why it's important, *Oso*. I just need to know."

"Well, that was the highlight of my morning, especially the ten minutes it took to convince the kid that the appendectomy scar wouldn't show when she wears one of those midriff things. Otherwise, it's been a steady stream, in one door and out the other. There's a little community down past Tres Santos that has some water problems, I think. We're seeing a bunch of nasty gastro stuff that sure reads like they're drinkin' something they shouldn't be."

Her arms began to ache. She loosened her grip and straightened his collar.

"I really need to get out there," he said and glanced at the book. "What'd you bring me?"

"Do you have time for a couple of questions?"

"Por supuesto, señora."

She clutched a fistful of coat fabric and led him over to the desk. "George Enriquez had this on the shelf of his office at home," she said.

Francis tilted his head and glanced at the cover of the pharmaceutical survey. "Ooookay."

She opened the book to the Post-it. "He has this section marked with this," and she tapped the note. "Or at least, this was stuck *in* this section. I was thinking that maybe the numbers he has listed here refer to page numbers?"

Francis leaned over, both hands on the desk, and frowned at the note. "Okay."

"So they could?"

"Well, of course, they *could*." He lifted a hand and riffled to the beginning of the gray section. "This section begins on page

305 and ends...on page 346. His list begins on 311, with the highest number 341." He shrugged. "As good a guess as any."

"There're eight numbers," Estelle said.

"I see that, Holmes."

"Would it be possible to look at each page and see if there's anything they have in common...or some kind of connection?"

"You don't have any idea what you're looking for?"

"No. Or even if I *am* looking." She reached out and brushed the right side of his face. "It's just that I'm curious. Anyone can own one of these books, for a million reasons. I'm curious, that's all."

"Por querer saber," he said. He glanced up at the wall clock and grimaced. "There's going to be a riot here soon." He opened to page 311. "Inhalers, stuff." He tapped a bicolored capsule. "Petrosin's a big seller. Fluoxetine hydrochloride? For depression. Anybody facing a grand jury probe would probably want several cocktails of that every day."

He frowned and leafed to page 315. "All kinds of neat stuff here. And that's wrong." He bent down, hands on either side of the book. "Which edition is this?" He lifted the front cover. "Okay." Flipping back to 315, he tapped a pill. "Some do prescribe a lot of this."

"Bicotin Six," Estelle read. "What's it for?"

"Pain reliever. It's just a mix of aspirin and codeine phosphate. There's a Bicotin Three, which has thirty milligrams of codeine, and Bicotin Six...which has sixty." He wagged his shaggy eyebrows.

"Okay."

"The problem is," and he slipped his hand into the page and flipped back to 311. "The problem is that Bicotin Six isn't yellow as it shows here." He bent closer. "And Petrosin isn't a yellow capsule, either. That's why I was wondering what edition this was." He glanced at the Post-it and then flipped to the next page. Estelle waited silently while her husband thumbed through the section.

Finally he straightened up. "Interesting stuff. On each page that's written down here," and he jabbed at the note, "you have what I'd call a popular drug listed. And in each case, the drug's yellow instead of white, or at least partially yellow."

"So he marked a particular drug, then. That's all."

"I guess. Talk about too much free time on his hands. But that's an interesting list. It's like a list of best-sellers, Estelle. Prescription best-sellers. I don't think George would be taking all those, at least not the oral contraceptives."

"Mrs. Enriquez said he was taking Somdex."

Francis shrugged. "That's just a muscle relaxant. For aches and pains. Like I said, he must have had a lot of free time."

"How so?"

"He's going to sit there with this book in his lap and use a yellow Hi-Liter to paint drugs new colors?"

He turned the desk lamp on. "Look at that," he said, and bent down so he was looking across the page at an acute angle. "You can't even see where he slopped over the lines. This guy must have been a master with crayons when he was in school. I couldn't do that if I worked at it."

"So the yellow drugs on those pages…from that list…are prescription drugs that are popular. Is that the only connection you can think of?"

"*Sí, corazón.* What's this guy doing, going into the supply side? I guess I should say, what *was* he doing."

"I don't know. It's just odd, that's all."

"You might talk to Louis. He works with this stuff on a day-to-day basis. Hourly, in fact. He might be able to give you some ideas."

"I might do that."

Francis closed the book and glanced at his watch. "I gotta go, *querida.*"

"Do you mind if I stay here a while?" she asked, and he smiled at her serious expression. He reached out with his thumb, gently trying to erase the wrinkle between her thick, black eyebrows.

"Much more of this, and you'll need some Petrosin yourself." She hugged him until he laughed. "Come on, *mi corazón.* If you don't let me go, I'm going to have to hang a stethoscope around your neck and make you deal with all the little snot-faces out there…and what's worse, their mothers.''

She released him instantly. ''I don't think so.''

''See you *anoche,* then?''

She nodded and watched him go. Like a magnet, the huge book filled with a world of wonder drugs drew her back. She settled in her husband's chair, breathing in the faint aroma of him that lingered. After a moment, she pushed his dictation equipment to one side and spread the massive book out in front of her.

For several minutes, she studied the book, leafing back and forth from index to product descriptions until she'd read each entry that had been marked. On impulse, she pulled open the center drawer of Francis's desk, but found no Hi-Liter.

Leaving the door ajar, she left the office and returned to the pharmacy. In less than a minute, she was back in her husband's office, a Hi-Liter in hand. She spread the book open and selected a large white tablet of Trilosec on a page that George Enriquez hadn't noted. The instant the ink from the marker hit the page, it clumped and bunched, as if she were trying to write on waxed paper. Yet, when she drew the marker across the pill, the photo of the product turned an even yellow. With her finger, she wiped off the ink; it disappeared from the waxy surface, leaving behind a perfect, yellow pill.

''*Caramba,*'' she whispered. ''That's neat.''

For the next several minutes, she highlighted a variety of medications. In every case, the result was the same. The ink wiped off the page just as it would wipe off waxed paper. But in each case, it left the yellow color intact on the product.

''Neat, neat, neat,'' she said. ''That would appeal to George's tidy nature.''

She reached out and picked up the phone, and dialed Frank Dayan at the *Posadas Register.*

TWENTY-THREE

FRANK DAYAN MET Estelle at the counter before either of the two girls who worked the front office could stir in their seats. She could see Pam Gardiner, the newspaper's editor, in one of the back cubicles, deep in a telephone conversation.

"Well, good morning," Dayan said heartily. He wore his habitual white shirt and narrow tie, looking like someone fresh from the '60s. He smiled as if Estelle had come to purchase a full-page ad. "We've got a whole slew of questions to ask you," he said.

"Frank, thanks for giving me a few minutes," Estelle replied. Dayan frowned at the massive book that she rested on the counter.

"Let's go back to the office," he said, and led her through the welter of activity.

"This is a bad day for you, I know," she said.

"Every day is a bad day for us," he laughed. "Come on in." His office was nothing more than another cubicle, the half-wall partitions providing the appearance of privacy. He gestured at a small chair that looked like a reject from the middle school and sat down in his own swivel chair, one elbow on the desk beside the computer keyboard. "First of all," he said, and then dropped his voice to a conspiratorial whisper, "what's up with the Kenderman thing? Pam said that when she stopped by the S.O. this morning, she couldn't find out a thing, other than that he'd been arrested in connection with the girl's death. Nobody's talking."

"We haven't had time to talk," Estelle said. "What you heard is correct," she added. "He was arraigned late last night. Judge Hobart set bond at fifty thousand dollars."

"Holy smokes." Dayan jotted a quick note as Estelle watched silently. "So what's the deal?"

"Officer Kenderman was on duty when he apparently was involved in an incident Monday night. Colette Parker was killed after her motorcycle crashed into a utility pole."

"We have that part," Dayan said quickly. "But high-speed chases don't end in bond and jail."

"The chase apparently occurred following a domestic dispute."

"You mean between the Parker girl and Officer Kenderman?"

"That's correct."

"How bizarre." Dayan raised his voice a notch. "Pam," he called over the partition, "did you hear that?"

The heavy-set young woman appeared as a wavy figure through the Plexiglass. She looked over the top at Estelle. "What prompted all this, anyway?" she asked.

"It's a domestic dispute," Estelle replied. "That's all I can tell you at the moment."

Pam's eyes narrowed. "So if bond was set, what were the charges?

"Vehicular homicide, at the moment."

"You mean there may be others?"

"That's a possibility." Estelle patted the cover of the heavy book on her lap. "I have an ink question that I need to ask you," she said. Pam disappeared, and in a moment Estelle could hear the keys of the editor's word processor.

"An ink question." Dayan watched her open the book.

"This is really trivia," she said, eager to think about something other than Perry Kenderman. "But I need to know."

"It's hard to imagine you spending your days with trivia," Dayan said easily, and when Estelle glanced up at him, he smiled broadly.

She spread the book open. "Why is it that when I mark this page with one of these Hi-Liters, the ink sticks to the image, but not the rest of the page?" She slipped the marker out of her pocket and uncapped it, then dashed a line of ink across the page, hitting a row of white pills as she did so. She immediately wiped off the excess ink with her thumb. The pills turned a perfect, even yellow.

Dayan's smile lingered. "Is this the way your day usually works?" He tapped his skull at the temple. "You must have some interesting tidbits filed away up there. It would make an interesting story."

"But why this?" Estelle asked doggedly, pointing at the page.

"You know what four-color process is, right? When we run a color picture, it's actually layered up out of four different plates—four different inks layered on top of the other?" She nodded. "Well, the slick, gray paper here in this book is actually *five* color. The gray tone of the paper is actually an ink wash, a fifth color. It isn't just gray paper."

"The white pill has no ink on it?"

"Absolutely correct," Dayan said, impressed. "The white pills are actually the color of the original paper stock. They didn't use white ink. Hardly anyone does."

"The ink from the markers beads up on the gray ink, then," Estelle said.

"Again, correct. The gray ink—any of the inks—is oil based. So it's like asking the Hi-Liter's ink to mark on oil. Doesn't mix. It beads up. Leave it there long enough, and it would dry. But you wiped it off before it had a chance to dry."

"And the rest soaks into the white paper."

"Just so." He folded his hands in his lap and grinned at the concentration on her face. "It looks like you had this pretty much figured out before you came here."

"I don't know," Estelle said, and snapped the book shut. "But thanks, Frank." She started to rise, and he held up a hand.

"Whoa, whoa, whoa," he said. "You can't do this to me." He affected a wounded expression, and Estelle smiled. "What's going on?" he asked. "And don't say, 'investigation is continuing.' Is this something with the Kenderman thing, or with Enriquez, or what? What's going on?"

"*Investigation continuing* would be the truth, Frank," she said. She relaxed in the chair and rested both hands on top of the closed book. "When's your deadline?"

Dayan glanced at his watch. "If we had something within the

hour, Pam wouldn't scream too much. We go to press at one-thirty. Even at this point, we'd have to pull something."

"Okay." She looked down at the book for a moment, then said, "The Posadas County Sheriff's Department is investigating the apparent homicide of George Enriquez, Frank."

"So it *is* homicide, then."

"Apparent." She watched him quickly jot notes. When he looked up, she said, "Enriquez died from a single gunshot wound, apparently from a magnum handgun. The revolver believed to be used in the shooting was recovered at the scene."

"You know, you should work for us."

"That's okay," she said.

"Motives?"

"Enriquez was currently facing a grand jury investigation, as you know."

"Stemming from the insurance fraud thing."

"Alleged improper practices," she said quietly.

"And can I attribute all this to you, by the way?"

"If you wish."

"I'd say 'according to Sheriff Bob Torrez,' but readers would never believe that." He chuckled. "The grand jury proceedings were cancelled?"

"Yes."

"You think somebody shot Enriquez because of some hanky-panky going on in his office, then?"

"I won't speculate, Frank."

"Suspects yet?"

"No."

"Witnesses?"

"No."

"Who found the body?"

"As I'm sure you've already heard," she said with gentle reproof, "one of his office staff discovered the body yesterday morning."

"Right there in the insurance office?"

"Yes."

"How long had he been dead?"

"We believe that Mr. Enriquez was killed sometime between

Monday morning and Tuesday morning, when his body was discovered.''

"Was it originally thought to be suicide?"

"There was always that possibility," Estelle said, and turned when she saw Pam Gardiner's shadow appear at the partition again. The girl apparently preferred peering over the translucent barrier like some large gargoyle rather than simply taking a step to her left and using the doorway.

"But that possibility was quickly dismissed?" Dayan pressed.

"I'm not sure how quickly, but yes, that's fair to say."

He looked down at his notepad, pursing his lips. "Where was he shot?"

"In his office."

"No, I mean where in the body?"

"A single gunshot wound through the head."

"While he was sitting at his desk?"

"It appears so."

"Who does the revolver belong to? Was it his?"

"It appears so."

Dayan regarded her in silence for a moment, then slowly shook his head. "Wow. You're heading up the investigation?"

"Sheriff Robert Torrez is in charge," Estelle replied.

"And what's he think about all this?" and Dayan immediately held up a hand to ward off the expected response. "I know, I know. I need to ask him. I'd get more out of this desk," he said, rapping the edge of the desk with his knuckle. "Well," and he took a deep breath, "this is going to help, don't you think, Pam? We had a little bit that we put together but no details." He nodded at Estelle. "We'll plug this in. Many thanks."

"You're welcome. As I know more, I'll let you know."

Dayan leaned forward conspiratorially. "So I'll ask again…what's with the ink thing?" He watched her get up, hefting the book. "How's that related to Enriquez—or is it?"

She nodded. "It's just one of those *investigation continuing* things, Frank."

"Oh, sure." He leaned back in his chair, face a study in skeptical resignation. "If anything crops up in the next hour and a half, you'll let us know?"

"Yes, sir." She nodded her thanks at both Dayan and Pam Gardiner. As she was making her way back toward the front of the office, she heard the publisher in hushed conversation with his editor. Estelle knew that District Attorney Daniel Schroeder's phone would be ringing in the next few minutes, and she knew exactly what Schroeder would tell the *Posadas Register* without the least bit of concern about when their deadlines might be.

TWENTY-FOUR

THE WEST WALL of Teresa Reyes's bedroom had been painted a soft, muted rose, called "sunset hue" on the color chart at the hardware store. The elderly woman had been adamant in her choice of colors when she and Estelle had discussed it. Estelle had been impressed but not surprised when Joe Tones had been able to find the perfect match.

Joseph Tones's world was the mind-boggling inventory of Posadas Lumber and Hardware, an impressive old-fashioned hardware store whose floors were still the dark and dented, oil-soaked pine that had been laid down before World War II. The hardware and its modest lumberyard took up half the block across from Tommy Portillo's Handi-Way on Grande. In that vast barnlike building with its sagging roofline, Tones moved among the crowded displays and vast bin arrays with effortless ease. He knew, always, where the most esoteric bit of hardware might be located.

Estelle parked the county car toward the rear of the hardware's lot, beside the white pickup truck with the store's logo on the door. She sat for a moment, letting her mind drift back over the conversation she'd had with Connie Enriquez. Connie had said that Tones had worked with her husband on chamber of commerce projects, that they had been friends for years.

Across the street, a group of five high-school students walked toward Portillo's store across Grande, enjoying the sunshine, enjoying their lunchtime escape from the confines of school. Estelle watched them and let the unhappy picture of Connie Enriquez bleed from her mind. As she watched, Estelle found herself wondering what Francisco and Carlos would be like when they were teenagers about to tackle the world. *Let that be a long time coming,* she thought.

Connie and George Enriquez together on the beach. The image in the photograph crept into Estelle's consciousness unbidden. A young couple enjoying the sun, water, sand, and each other, spared the agony of a crystal ball that would show them where their lives were headed. Estelle watched the five high-school kids until they disappeared inside the convenience store.

She opened her briefcase and put a fresh, labeled cassette in the recorder, then slipped it into her pocket.

As she was closing and locking the briefcase, an orange pickup truck with state highway department emblems on the doors pulled into the slot beside her county car. She glanced up and saw the large woman who got out, hard hat and all. Estelle had been reaching for the door handle but paused. There was always a chance that Leona Spears hadn't recognized her…but then that didn't count for much. She'd be ambushed inside the store instead.

Leona smiled brightly and twiddled her fingers at the undersheriff. A robust woman, she stood nearly six feet tall, broad through the shoulders and thick waisted. Her amazingly thick blonde hair was pulled into a tight Heidi braid that could be tucked up under the aluminum hard hat if necessary.

Estelle got out of the car and smiled pleasantly at Leona, who waited by the low parking barrier.

"Hi there," Leona said cheerfully.

"Good afternoon, Leona," Estelle replied. She turned to make sure the county car was locked, giving Ms. Spears a final chance to find something else to do. When Estelle turned away from her car, Leona smiled again, in no hurry to move on. Just as quickly, the smile faded, her thick blonde eyebrows gathered, and she stepped toward Estelle.

"I heard about Mr. Enriquez," Leona said.

And what did you hear, Estelle almost said but settled for a neutral nod.

"And that right on top of the incident with the Parker girl," Leona added, making it clear there was more to the *incident* than was apparent through the rumor mill. "What an awful week it's been."

"Yes, ma'am," Estelle said. Leona had managed to position herself to effectively block the undersheriff's path, and Estelle knew exactly what the woman wanted.

"Did Matt White call you?"

Estelle frowned, startled by the question since, on the surface at least, it had nothing to do with prying into the sheriff's department's business—Leona's principal hobby both before November 7, when she had been campaigning for the sheriff's position, and even after that, when she had been digging out from under Robert Torrez's landslide.

"You mean today?" Estelle asked. She had spoken with Highway Department District Manager Matt White on numerous occasions in past months.

Leona nodded. "He was going to call you folks about the gravel we've been losing," Leona said.

"Ah," Estelle said. "If he called, he didn't talk to me."

"He was going to. I told him that he should ask for you specifically if he wanted something done."

"I haven't seen the inside of my office very much this week," Estelle said. "Someone's been stealing gravel from the state yard, you mean?"

"No. From the roadside stock, down near the intersection of County Road Fourteen. From the tire tracks it looks like somebody just backs a trailer right up to the pile and helps themselves."

Estelle managed to keep a straight face. Leona would know about the tracks. She would climb out of her state truck, tape measure and sketch pad in hand, and draw her version of the crime scene, ready to file a report.

"That's easy to do," Estelle said. "With those unfenced piles, it's sort of an invitation. Unless a deputy just happens by and catches them in the act, there isn't much chance that they'll be caught." That wasn't the answer Leona wanted to hear, Estelle knew. Better to create a gravel profile and match it to freshly spread evidence in someone's driveway.

"I was thinking that maybe a deputy could watch from either

the parking lot of the saloon across the way or from a little ways up Fourteen. It'd be easy to spot them from either place."

Estelle smiled despite her best effort. "That's not going to happen, Leona."

"What do you mean?"

"We're not going to assign a deputy to baby-sit a gravel pile. Most of the time, we only have one deputy working the entire county. At night, anyway."

"I heard that Perry Kenderman was arrested," Leona said.

"But not for gravel theft," Estelle said and instantly regretted the amusing remark, prompted as it was by the abrupt change in subject. Predictably, Leona's eyes narrowed with that characteristic are-you-making-fun-of-me expression. "You're right. Officer Kenderman was arrested last night," Estelle said, keeping her expression sober.

"So…" Leona said and as abruptly stopped while the mental gears ground and then meshed. "Bring me up to speed on this Enriquez thing," she said, wonderfully unaware that the "Enriquez thing" was none of her business.

"Other than that he's dead, I really can't tell you much, Leona." Estelle reached out a hand and touched the woman on the arm, moving her gently out of the way so she could squeeze past. "And I really need to go. It's nice to see you again."

"Oh, and by the way," Leona said, turning in perfect synchronization to follow Estelle, "how's that new clinic going?"

"Wonderful," Estelle said.

"You know, that pharmacy is amazing." She fell in step, reached for the front door, and opened it for Estelle. "I have to take a couple things, you know? I bet the prescription prices are twenty percent lower than old Trombley's." She reached out and touched Estelle's shoulder. "Now I have to admit, I haven't been in all that often." She made a face. "I'm one of those loyalists, I guess. It's hard to change my ways." Leona leaned a little closer. "I think old Guy Trombley understands me, so I don't mind paying his prices, you know? For one thing, I have this absolutely *horrible* memory. I run out of something, and he'll just shrug and keep me going until I can have my physician call from Deming."

"I'm sure he's most understanding," Estelle said.

"But I'm so pleased the new place is doing well. It's needed, you know. It's needed. And it may be my imagination, but I think that maybe I'm already paying a little less for some things at Trombley's. The competition is a good thing...although I suppose Guy would argue that."

"Well, perhaps," Estelle said with considerable resignation. "I'm glad things are working out for you, Leona."

"Hi, ladies," the pudgy girl at the front counter said. "What can we help you find today?"

Loath to say anything in front of Leona, Estelle scanned the store, hoping to see Joe Tones. As she did so, Leona said to the girl, "I just need a key made." She dug the sample from her front pocket and handed it to the girl.

"Leona, nice seeing you," Estelle said, taking advantage of the distraction. She strolled away from the front register, putting as many aisles between herself and the front desk as she could.

Back by the toilet repair kits, she found Joe Tones down on his hands and knees, pliers in hand. He glanced up, saw Estelle, and pushed himself up to a more dignified position.

"Somebody stepped on the front of this bin and broke it, would you believe that?" he said. "Can I help you find something?"

"Actually, I was looking for you, Mr. Tones."

"Oh. Well, how delightful." His smile was snaggle toothed and quickly vanished as he grunted first to one knee, then to his feet. "Take my advice, and don't get old," he said.

The first time that Estelle had entered Posadas Lumber and Hardware, she had been a junior in high school, less than a month in the United States, and accompanied by her great uncle Reuben. She didn't remember what Reuben had purchased that day, but it seemed to her that the Joe Tones standing in front of her now was unchanged from the man who had waited on them then, unchanged except for a bald spot that had expanded over the years.

He thrust the pliers in his back pocket and dusted off his hands. "What can I help you with?"

"I'd like to ask you a couple of questions about George En-riquez," she said.

Something flashed across Tones's face and was gone so quickly that Estelle couldn't tell if it was sorrow, anger, or irritation. Tones leaned an elbow against the front lip of a bin holding short lengths of threaded galvanized pipe. He appeared to be studying the price tag on the front of the bin.

When he turned to look at Estelle again, his expression was guarded. "What did you want to know? This hasn't been an easy thing to deal with, I can tell you that for a fact."

"Mrs. Enriquez said that you and George worked together in various chamber of commerce ventures. Is that correct?"

"Sure, over the years. All the time. He did a lot for this community. A lot of folks are going to miss him. I don't care what anybody says."

"Did you know him really well, sir?"

"I thought I did. But we know how that goes, don't we."

"Meaning?"

"It kind of threw me for a loop, you know…hearing about him shooting himself that way." He shrugged. "That's why I'm hiding back here. Easier than trying to talk to folks who come in."

"Had you seen George during the past few weeks?"

"Sure. I see him all the time."

"How did he seem to you?"

Tones shook his head. "Well…you know. He had his share of troubles, with that grand jury thing hanging over his head. I know that worried him."

"He talked to you about that?"

"Yeah, sure he did. Some."

"Were the two of you planning to go elk hunting some time this fall?"

Tones jerked his head in surprise and frowned at Estelle. "I was the one who told George that it'd do him good to get away for a little bit, *especially* before…before, you know. That damn jury thing. Christ, that hung over his head like some big cleaver."

"George wasn't much of a hunter, was he?"

"No." Tones managed a tight smile. "That's the understatement of the year."

"How'd he come to decide on an elk hunt, then? That's a pretty rugged undertaking, isn't it?"

"Not the way we do it," Tones said. "The four of us have reservations at one of those fancy game ranches north of Chama." He smiled. "It isn't exactly roughing it, if you've ever seen their lodge."

"This is a captive elk herd we're talking about?"

Tones nodded. "That ranch is big enough, so you'd never know it. Guides take you as close to the herd as you want…or you can hike or ride horseback all day, if that's what you're after. George was pretty excited about the idea."

"Had you actually made reservations, or was all this just in the dream stages?"

"Oh no. No dream. Once George decided that this was something he wanted to do, bingo. He made all the arrangements with the lodge up there. We were originally going to use that big camper of George's, but then we decided that was kind of dumb, the lodge being available and all. George…he took care of it." He sighed. "I don't know now. I guess we'll cancel out."

"Who's the we, Mr. Tones? You said that four of you planned to go."

He looked askance at Estelle. "How's all this related to George's death, anyway?"

"I'm not sure that it is, Mr. Tones."

He adjusted the rack of pens in his pocket protector. "It was me, George, and Glen Archer. I guess you know him."

"Indeed I do."

"And Owen Frieberg, from Salazar's." Tones glanced past her shoulder at the same time that she heard soft footsteps behind her. She turned and saw the girl who had been grinding the key for Leona Spears.

"Joe, I can't find the right blank for this." She held up the key. From six feet away, Joe Tones glanced at the key and shook his head. "That's a Yale security lock, Donnie. We don't have blanks for them. Who's it for?" He peered around the counter. "Oh. Tell Leona she needs to see a locksmith."

Donnie nodded and turned away.

"Let's find some privacy before that crazy woman corners me," he said. "We can use John's office." He led Estelle through the fencing and garden tool section, and ducked into a large back workroom. They wound their way through stacks of boxes and rolls of wire, finally finding a cubbyhole in the distant back of the store. John Hildebrand's office was a study in things fresh and new in 1950. The old man, sole owner of the hardware business, came to work when he felt like it—as much as ten hours a week at times.

Tones dumped a load of catalogs off a small swivel chair and scooted it toward Estelle. "Sit," he said, and pulled out the captain's chair behind the desk. It groaned when he sat down. The sleeves of the jacket that had been thrown across the arm dragged on the floor as he leaned back. He immediately picked up a pencil and drilled the point into the remains of the desk blotter.

"Fire away," he said.

"I understand that the chamber of commerce organizes a couple of trips to Mexico each year."

"Yes, we do. One about the first week of Christmas, one on the *Cinco de Mayo*. Fifth of May."

"Is this part of the sister-village project?"

"Yep."

"And that's with…"

"Acámbaro. It's a little place about a two hours' drive south of the border crossing at Regál." He grimaced. "I don't know why I'm telling you all this. I'm sure you know Mexico far better than I do."

"Actually, I've never been to Acámbaro, Mr. Tones."

"Well, you haven't missed much. It's a lot like Palomas, only smaller. Maybe two hundred people on a good day. More like Tres Santos. Poor as dirt."

"What's the main objective of the Christmas trip?"

"Party time," Tones said. "We work with the middle school, you know. It's really a student-council project, and the chamber tags along and gives what we can. We take bags of groceries, toys, clothes, anything we can scrounge. Then we have a hell of

a Christmas party in the little gymnasium next to the school."
He leaned back and rubbed the bald spot on his head, closing
his eyes as he did so. "I use the term *gymnasium* advisedly. It's
a cinder-block barn. Last time we were there, they were trying
to raise money to close in the one end they haven't finished."

"Who goes on the trip? Just the chamber and the school?"

"Posadas Middle School Student Council. They're the main
drive behind it. I always go, representing the chamber, since
we're the ones who raise a lot of the money for the kids' gifts.
A couple of years ago, I told George that he needed to go along,
that it'd be good for his soul." Tones grinned. "I didn't think
he would. But you know, he did. He even talked his insurance
company's home office out of about a thousand pencils and pens
to take along. He went over and hit up the Forest Service for a
couple hundred of those wooden Smokey Bear rulers—all that
kind of thing is big stuff if you don't have it. We got another
case of pencils from the Bureau of Land Management. It's quite
a bash." He leaned forward, the chair protesting every move.
"You should go with us sometime. It's something to see the
kids' faces—from both sides of the border. Most of our kids
have never seen poverty like that. It's an eye-opener."

"When the boys are a little further along in school, I'm sure
I'll be doing all sorts of things like that," Estelle said. "And
that's it? You, the school kids, George Enriquez…anyone else?"

"Well, the superintendent always goes, like I said. When they
start dancing, Glen's the biggest kid of all, I think. This year we
took down about ten older-model computers that the school was
surplusing out. I don't know what the Mexicans will plug 'em
into down there…in fact, I don't even know if the electrical
wiring is compatible, but Glen said they'd figure it out and make
whatever adjustments were needed."

"Just him? From the school, I mean?"

"Oh no. Let's see." Tones closed his eyes again and resumed
stroking his bald spot. "The student-council advisor goes. What
the hell's his name." He leaned forward and stared at the floor
intently. "Barry something."

"Barry Vasquez?"

"That's him. Him and about twenty kids, I guess."

"And you mentioned Owen Frieberg."

"And Owen, right. His daughter's in eighth grade. In fact he drove one of the buses."

"Bu*ses?* For twenty kids? How many did you take?"

"Two full-sized buses, crammed to the gills. And we barely fit, too. All that junk, plus the computers, plus..." He waved his hands in the air above his head. "And in some ways, the buses make it easier. The guys at the border crossing all know us."

"Sounds like fun. What's the purpose of the *Cinco de Mayo* trip?"

"Turn about," Tones said with satisfaction. "They throw us a party as sort of a 'thank you' for the December gig. Unbelievable. Where some of those kids come up with some of those dance costumes, I'll never know. Out of thin air and dust, I guess. They can't come to Posadas, so we go back down there."

"George went on that trip as well?"

"Yes. Basically the same crew."

"Archer went along, too?"

"He drove one bus and Frieberg drove the other, just like in December."

Estelle looked down at her notebook. "During the past few months, were you aware of any friction between George Enriquez and anyone else?"

"Friction? I don't think so. George was about as affable a guy as you could want. Good hearted." He shrugged. "I still don't understand all this shit that was being thrown up in the newspaper about insurance scams."

"Did you know Connie Enriquez, Mr. Tones?"

"Sad, sad woman." He shook his head slowly, his lips pressed tight. "George had the patience of a saint."

Estelle flipped several pages back in her notebook. "I'd like to return to the hunting trip for a moment, Mr. Tones. Do you happen to know what rifle George was planning to use? Did he own one?"

Except for the rhythmic stroking of the top of his head, Tones might have been asleep. The hand came down, the pencil stopped tapping, and he regarded Estelle with curiosity. "It would be interesting to know which of the questions that you're asking already have answers in that little book," he said.

He leaned forward, resting his elbows on his knees. He held his hands about a foot apart. "It was a rifle involved in his death?"

"Actually, no, it wasn't. I was just curious about the hunt. His wife made it clear that firearms weren't allowed in the house."

"Yeah, well," Tones said, and shrugged. "I heard about that, more than once. George liked guns. It was one of those things, like a guy who wants a toy of some kind and can't have one, because it's his *wife* that doesn't approve."

"Are you aware that at one time he purchased a .41 magnum revolver?"

"Sure. From George Payton."

"You knew about that, then."

"Uh huh. He showed it to me once when I was over at the house. He had it in his desk, there." Tones's face sagged. "Is that what he used? The handgun?"

"We think so."

"Geez," he said wearily, and looked off into space. "Look. I don't *know* what drove George Enriquez to shoot himself. If I did, well…I just don't know." He shrugged and held up his hands helplessly. "Detective, *I don't know.*"

"I appreciate your talking with me, Mr. Tones."

He sighed heavily. "Anytime. Especially if it's helping that wonderful mother of yours choose paint colors. That's the sort of thing I *like* to do. Trying to figure out why old friends end up dead just isn't up my alley."

Estelle stood up, pushing the old chair gently under the typewriter table.

"I appreciate your help, sir."

Tones stood up and stretched his back. "That doesn't mean that I wouldn't like to know…when you find something out," he said. "Good luck with your investigation. God knows, George Enriquez sure deserved better than what he got. And that's a fact."

TWENTY-FIVE

As SHE WALKED back down the center aisle, past the bin displays of two-dollar Taiwanese hammers and seven-buck sets of six pliers, Estelle saw that Leona Spears and the patient salesgirl were still lost in the world of key blanks. The highway engineer looked up and saw Estelle approaching. Immediately, she began to move away from the current key problem, homing in on the undersheriff.

"Have you stopped for lunch yet?" Leona asked.

"Lunch isn't on the schedule for today, Leona," Estelle answered with a rueful smile. The statement was perfectly true unless Francis could break free for a few minutes.

Leona looked wistful. "Well, someday, then," she said, and drifted toward the door after Estelle. "Would you please tell your husband how much we all appreciate his efforts with that new clinic and pharmacy?"

Estelle nodded. "I'll do that. He'll be pleased to hear it."

She exited the store, feeling the warmth of the early afternoon October sun bouncing off the roof of her car. As her hand touched the door handle, her cell phone chirped as if car and phone had somehow made electrical contact. She slipped inside the sedan and closed the door.

"Guzman."

"Estelle?"

She didn't immediately recognize the voice. "Yes."

"Listen, this is Owen Frieberg, over at Salazar and Sons Funeral Home. Are you going to be around this afternoon sometime? I tried to catch you at the office earlier, but I missed."

"I would think so, Mr. Frieberg. What may I do for you?"

"Well…" and he hesitated. "There's kind of a tricky matter that I need to discuss with you. Won't take but a minute." Even as he spoke, the radio barked. Estelle didn't respond immediately but sat quietly, trying to imagine what kind of "tricky matter" a funeral director might have that would demand her attention.

"Just a second, sir," she said. Even as she reached for the mike, Sheriff Robert Torrez's clipped voice broke through again.

"Three ten, three oh eight."

She pulled the mike off the dash clip.

"Three ten. Go ahead."

"Three ten, ten nineteen," Sheriff Robert Torrez said cryptically.

"Ten four," she said. "ETA about two minutes."

"Interesting morning," she said to no one in particular as she hung up the mike. "Mr. Frieberg, I'll be back in the office in just a few minutes. Do you want to touch bases there, or do you want me to swing by your place later this afternoon? Would that work for you?"

"That would be fine."

"I'm not sure what time that will be."

"That's okay. I'll be here most of the day. I'll see you then."

She switched off and saw Leona Spears push open the hardware store's front door, and for a brief moment it looked as if she was headed toward Estelle's car once again. Estelle lifted two fingers off the top of the steering wheel in acknowledgment, farewell, or however Leona wished to interpret it, and pulled the car into reverse.

The Public Safety building was one block north on Grande, and one block east on Bustos. Well under the two-minute estimate, she thudded the county car's door shut and entered the back door of the sheriff's department.

"Oh, here you are," Gayle Torrez said. She was standing in the dispatch island and appeared to be trying to explain something to Dennis Collins, who held a thick envelope open for her. "Bobby's huddling with Chief Mitchell," she added, nodding toward the sheriff's office.

Estelle nodded, ignoring Collins's slack-jawed gaze, recognizing the expression of a young man who found it hard to look women in the eye. Nothing above a woman's neck seemed worthy of his attention.

The sheriff's tiny office looked like a transplant from a Marine Corps barracks, with neutral, institutional colors, metal desk, files, and a scarcity of chairs. Torrez was sitting behind his desk, one brown hunting boot across the corner, the other propped against the heating duct that ran up the wall. The back of his chair rested against the lower window frame behind him, and as Estelle entered he was thoughtfully rubbing the end of his nose.

Chief Eddie Mitchell turned from his perusal of the county map on the wall and flashed a quick grin at Estelle.

"Howdy," he said.

"Good afternoon," Estelle said. She leaned her black briefcase against the nearest chair, an uncomfortable steel folding thing with a county inventory sticker on the back. Mitchell glanced at the sheriff, and Estelle read the you-tell-her expression accurately.

Torrez frowned at his boot. "Some interesting things about the revolver," he said after a long moment. His eyes clicked to Estelle's and then to the door. "You want to make sure that's shut?"

She turned and nudged the door closed, curious. "You mean beyond its original purchase from George Payton's gun shop?"

"Way beyond. At one point, George Enriquez loaned the revolver to Owen Frieberg," the sheriff said. He let the unadorned sentence hang there. His fingers finally abandoned the problem on his nose, and both hands relaxed in his lap, fingers intertwined.

Both Estelle's eyebrows shot up, and the trace of a smile touched Torrez's face.

"Frieberg called me a couple of minutes ago," Estelle said. "Just now, when you were on the radio."

"He beat me to it, then. Your phone was busy when I dialed," the sheriff said. He swung his boot off the desk and let the other slide down the heating duct to the floor.

"Did you talk with him, or what?"

"The chief and I stopped by Salazar's this morning, at Frieberg's request."

"How did this connection come up?"

Torrez looked across at Mitchell. The chief turned the other small chair around and sat down, his arms crossed over the chair back. "The kind of brilliant detective work from which legends are made," he said dryly. He waited for the count of three. "Frieberg called me at home and told me that he had borrowed a handgun from George a while ago. He says that George had shown him the gun a time or two and even offered to loan it to Frieberg if he ever wanted to take it hunting. Frieberg says he did just that. He recalls offering to buy the revolver from George at one point, but George didn't want to go for that. Frieberg took the thing javelina hunting a couple of weeks ago."

"And he called you this morning, just to tell you that?"

Mitchell nodded. "That's what he did."

"So how…"

"He borrowed it quite a while ago, he doesn't remember exactly when, and then returned it late last week. He thinks it was Wednesday or Thursday."

"That's interesting," Estelle said softly. "I can understand his eagerness to call, then. The revolver he used for who knows how long is returned, and then used in a crime. And guess whose fingerprints should have been all over it."

"Except they weren't," Mitchell said.

"He cleaned it when he was finished," Torrez offered. "No big deal."

"That's interesting," Estelle repeated. "They'd have to be pretty good friends."

"George was good friends with half the town," Mitchell said and smirked. "And that's in addition to all the people he fleeced over the years, good friend that he was."

"And speaking of small towns, Salazar and Sons is where the body is headed when the medical examiner releases it," Torrez said. "Anyway, Frieberg heard the news, heard the rumor that George had shot himself with a large-caliber handgun, and put two and two together. He decided it might be wise to check with Chief Mitchell."

Mitchell shrugged philosophically. "It would have been embarrassing if he decided to stay quiet and then had to explain himself when we knocked on the door. If a print showed up, we'd trace the thing.''

"Maybe that,'' Torrez said. "Or someone might know about Frieberg borrowing the gun and mention it. All kinds of ways for the rumor mill to work. Frieberg just decided to get a jump on it all.''

She felt the sheriff's unblinking gaze as if he were inventorying the movement of every fine muscle in her face, inventorying every expression. If she were a contender for Boone and Crockett points, he'd be waiting for her to step out from behind the tree.

"What did George tell the district attorney when he telephoned him on Sunday?'' Torrez asked.

The question caught Estelle by surprise. She felt a quick swelling of anger at the district attorney and as quickly dismissed it. That was replaced with a twinge of irritation at the sheriff, but she knew it was only natural that he would compare the D.A.'s version of the story with her own.

"Schroeder says that George told him that he could, quote, *Give you Guzman,* unquote.''

When she didn't elaborate, Mitchell asked, "What's that mean?''

"George was trying to weasel his way out of facing a grand jury,'' Estelle said. "The implication, at least in Schroeder's mind, was that Enriquez knew something incriminating about 'Guzman' that he could somehow trade for immunity from the grand jury—partial or entire, who knows.''

"Huh,'' Mitchell said. "That's interesting. What else did he say?''

"Nothing, according to Schroeder. They were going to meet and talk about it sometime Monday.''

Mitchell's round face broke into a grin that didn't include his eyes. "So what did you do that's so incriminating it would get Georgie off the hook if it went public?''

"I don't have a clue,'' Estelle said.

"Wrong Guzman, maybe,'' Torrez said quietly, and the words wrenched Estelle's stomach into the same knot she'd felt when she'd discussed that very possibility with Bill Gastner the previous evening. She would have thought less of Bob Torrez had he not voiced the realization, but that didn't make it hurt any the less. A dawning of comprehension pulled Mitchell's mouth open in a soundless "Oh."

"*Doctor* Guzman," he said.

Estelle took a moment and sat down, carefully moving the briefcase so it wouldn't tip over. Her mind spun, refusing to focus on the obvious, the chaos in her mind fueled by the single, terrible possibility that George Enriquez somehow had been trying to save his own skin at the expense of her husband's new clinic.

"Look," Torrez said, leaning forward with his beefy forearms resting on the desk. "If George is willing to work his little insurance scam…"

"Not so little, either," Mitchell observed.

"Right. But if he's willing to work that, what's to keep him from dabbling in something else? He'll do one thing, he'll do another."

"A crook's a crook," Mitchell said. "What's he got going then, some kind of health insurance deal?"

"I don't know." Torrez relaxed back as if the conversation was over, with the others left to make their own connections.

"You're saying Enriquez was into something else," Mitchell said when Estelle made no response. "Well, of course he was. Why else would somebody shoot him? For fake insurance? I don't think so." He grinned. "Of course, if old Denton Pope hadn't blown himself up and managed to kill his mother in that fire the way he intended, *he* sure as hell would have been torqued to find out his home-owner's insurance was fake. But it wouldn't do much good to shoot Georgie."

"Look at the timing," Estelle said, feeling as if her words were spoken through wads of cotton. "The grand jury that would investigate George Enriquez convened on Tuesday morning. Who's the leadoff witness?"

"Undersheriff Estelle Guzman," Mitchell said.

"Exactly. George's object might have been to prevent *me* from testifying. It had nothing to do with my husband. So he tries to frame *me* for something, whether he had anything concrete or not."

"A couple of minutes ago, I brought up the possibility that Enriquez meant your husband, not you," the sheriff said. "We still don't know about that."

"And that doesn't make any sense," Estelle said. "I was the main grand jury witness. If Enriquez could throw a hammer into *my* testimony, he'd gain a little time."

"So you think he was just talking."

"Maybe."

"There's a simple fact remaining in all this," Mitchell said. "Someone obviously wanted George Enriquez dead. Now, it may be coincidence that it happened the day before the grand jury convened. And maybe not. It may be coincidence that the revolver that killed him was in someone else's possession for a few days prior to his death. And maybe not."

"Somebody didn't want George's story to go public," Torrez said.

"That's right. Lots of dirty laundry comes out after a grand jury indictment. And maybe his wife just got sick and tired of the whole circus," Mitchell said. "Maybe she waddled down there and popped him a good one."

Torrez rapped the desk gently. "The other possibility is that George really did have something to tell the district attorney. Something to trade. Something big enough, valuable enough, that even Schroeder would sit up and take notice...that he'd be willing to deal."

"I don't like coincidences," Estelle said, her voice almost a whisper. Both men looked at her, waiting. "I want to know more about the revolver. I told Frieberg that I'd stop by this afternoon. Now I'm thinking that it might be better if I left him hanging for a little bit. He already told you about the revolver, Bobby. I don't understand why he feels the need to tell me, too."

"Maybe he wants to talk about something else," Torrez said.

She reached for the briefcase. "Maybe. In the meantime, let me tell you about George Enriquez and Mexico."

TWENTY-SIX

THE RECEPTIONIST looked up to see the sheriff and undersheriff of Posadas County step through the inner door. The central office of Posadas Municipal Schools was the hushed silence of carpet and paperwork. The woman turned her pencil just so and laid it down on the blotter as if afraid the thud of its landing would be offensively loud.

"Well, good afternoon," she said, favoring them both with a broad smile.

"How you doin', Minnie," Torrez said.

"Just fine." The smile faded a watt. "You two look awfully official today."

"We need to talk to Glen," Torrez said.

Minnie's hand reached for the telephone. "Let me see if he's in." She pushed the appropriate button and waited, then actually smiled at the telephone as she said, "Nancy, Sheriff Torrez is here to see the superintendent. Has he come back yet from the middle school?" She nodded. "Uh huh. Sure." The smile widened. "Sure. Okay. Thanks, Nancy." She hung up the phone, and her face took on that professional I'm-*so*-sorry expression. "He's still over at the middle school, Sheriff. Do you want me to tell him to give you a call? Is there something I can help you with?"

Torrez rapped the counter once with his knuckle. "No, that's all right. We'll go on over and find him."

"Well, I think he's speaking at an assembly," she said, and the hint of worry in her tone amused Estelle. Perhaps the woman had visions of Sheriff Torrez striding into the assembly and tapping the superintendent on the shoulder just as Archer was about to introduce the Football Mom of the Year.

"*That'll* be interesting to hear," Torrez muttered. "Thanks, Minnie." Outside in the sun, he stopped halfway up the sidewalk. It appeared that he was examining one of the lawn sprinkler heads as it jetted pulses out across the putting green approach to the school superintendent's office. "Glen Archer and Owen Frieberg drove the buses to Mexico," he said, still watching the water. "George Enriquez and Joe Tones went along. Somebody from the school as well."

"Barry Vasquez, the student-council sponsor," Estelle said.

"Vasquez," Torrez repeated. "I know him. He's one of the varsity's offensive coordinators."

"That could be."

"Tones didn't mention any other teachers?"

"No. The five adults and a couple dozen kids."

Torrez nodded. "Okay." He turned and Estelle watched the muscle twitch on his cheek as he squinted at the grill of the county's Expedition.

"That's what I mean about coincidence," Estelle said. "As far as I can determine, the only three unusual things in George Enriquez's life recently have been this school deal in Mexico, the hunting trip that he was planning, and the grand jury staring him in the face."

"Uh huh."

"And two of the three have the same players."

"Okay," Torrez said. He turned abruptly and strode to the truck. They drove across the broad macadam parking lot the hundred yards to the front door of the middle school. The moment Estelle got out, she heard the volley of screams from the gymnasium, off behind the flat-roofed classroom wing.

"Mayhem," she said. "Brings back memories."

"All of them bad," Torrez replied. "This place hasn't changed much." Estelle tried without success to imagine Robert Torrez as an eighth-grader in the middle of a public speaking unit. They entered through the door whose sign admonished all visitors to check in with the principal's office—Glen Archer's domain at one time before he'd taken on first the high school and then the superintendency.

A grandmotherly-looking woman with a telephone glued to her ear beckoned at the same time as she quickly concluded her conversation on the phone. She arose, frowning. "Is that Bobby Torrez?" she asked.

"Yes, ma'am," the sheriff replied.

"I don't think I've had a chance to talk to you since the wedding," she said, referring to Torrez's marriage to Gayle Sedillos. "How's my favorite gal?"

"She's doing fine." Torrez glanced at a dour-faced youngster who walked by, bulging knapsack pulling one shoulder low, then turned back to the principal's secretary. "This is Undersheriff Estelle Guzman," he said. "Iona Urioste."

"Hi," Iona said, and offered Estelle her hand. "I've seen your picture in the paper."

"Central Office tells us that Glen Archer is over here today," Estelle said.

"They're all down in the gym," Iona replied. "Did you need to speak with the superintendent?"

"Yes."

Iona turned and looked at the clock on the back wall of her office. "They should be out of there in another ten minutes or so."

"We'll just go on down," Torrez said.

"You know the way," she said with a smile. "Good to see you again."

They walked down the empty polished hallway toward the intersection where the battered school seal adorned the wall, then turned toward the swelling cacophony of voices. Thirty yards ahead, a sea of students appeared through the double doors.

"It's like swimmin' upstream," Torrez observed as they made their way along the right-hand wall while the flow of chattering middle-schoolers flowed past, for the most part oblivious to their presence. One gaggle of five girls, lost in conversation, cruised down the wrong side of the hall. Torrez stopped and waited, forcing the girls to change course or collide. The bottleneck of oncoming traffic reached critical proportions at the double doors, and Torrez slowed, letting the tide of youngsters figure out for themselves how to either maneuver around or bounce off him.

School Superintendent Glen Archer was standing near the gymnasium doorway, beaming at the flow of children and talking with a short, chubby woman with close-cropped hair and enormous dangling earrings. Archer was the first to see the officers. A quick frown touched his open, kindly face.

Archer reached out to touch the woman on the elbow, mouthed "Excuse me," and walked across the foyer to meet the two officers.

"You missed all the excitement," he said, stretching out his hand. "They sure get wound up, don't they? Like to break my eardrums."

"What's the occasion?" Estelle asked.

"End of the first marking period," Archer said. "We gave away four bikes for perfect attendance." He nodded at a straggling gaggle of students as they filed out of the gym. "Good group of kids." He turned back to the officers. "What can I do for you?"

"We need to talk with you for a few minutes."

"Sure." He turned and caught the eye of the pudgy woman with the earrings, raising his voice just high enough to carry across the foyer. "Use your office for a minute, Mrs. Dooley?" The woman nodded and made a you-go-right-ahead shooing motion with her hand at the same time that she reached out with the other hand and stopped a harried-looking student who was trying to stuff papers back into a rumpled manila folder and walk at the same time.

"Follow me," Archer said. He grinned at the two officers. "Been a while since you guys wandered the halls, eh?"

"Not long enough," Torrez said.

Archer laughed. "Robert, all we ever had to do to find you was figure out which hunting season it was." He led them up the hall, through the crowd of kids, each of whom seemed to be slam-testing locker doors. In the front office, Iona Urioste was back on the phone, and Archer paused at the corner of her desk until she put a hand over the receiver. "We'll be using Mrs. Dooley's office for a few minutes," he said, and Iona nodded.

He pushed the inner door open, and Estelle glanced at the large spot marked on the wall, labeled STRESS RELIEF: BANG HEAD HERE.

The superintendent closed the door securely behind them, blocking out the hubbub. "Let's use this," he said, indicating the long conference table. "Now…which of our kids do you have in jail?" He managed to make it sound like a joke. "And by the way, when do your kiddos start school?" he asked Estelle.

"Francisco starts kindergarten next year," she said.

"Wow." He shook his head. "How the years go by."

"Glen," Bob Torrez said, eager to halt the reminiscing, "we need to know some details about the trips down to Acámbaro." His heavy-featured face was impassive, eyes heavy-lidded.

"You mean last year?"

"Yes."

"Well," and Archer drew a circle on the polished table. "We go twice a year, as I'm sure you're aware. Once in early December, once on the *Cinco de Mayo*. And I gotta tell you, it's a really big deal for the kids."

"On both sides of the border, I would imagine," Estelle said.

"Oh, sure. You wouldn't believe…well, I guess maybe *you* would, eh? What exactly did you need to know?"

Estelle slipped the small recorder out of her pocket and slid it across the table so that it faced Archer. "Do you mind?"

"Of course not." His forehead furrowed. "This is about George Enriquez, isn't it."

"Yes, it is."

"Wow."

"Mr. Archer, what adults went on the trip in December?"

"Well, it was the same crew both times, actually." He drew another circle that linked with the first. "I've been going now for eighteen years. I wouldn't miss it. Usually, the middle-school principal goes. At least in the past. This is Mrs. Dooley's first year. She didn't feel that she could take an entire day, so she didn't go along. I told her to plan for next year, though. It'd be good for her."

"Who else?"

"Let's see. Barry Vasquez went, of course. He's the student-council sponsor, and the program is his baby, so to speak. Do you need to talk with him?''

"Not just now."

"Okay. Let's see. Me, Barry, George Enriquez from the chamber of commerce. You wouldn't believe the load of stuff that group got together to take on down. George and our other buddy, there. Owen Frieberg. Both with the chamber. We couldn't do it without them, let me tell you.'' He grinned. "For one thing, we were *really* short of bus drivers last year. I ended up driving one, and Frieberg the other. He got his bus driver's license a couple of years ago, when he was helping out with the track team."

"That's four," Torrez observed dryly.

"Let me think. Am I missing someone?" He regarded the ceiling tiles for an instant. "Well, sure. Joe Tones. He's with the chamber, too. In fact, I think he's president this year. Can't leave him out." He nodded vigorously. "That was the crew. Me, Barry, Joe, Owen, and George."

"Two buses?"

"That's right. We took the two new activity buses. Two buses and the van."

"Which van is that?"

"George Enriquez borrowed the van from the senior citizen's center. That big twelve-passenger thing. We had a whole bunch of computers, and he suggested using the van. A whole lot easier to load and unload from that than trying to lug all those components up into a bus. Plus we had about a hundred sacks of food, clothes, and toys, so we needed the room."

"You drove one bus, Owen Frieberg drove the other, and George Enriquez drove the van."

"That's correct."

"Joe Tones rode with the van, or in one of the buses?"

"He rode down and back with me," Archer said. "That way Barry covered the other bus with Frieberg. Not that there was going to be any kind of problem. Not with the twenty-two best kids in school."

"They were all on one bus?"

"We had most of them with us. There were three, I think, on

the other bus. It was kind of crowded, with all the groceries, gifts, stuff like that. You wouldn't believe how much stuff went down there. We even had an older-model copier shoved in the back of my bus. I wasn't sure we'd clear the border checkpoint there at Regál, but we had no trouble. If you looked in the van or the bus, either one, it looked like we had a used-electronics ring going. But we've been doing these trips long enough that we've got some friends on both sides of the border.''

"What time in the morning did you clear the border crossing?'' Estelle asked.

"Let's see. We got out of here about nine, so we hit Regál what, at about nine forty-five or so? Maybe a little before.''

"And came back into the country…?''

"Right at three,'' Archer said. "That gives us a full three hours in Acámbaro, which is plenty. And we like to have the kids back in time to catch their regular bus home. Saves us and the parents a lot of headache.''

"Any complications at the border crossing coming back?''

Archer leaned back in his chair and spread his hands. "Neither time. In December, one of the officers stepped onto my bus…I was first in line, then the van, then the second bus. The customs guy looked at the kids all seriouslike for a couple of seconds, then said, 'Welcome back.' That was it. In May, we were just waved on through.''

"And you traveled as a group, both times? Two buses and the van.''

Archer nodded. "Both times. Well, in May, we didn't need the van. Just the two buses.''

Estelle looked down at her notebook for a moment. "You were in Acámbaro for about three hours, is that right?''

"Just about. In December, there's lots of music and dancing with the kids. Then we give out the gifts, have a snack, and hit the road. During the May trip, it's mostly a show put on by the kids at the Acámbaro school. We have a picnic afterward, and that's it.''

"You said that George Enriquez went on both trips, Mr. Archer?''

"Yes, he did. Same crew both times.''

"What about the year before that?"

"No, this was George's first trip. Joe Tones has been going for a decade or more. I think this is Owen Frieberg's...I don't know, maybe fifth year?" Archer grinned ruefully. "You got to be careful when you let the school district find out that you've got a bus driver's license. Once we've got our claws in you, it's hard to escape."

"In May, where did you park the buses when you got to the school in Acámbaro?" Torrez said. "Right in front on the street, or in that space back by the gym?"

Archer looked puzzled. "The one bus—the one I was driving? We drove it around back, since we were the one with the heavy copier. That was the nearest point to their office, where it was going. The other bus just pulled up in the street, right at the curb."

"And the van?"

"He went around back with me."

"And the vehicles were parked there the whole time?"

"Well, the bus was. After they unloaded all the computers from the van—and I think they also had some of the old toner cartridges and stuff like that for the copier—George parked it back out on the street with the other bus."

"Did Mr. Enriquez appear to enjoy himself?"

"I think he had a good time," Archer said. "He seemed to have a real affection for the kids, you know? And he's fluent in Spanish, so that helped. I noticed that he spent quite a bit of time talking with a couple of the little Indian children. Tarahumara, I think they are. They were kind of spooked by all the activity."

"He was there the whole time?"

"That I couldn't say, Estelle. Things get so hectic, with so much going on, the last thing I spend my time doing is trying to keep track of the *adults*. You know what I mean? I figure they can take care of themselves." He leaned his arms on the table. "I was sorry to hear about the man's death, guys. A real shock, you know? He's done a lot for the community."

Estelle nodded. "Yes, sir, he has." She reached over and

turned off the tape recorder. "May we have a list of the twenty-two youngsters who went on the trip?"

"Of course." His expression became wary. "I hesitate a little bit with that. You can talk to me all day, if you want to, and to Barry Vasquez, if you like. But with the youngsters, it's a little different. One of the school staff needs to be present for anything like that." He paused. "And you know, the eighth-graders who went on the two trips last year are in ninth grade now, so they're over at the high school. That shouldn't be much of a problem, though. Can you tell me what you're looking for? If I knew, maybe I could be of more help."

Estelle glanced at Torrez, who nodded slightly. "Sir," she said. "It's a possibility that one or more of the students saw something that could assist us in this investigation. The adults are busy watching kids, and might not notice anything of interest beyond them. Kids see some interesting things, sometimes."

Archer's smile was tight-lipped. "But you don't want to say just yet what those interesting things might be. Do I read that correctly?"

"Yes, you do."

Archer pushed himself back from the table. "If you don't have any more questions for me, let me get you that list. We'll go from there."

"This could be a real wild goose chase," Torrez said quietly when Archer left the office.

"I hope so," Estelle said.

"You're planning to talk to all twenty-two kids?"

"If I have to."

TWENTY-SEVEN

ESTELLE KNEW THAT once planted and fed, the rumor grapevine grew at the speed of sound. With that in mind, she and Torrez elected to interview the students in school the following day, rather than in individual homes. Despite admonitions to keep the experience to themselves, it was a certainty that the students would talk with one another after the interviews—and that some would talk with parents when they arrived home from school late Thursday afternoon.

That gave Estelle a window of opportunity when any information that the students might possess would not be general knowledge in the community—one brief school day.

Six of the twenty-two students on the trip had been seventh-graders, and five of those had returned to Posadas for the following school year. The sixth had moved to San Diego.

Estelle met with the five, one at a time, in Tessa Dooley's office at the middle school. Mrs. Dooley sat at the head of the conference table and greeted each student with an expression that was half glower and half affectionate empathy—an expression that told them they'd better provide answers, and fast.

By nine-thirty Thursday morning, Estelle had heard the same wandering, vague recitation of the Mexican experience: the embarrassed dancing, the gift giving, the food. For several of the students, the high point of the trip appeared to have been listening to their boombox headphones on the bus ride down and back.

All five remembered "those guys" from the chamber of commerce. Not one recalled a name. Two of the five students had no idea who school superintendent Glen Archer was—much to

Mrs. Dooley's exasperation—despite Archer's appearance at the middle-school assembly just the day before.

One of the five, a slender little girl with enormous blue eyes and a mouthful of braces, recalled the poverty of the Acámbaro area. What stuck in her memory was the lack of a sidewalk from the classroom building to the uncompleted gymnasium.

Estelle and the principal watched the last child slip out of the office. "Close the door behind you, dear," Tessa Dooley said, and when the child left without latching it, the principal arose with a grunt and pushed the door closed herself.

"Impressive, don't you think?" she said, the sarcasm heavy.

Estelle glanced up at Dooley as the principal maneuvered her way back to her place at the conference table. "I'm always amazed at what children see, or maybe I should say, *how* they see," Estelle replied.

"It's very different, that's for sure. Maybe with a little prompting, they'd remember more, but it's been a long time for them." She flashed a quick smile. "By their standards, a long time. I wish I had gone along. Of course," and she hunched forward into a self-deprecating shrug, "I probably would remember less than they did."

Estelle reached across and turned off the tape recorder that had been nestled discreetly beside a large box of tissues, simply so that it hadn't been the sole, intimidating object on the table.

"Wouldn't it help if we knew what you were looking for?" Mrs. Dooley asked. "I feel like we're stumbling around in the dark here."

"I'm sorry it's frustrating," Estelle said, "but it's important that the kids don't pick up on a particular direction from us. They're wonderfully adept at figuring out what adults want to know and bending their stories accordingly. I'm sure you know that better than I."

The principal laughed with resignation. "Oh, yes." She studied Estelle silently for a moment. "You must have kiddos of your own?"

"Two boys."

"Mr. Archer tells me that you were born in Mexico?"

"Yes."

Mrs. Dooley's mouth pursed a little with amusement at Estelle's cryptic answers. "Here I go, asking all the questions," she said. She stood up quickly and extended a hand, glancing at the clock at the same time. "If there's anything else we can do, you know where to find me."

Locating the remaining sixteen students at the high school was not so simple. Two had moved out of district during the intervening year. Three were absent from school, as was the high-school principal himself. Estelle met first with Barry Vasquez, the sponsor of the trip. He had transferred to the high school for the new school year.

In his late twenties, broad-shouldered and full-bellied, Vasquez settled uneasily onto the leather couch in the principal's office. He placed an enormous wad of keys secured on a long lanyard on the couch beside him, then looked warily at the tape recorder. He glanced at the door as if weighing his options for escape. Estelle turned the chair beside the principal's desk so that it faced Vasquez.

"Mr. Vasquez," she said, "we're interested in certain aspects of the two trips that you and your students took to Acámbaro last year. The one at Christmas, the second the following May."

"What's the deal?" Vasquez asked, his accent thickly west Texas.

"You rode on one of the buses?"

"Gol dang, I don't remember which bus I rode on. That's a long time ago." His smile was immediate and faded just as quickly. He glanced at the door again, then at his watch. Estelle leaned back in her chair, her right hand resting comfortably against her cheek.

"I'd like to know if your recollection agrees with Superintendent Archer's, Mr. Vasquez."

"I'm sure it does," Vasquez said. "What's this all about, anyway?"

"Mr. Vasquez," Estelle said patiently, "we can dig our way through this one painful step at a time, or you can speed things up immeasurably. I need to know anything you remember about the two trips to Mexico. I want to know how you got there, what you did while you were there, what you saw. I'm interested in your impressions, Mr. Vasquez.''

"Some of our kids in trouble?''

"No, they're not.''

"And that's all I get to know?''

Estelle nodded and remained silent.

"Is this tied in with that Enriquez thing somehow? He went along with us, both times.'' He pushed himself forward on the couch so he could rest his forearms on his knees. "Look, this is a trip that the school has been taking for years…since way before my time here.''

"I'm not interested in any trips except the two last year,'' Estelle said. "The one in December, the one in May.''

"Okay,'' Vasquez said, and settled back on the couch, twisting so that he could throw one arm over the back and rest his left knee on the cushion. He pulled up his sock and smoothed the trouser leg over it. His recitation of the trips was a high-speed synopsis that began with how the student council chose which students could go along, how the preparations were made, and the schedule of the actual trip.

As he warmed to his topic, Estelle could see that Barry Vasquez was one of those people who would spend thirty hours a day at school if he could. His eagerness to help students organize themselves was his major motivation, and talking about the challenges of taking twenty-two middle-schoolers to Mexico, along with a ton of food and gifts, loosened his tongue.

As far as he was concerned, both trips had been completed without a hitch. The students had been where they were supposed to be, when they were supposed to be.

"Mr. Vasquez,'' Estelle said as he wound down, "did George Enriquez appear to enjoy himself?''

"Which time? December?'' He pulled at his sock again. "Yeah, I think so.''

"He drove the senior citizens' van for the December trip?''

"Yes ma'am, he did. Both times.''

"What did the chamber take down in December? Why was the van necessary?''

"Ah…'' Vasquez paused and rubbed his forehead vigorously.

"The copier and all that surplus junk. The junk computers and stuff." He frowned at his sock. "The van was where most of the food was, I think. At least a lot of it. Yeah." He looked up quickly. "The food was in the van. We had it packed in plastic bags."

"Did Mr. Enriquez stay in Mexico with the group the whole time?"

"Sure. We all crossed the border together. Two buses and a van. We traveled as a group."

"Both times."

"Yes. Except no van the second time. We didn't need it."

"Was there ever a time, either trip, when you noticed that Mr. Enriquez was *not* at the school with you?"

"What do you mean?"

"You explained that you arrived at the school in Acámbaro in the late morning and left sometime between one and two that afternoon. That's three hours or so. During that time, was Mr. Enriquez always present?"

"Sure. As far as I know. I remember that on the December trip, we forgot the ice. He and one of the other guys went to get some. There's a little sort of gas station-grocery store-gift shop just a couple of blocks down from the school. He drove the van down there, I remember."

"And someone else went with him?"

"I *think* so, but I don't remember for sure. I really don't." He leaned his head back and closed his eyes, then abruptly shook his head. "I just don't recall. I *do* remember that in May, we didn't take any ice along, because we knew we could get it right there."

"But all the years previous you took ice with you?"

"Sure." He shrugged. "We took *everything*, Sheriff. Right down to bottled water." He grinned sheepishly.

"Who went to get the ice in May?"

"Good God, I don't know." He started to shake his head, then as abruptly stopped and held up a hand. "I think it was Mr. Enriquez. In fact, I know it was. I remember seeing him and Owen Frieberg carrying the four bags into the gym when they got back."

"Frieberg went with him?"

"I don't know if he went or not. I'm just assuming that he did. I just remember seeing them carry the bags into the gym. I remember Frieberg saying something like, 'You think this stuff is safe?' and Mr. Enriquez just laughing."

Estelle toyed with the tape recorder, shifting its position a fraction of an inch. "What did you bring back with you, Mr. Vasquez?"

"How do you mean?"

"Just that. Did you guys do any souvenir shopping anywhere? In Acámbaro or anywhere else? Did you let the students out for a break?"

"No. We didn't have time for that. It's a short drive, anyway. Just a bit over an hour. If there'd been a mall, the kids would have rioted if we didn't stop. But I think they were kinda happy to get back across the border and onto home turf."

"No stops in Tres Santos, for instance?"

"There's nothing there."

"I was thinking about some of those neat woodcarvers' places."

"No. We came right through."

"A return trip with two big empty buses and an empty van," Estelle said.

"We had lots of room to stretch out," Vasquez said. "The chamber guys put all the trash bags in the van for us, so we didn't even have to mess with that."

"Lots of trash?"

He nodded. "We trek it in, trek it out. There must have been ten of those big black trash bags full. Gift wrapping, bottles, cups…just all kinds of stuff. I always tell the kids that no one in Mexico wants to pick up after a bunch of little rich kids from the States." He grinned. "That always gets their attention. They don't like being called *Lurks*."

"Lurks?"

"Little Rich Kids."

"Ah. That's neat. In December, Enriquez drove the van by himself? Both ways?"

"Yes, ma'am. As far as I recall." He leaned his head back

again. "The superintendent and that other chamber guy, Joe Tones, were in the one bus. I rode on the big activity bus with Frieberg so we'd have someone from the school with the kids. That's where most of the stuff was. And Enriquez drove the van."

Vasquez picked up his bundle of keys and wrapped the lanyard around his fingers, looking at Estelle expectantly. She reached over and turned off the tape recorder.

"I don't know what exactly you're looking for, but a lot of the trip in December is on tape," Vasquez said. "The kids put out a video yearbook, and one of the yearbook kids is on the student council. Lori Schmidt? She's the council historian, in fact. Old Lori was always stickin' that camera in our faces. I think she used up an entire tape."

"I'd like to see that."

"When the clip came out in the video yearbook, it was about three minutes long," Vasquez said. He laughed. "Chop, chop, chop."

"What teacher works with the yearbook crew?"

He ducked his head with a touch of pride. "My wife." It came out *ma waff*, and Estelle smiled. "She's still at the middle school. Emily Vasquez? Teaches math and art."

Estelle made several quick notes. "Okay. Thanks." She smiled at Vasquez. "I appreciate your cooperation. I'm sorry to keep you so long."

He practically lunged to his feet. "That's all right. You all got a job to do, same as us." He shook hands, his grip crushingly strong. "Lemme know." He nodded and left the office, keys jangling.

TWENTY-EIGHT

ESTELLE WALKED THROUGH the front door of the middle school in time to hear Principal Tessa Dooley's voice booming over the P.A. system, reminding students that Friday was yearbook picture day and that they should dress appropriately. The woman turned and saw Estelle, hesitated, and then carefully stowed the P.A. microphone back in the cabinet.

"Good morning again," she said, and her eyes shifted beyond Estelle and down a notch. She beckoned, and Estelle stepped to one side to allow two girls into the office.

"We're supposed to pick up some tag board for Mrs. Tyler," one of the students announced. The two girls glanced at Estelle, and one of them smiled shyly.

"Right there," Dooley said, and pointed a fair collection of rings in the direction of a flat box leaned up against one of the office chairs. "You guys be careful," she admonished as they struggled with the awkward box so that they could carry it between them. "Child labor," she said as the two disappeared down the hall. "No school can run without it." She took a deep breath and exhaled noisily. "What can I do for you? Sorry about the mayhem. My secretary is out today."

"Mrs. Dooley, I need to speak with Emily Vasquez."

"That shouldn't be an impossibility," the woman said. "And I won't even ask you why." She pulled out the right-hand sideboard of her secretary's desk and ran a finger down the list of faculty. "This is…"—she looked up at the wall clock—"third period." Her finger found the appropriate column. "Her prep's fifth period, right after lunch. Right now she's got a pre-algebra class."

"Will you point me in the right direction?"

"Better'n that. Let's take a hike. That way, I miss a couple of phone calls." She rolled her eyes and lowered her voice. "Damn thing is driving me nuts this morning."

Despite her short, roly-poly stature, Tessa Dooley set off at a brisk clip, head down and taking her lane out of the exact middle of the hallway. "You guys have been busy, I understand," she said.

"Yes, ma'am."

"Nasty stuff."

"Yes, it is."

"I'm always surprised at the conditions some of our kiddos have to put up with outside of school," the principal said. "It's amazing they can function at all."

Before Estelle had a chance to answer, Tessa abruptly changed course, hitting the door of the girls' restroom with the heel of her hand. "Two seconds," she said, disappearing inside. She reemerged and grinned at Estelle. "You just never know what interesting things you can interrupt in a middle-school restroom." She set off again, motioning toward the end of the hall. "One sixteen is the last room on the left. We'll see if Mrs. Vasquez can break away for a few minutes. I can sit her class if it comes to that."

They reached 116 and the principal paused, looking through the door's narrow glass light. Estelle could see a classroom full of students, a white-board full of mathematics, and a young woman working with a student in the third row toward the back.

Mrs. Dooley opened the door gently, as if the students were a herd of gazelle that might bolt at the slightest disturbance. Emily Vasquez looked up and saw her, nodded, and continued her conversation with the red-haired eighth-grader whose freckled face was screwed up in frustrated anguish. The principal waited patiently until the discussion between student and teacher wound down.

"If you write it out, you'll see why you have to add the exponents," Mrs. Vasquez said as she moved away. The student didn't look convinced. Three other hands instantly shot up, but the teacher ignored them and smiled pleasantly at the principal.

"Do you have a few minutes?" Dooley asked. Her broad body still blocked the doorway, and Estelle stepped back into the hallway. "Mrs. Vasquez, this is Deputy..." and she hesitated. Estelle reached out a hand.

"Undersheriff Guzman," she said, and Tessa Dooley grimaced.

"Well, I got that right, didn't I. Anyway, Emmy, can you talk with the officer for a few minutes?" She glanced over her shoulder. "Jane's not here today, so you can use her office."

"Sure."

"I'll keep the hoodlums under control," Dooley said with relish. "I can add and subtract as well as any eighth-grader." She bustled across the hall, selected a key from the wad, and opened the nurse's office door. "There you go. Enjoy."

Estelle followed Emily Vasquez into a small office wallpapered with charts of various parts of the perfect human's anatomy. As she was closing the door, they heard an explosion of laughter from across the hall.

"She's a hard act to follow," Emily said.

"An interesting lady."

"Just incredible. Anyway," she said, and sat down with her hands folded in her lap. "What can I do for you?" Another peal of laughter drifted to them, and Emily Vasquez smiled. She had the athletic build of a runner, as trim and fit as her husband was porky.

"Mrs. Vasquez, it's my understanding that you were sponsor of the yearbook last year. Is that correct?"

She nodded. "Not a yearbook, actually. Two years ago, we decided to try making a year-video kind of thing. It seemed like a good project for mid-schoolers to try. The kids film the various activities during the year and then try and edit the segments down so that each spot is just a minute or two long. It actually works pretty well. This will be our third year."

"And then you sell the tapes?"

"Yes. The first year, we sold only about fifteen. Then fifty last year. We'll do even better this year, I think." She cocked her head warily. "Is there some problem with the tape?"

"None whatsoever. I wonder if I might see the original tape from the student council trip to Mexico."

"Oh, God." One hand drifted up to cover the teacher's mouth. "What happened? What'd we do?"

Estelle shook her head quickly and held up a hand. "Please...don't misunderstand. We're investigating an incident that *might* have involved one of the adults who went on the trip, not the students. There's a possibility that in filming during the day, the student photographer might have caught something on tape that would be of interest to us."

"My husband was on that trip."

"Yes, ma'am." *And I know exactly how you feel,* Estelle wanted to add.

"Wait..." Emily Vasquez held out a hand. "Barry said that one of the men from the chamber of commerce who went on both trips is the one who shot himself the other day. Is that true? Is that what this is all about?"

Estelle nodded.

"What could possibly be on that tape?" Emily asked. "The raw tape was almost three hours of a gym full of kids whooping and hollering."

"May I see it?"

She frowned. "You don't want to see the year-video version then, the three-minute finished program."

"Both would be fine."

Emily put both hands on the arm of the chair and pushed herself halfway up. "One's easy. You can *have* a copy of the year video. I don't know for sure if we still have the raw tape. We'll see. They're all in the back closet in my room."

She led the way back across the hall, and as she opened the door of 116, Estelle could hear Mrs. Dooley's twang as she explained her own version of exponents to a student.

"I'll wait out here," Estelle said. "That would be better." Emily Vasquez nodded and disappeared into the room. Less than a minute later, she returned with two videotape cassettes in hand.

"This one is the raw footage," she said. Estelle saw the ACÁMBARO, CHRISTMAS 2001 label on the spine. "And this is the year video. You're welcome to keep that if you like. We'd like the file footage back. Sometimes we use a clip for some other project.''

''I'll be careful with it,'' Estelle said.

Emily reached out and touched her arm. ''Did you talk with the student who filmed the trip yet? She's a freshman this year.''

''Lori Schmidt,'' Estelle said.

''Yes. She's a wonderful girl.'' She started to say something and hesitated.

''We'll do our best not to involve any of the youngsters,'' Estelle said. ''That's one of the reasons I wanted to view the tape first, before I talked to her.'' She held out her hand. ''Mrs. Vasquez, I appreciate your help.''

The teacher grimaced. ''I don't much like it when the outside world comes into this building, Sheriff. I like to be able to pretend that it's not out there sometimes.''

''I can understand that.''

''And I don't know what I'm going to tell students when they ask me why I let you have those.''

Estelle held up the tapes. ''Mrs. Vasquez, I don't think that this is one of those First Amendment questions where you're correct to protect a source. What I'm looking for is something the *camera* might have seen, perhaps in the background—something that Lori didn't even realize was there, or was important.''

The teacher nodded.

''I can get a court order, if that makes you feel better.''

''No, no,'' Ms. Vasquez said with a quick shake of the head. ''That would be a waste of your time. I just want to be sure that the youngsters are protected.''

''That's my first concern,'' Estelle said. ''I'll bring these back as promptly as I can.'' She left the building through the side door, hearing a final peal of laughter as Tessa Dooley relinquished her hold on the math class. It was a comforting sound to hear.

TWENTY-NINE

SHERIFF ROBERT TORREZ settled into the chair at the end of the conference room opposite the television monitor and folded his hands across his lap. Linda Real popped the zip top on a can of soda. "Anyone bring popcorn?" she asked.

"I'd settle for dinner," the sheriff said. "Perrone called, by the way. About half an hour ago."

Estelle stopped rummaging for the TV's remote. "What did he say?"

"Someone popped Enriquez on the right temple hard enough to fracture his skull. Perrone is sure it happened *before* the gunshot. The body's gone to the M.E.'s in Albuquerque."

"And the gun?"

"That, too," Torrez nodded. "It's lookin' like someone hit George with the barrel of the .41, which would explain some of the hair traces. We'll see."

Estelle straightened, remote in hand. She placed it carefully on the TV stand. "If he was struck, his hands would go to his head out of reflex," she said. "That would explain why his head was back against the chair and his left arm raised." She mimed the motions of someone clutching the side of his head. "That's how he was sitting when the shot was fired."

"That could be," Torrez said noncommittally. He nodded at the television. "Show time," he said. "How long is this thing?"

"Three hours," Estelle replied. She looked down at her legal pad at the list of footage. "But we're just going to make some brief stops along the way."

"You want sound?" Linda Real asked.

"Sure."

A bright image of the Posadas Middle School's parking lot flashed onto the large screen, and Estelle immediately pressed the Pause button. "Two buses and a van," she said. Surrounding the vehicles was a swarm of students. The bulky figure of Barry Vasquez could be seen in the back of one of the buses, partially hidden by the yawning door. Tessa Dooley was frozen in mid-stride halfway between the school's side door and the vehicles.

"This is George Enriquez," Estelle said, touching the screen with the tip of her pencil. She indicated a dark shadow inside the van. The vehicle's two doors were open wide, with a variety of bags and boxes already filling the empty space behind the last seat.

"Okay," Torrez said.

Estelle pressed Play, and the scene jumped into motion. In a flurry of disorganization, the van and buses were loaded, the students forming an unruly ant line back and forth into the school. "This is first thing in the morning," Estelle said. "They actually started loading about eight-fifteen or so. They were on the way by about five minutes after nine."

"What am I looking for?" Torrez asked.

"I want you to look closely at the van," Estelle said, "especially in a couple of minutes when the camera moves in closer."

For almost ten minutes they watched the loading process. It appeared that George Enriquez was good-naturedly directing the stuffing of the van, starting with the first of the three bench seats in the back, and then filling the remaining space between the final seat and the doors.

"Who was running the camera?" the sheriff asked.

"An eighth-grader named Lori Schmidt," Estelle said.

"She's a patient girl."

"Yes, she is."

"And she used a tripod," Linda Real said. "That thing's rock steady. And it's a good camera. Nice and clear."

The scene abruptly shifted to a bus pulling out of the parking lot, with hands waving out the windows. Estelle put the tape on Fast Forward. "There's a lot of footage of kids doing kid things," she said. "Lori has a good eye. Lots of smiling faces, lots of neat expressions. She shot about five minutes of tape just of the kids on the bus. Mostly nonsense stuff.''

Estelle pressed Play again, and the border crossing at Regál sprang into focus, the video shot through the window of the second bus.

"This is interesting," Estelle said. "The van is between the buses. The Mexican border officials know the program, and they've seen the same buses before, so it's nothing new." They watched the first bus as it was waved through. The Mexican border guard appeared to chat with George Enriquez for a few seconds and then grinned broadly, looking toward the second bus as he stepped back.

"Who's driving the lead bus?"

"That's Frieberg," Estelle said. "You'll see him later, when they're unloading. As far as I can tell, he just sat in the bus when they loaded in Posadas. Glen Archer is driving the bus that Lori's on. In fact, there's a place where he tells her that she needs to stay seated when they're on the road. He tells her that about five times."

The Fast Forward spun the students into a blur, and Estelle abruptly slowed the tape and put it on Pause. "Now. We see one van and one bus, parked in front of the school in Acámbaro." The front yard of the school was packed clay, and every now and then the wind would kick a small whirl of dust through the legs of the students, enough of a breeze that it plastered clothes and ruined perfectly prepared hair.

"Barry Vasquez told me that the bus Frieberg was driving pulled into that dirt lane beside the school and that the other remained out front. The same thing that Archer told us."

She pressed the remote, and the tape paused, a group of smiling youngsters frozen with their arms laden. Behind them, the doors of the van gaped open. George Enriquez stood beside the back door, one hand on the corner of it as if holding it against the wind. "Lori took just enough film outside to show that they unloaded," Estelle said. "Then she got out of the wind." She fast-forwarded and just as abruptly stopped. "I want you to look at this picture in particular."

Torrez leaned forward, expression puzzled.

Using the eraser of her pencil, Estelle marked a circle around a portion of the scene, including George Enriquez putting two bags into the waiting arms of a stout middle-schooler. The kid's face was scrunched with determination, as if enough concentration would keep the sand out of his eyes.

"When he steps back, I want you to look right there. Right under the backseat." She looked back at the sheriff, pencil eraser still touching the screen.

"Okay," he said.

She stepped to one side and pressed Play. The kid hefted the two bags, George Enriquez said something that the camera microphone couldn't pick up over the growling of the wind, and then the youngster turned away, disappearing out of view. Enriquez beamed at the camera, tossed a salute for the fans, and turned to slam the two doors.

Estelle stopped the tape, with Enriquez frozen in mid-stride, one arm trailing back toward the van.

"What did I see?" Torrez said.

"That's right."

"An empty van."

"Let me play it once more, and this time look at the space directly *under* the backseat." She played the tape backward, and they saw Enriquez waddle back, pull the salute out of the air, and smile. The youngster arrived with the bags and gave them back.

"Ready?"

"Sure."

The scene played once more. "All right," Torrez said when she halted the tape, Enriquez frozen again in mid-stride. "There's nothing under the seat."

"Exactly right."

"Shit," Torrez muttered.

"Sir?"

He waved a hand in disgust. "It's just that I know exactly where this is going," he said. "This is going to be the biggest damn nightmare we've had around here in a long time." He flicked a go-ahead gesture.

Estelle ran the tape on Fast Forward for what seemed like a

long time. They watched kids scuttling at high speed this way and that, long lines of kids in some kind of exotic dance, un-collected crowds of kids doing who knows what, some in-tight and personal shots of enormous smiles, flashing teeth, and the Mexican school principal making a speech that lasted altogether too long.

Finally, the youngsters all flowed to one end of the gym, the grown-ups gesticulating wildly.

"What are they doing?" Torrez murmured.

"You want me to slow it down?"

"No, please," he said instantly. "Just tell me."

"They're sweeping for trash," Estelle said. And sure enough, the line moved across the gymnasium, backs bending and heads bobbing.

"They don't have floor mops?" Torrez asked.

"That's not the point of the exercise," Estelle said. "Now they're going outside, and they'll do the same sweep all around the school grounds."

"Absolutely fascinating."

"Just be patient, Roberto."

"The kid who shot all this must have a permanent black ring around her camera eye," Linda laughed. "She's *really* good." She glanced at Torrez. "We should hire her, sir."

"Oh sure. We can't even afford to pay you."

"Now," Estelle said, switching the VCR to the Play mode. Instantly, the humans on-screen slowed to a sane pace. At least a dozen black trash bags, bulging fat, were lugged across the camera, the kids taking the opportunity to wave at the lens.

A smiling George Enriquez, this time with Owen Frieberg standing on the other side of the van's side door, accepted one bag at a time, stuffing the van full of trash. When the seats were apparently full, they moved to the back doors.

"Watch closely," Estelle said. The remaining four kids, wad-dling with their loads, lined up. Enriquez stood on the driver's side of the door, Frieberg on the other. Enriquez took the first bag from the youngster. As the boy turned away, Enriquez turned and swung the bag up and into the van.

"There," Estelle said. The scene froze. She moved close and tapped the screen with the pencil. "Right there."

"Yup," Torrez grunted.

"It's there for just an instant, and then the rest of the bags cover them up. I can see two distinct white cardboard boxes under the seat. Maybe a third." She held her hands up, eight inches apart. "About like so."

"Christmas gifts for his wife," Linda said.

"Bullshit," Torrez said instantly. "If those were gifts, or something legit, he'd have them up on the front seat, not piled under an avalanche of trash."

"The other problem is, we can't see under the other seats. The one right by the door," and she rewound, the figures dancing backward and unloading the van, "right here? The seat's got a skirt of some kind on the side, so we can't see."

Estelle stopped the tape, the blank blue screen staring out at them.

"What do you think?" Torrez said. "What's the simple explanation?"

"I don't know. Like you said, if it was something small and simple, why bury it under the seat?"

"Did this camera girl film the group crossing back into the States?"

"No. According to Barry Vasquez, they were waved right on through."

"So Georgie didn't have anything to declare."

"Right. What bothers me the most is that they had an opportunity to make a pickup, if that's what they did. They forgot ice for the party, and Enriquez told them they'd get it at a little mercantile right there in Acámbaro. He and Frieberg went and got it. Both trips. Certainly in December, anyway. In May, they didn't have the van, so maybe it came to them while everyone was busy inside."

"That doesn't give us much," Torrez said.

"No. Except it points to opportunity."

"It's not booze," Torrez said. "The boxes are too small. I don't think he's going to try to carry something like grass or coke that way. Hell, the first drug dog that sniffed the van would hit. I don't care how many tons of garbage were dropped on top of it.''

"The simple fact is that when they loaded the van at the middle school, there was nothing under those seats," Estelle said. "When they left Acámbaro with a load of rubbish, there was." She turned off the monitor. "That's all. First there wasn't anything, and then there was." She shrugged and watched Torrez's cheek muscles flex. "There may be a simple, innocent explanation, Bobby. Maybe it was nothing. I just need to know."

Torrez leaned forward, his chin cupped in his hand. "Our problem is that we *think*—well, that's wrong—we *know* Enriquez was murdered. But before somebody whacked him, he mentioned your name, or your husband's, to the D.A. And then he turns up dead." The sheriff fell silent, as if the three sentences had exceeded his allowed maximum for one outburst.

"Frieberg is eager for us to know that he handled the revolver," Estelle said. "I can understand that. But we have two connections between Enriquez and Frieberg: this trip to Mexico and the elk hunt thing."

Torrez shrugged and pointed an accusatory finger at the dark screen. "That's a little problem right there, and it involves George and Frieberg…*again*." He shrugged. "You're right, Estelle. I want to know what was in the boxes, too. I'm willing to bet that you've got some ideas."

"I wish I didn't," she said, and let it go at that.

THIRTY

THE DRIVE FROM the sheriff's office to the clinic on Escondido was scarcely more than a mile, but it took Estelle Reyes-Guzman fifteen minutes. She walked out to her car and then sat in the silent interior for a few minutes, the radio and telephone off, windows tightly rolled up. Her mind refused to focus on a specific direction, instead circling from all points of the compass.

There could be such simple explanations. The boxes under the seat of the van could be innocent gifts, perhaps fragile wood carvings or spicy Mexican candies. George had packed them securely so they wouldn't be jounced on the rough ride north from Acámbaro to Regál. That could be.

George might have been fascinated by the world of medications and read the drug reference guide as a hobby, idly marking various drugs that caught his fancy or that he'd taken over the years. That could be.

He had loaned Owen Frieberg an expensive handgun to take along on a hunting trip or maybe just to blow holes through cans. Frieberg had returned it after a short time, and when he'd heard that the revolver had been involved in Enriquez's death, had felt compelled to tell police that he'd used the gun earlier...a logical thing to do if he feared his prints would be found on the weapon. That could be.

It *could* be that beyond those possibilities, the affairs of George Enriquez and Owen Frieberg were not related in any way.

"*I can give you Guzman,*" Estelle whispered. She glanced in the rearview mirror, as if Enriquez might be walking across the small parking lot toward her at that very moment. "George, what were you doing?" she said.

Estelle started the car and backed out, turning first west on Bustos and then south on Grande. Less than a block down that street, she pulled into Tommy Portillo's Handi-Way convenience store. With her mind still wandering through the field of *"coulds,"* she ambled into the store, purchased a bottle of flavored tea and a package of fudge chocolate-chip cookies. The young man behind the counter could have fleeced her out of most of the change for the twenty-dollar bill that she handed him. She pocketed what he gave her without a glance and left the store.

Back in the car, she opened the tea, took a drink, and grimaced. "Yuck," she said aloud. She started to open the cookies, and stopped, looking at the package as if surprised that they'd materialized in her hand.

The trouble was, all the innocent *"coulds"* might as easily be replaced by sinister ones, and a troop of worst-case scenarios trooped through her mind, with those scenarios focused on the only connection that she could imagine that might involve her husband.

She dropped the unopened package of cookies into the center console, screwed the top onto the tea, and started the car. The dashboard clock reported ten minutes before six. Irma Sedillos would already have started dinner for the boys and *Mamá.* With any luck at all, Francis would be finished at the clinic, with no calls waiting at the hospital. She should have been walking through the front door of her home, before her family forgot what she looked like.

But the itch remained, and she pulled out onto Grande again and turned south. A few minutes later, she saw Louis Herrera's Mustang convertible nosed into its reserved slot in front of the clinic's pharmacy, shaded by a grove of small oaks that the bulldozers and various contractors had avoided. She parked beside his car and sat quietly, looking at the oak grove. She remembered them clearly before the construction, when *Padrino*'s five acres had been a tangled, scruffy woodlot buffering his old adobe home from the drone of the interstate.

She closed her eyes, almost a flinch as if someone had jabbed her, as the dark possibilities crept into her mind. "Ay," she said softly and then shook it off. She reached across for the massive prescription-drug text and let its weight fall against her chest as she got out of the car.

Estelle trusted Robert Torrez implicitly, yet she hadn't shown him the book of drugs. When he knew about it, his agile mind would make the same connections she had, and she knew that she wasn't ready for that. Why would George Enriquez bother to study a drug book, using a Hi-Liter to mark the best-seller list as if he were studying for an exam?

An elderly man carrying a plastic bag of purchases held the door for her as she entered the pharmacy. The store was bright with wide aisles and low shelves, designed so that no products were either lower than twenty-four inches from the floor nor higher than five feet. The woman behind the register smiled at Estelle.

"I didn't have the chance to say hello when you were in yesterday," she said.

"Ella, we were so busy yesterday, *I* didn't have a chance to say hello to me," Estelle replied, and the woman laughed. "I need to see Louis for a minute, if he's still here."

Ella raised her short, matronly frame on her tiptoes, looking over the sea of racks and displays toward the pharmacy. "I see his pointy little head," she said. "Go back there and catch him before he slips out the back door."

"Thanks."

Herrera was bent over, both hands grasping the edge of the work counter, a thick ring binder open in front of him. Estelle stood quietly at the end of the counter, watching him as his lips worked. After a moment he shook his head impatiently, looked up and saw Estelle, and immediately brightened.

"Hey, guy," Estelle said. "You look seriously busy."

"That's okay, that's okay," Herrera said. He frowned at the big drug reference book that she thudded onto the counter. "You've grown a new appendage," he said. "That thing was stuck to you yesterday, too."

"*Oh sí,*" she said. "This baby and I are becoming old pals."

He sighed and straightened up. "Is there something I can help you with, or are you just thinking of changing professions?" he asked, nodding at the book. "We could use the help."

"I had a couple of questions I needed to run by you," Estelle said. She opened the reference to the illustrated pages, turning first to page 311. "Francis tells me that Petrosin is a popular drug."

Herrera frowned and nodded. "Sure. Depression is a popular condition, whether the customer actually has it or not." He grinned. "He's thinking of putting you on it, or what?"

"I think I'm getting closer all the time," Estelle said. She turned to page 315. "And Bicotin Six?"

"What about it?"

"It's popular?"

"Well, I don't know that I'd use the word *popular,* Estelle. It's prescribed a lot, yes. Both Bicotin and Petrosin are."

She idly turned several pages, stopping as if at random. "I've never heard of this," she said, and turned the book toward Herrera, pointing at the capsule. "Watrusil?"

"You don't need it," he said, with mock severity.

"What's it for?"

"An appetite suppressant."

"Ah."

Herrera watched her with amusement. "And yes. We sell a lot of it."

She stopped at page 332. "Deyldiol?"

"Sure. Oral contraceptives. Do I get to ask what it is that you're after?" He glanced at her sideways, half smiling.

"Four more first," she said, and stopped at each of the remaining highlighted drugs. In each case the answer was the same. Francis had been right. The eight prescription medications topped the list of brisk sellers.

"Now," Estelle said, and abruptly stopped. "You have some time?"

He held up his hands in surrender. "I'm yours. You've only marked the eight?"

"I didn't mark any of these," Estelle said easily.

"Well, highlighted, then." He tapped the last page, indicating the large capsule of Diamitrol. "This is white, not yellow. That's true of all the ones you've showed me."

"Ah," Estelle said. "Okay. But that's not what I wanted to ask. Let's say I had a prescription for…" and she leafed backward. "Petrosin." She looked up at Herrera. "How much would that cost me?"

"How much would it cost *you?*"

"A customer. A regular customer, no prescription insurance. No co-pay thing."

Herrera pooched out his lips in thought. "Normally? Probably about thirty-six bucks for thirty caps."

"That's what the insurance company is charged?"

He nodded. "We don't have separate pricing, Estelle." He straightened up. "I won't mention any names, but you can check with the competition, and I'll bet my month's salary that we're lower. We decided—Francis, Alan, and me—that we were going to keep prices as low as we can. And a lot of the time, as I'm sure you're aware, we don't get paid at all. A lot of our Mexican friends, for example."

"So thirty-six dollars for thirty."

"Yup."

"Of the eight, what's the most expensive one?"

"No contest,". he said without looking at the book. "Daprodin. That stuff is almost four bucks a pop. It's one of those new powerhouse antibiotics that hit the best-seller's list after the anthrax scare."

"So thirty pills would cost me more than $120."

"Just about."

"What if I went to Mexico and bought them there?"

He grinned broadly. "I'd be unhappy with you."

"No, really."

"You don't even need to go to Mexico, Estelle. You can buy almost anything on-line from a Mexican pharmacy that's dipping into that business and have it shipped right to your door. The loophole will be plugged some day, but right now, it's wide open."

"How do the Mexican pharmacists handle validating the doctor's prescription?"

"Many of them don't. That's part of the trouble." He turned and tapped the keyboard of the computer beside him. *"Mira,"* he said. In a moment, he'd accessed the search engine and typed in the name. "I know about these guys," he said. "Let's see what they have. I'd be surprised if you could get Daprodin from them. But maybe."

Estelle waited while the computer thought. In a moment a flashy web page advertising pharmaceuticals appeared on the screen. Once past the promises of instant delivery and lowest prices, the site became a simple typed list of drugs and prices in dollars.

"Well, I was wrong," Herrera said. "There it is right there. Daprodin: eighteen bucks for thirty, thirty-two bucks for sixty." He turned and looked at Estelle. "Eighteen bucks, compared with $120."

"The $120 is your price? The price you charge?"

He nodded. "And that's below market," he said. "At least in this country."

"Wow."

"Uh huh." He ran the cursor down the list. "Here's Petrosin MN, which is the same thing as you've got there. Seven-fifty for thirty. That's instead of the thirty-six bucks that we charge."

Estelle studied the screen.

"Where do you get your pharmaceuticals?"

"Our wholesale supplier, you mean?" He glanced at Estelle sideways, and she felt as if she'd just stepped into deeper water. "We have regular distributors, like anything else," Herrera said easily. "The companies lobby us pretty hard all the time. Lots of samples." He patted his pocket and grinned. "Tons of nifty pens."

"Why not just order it there?" she said, pointing at the computer.

"Well, for one thing, that would be illegal for us. For another, most of those Mexican companies try to be legit. So they're going to sell individual prescriptions, but they're not going to ship a couple thousand caps of Petrosin MN across the border." He glanced back at the computer. "Although I'm sure that you wouldn't have to look very hard to find a site that would. There's one for anything, I think. But like I said, it's only a matter of time before shipments across the border are blocked, *especially* for pharmaceuticals.''

"There might be questions of drug purity?''

"Of course. That's already a problem.'' He pushed himself away from the counter. "So what's going on? You found a car full of best-sellers, or what?''

"Nothing that simple, Louis.''

"Well, if I had to list the top ten or twenty most popular drugs, the eight you marked there would be on the list.''

Estelle patted the reference book's cover. "Popular stuff.''

"Yes, indeed. More so all the time. It's a good business to be in.''

And someone convinced George Enriquez of that, Estelle thought.

She chatted with Herrera for a few more minutes, then drove straight home from the pharmacy, torn by conflicting emotions. On the one hand, moving prescription drugs north out of Mexico fitted what little she knew of George Enriquez's recent activities. It would have been simple, during the three-hour window of opportunity in Acámbaro, to rendezvous with a supplier and load the van.

The number of individual capsules of Petrosin or any other medication that would fit in an eight-inch cardboard box boggled the mind. In Lori Schmidt's video, there was no way to accurately judge the number of boxes stowed under the seat of the senior citizens' van, but there would be room for more than a dozen under the three seats, maybe more.

Crossing the border staffed by custom agents familiar with the Posadas Middle School outing to Acámbaro, the van was in good company with the two school buses. On top of that, it was filled with a load of trash from a children's party. The setup hardly matched the illicit drug trade "profile.''

There was also the possibility that George Enriquez carried an invoice with him for the drugs. If the order for the medications was from a pharmacist and the drugs were accurately invoiced, there was no smuggling involved, only the government's cut to be paid at the border.

Once in the States and in possession of a pharmacist, the prescription drugs were virtually untraceable, and when dispensed through a physician's prescription, they'd be laundered to the consumer. The state board of pharmacy was like any other state agency, Estelle knew—understaffed and underfunded. It would be impossible for state inspectors to conduct inventories of common drugs that were not controlled as stringently as narcotics were. But birth control pills? Antibiotics? Antidepressants? All flowed in a river from vendor to pharmacy to patient as the doctors ordered.

I can give you Guzman. The drugs needed a vendor on the American side of the border. If George Enriquez had thought that the drugs he brought back from Mexico were headed for the Posadas Clinic and Pharmacy, if he had thought that physicians like Francis Guzman and Alan Perrone were crafting prescriptions to favor drugs whose Mexican wholesale cost produced soaring profits even at discounted retail prices, then his cryptic promise to District Attorney Daniel Schroeder made sense.

The thought curled Estelle's gut into a tight ball as she pulled the county car into her driveway. More than anything else, she wanted to find a quiet corner and talk with her husband, to listen as his soft, husky voice assured her that her nightmares weren't true.

She sat in the car, its engine silent. She gazed at the house, knowing every smell, every sound, every soft touch inside. George Enriquez was a persuasive salesman. Her eyes narrowed with anger, and she twisted the ignition key. The county car started at the same time that the front door of her home opened.

Francis Guzman peered out at her and then stepped out on the stoop, closing the door behind him. She rolled down the window as he approached. He bent down, both hands on the door.

"You lose your way?" He reached out and touched her cheek.

"No, I don't think so, *Oso.* But I forgot something. Half hour. I promise."

"One of the other docs is covering for me tonight," he said and thumped the door gently with the heel of his hand. "As soon as the kids are done with dinner, I'm going to send Irma home. Okay? Maybe we'll get lucky.''

"Fine. I'll be right back. But there's one more thing I need to do."

"*Siempre uno más, querida.* Always one more."

She nodded.

"Did you make some progress today?" He watched her face, his gaze almost clinical.

"I think so."

"We'll talk about it when you get home."

She nodded, and he leaned toward her. When their lips touched, she had the urge to pull him through the window, and some of her urgency must have been transmitted through her grip on his arm. "Be careful," he said.

"You bet."

He stood by the driveway and watched as she backed the car out into the street, then lifted a hand in salute as she pulled away.

THIRTY-ONE

GUY TROMBLEY'S Rite-Brand Pharmacy, Cards and Gifts shared the corner of Pershing and Bustos with Bascomb Auto Parts. The two stores shared more than the corner. Both were dark, cluttered, and soaked in the odd smells of their merchandise.

At one time, Trombley's had included a six-stool soda fountain, but the vending machines down the street outside of Tommy Portillo's Handi-Way—along with the racks of junk food inside that convenience store—had made the soda fountain obsolete. Trombley had refused to remove the stools or the counter. And he hadn't set foot in Portillo's store during the twenty years it had been open.

Estelle had no difficulty imagining how Guy Trombley must have felt about the new Posadas Clinic and Pharmacy, after being what Bill Gastner was fond of calling the "stud duck" for three decades.

Shortly after six, Estelle parked on Pershing two car lengths from the corner. The drugstore's large windows fronted Bustos. The concrete-block wall that faced the cross street had blistered and peeled like skin in critical need of a dermatologist.

She hefted the drug reference volume, hesitated for just a moment, and then left the car. The posted hours on the door announced that closing was six minutes overdue, but the OPEN sign that nestled in the corner of the window hadn't been turned. A tiny bell chimed when she entered the drugstore.

"Just under the wire," Guy Trombley said without looking up. He stood behind the cash register, the drawer open and a bank bag laid across the change tray. He was frowning at a fistful of bank-card receipts. He shook his head and stuffed them into the bag, glancing up at Estelle for the first time as he did so.

"Well, well," he said. Tall and slender, with the exception of a neat watermelon-sized pot belly, Guy Trombley was stoop-shouldered from forty years spent bending over the prescription counter. He wore the sort of half glasses that came ten to a display card, $3.95 apiece. He regarded Estelle over the top of them, hands poised over the cash drawer.

"And what can I do for you?" His tone was neither particularly gracious nor impatient, just faintly surprised.

Estelle placed the heavy volume on the counter. "May I ask you about a couple of drugs, Mr. Trombley?"

"Of course." He stepped away from the register, leaving the drawer open. "I'm not sure what I can tell you that your husband can't." It was said as a simple statement, without inflection, and Estelle ignored it, unwilling to test what was left of Guy Trombley's generous spirit.

"Daprodin," she said and opened the large book to the appropriate product identification page. "That's made by Thacker-George Pharmaceuticals, according to this."

Trombley waited patiently, the half glasses perched at the very end of his patrician nose. His eyes were brilliant hazel, probably changing hue, depending on light or mood. He watched Estelle rather than the glossy pages displaying the colorful drugs.

"Are they also manufactured in Mexico?"

A faint smile touched Trombley's full lips. "I have no idea. But I wouldn't be surprised."

"Is there any way to tell the difference between the capsules made in Mexico, for example, and the ones made domestically?"

"You mean just the tablet itself? It's called a *tablet*, by the way, not a capsule. You're not talking about the labeling on the bottle?"

"Maybe both."

"The only thing on the tablet itself," and he pointed a long, slender finger at the image on the page, "is the lettering T-G. In this case. Most manufacturers use something that makes a pill distinctive…although not always."

"May I look at one?"

"One what? A Daprodin tablet? Sure." He reached back and shoved the drawer closed. "Let me lock up first," he said. His stride was unhurried, almost thoughtful. He snapped the dead bolt on the door and turned the sign to CLOSED. "Come on back."

She followed him through the store to the pharmacy. He stepped up into the area, avoiding two five-gallon jugs of drinking water that had been parked by the steps. With the perfect precision of someone who could count and name each bottle in his sleep, he selected a large milk-white plastic bottle from the shelf, turned to the counter, and deftly shook out a single tablet onto the blue plastic counting tray. He screwed the top tightly back on the bottle.

He stepped back without comment. "And, as you can see, it's white, not yellow. Somebody's been coloring in your book."

The large tablet was marked only by the incised letters of the manufacturer, and when Estelle didn't respond to his comment, he added, "How are the kids, by the way?"

"They're well, thank you."

"Growing fast, I imagine."

"Too fast," Estelle said. "I wish they'd stay just the way they are."

For the first time, Guy Trombley smiled, showing the even, too-white of his dentures. "No, you don't. They're going to accomplish all kinds of wonderful things in their lifetimes. You want to see all of it." He leaned his hip against the counter, waiting. "Do you need that as a sample?"

"May I?"

"Either that or it goes in the trash. Did someone find some of those loose at school or something?"

"You wouldn't believe where we find things," Estelle said.

"Oh, yes I would."

"What would a prescription of those cost. Say thirty tablets?"

He looked over his shoulder. "My computer's not booted up just now, so I'm ball parking it. I'd guess right around $140, maybe $145 or 50, plus the governor. Pricey stuff. If you've got insurance, the co-pay is right at $40."

"And it's an antibiotic?"

He nodded. "Great stuff, or so the salesmen would have us believe. It's used primarily for really pesky urinary tract and kidney infections, even something dangerous like endocarditis. And anthrax doesn't like it much." He watched Estelle slide the tablet into a small plastic evidence bag. "It's interesting you asking about whether or not Thacker-George has a plant in Mexico. One of the troubles, and I blame that thing, by the way," he turned and nodded at the computer, "is lots of fake stuff on the market now. Just like you can buy a Rolex watch on a street in Hong Kong for thirty bucks, or a pair of Adidas shoes for ten that should cost a hundred? The old knockoff racket."

"Fake medications, you mean?"

He nodded. "Sure."

She looked down at the plastic bag. "How would you tell if it was fake or not?"

"Unless it was crudely done, you couldn't," Trombley said. "And some of them are pretty crude, I'm told. We were shown some at a seminar not long ago that looked as if they'd been carved with a pocket knife. But otherwise, you couldn't tell…not without sophisticated lab analysis. And we're talking human nature here, too, you know." He grinned. "I don't mean to cast aspersions on our eminent medical profession," and he laid a hand on his chest, "or on us, either, but let's face facts. We're in the feel-good business most of the time. If you've got a whopper of a head cold, you gulp down fifteen or twenty bucks worth of medications, and in eight or ten days, you start to feel better. Or you can save your money, and guess what? If you take care of yourself, in eight or ten days, you'll start to feel better."

She lifted the plastic bag. "But you normally wouldn't take this for a head cold, would you?"

"Indeed not. But if the first prescription doesn't work, what does the physician do in ten days' time?"

"He tries something else."

"Exactly," Trombley said, sounding indulgent. "So if that drug is actually nothing more than a little bit of sugar pressed into the shape of a tablet, well, cheer up. In ten days' time, the doc will give you something else that *might* work."

He glanced toward the front of the store as if someone might be leaning with their ear pressed against the door. "As I'm sure Louis Herrera would tell you, should you have this same conversation with him, that's the problem with doing business with some of our pharmaceutical brethren south of the border, especially over the Internet, where you don't know who you're talking to." The humorless smile lingered on his face, as if to say *Do you understand what I'm saying?*

Estelle took her elbow off the drug reference guide and opened it to page 332. "You're not telling me that they make fake Deyldiol? Pregnancy is a little more serious than a head cold."

Trombley chuckled. "My wife used to say something very similar to that, bless her soul." He tapped the page thoughtfully and then stopped his finger at the head of the column. "Deyldiol is made by Peekskill Laboratories. And they *do* have a lab in Mexico. I happen to know that for a fact. We used to pass it every time we drove down to Chihuahua to visit our daughter."

"The lab is in Chihuahua?"

"On the outskirts of town. In one of those new little industrial parks that Mexico is trying so hard to make work."

"Do you do business with Peekskill?"

"No." The answer was flat and unqualified.

"Any special reason?"

"I'm happy with the suppliers that I use now. Half a dozen companies make that particular birth-control formula. There's nothing proprietary about it."

"What if a customer comes in and has a prescription specifically for Deyldiol?"

"Then I call the doc and suggest that he make a change. Go generic, or at least go with something I have in stock. They're usually pretty good about that." He relaxed against the counter, leaning his weight on his elbows, hands loosely clasped. "What you do is not my business," he said, "but it sounds like this is the sort of thing that might attract the state board of pharmacy...what you're looking into."

"It might."

"Am I going to be sorry I talked to you?" He didn't smile.

"I don't think so, Mr. Trombley. At least I hope not." She

closed the book. "Can I ask you one more thing, not necessarily related?"

"Sure."

"How well did you know George Enriquez?"

Trombley took a long time answering, first drawing little invisible circles on the shiny black counter top. "Old George," he said finally, and lapsed into silence again. Estelle waited. Trombley sighed with resignation. "Connie is a good customer—too good sometimes. I manage to talk her out of about half of the junk that she wants to take." He flashed a quick, conspiratorial smile. "George and I are...were...both in Lions Club. And Optimists. We're in the chamber of commerce." He straightened away from the counter. "He wasn't the sort of man who impressed me as suicidal, Estelle. I didn't need to see the headlines in the paper yesterday afternoon to know that."

He looked at the undersheriff for a long time while his jaw worked. "For one thing—and I think I'm one of the few who are privy to this—you can't imagine how much George truly loved his wife. He was so protective of her, of her faults, of her troubles, of her...her whatever." He waved a hand helplessly. "I'm not so sure that any of that was reciprocated, which makes it all the more tragic, somehow. I can't imagine him saying, in effect, 'Well, I'm leaving you now, Connie, mess and all. Deal with it, sweetheart.' I can't see him doing that."

"Maybe he just reached a point."

"The paper implies that you don't believe that, Mrs. Guzman. I know he had his legal troubles, but this is going to be a bigger mess than he *ever* imagined."

She hefted the large volume and extended her hand. "Thank you, sir."

"You bet. Any time. I hope things work out, whatever those things are." As Estelle was turning to step down past the two water bottles, he added, "And by the way, under the not-*necessarily*-related category—and I hope I don't regret telling you this—but I've always liked your honest face." He approached and leaned on the stub wall partition that fronted the counter. For a long moment he stood silently, examining the paint job on the top edge.

"George approached me once a year or so ago. I think it was when I stopped by his office to have the insurance changed on the new car. He said a friend of his was getting into the prescription-drug distributor's business, and he wondered if there was anything I needed that I was having trouble getting now. He said that he could guarantee prices that would beat anyone's."

"He asked you that?"

Trombley nodded. "Yes, he did. I said no. I've got enough pharmaceutical salesmen who call on me now. I didn't need one more, especially a friend of a friend, if you follow what I mean. That's what all this is about, isn't it? George Enriquez?" He flashed the denture smile again. "The 'not necessarily related' part?"

"He didn't happen to mention who this distributor friend was, did he?"

Trombley's smile disappeared. "No, he didn't. And I guess I should be wishing about now that he had?"

"I'd appreciate it if you'd give me a call if you recall anything else, sir," Estelle said.

"About George Enriquez, or about the drugs?"

"Both, sir."

He nodded with satisfaction. "That's what I thought." He ambled after Estelle as she walked toward the front door. She waited for him to snap the dead bolt. "Give your husband my regards," he said. He smiled, an expression that was almost kindly. "Tell him that I'm proud of what he's doing."

"He's working with a good crew," Estelle said.

"For the most part," Trombley said. "You take care, now." He nodded and closed the door before she had an opportunity to respond. But she knew what he meant, and as she walked out to the car, her heart felt heavy, like an old cinder block tied on the end of a stretched and frayed cord.

THIRTY-TWO

"YOU LOOK EXHAUSTED," Francis said. "For three months, no-body in town so much as double-parks, and then all of a sudden the whole town dips into the funny water." He frowned at Es-telle, taking her chin in his hand so that he could turn her head gently this way and that.

Estelle opened her mouth wide as if waiting for the tongue depressor. "Ah."

Francis laughed softly. "That's just the way it goes, I guess," he said. Estelle watched his handsome face as his eyes read hers. Hours and hours ago, during the late-night walk home after ar-resting Perry Kenderman, *Padrino* had given her one of his rare bits of advice, and so far, she'd done a good job of ignoring it. But she knew that Bill Gastner was right.

"What's aching to come out?" her husband asked. The index and middle fingers of each hand rested on her temples, a feath-erlight pressure that prompted her to close her eyes. For a long time, she didn't say anything, as if satisfied that her thoughts could simply flow through barriers of bone and tissue, to be absorbed by her husband's fingertips.

"I'm that transparent, *Oso?*"

"*Sí.*"

She reached up, sliding a hand around each of his wrists, glad that they were alone in the hospital hallway. Behind her husband, the door to radiology stood open, and she heard the abruptly truncated swish and snap as one of the technicians stabbed an X-ray film up into the light board for viewing. Quiet voices drifted out to them as the technician and radiologist conferred.

"My pictures are ready," Francis said, but she didn't release his wrists. If the bruised and battered college student waiting in the emergency room was lucky, the X-rays would show nothing more than a badly sprained ankle. That wasn't a bad price to pay for falling asleep while driving on the interstate. Her car had drifted across the shoulder, then battered back and forth between the concrete overpass barriers like a pinball. "Can you wait a few minutes?" he asked.

"Sure." Any excuse to put off heeding *Padrino*'s advice was welcome. The doctors' lounge was quiet, and she curled up on one of the overstuffed couches, feet under her, head back against one of the cushions, eyes closed. She forced her mind to sift through what she knew, to look for connections and links. No matter what path her thoughts took, she found it inconceivable that Francis knew anything of George Enriquez's activities.

Each one of the faces of Enriquez's friends and family in Connie Enriquez's kitchen looked back at her passively. She found herself asking each one the hopeless question: *What do you know?* And each face turned away.

Something light touched the side of her face, and she jerked awake. Her husband settled onto the couch beside her. "I probably shouldn't have disturbed you," he said. "You were just settling in to a pretty good session blowing z's."

"That's okay," she said. She stretched her arms straight out and rested her hands on her knees. "How's the ankle?"

"Sprained," Francis said. "*Really* sprained. It might have been less painful if she'd broken it. A few cuts and bruises otherwise. She's a lucky kid. And by the way, Tom Pasquale said that he'd be staying central if you needed anything."

She nodded absently. "I need to talk with you, *Oso*."

"Here I are." He turned sideways on the couch with his right elbow on the backrest, head resting in his hand. He reached out and touched her cheek again, just a tiny, single stroke with the back of his left index finger.

Estelle sat upright and shook the sleep away. She glanced at the lounge door to make sure that it was closed. "Last Sunday evening, George Enriquez called the district attorney. He offered information in exchange for a plea bargain that would get him off the grand jury's hooks." She turned and looked at her husband. His expression was patiently expectant. "Enriquez wanted to set up a meeting with Schroeder for Monday afternoon, to discuss what he knew. Or supposedly knew."

"And that would be?"

"We don't know."

"Because he never showed up for his meeting," Francis said.

"Correct."

"He never told the D.A. what sort of information he had? When they were talking on the phone?"

Estelle hesitated. "Not directly, no."

"Well, indirectly, then."

"A hint." Estelle shook her head in disgust that the words refused to tumble out without a struggle.

Francis cocked his head sympathetically and waited.

"According to Schroeder, George Enriquez told him on the phone that, quote, *I can give you Guzman,* unquote."

The physician's face was blank. "What's that supposed to mean? *Give you Guzman* how?"

"I don't know, *Oso.*" She held up a hand, but the words that would have accompanied the gesture stuck in her throat. After a moment, she said, "We've found evidence that indicates that George Enriquez might have been involved in bringing bulk prescription drugs into the country from Mexico. That's just a guess. We don't know for sure."

Francis Guzman's head tilted back as he mouthed a soundless *ah.* "The top best-sellers we were discussing earlier," he said, and Estelle nodded. "*That's* what you were looking at with the drug reference guide."

"That was George's book, *Oso.* He marked a total of eight drugs—the ones you and I talked about. Now why would he do that?"

"Maybe he kept a tally of what pills he popped," Francis said. "There's nothing illegal about that."

"We think that he picked up *something* during the school trip to Acámbaro at Christmas time. Perhaps at other times as well."

"Last year, you mean."

"Yes. And perhaps again in May, when the school attended the *Cinco de Mayo* festivities there. Maybe others."

"How'd you find that out?"

"Well, that's the trouble. At this point, it's nothing more than a wild guess on my part. I know that *something* was brought back into the States during that trip. We've got video evidence that's the case."

"But you don't know what it is."

"No."

"It could as easily be heroin or cocaine or Christmas tree ornaments."

"I suppose."

"Except when Enriquez told the D.A. that he could hand over information about the nefarious Guzman, that kind of leaves out the ornaments," Francis said.

"The prescription drugs make sense to me," Estelle persisted. "Whatever he had was packed into neat little white cardboard containers and stowed under the seat of the van. I can't imagine him trying to move hard drugs that way. And there's the book."

"Shipping prescription drugs is not necessarily a crime, is it?"

"No. Not if there's appropriate paperwork to cover the shipment and all the proper fees and so on are paid at the border. But that's not what happened. And we're talking boxes and boxes of the stuff. Cases. And if the drugs are fake, or counterfeit, that's a whole new game."

Francis regarded her silently. "You're wondering what happened to them after they reached the U.S., right?"

She nodded.

"There are two logical paths, as far as I can see," Francis said. "They could peddle the drugs on the street, and that would be sort of dumb, I would think. Certainly not very efficient, anyway. I can't imagine anyone paying much for a hit of Petrosin, or whatever. The logical thing to do would be to find a pharmacist who would dispense the meds as prescriptions call for them." He shrugged. "Buy the drugs for a reduced, bargain price in Mexico, jack up the retail, and you've got a good profit margin." He frowned. "And you know, one of the troubles with drugs from some fly-by-night outfit south of the border is that there's no FDA controls…no quality assurance that you're getting what you paid for. Talc and sugar pills for a penny apiece, sell 'em for whatever you want.''

He tilted his head, trying to assess the expression on Estelle's face. ''And we're back to what Enriquez told the D.A., aren't we.'' He leaned back and put his arm on the couch behind Estelle. ''Let's cut right to the chase, then. If the drugs were going to *our* pharmacy, and someone turned us in, we'd be nailed,'' he said.

''What if George Enriquez was selling bulk Mexican pharmaceuticals to Louis,'' Estelle said. ''Would he do that?''

''Would George do that? Or would Louis, you mean?'' She nodded. ''I would hope not.'' His eyes narrowed. ''We might as well go all the way, and assume that if George was dealing prescription drugs, he was hitting *both* pharmacies in town. Louis and old man Trombley, too. Why not, *querida*. Bulk prescription drugs from Mexico don't bother me half as much as the idea of fakes…that would be where the money is. And there are lots of other drugstores around the area, too—not just the two in Posadas. Maybe he wasn't crapping in his own nest, so to speak.''

''*Oso,* the implication was that George could turn over evidence that the D.A. would be interested in, something that had to do with Guzman,'' Estelle said. ''That wouldn't point to a drugstore in Las Cruces. *Guzman* means you or me.''

''And you're thinking, *Why didn't Enriquez just say 'I can give you Herrera,'* if he knew my pharmacist was caught up in something.''

''Yes.''

''Because I'm the one who runs the clinic,'' Francis said. He shrugged. ''Alan Perrone and I. Alan isn't married to the leadoff witness in a grand jury investigation. If Enriquez thought he had information that would make your life miserable, then it's logical that he might use it to save his own sorry hide.''

''Well, I'm miserable. He succeeded.''

Francis reached out and gently massaged the back of her neck. ''Do what you always do, *querida*.''

''I'm finding that hard.''

''Just turn over all the stones. All I can tell you is this: I went to school with Louis, and I think I know him pretty well. I can't imagine he'd risk something so stupid. But," and he shrugged helplessly. "We don't know, do we? I don't pay attention to how he runs the pharmacy, any more than he watches over what Alan and I do down the hall. Too trusting, I suppose."

"There was an understanding between the three of you that you'd sell prescriptions as inexpensively as you could."

"Yes. And there's a fair-sized clientele that pays nothing at all, for drugs or services, either one…or maybe a few token pesos. But we knew that would happen going in. That was part of the deal."

Estelle fell silent.

"By the way, I don't know anything about Guy Trombley, other than what the rest of the town knows: He and his drugstore have been here forever. I've never had a patient complain to me about anything he does…except once in a while about the price of things. On a few occasions, I've been a little irritated with his second-guessing the doctor's orders, but there's probably not a pharmacist on the planet who doesn't do that once in a while."

"That's not what worries me," Estelle said.

"It sure worries me, *querida*. We have a lot to lose."

She turned and looked at her husband. "George Enriquez knew something. We don't know what. He contacted Dan Schroeder. And then someone blew George's brains out. It's not about the drugs, *Oso*. It's about murder."

"You're telling me that somehow Louis Herrera might be involved in Enriquez's death?"

"I don't know what I think."

"You could as easily imagine that Dan Schroeder is involved."

Estelle's face went blank. "Why would I think that?"

"Enriquez called him, then ended up dead. It's a fair assumption."

"The district attorney did not kill George Enriquez," Estelle said.

"And how do you know this?"

"I just do."

"Ah. *La intuición femenina*. But remember, he had a great

alibi. In court, busy with the grand jury that was supposedly seeking an indictment against Enriquez...''

"*Oso,* get a grip. If that were the case, there would have been no reason for Enriquez to call Schroeder, or in the bizarre event that he did, no reason for Schroeder to tell me about the call in the first place."

"It was just a thought." He held up both hands. "What do you want to do, then?"

"I'd like to look through the drug inventory down at the clinic." She watched his left eyebrow drift upward. "Will you help me do that?"

He shook his head wearily. "This is really scary, *querida.*" He drew in a deep breath and glanced at his watch. "This is in the category of 'no good deed goes unpunished.'"

"I need to know," Estelle said.

"We'll do whatever you have to do," Francis said. He reached out and squeezed her leg just above the knee, rocking her gently back and forth. "This is going to work out, one way or another. We do what we have to do. You want to focus on the drugs that Enriquez marked in the book?"

"I think that was his study guide," Estelle said, nodding. "That's a good place to start. That will tell me if I'm crazy or not."

"Louis should be there, you know. The pharmacy is his bailiwick. But I guess that's not what you had in mind."

"No."

Francis smiled and held up a hand. "Which prompts a question. I have a key that will get us into the pharmacy, no problem. Should you then decide to go through all of Guy Trombley's stock, too, how are you going to do that? He's not going to be overjoyed at that prospect."

Estelle pushed herself up off the couch and straightened her suit. "I hope it doesn't go that far, *Oso.* I have no connection with Guy Trombley. I *do* have a connection with Louis Herrera. That's why I want to start there. If it does go further...that's the nice thing about a warrant. It won't matter if Trombley is overjoyed or not."

THIRTY-THREE

"WHERE DO YOU want to start?" Dr. Francis Guzman held open the heavy door that separated the pharmacy from the clinic. Estelle stepped into the darkened pharmacy and paused. She didn't want to start at all, and even more than that, didn't want to find anything once she did.

"The best-sellers," she said, without enthusiasm.

Her husband switched on the panel of lights directly over the pharmacist's work counter. The pharmacy was tidy. Rows of white boxes and bottles trooped on narrow shelves as if they'd been lined up with a laser. Estelle lifted the weighty pharmaceutical reference book and laid it on the counter.

"Of the eight that were marked, which ones do you prescribe the most often?"

"Me, personally, or physicians in general?" Francis asked. He saw the impatience flick across his wife's face. "I'm just asking, *querida.* There are some drugs that some physicians prescribe a lot, that I don't," he continued. "I don't know if that makes a difference or not in this case."

"I don't either."

"Petrosin is an example." He folded his arms across his chest. "To me, it's sort of like using morphine to counter the pain of a stubbed toe. Obviously, not everyone agrees with me." He shrugged. "Of the eight drugs that you've marked there, I commonly prescribe Deyldiol. When they remember to take it and stay on schedule, it's pretty dependable."

"It's fairly inexpensive," Estelle said.

"Well, remember that 'inexpensive' is a relative thing," Francis said. "Of all the prescriptions we give out that we *know* we're not going to be paid for, Deyldiol probably heads the list. That wasn't always the case.'' He shrugged. "Birth control by chemical wasn't always an option, especially south of the border. It's interesting,'' he added, and then frowned as he fell silent. Estelle waited, watching her husband's face.

After a minute, he said, "You know, that's an interesting spectrum. I was going to say that the other drug that is prescribed frequently is Daprodin. It's a real powerhouse antibiotic, and so far we haven't seen too many side effects. But we're getting good results with it—sometimes even spectacular—with really tough, persistent infections. Urinary tract, prostate…things like that. It's really effective against some of the strep infections. On top of that, Daprodin is the most expensive of the group that you've got there, by far. Four, five bucks a pop.'' He held up a hand. "But even that isn't near the top of the list as far as expense is concerned. We can hit forty grand a year with some of the injectable drugs that AIDS patients take as part of their daily smorgasbord.'' He reached out and tapped the book. "But none of those are on your list.''

"Let's start there,'' Estelle said. "With Daprodin, I mean. If they were counterfeit pills, could you tell the difference?''

"That depends,'' Francis replied. "People counterfeit things as complicated as currency all the time. I don't see why it would be hard to knock off a fake tablet that would fool most patients. Probably their doctors, too.''

He stepped to the shelves and ran his hand along the edges, reached the end of a section and turned the corner. After a moment he straightened up with a large white plastic bottle. "Daprodin DG.''

"What's the DG stand for?''

"'Damn good,' at this price, I suppose.'' He flashed a quick grin. "I don't know, querida. If it's not in that tome that you're carrying around, you'd have to ask the company.'' He turned the bottle so he could read the bottom of the label. "Kleinfelder and Schmidt Laboratories, Darien, Connecticut.''

"Is that the way it's normally shipped? In an opaque bottle like that?''

"I don't know. I would suppose so. Those are questions that Louis could answer."

She reached out and took the bottle. "One thousand count. Ay. This little bottle is four thousand bucks."

Francis nodded. "Sure enough, but a thousand pills means *a lot* of dead bugs, *querida*." With the tips of his fingers, he rolled a second bottle, the same size as the first, forward toward the edge of the shelf. Estelle saw the Kleinfelder and Schmidt label.

"Why would both bottles be open?" she asked.

"Are they?"

"Yes, they are. This one has the remains of a heat-shrunk sealing band. That one has nothing at all."

Francis made a face. "Sharp eyes." He handed her the second bottle.

"May I look?"

"Sure. Use the thingy, there." He pointed at the counter behind her. "The counting tray." He thrust his hands in his pockets. "And they don't go back in the bottle once they're out."

Estelle opened the first plastic bottle and carefully shook two of the white capsules onto the plastic grid. With the small white spatula, she flipped over one of the pills. "Daprodin DG," she said, and then examined the second pill. "And five hundred on the other side." She leaned against the counter, regarding the two pills. Her free hand idly screwed the cap back on the jar and then reached for the second container. She pushed the first two pills to one side, neatly lined up on the grid, and then deftly shook out two pills from the second jar. "Daprodin DG, five hundred," she said, and frowned. "I took this stuff last year, didn't I."

"Yes, you did."

"Horse pills. I can remember trying to swallow them without gagging."

"Break 'em up first."

"I did that." She reached out and tapped one of the pills with the spatula. "And they taste awful." She looked up at her husband. "You'd have to counterfeit the taste, too. Otherwise, they wouldn't fool anyone."

"Quinine," Francis said.

"That's what's in them?"

"In part. Daprodin is a quinolone, one of a fairly large family of drugs that's derived from quinine."

"Ay. Four dollars a pill for powdered bark."

Francis laughed gently. "Almost. Rare powdered bark, though." He frowned as Estelle took one of the pills from the first bottle and touched it to her tongue. For a moment, she closed her eyes.

She made a face. "Oh, *sí*." She regarded the damp pill for a moment, then dropped it into a small plastic evidence bag. After jotting a note on the label, closing the top, and tucking the bag into her jacket pocket, she pushed one of the pills from the second bottle to the side of the tray and picked it up.

"The scientific tasting test," Francis said.

"You bet. Sophisticated laboratory analysis, as Guy Trombley would say. Let's hope it's not rat poison."

"I don't think so," Francis said.

She let the capsule rest on her tongue, eyes closed. After a moment, without moving the pill or closing her mouth, she opened her eyes and looked at her husband.

"Well?"

She dropped the capsule into her hand and nodded at the tray. "Try one."

"You're serious?"

"Oh, *sí*."

Francis Guzman picked up the remaining pill and popped it into his mouth. Almost instantly, his eyebrows crumpled together, meeting over the bridge of his nose. "Talc," he said. "That's what it tastes like. That kind of musty, sweetish…" he waved a hand and then spat out the pill. He turned it this way and that, inspecting it. "Ain't Daprodin, *querida*."

"Most definitely not." Estelle fell silent for a moment.

"Now what?" he asked, sagging his weight against the edge of the counter. "Christ, Louis," he whispered. He hefted the second jar and turned it slowly, reading the label. "I can't believe he'd do this. I mean, this means we've got patients out there who might as well be taking sawdust, as much good as this crap will do them."

Estelle started to reach toward the second jar of capsules with the spatula when her cell phone rang, a shrill warbling. She looked heavenward. "Guzman."

The phone remained silent long enough that Estelle repeated herself. The voice was tentative. "Is this…Undersheriff Guzman?"

"Yes, ma'am." She recognized Barbara Parker's light alto, complete with the woman's characteristic waver of indecision. "How can I help you?" She glanced at her watch.

"Well, I…" the line fell silent, and Estelle waited, able to hear the woman's breathing. "I probably shouldn't have called," Mrs. Parker said. "But I…well, I just don't know."

"Mrs. Parker," Estelle said, "what is it?"

"You said to call, and then I wasn't going to, and now I think I should say something," Barbara Parker said. "Rick was here not too long ago. He wanted to talk, and I didn't see any harm in that."

Estelle felt her stomach tighten. The hand with the plastic spatula sank to the counter. The woman continued quickly now that she'd breached the dam. "We talked for nearly an hour, Undersheriff. Now it turns out that there's a really good daycare center in Las Cruces that's just a few blocks from Richard's apartment, and he thought he'd be able to place Ryan there right away."

"Mrs. Parker…"

"I knew that you wouldn't approve, but…"

Estelle tossed the plastic spatula on the counter in disgust. "Mrs. Parker, it's not whether *I* approve or not. *You're* the guardian of your daughter's children at the moment. We placed them in your custody because we believed they'd be safe there. That would be the best place for them. Richard Kenderman has no legal claim until a paternity test establishes that he's the father. For both children. He hasn't been living in the household. He hasn't been contributing in any way toward child support."

"I know," the woman said, sounding as if she clearly *didn't* know.

"Do you believe that Richard Kenderman is Ryan's father, Mrs. Parker?"

"Well, I don't know."

"And I don't think he does either, ma'am. Perry Kenderman is also claiming that honor."

"He is?"

"Yes, he is. And I think we've had this conversation before."

"Well…"

"And when Ryan isn't in that wonderful day-care center down in Las Cruces, when he's stuck in Richard Kenderman's apartment the rest of the day, during the evening, at night, what then, Mrs. Parker? You trust Richard with Ryan?"

"No," Barbara Parker said, and for the first time she sounded positive of something.

"That's why it seemed reasonable to leave the children with you, Mrs. Parker. I'm as sorry as I can be about your daughter, but the fact remains that *you're* Ryan and Mindi's grandmother. They've been living in your home all along, and there's no reason to change that now. Richard Kenderman might be the father of one or both of the children, and he might not be. If he wants custody, then he's going to have to agree to a paternity test to establish his claim. Then, the courts will decide. Otherwise…"

"That's why I called. Rick can be so persuasive, you know. Everything he said made sense, and he sounded so earnest. And he loves Ryan so, I think that's clear. But now I think I made a mistake. In fact, I had decided that before he left. I told Rick that I'd consider it…what he was talking about, I mean. And apparently he didn't like that very much. You know that temper of his."

"Well, no I don't, Mrs. Parker. I've met the young man once, and that wasn't under the best circumstances. What happened?"

"I told him that I didn't want Ryan going to the city, especially at such a late hour, and that we should talk about it more later. That I wanted to talk with you."

"Mrs. Parker," Estelle said, and glanced at her husband. "What happened?"

"Well, Rick took my grandson, Undersheriff. I told him that he shouldn't, but he didn't want to listen. He's such a strong-headed young man. And I could smell alcohol on his breath, and I *know* what he can be like when he's drinking."

"He took Ryan, Mrs. Parker? He took the boy from your home?"

"Yes." The woman choked on the single word.

"How long ago did he leave, Mrs. Parker?"

The woman hesitated. "I think no more than ten minutes. But it could have been longer."

"He was going to Las Cruces?"

"I think so. I don't know anywhere else that he'd go. I mean, that's where he lives, after all."

"Mrs. Parker, if you voluntarily relinquished custody to Richard Kenderman, then that's your business. There's nothing I can do about that."

"But I haven't done that. I mean…"

Estelle leaned heavily against the counter and rested her head in her free hand. "Let me ask you a yes or no question, Mrs. Parker. Did Richard Kenderman take your grandson after you specifically told him not to?"

"Well…it's more complicated than that."

"I'm sure." Estelle took a long, slow breath. "Mrs. Parker, let's see if we can make it uncomplicated. Did Richard Kenderman take your grandson from your home against your will?"

"Well…"

"Mrs. Parker, please." The phone fell silent. "Did you try and restrain him in any way?" The silence continued. "Mrs. Parker, if you *allowed* Richard Kenderman to take Ryan, that's one thing. If Richard Kenderman *kidnapped* your grandson, that's another story."

"Kidnapped?"

"That's what it's called, Mrs. Parker. If Kenderman came to your home and took your grandson against your will, then it's kidnapping."

"If he contends that he's the boy's father…"

"It doesn't matter what he *contends,* Mrs. Parker."

After another long silence, Barbara Parker sounded both irked and resigned. "I don't know what to do. I mean, it's not kidnapping in this case."

"All right. I'll take your word for it." Estelle turned and looked at her husband. He shrugged helplessly.

"What do you think I should do?" Mrs. Parker asked.

"What I think is not at issue," Estelle said. "If you say that Richard was drinking, that's enough probable cause for us to stop him."

"I want Ryan back, that's all," Barbara Parker said. "I made a mistake. All right, now I want to correct that."

"Mrs. Parker, if you swear out a criminal complaint that your grandson was kidnapped, we'll go find him and bring him home. And we'll put the person responsible in jail. And then the courts will sort out who's who."

"A complaint?"

"Mrs. Parker, much as there are a dozen things we'd *like* to be able to do, there's nothing we *can* do if you willingly gave custody of Ryan to Mr. Kenderman. If we stop him on the highway, and then it ends up that he doesn't blow at least impaired, then we have to let him go. It's that simple. And then the whole mess starts over again. If Mr. Kenderman *took* Ryan from your home, against your will, then yes, there's something we can do about that. If he threatened you in any way. Make up your mind, Mrs. Parker. And I wish you'd do it quickly."

"I want Ryan back," Barbara Parker said.

"I'll ask you again." Estelle pulled the microcassette recorder from her pocket and deftly punched the tiny controls. "And Mrs. Parker, my tape recorder is turned on now. Think before you answer." She hesitated, letting the phone fall silent. "Did Richard Kenderman take Ryan Parker from your home against your will?"

After the barest hesitation, Barbara Parker replied, "Yes, Undersheriff, he did."

"Did you try to restrain him in any way?"

"I don't see how I could. The more we talked, I could see that he was getting angrier."

"He threatened you?"

"Well, not in so many words, but his meaning was clear. He was determined to take Ryan."

"Was he driving the old red Mustang?"

"Yes, I believe that he was."

"I'll be back to you," Estelle said, and flicked off the phone and then the tape recorder. She stood silently for a long time. "What a mess."

"What's this character want with the boy?" Francis asked. "I gather that paternity is an issue?"

Estelle nodded. "And I don't know what Kenderman wants. I don't know what's wrong with Barbara Parker that she can't seem to stand up to this kid. All I know is that the whole thing scares me to death. All I see is lose-lose."

"You can put Ryan with the state's protective services division for forty-eight hours," Francis said.

"I know that. And that's exactly what I *would* do if I was holding his hot little hand in mine right now. But that's not the case." She flipped the drug I.D. book closed. "Right now, we've got a four-year-old riding on the interstate in an old hot rod driven by a drunk. And it goes downhill from there."

"What do you want to do about all this?" He watched as she folded the small plastic evidence bags and slipped them into her pocket.

With the heavy book under one arm, she turned toward the door. "They're going to have to wait," she said. "Can I drop you off at *Padrino's*?"

"I'll walk over," Francis said. "Don't worry about me. But you be careful with this guy."

"Right now, it's Richard Kenderman who needs to hear that. And what I know about him scares me, *Oso*. Listening isn't his strong suit."

THIRTY-FOUR

THE COUNTY CAR nosed down against the hard pull of its brakes, then swung right onto Grande, followed by an almost immediate sweeping turn onto the eastbound entrance ramp of the interstate. If Barbara Parker's "ten minutes" was accurate, Kenderman would have a substantial lead, even if he wasn't pressing the speed limit.

"Posadas, three ten." Estelle waited for dispatcher Ernie Wheeler's foot to find the transmit remote.

"Three ten, Posadas."

"I need a BOLO on a 1968 Mustang, color red, license Ida Mary Boy Adam David. Operator is Richard Kenderman. One passenger, a four-year-old male. Ten eighty-five. Make sure the state police out of Deming understand the situation."

"Ten four."

A second voice broke in. "Three ten, three oh six."

"Go ahead, three oh six."

"Three ten, I'm parked on Alamo Drive, looking across Grande at the parking lot of Portillo's. The vehicle in question is parked there. The driver is out of the car and inside the store."

Estelle glanced in the mirror, stabbed the brakes, and dove the car across the rough center median of the interstate. With a howl of tires, the Ford leaped back up onto the pavement and headed back toward Posadas. "Three oh six, can you tell if the little boy is still in the vehicle?"

"Affirmative. I can see the kid. He's standing on the front seat."

"Box the car in and take the child into custody. Keep the

subject away from him and don't leave him unattended. ETA one minute.''

"Ten four."

The unmarked car swept down the exit ramp from the interstate, and Estelle looked far ahead down Grande Avenue. The wide, four-lane street that formed the north-south arterial through Posadas was deserted. A mile ahead, Alamo Street, a tiny alleyway behind the hardware store, provided a diagonal view of the Portillo's convenience-store parking lot, a popular hangout that was one of Deputy Thomas Pasquale's favorite hunting grounds.

As she passed the intersection of Grande and McArthur, Estelle saw Pasquale's unit far in the distance, the glint of streetlights off its broad, white roof as he eased across Grande and into Portillo's parking lot.

"Posadas, three oh six is ten six Portillo's."

Estelle's radio barked again, this time the voice of Chief Eddie Mitchell. "Three ten, P.D. 1 copies. I'm north of the hospital. ETA about a minute."

"Posadas, three oh six, ten seventy, ten twenty-six." Deputy Pasquale's voice was calm despite the code for crime in progress and the request that responding officers not use lights and siren. Estelle's pulse leaped. "He's after more than Twinkies," Pasquale added.

Estelle leaned forward, trying to will the last half mile away. "Tom, I want the boy out of that car."

"Ten four. I've got him. Kenderman saw me. He's going out the back of the store."

Estelle stood on the brakes and wrenched the steering wheel hard to the right, lunging the county car into Rincon Avenue, the narrow lane south of Portillo's. She had a brief glimpse of Deputy Pasquale bundling little Ryan Parker out of the Mustang. "Don't leave the boy alone, Tom," she snapped, and then tossed the mike on the seat.

Traveling too fast when it hit the gravel of the lane between Portillo's and the *Posadas Register* building, the unmarked car slid sideways and smacked into the concrete-block wall hard enough to thump Estelle's head against the driver's side window.

She mashed the accelerator, and the car shot forward toward the intersection of Rincon and the alley behind the buildings.

Richard Kenderman had dodged out of the store's back door and turned right. He appeared at a full sprint just as Estelle's car slid into the alley. Unable to stop, he crashed into the front fender of her car. He catapulted across the hood, arms flailing, white T-shirt bright in the glare of headlights.

Estelle jammed the gearshift into Park and threw her weight against the crumpled door. It groaned open enough that she could slide out. With flashlight in one hand and Beretta in the other, she darted to the front fender.

Richard Kenderman had managed to land face first on the broken asphalt of the alley, and he staggered to his feet. Blood ran into his right eye, and when he raised his right hand to wipe the blood away, Estelle saw the gouge in the muscle of his forearm. He backed up awkwardly until he could lean on the concrete-block wall. He turned at the sound of Chief Mitchell's patrol car as it nosed into the other end of the alley, then looked up the alley in the opposite direction, beyond Estelle.

"Don't make things worse for yourself, Richard," Estelle said as she advanced around the mangled fender of her car. "Turn around and put your hands on the wall."

Kenderman slumped a little lower against the wall, arms against his sides. He blinked hard. "What?" he panted. "You're going to shoot me, or what?" His eyes flicked to Eddie Mitchell. The chief was using his own squad car for cover, advancing along the wall. Mitchell's left hand rested on his holstered service automatic.

"Turn around and put your hands on the wall," Estelle repeated, but even as she said it, she saw the motion of Kenderman's right hand, a slight curling of the wrist toward the tail of his T-shirt. Kenderman's body blocked the movement from Mitchell's view.

As soon as she saw the hand move, Estelle flicked off the Beretta's safety, and her right index finger curled into the trigger guard. Her wrist locked.

"Don't," she barked, but somewhere deep in his mind, Richard Kenderman had made all of his decisions. Drunk as he was and shaken from his fall, he still managed to slide the heavy revolver out of the waistband at the small of his back, out from under his T-shirt. The weapon swept up and out, the threat directed toward Mitchell. As Estelle's index finger began the long zip of the Beretta's heavy double-action trigger stroke, the chief's figure to her right moved in a blur. The Beretta bucked back and Kenderman twisted right as the 9-mm slug smacked into his upper arm three inches below the shoulder, yanking the gun to the side. An instant later, two shatteringly loud explosions came as one, and Kenderman spun back against the wall. The handgun skittered away. Estelle froze, the Beretta's trigger a twitch from release.

The young man's hands flexed against the cold blocks as he settled down on his knees, face against the wall. One of the two .45 rounds from Mitchell's automatic had exited high on his back to the left of his spine. In seconds, bright arterial blood soaked his T-shirt to the waist. One hand drew back as if the wall were hot to the touch at the same time as a long, rattling gurgle escaped his throat. He coughed hard, and as she moved cautiously toward him, Estelle saw bright blood splatter the wall. His body sagged even as Estelle kicked the revolver further out of his reach, and knelt beside him.

His eyes were closed, and he had stopped breathing.

Behind her, she heard the chief order an ambulance. "Come on, *hijo*," she whispered. She gently rested two fingers on the side of his neck as she holstered her automatic. His pulse was thready and weak, and then skipped several beats, to pick up again with a surge, miss again, and stop. A deep sigh bubbled up through his blood-choked windpipe.

She heard Mitchell behind her, and off to the left, the back door of Portillo's was yanked open. "He's gone," she said to the chief. She pulled Kenderman's right shoulder away from the wall to make sure that his hands were empty. She could feel the grating of the shattered upper arm bone. The two rounds from the chief's weapon had struck an inch apart, two inches below the juncture of sternum and clavicles.

Mitchell knelt down and examined the revolver without touching it.

"You guys all right?" Tom Pasquale was breathing hard, handgun held high.

"It's over," Estelle said. She turned to glance up at the deputy. "Where's the boy?"

"He's okay," Pasquale said. His face was pale.

"All right. Don't leave him alone in your unit, *Tomás*. And while you're at it, put the call in for Bobby and Dr. Perrone."

"And Schroeder," Mitchell muttered. He stood up, the revolver still lying at his feet. "This kid wasn't the sharpest tool in the box. He had three rounds in the gun, none of 'em under the hammer."

"That's not the first mistake Richard Kenderman ever made," Estelle said. She stood up and reached out a hand to take Pasquale's sleeve as he turned away. "And you might as well stay here, Tom. I'll take the boy home." Pasquale handed her the keys to his unit.

"What was he up to inside?" Mitchell asked.

"The clerk said Kenderman threatened him, took a swing at him, and then reached across the counter and riffled the cash register."

"Kenderman threatened the clerk with the gun?"

"I don't know," Pasquale said. "I haven't had time to ask."

Mitchell turned and gazed at Estelle for a moment, then turned and shook his head in disgust. "You didn't see a weapon when you looked through the front window?" he asked the deputy.

"No, sir."

"Where the hell did he think he was going to go?"

"He wasn't thinking at all," Estelle said.

"Three ten, Posadas. Ten four?"

Estelle's hand drifted down to the radio on her belt. The sheriff's department was a handful of blocks east, and if Ernie Wheeler had a window cracked, he probably would have heard the gunshots.

"Posadas, three ten is ten six. Ten sixty-three alley behind Portillo's. One adult male. Contact Perrone and Sheriff Torrez." She started to lower the small radio. "And cancel the BOLO."

The radio fell silent for the count of four, and then Wheeler's subdued voice replied, "Ten four, three ten."

Estelle pulled the small cell phone out of her jacket pocket and dialed Barbara Parker's number as she walked back toward the convenience-store parking lot. If he was very lucky, little Ryan Parker wouldn't understand what the loud noises had meant as they echoed from the alley behind the convenience store.

The phone rang nearly a dozen times before Barbara Parker answered it, her voice small and tremulous.

"Mrs. Parker, this is Undersheriff Guzman. I have Ryan with me. I'll be bringing him home in just a few minutes."

"Oh…" the woman sighed. "Thank you, Sheriff. Thank you so much." She hesitated. "I hope that Richard understood."

"No, ma'am, he didn't understand," Estelle replied, and broke the connection. In the distance, she heard sirens, one of them from the direction of Sheriff Bobby Torrez's home on McArthur, another from far to the west, where Sgt. Tom Mears had been working traffic on State Route 78. As she walked across the lot toward the Expedition, she saw that Ryan was standing on the back seat, peering through the side window. With the security screen between front and back seats, the child looked like a small, caged animal.

As Estelle approached, he backed away from the window and sat down on the seat, both hands clasped tightly between his legs. She opened the door.

She extended her hand toward the child. His eyes were wide and frightened. "Come on, Ryan. You don't want to ride back there."

He didn't move, but both hands came up and cupped under his chin, his tiny, thin arms tight against his chest as if warding off a ripping, cold wind. In that moment, Estelle knew that Ryan Parker realized exactly what had happened. She gathered him up off the seat and felt the shaking through his tiny frame.

THIRTY-FIVE

"POSADAS, THREE TEN." Estelle made a notation in her log as she waited for dispatcher Ernie Wheeler to respond. Ryan Parker sat silently, a blanket wrapped around his tiny shoulders, shaking so hard that his teeth chattered.

"Go ahead, three ten."

"Three ten will be ten six at seven oh nine Third Street. Ten five, one juvenile that location."

"Ten four, three ten," Wheeler replied. "And three ten, ten twenty-one 4570 when you have the chance." Estelle recognized Bill Gastner's home phone number. She glanced at her passenger. The little boy had focused his attention first on the complexities of the child-restraint system that held him securely in the front passenger seat—the same device that drove five-year-old Francisco Guzman wild when he was forced to use it—and then had stared wide-eyed at the array of unimaginable things that filled the front-seat compartment of the patrol car.

"You talk f-f-f-funny," he stuttered soberly. Estelle could hear his teeth chattering.

"Yes, we do," she said, and tried to smile. The number jabber on a police radio had been the source of more than one stand-up comedian's routine.

"My daddy's car is fast," he said matter-of-factly, and squirmed against the straps of his seat. "Are we going back to grandma's now?"

"Yes, we are, Ryan." She found the cell phone and selected the speed dial for former Sheriff Bill Gastner's home. He answered on the second ring, and she could picture him standing in the kitchen while he watched a fresh pot of coffee brewing. "Gastner."

"Hey, there," she said. "It's me."

"Hey, you," Gastner said. His gruff tone softened a little. "You okay?"

"I'm all right," she said. "I'm taking a small passenger home right now. After that, it's going to be a long night. Things didn't go well."

"If you need me for anything, you holler, all right?"

"Thanks, *Padrino*." She knew the former Posadas County sheriff hadn't called to commiserate. "Is Francis still there?"

"Oh, yes. He and I were up to no good, I'm happy to report. You got thirty seconds?"

"Sir, I need to take Ryan home and then get back to the scene." She lowered her voice. "I fired one of the shots, so there's going to be a lot of questions."

"Shit," Gastner said. "You shouldn't be leaving there now, then. And this'll give you something else to think about, sweetheart. This is what comes of leaving two delinquents to their own devices," Gastner said. "Here's Francis. Give him a couple of seconds to fill you in. You need to know about this."

Before she could protest, Dr. Francis Guzman came on the line. "*Querida?* Is the boy all right?"

She glanced at Ryan again. "Yes. I'm taking him home."

"Thank God for that, at least. We heard all the sirens."

"It didn't go well, *Oso*. I'm going to be a while." Francis Guzman read the tone of her voice correctly.

"You have Kenderman in custody, or…"

"I'm afraid it was 'or,' *Oso*." She glanced at Ryan. He didn't appear to be listening, but she lowered her voice a bit anyway and turned away. "He pointed a weapon at the chief."

"Uh oh."

"Yes." She slowed the large vehicle to a walk as she turned left at the end of Pershing Park. "I'll talk to you later about it. But it's going to be late, *Oso*. The D.A. isn't going to want to wait until morning." After the boy was safely home, she would spend hours in the alley until every scrap of evidence involved in the shooting of Richard Kenderman was recorded, photographed, and collected. The rest of her night would be filled with the ceremonial paperwork that would make Richard Kenderman's death an official statistic: reports, depositions, and not the least of all, answers to District Attorney Dan Schroeder's questions. Francis Guzman knew the drill.

She paused at the Stop sign at Third and Pershing. "What have you and *Padrino* been up to? I'm almost afraid to ask."

"And I almost wish I hadn't looked," Francis said.

"Looked where?"

"We were standing in Bill's kitchen, and you can see the clinic parking lot from the window over the sink. That's where I'm standing now. Anyway, about thirty minutes after you dropped me off here, I saw Louis's Mustang pull in, along with another vehicle."

For a fraction of a second, Estelle almost asked, "Louis *who*," before the mental gears meshed. Her taste testing on the flavor of counterfeit Daprodin seemed an episode during some other lifetime.

"Start over," she said.

"Louis Herrera showed up at the pharmacy," Francis repeated. "Not that that's unusual. Then the other car arrived, and we got curious."

Estelle slowed the car in front of Barbara Parker's home. "*Oso,* I'm just pulling into Parker's now. I'm going to have to go."

"Sorry, *querida.* I'll cut to the chase. It was Owen Frieberg. It was too far away for us to see who it was, but we got lucky with the license."

"Ay," she sighed. "It's not possible to see a license plate in the clinic parking lot from Bill's house, either, *Oso.*"

"True. We kinda went on over there. Discreetly, so to speak."

"Uh huh. *Los dos Osos.*" She could picture the two bears sneaking through the bushes.

"And then after about fifteen minutes, Frieberg…I guess it was him, we couldn't tell for sure…Frieberg came out carrying a bunch of stuff. Three guesses what it probably was."

She stopped the car. "Give me about ten minutes, *Oso.* Don't go anywhere. And tell *Padrino* not to go anywhere, either."

"We'll be here, *querida*."

"While you're waiting, give Irma a call, okay? Make sure the kids haven't…" She drifted off, realizing that Carlos and Francisco were no match for their nanny, Irma Sedillos, even on her worst day.

"I did that," Francis said. "Everything is fine."

"Ten minutes, then." She saw Barbara Parker's front door open. "Love you, *Oso*." Ryan scrambled to climb out of the harness as his grandmother approached the car. "There you go, *hijo*," Estelle said as she popped the last buckle restraining the youngster. She reached across and pulled the door handle to turn the small hurricane loose. His grandmother staggered backward at the rush of the little boy into her arms, and Estelle remained in the car to give Barbara Parker a few moments' privacy with her grandson. She took the opportunity to finish her log notations and stowed the clipboard. *Everything boiled down to numbers and notations,* she thought wearily.

Mrs. Parker untangled her hug with the boy and scooted him toward the house, and Estelle got out of the car. The woman turned toward her, and Estelle clearly read the anguish on her face.

"What did Richard say?" she asked.

"Mrs. Parker," Estelle said, and she stepped close to the woman and lowered her voice, "Richard Kenderman was apprehended at Portillo's, but we don't have the full story about what happened there. He left Ryan in the car when he went inside. There is reason to believe we interrupted a robbery in progress. When we arrived, he fled out the back of the store." She paused as she saw the tears welling up in Mrs. Parker's eyes. "He didn't want to talk with us, Mrs. Parker. When we attempted to take him into custody, he pulled a weapon and pointed it at Chief Mitchell."

"Those sirens I heard…"

Estelle nodded. "Mrs. Parker, the district attorney will want to talk with you later tomorrow morning. Sergeant Tom Mears from our department will probably be over later tonight. He'll need a deposition from you."

"And you'll charge Richard?"

Estelle frowned. She looked at Barbara Parker for a long moment, trying to imagine what the woman's thought processes might be.

"No ma'am. Richard Kenderman is dead."

Mrs. Parker's hands drifted together palm to palm as if ready for prayer, and she pressed her fingers to her lips and closed her eyes. "Oh…"

"I'm sorry," Estelle said.

Barbara Parker's eyes remained tightly closed as she shook her head repeatedly. Finally the oscillation stopped, but her eyes remained closed. "And Perry?"

"I don't know yet how that will turn out. Perry is in custody. The district attorney is pressing charges against him. That's all I can tell you."

"If I'd…" the woman started, and bit it off with another shake of her head.

Hindsight is a wonderful thing, Estelle thought, but she remained silent. Mrs. Parker turned toward the house, hands still pressed to her lips. "I need to be with Ryan," she said.

"Yes, ma'am," Estelle said. "You certainly do." Mrs. Parker heard the clipped edge in the undersheriff's tone and grimaced. "And Mrs. Parker, if establishing paternity for Ryan is important to you, then you need to contact Judge Hobart first thing in the morning for a court order. Once the body is buried or cremated, there isn't much that can be done."

The woman looked as if she'd been stabbed with a fork. "Oh, my," she breathed. "Would it be possible for you…"

Estelle shook her head. "No, it wouldn't, ma'am. That's something that *you* need to do, Mrs. Parker. Regardless of how we feel at the moment, someday it might be important to Ryan and Mindi to know. Right now, that's *your* job."

"I'm so sorry," Mrs. Parker said. Her shoulders slumped.

"We all are, ma'am," Estelle said. She nodded toward the house. "Ryan's going to need a lot of attention."

"Will you keep me posted about Perry?"

Estelle took a deep breath, forcing herself to say exactly the right thing. "No, Mrs. Parker, I won't. You know exactly where Perry Kenderman is. You're free to visit him at the county lockup during regular visiting hours any time you wish. If you want a blood test to establish whether or not he's Ryan's father, feel free to ask him to comply. If he refuses, then your next avenue is Judge Hobart.''

"I'm sorry. I didn't mean to…" Barbara Parker hesitated as she glanced toward her house. "He could go to prison, couldn't he."

"Yes, ma'am. He could."

Barbara Parker nodded and gazed off toward the house. "Okay," she said, and turned to Estelle with a tight, painful smile. "Thank you."

"Expect either Sergeant Mears or one of the other officers later this evening," Estelle said. "I'll be in touch."

As soon as the car door slammed, she keyed the mike and cleared with Dispatch, her thoughts already back in the dark alley behind Portillo's.

"Three ten, ten twenty-one Sheriff Torrez," Ernie Wheeler said.

She acknowledged and switched from radio to telephone, pushing the car back into Park. The sheriff was difficult enough to hear under the best of circumstances, but this time his voice was soft and delivered one notch above a whisper.

"Are you all right?"

"Yes, sir. Ryan's home and safe. I just left there."

"Good enough. We've got a convention going on over here. Schroeder will be here in a few minutes," the sheriff said. "You're on your way back over?"

"In a bit. Can you give me some time?"

"Time for what? The place you need to be is right here."

"I know that, Bobby, but I just talked to Francis," she said. "I left him at Bill's earlier when we went after Kenderman. He says that both Frieberg and Herrera are up to something at the pharmacy. We need to know what's going on."

"Great timing."

"We need to move on that, Bobby. Tonight."

A long silence followed. "Look, Estelle…Schroeder's going to have some questions. I got a few of my own. In the first place, any number of people could have taken the kid home. You shouldn't have left here to do that. You're one of the principals in this.''

"I understand that, sir," Estelle said, making an effort to keep her voice even. "But what's going on at that pharmacy is somehow related to George Enriquez's murder. There are a number of people who can give you an accurate version of what happened with Richard Kenderman. Give me a few minutes and I'll get back to you. If there's something urgent, you'll be able to reach me."

"Just a second." She heard the phone muffled and voices in the background. "You keep the phone handy," Torrez said when he came back on the line. "Don't be goin' Lone Ranger on us. Taber's comin' in early to give us some coverage on the road, so you can use her. We'll clean up the mess here. If Schroeder needs to talk with you right away, I'll let you know. I don't think there's too much question about what happened. The store clerk looked out the back door just as the first of the shots was fired." Torrez hesitated. "For once everyone agrees. You're sure you're all right?"

"Yes, sir." *All right was relative, of course,* she thought.

"Okay. Don't be goin' without the cavalry. And stay in touch."

The drive from Barbara Parker's home on Third Street south to Bill Gastner's rambling adobe on Escondido, where Francis Guzman waited, was no more than two miles. During those four minutes, Estelle tried to push the Parker family out of her mind. She knew that she could spend fruitless hours wondering and worrying about Ryan and Mindi's care…about Barbara Parker's various failings as a guardian, about what Perry Kenderman's next move might be should he ever be able to post bond.

She also knew, despite the powerful tugs of affection she felt for the children caught in the middle, that the family's various troubles were none of her business until laws were broken. There was nothing in the statutes that prevented a guardian from doing all the wrong things.

To force the crumpled, bloody figure of Richard Kenderman from swimming back into focus, she concentrated on the mistakes made by George Enriquez—and the mistakes made by the person who had murdered him.

THIRTY-SIX

As SHE TURNED LEFT on Guadalupe Terrace, Estelle switched off the headlights. She let the Expedition drift along Guadalupe so slowly that a power walker would have left her in the dust. The mobile-home park on the left was quiet, most of the porch lights on, a smattering of vehicles snuggled in beside the trailers. She passed Escondido and saw Bill Gastner's Blazer parked in his driveway, fifty yards down the lane.

Ahead on the right, just around the gentle southward curve of Guadalupe, the Posadas Health Clinic's bulk cast a low, squat shadow against the trees. The front of the building featured a series of tall, narrow slots that passed for windows, perhaps the architect's reminiscence of crevasses in the sides of red sandstone mesas. The clinic doors faced east, into the parking lot.

That apron of macadam curved around the building where the pharmacy's front door opened to the south. The outside security light over the door washed out any possibility of seeing furtive lights inside, an interesting phenomenon that she had pointed out to the architect during the early planning stages of the building. The architect hadn't believed her, and neither had the insurance company.

As she approached the clinic's parking lot, Estelle braked to a gentle stop on the shoulder of the street. She could see the back of Louis Herrera's yellow Mustang, nosed in close to the private staff entrance on the east side of the pharmacy.

With the driver's-side window down and her engine switched off, she listened to the neighborhood, dominated by the intermittent howl of tires on the interstate just to the north. Somewhere to the east, a ringing telephone prompted a small dog to comment.

For five minutes, Estelle sat and watched her husband's clinic, loath to do any more, even though she knew that every moment she waited worked in the meticulous, organized Louis Herrera's favor. Could he actually be unaware that some of his pharmaceuticals were nothing but pressed talc or sugar? Believing that Louis Herrera had been duped was too comfortable.

After a moment she pulled her cell phone out of her pocket and dialed Dispatch. "Ernie," she said when the deputy answered, "I'll be at the clinic for a while, talking with Louis Herrera."

"Roger that," Wheeler replied. "You doing all right?"

Estelle almost laughed despite the helpless feeling that this night was headed downhill on a rocket sled. "Just wonderful, Ernie."

"Jackie came in early. Everybody's still tied up over at Portillo's, so she's the only one on the road."

"You might have her stay central for a while," Estelle said. "No mention of this location on the air, *por favor.*"

"You got it."

She switched off the phone, started the Expedition, and eased forward, circling the outside of the parking lot until she pulled to a stop broadside behind Herrera's compact. She saw the movement in the trees just as she was about to open the door. A large, slow-moving figure appeared, hands thrust in his pockets, head down...one of the clinic's neighbors out for a stroll before bedtime. She waited until Bill Gastner was within a dozen steps before she slipped down out of the tall vehicle. She eased the door shut and stood silent.

The former sheriff waited until Estelle was within touching distance before speaking. "I thought you were going to stop by the house."

"If I did, Francis would have wanted to come with me. I didn't want that."

"Well, he wanted to come anyway," Gastner said. "He knows that he's got a hell of a stake in all this, but I told him as undiplomatically as I could that now was a really good time to stay out of the way." He nodded toward the pharmacy. "You want some company?" Gastner flashed a grin. "Or should I stay out of the way, too?"

Estelle reached out and squeezed the older man's arm. When she didn't release her grip, he chuckled, "Anyway, you never know when you might need a livestock inspector. There might be an unbranded calf or something inside."

A set of headlights appeared on Escondido and just as quickly winked out. Estelle watched as the vehicle coasted through the shadows. When it passed under the streetlight on the curve, she recognized the older Bronco that Deputy Jackie Taber drove on the graveyard shift.

"The cavalry," she said, and reached around to double-key the radio on her belt so that the two barks of squelch would alert the deputy that Estelle had seen her approach.

"Herrera has a scanner in the pharmacy, as I remember," Gastner said.

"Yes, he does. I told Ernie."

The employees' door was painted turquoise to match the building's trim, but the color did nothing to hide the plain, utilitarian nature of the steel construction. Estelle rapped hard, the sound an intrusion in the quiet night. She and Gastner waited for a full minute before he said, "Try mine." He walloped the door four times, and by the fourth knock they heard the dead bolt slide out of the striker. The heavy door opened noiselessly, and Louis Herrera peered out cautiously. He saw first Gastner and then Estelle, and his face brightened.

"Ah," he said. "You guys out for a walk?" He looked past them and saw Estelle's county vehicle parked behind his. "I'm getting some paperwork done," he said. "Some stuff that I've been ignoring for too long."

"Louis, we need to talk," Estelle said, and her abrupt tone wasn't lost on the pharmacist.

Herrera frowned, his glance shifting from Estelle to Gastner and back. "Well, sure. Any time. You know that." He stepped to one side, holding the door open wide. "Come on in." As she slipped past him, he said, "Any progress on that big book?"

"Yes," she said.

"Well...good. Come on in." A few steps brought them to his work station. The computer was on, its screen saver just starting a display of pipes building into a vast plumbing snarl. Herrera flipped shut a thick computer readout and pushed it out of the way. He glanced at Bill Gastner, as if expecting the former sheriff to say something, but the older man's face was placid as he scanned the various drugs on the shelf to his left.

"So, what's Francis up to tonight?" Herrera said.

"He's waiting over at my house," Gastner said before Estelle had a chance to answer. He continued his calm examination of the shelf's inventory, and Estelle could see that Francis had outlined for Gastner what she and her husband had looked at earlier in the drug reference guide. Gastner fell silent, not bothering to explain why Francis was waiting. It was the sort of flat statement that drew the conversation up short, and Estelle watched the pharmacist's face.

"This is going to be hard enough on him as it is, Louis," Estelle said. His right hand drifted out to the counter beside him in what ordinarily would be a casual move but this time looked as if he was searching for balance.

"What's going on?" he asked.

Estelle regarded him for a moment. He held her gaze for ten seconds or so, then his eyes darted first toward Gastner and then to the floor. Estelle pulled the small evidence bags from her jacket pocket. "I know about the drugs, Louis," she said, and even as she spoke she felt a wellspring of anger against this smooth young man. "These two are Daprodin DG." She tossed the bags on the counter so that they landed just in front of Herrera's outspread fingers. He didn't move. She held up the second set of bags for a moment, then tossed them on top of the first set. "And those are counterfeit Daprodin DG."

Louis Herrera stood perfectly still, his eyes riveted on the four evidence bags. If he was still breathing, Estelle couldn't tell.

After a moment, he pulled his hand away and Estelle saw the streaks of moisture left behind on the counter.

"Should I ask where you got those?" he whispered.

"I think you already know, Louis."

Gastner had moved down the shelf a bit, and now leaned back, neck cricked as he looked through his bifocals at the white bottle in front of him. "That Daprodin is popular stuff," he mused as if talking to himself. He pulled a pencil out of his shirt pocket and with the eraser end moved the stock bottle of Daprodin half an inch to the right so he could scrutinize the label. Estelle could see that there was no second bottle behind it.

"Why would I know?" Herrera said. He watched Gastner instead of Estelle.

"Louis," Estelle said, "Francis and I were in here earlier. The real Daprodin DG came from that bottle on the shelf. I took two samples." She separated the bags. "These two were taken from the second jar. Earlier, the second jar was stowed behind the first, on that shelf." She nodded across the room, and Gastner tapped the shelf in front of him with a knuckle. "Whoever manufactured this second batch didn't get the taste quite right."

The young man's round face had gone from flushed to pale. His lips tightened. "You were in here going through my inventory? What do you think…" He settled his fists on his hips in a half-hearted show of umbrage.

"It's too late for that, Louis," she said quietly. "Do you want to tell me about it?"

He shrugged helplessly. "What's the 'it,' Estelle?"

"Let me make it crystal clear for you, Louis. You can either help us, or you can be arrested right now and try to tough it out." She smiled without humor. "I'd sort of like to see you do that."

She saw Herrera's weight sag against the counter, and he closed his eyes.

"You tell me what you want to do," she said. "Just don't take too long to do it."

The room was so silent that Estelle could hear her pulse. She could see Louis Herrera's, pounding through his left carotid artery as he regarded the counter and the four little bags. Bill Gastner had finished his examination of drugs that interested him not in the least, and he stood with his hands loose at his sides, watching Herrera.

After a moment, the pharmacist appeared to reach some sort of conclusion with a little shake of his head. He drew in a long breath, one hitch halfway sounding almost like a hiccup. "This isn't about the drugs, is it."

"No, it's not."

Herrera's right index finger traced little circles on the counter. "I don't know what I'm going to do," he said, sounding pathetic. Estelle didn't respond. "Francis had nothing to do with any of this," Herrera said. "He didn't."

"I know that," Estelle said.

"He didn't know anything about any of it."

"Right now, I have only two concerns," Estelle said. "I want you out of my husband's clinic so he can start repairing the damage you've done. And I want to know who killed George Enriquez."

Herrera flinched as if he'd been struck. "I don't know," he whispered.

"How well do you know Owen Frieberg, Louis?"

He shook his head. "Not well...but I mean, well *enough*. He didn't do it, Estelle."

"You're sure of that?"

"No. I guess I'm not sure of anything." He hunched his shoulders high and held them there. "I don't know what I know." He let his shoulders sag. "Owen came and got the drugs just a little bit ago. He said he had tried to reach me at home, then drove by the clinic to see if I was here." Herrera shrugged. "I'd gone out to get something to eat, so he missed me. Frieberg said that he'd driven by earlier and seen your county car parked in the lot. I told him I didn't know anything about that, but that you'd been to see me earlier with the pharmaceutical reference, so we knew that you were on to something." He paused and made a face. "Funny."

"What's funny?"

He looked up and tried to smile. "Yesterday, Francis and I were talking about the Kenderman thing, you know? About that young cop being so stupid. I remember saying to Francis, 'I'd hate to have her after me.' Herrera sighed. "And I guess you are, right?"

I'm fresh out of sympathy, Estelle wanted to say. "Owen came here and picked up the counterfeit drugs. That's what happened?''

''Yes. He figured that we should stow them, just in case.''

''Just in case what?''

''Just in case that's what you were after.''

''And if it wasn't, you were going to put them all back on the shelf? Is that it?'' Estelle felt the flush on her face. ''Why did Frieberg call you in the first place?''

''I don't know, Estelle. I really don't. And I'd tell you if I did.''

''Tell me what you *do* know, Louis.''

''About?''

''Frieberg and Enriquez were bringing the counterfeit drugs into the country. Is that correct?''

''Yes.''

''Where do they get them?''

''He never said. And I didn't ask. In Mexico someplace.''

''Who else was in on this?''

Herrera shook his head vehemently. ''I don't know. I really don't. And like I said, maybe I didn't *want* to know. It could have been just them…just Owen and Enriquez. I don't know.''

''You knew the drugs were counterfeit.''

He nodded. ''But they had regular ones, too. The counterfeit part only started a few months ago.'' His cheeks flamed scarlet. ''Sometimes, a patient would come in, and I'd know just as well as anyone that the drugs were a waste on 'em, you know? And sometimes, the medication might be actually counterproductive. So I'd slip in a placebo.''

''Did Frieberg and Enriquez peddle the drugs to anyone else?''

''I don't know.''

''To Guy Trombley, for example?''

''Estelle, if I knew that, I'd tell you. But I don't. I didn't ask, and Frieberg never said.'' Lifting both hands in the air, he looked at the undersheriff beseechingly. ''Tell me what to do.''

''What does Joe Tones know about all this?''

''Tones? You mean the hardware guy? How would I know anything about him? I told you…I accepted some of the pharmaceuticals from Freiberg. I knew where they came from...I mean, in general, I knew. And I knew some of them were fake. That's it.'' He held out his hands. ''You gotta tell me what to do.''

''Find yourself a *really* good lawyer, Louis. That's the first thing you might want to do.''

''I'll cooperate any way I can. You know that.''

''That's nice,'' Estelle said. She chose her words carefully. ''Let's start with what Dr. Guzman would want you to do.'' She didn't add *step in front of a bus,* which is what she wanted Louis Herrera to do just then.

She pulled the portable radio off her belt. ''Three oh three, three ten.''

Deputy Taber responded instantly. ''Three oh three.''

''Three oh three, ten eighty-seven this location.''

Estelle slipped the radio back in its clip. ''Louis, Deputy Taber will be here in a few minutes. She's going to assist you in any way she can. I want a list compiled of every prescription drug, fake or not, that you received from Freiberg. Date, name, amount. And then I want a list of every patient to whom you dispensed those drugs. Every last one.''

''I don't know if I can remember that,'' Herrera said.

''If you can't, then the computer can,'' Estelle said icily. ''When you're finished here, Deputy Taber will escort you to the Public Safety Building. The information you provide from here and what you say in your deposition will determine in part what course the district attorney may wish to take against you.''

''It has to go that far?''

''Yes, it does.'' She nodded as she watched him listen to the faint sound of a car door closing outside. ''You're free to take some other route if you wish.''

''I don't have much of a choice, do I?''

''You always have a choice, Louis. But we're not leaving you alone here.''

''You think that after all this, I'd do something to try and...'' Herrera waved his hand hopelessly.

''That's just the trouble, Louis. I don't know what you'd do.'' The door opened and Deputy Jackie Taber stepped inside. Her eyes locked on Louis Herrera, her face expressionless. "As far as I'm concerned, you have two choices," Estelle said. "You can cooperate with us, or you can be arrested and spend the night in the lockup until Judge Hobart decides what to do with you." She glanced at her watch. "That's the only break I'm going to give you. And we're wasting time."

Herrera held up his hands. "I'll do whatever I can to help."

Estelle nodded curtly and then quickly explained to the deputy what she wanted. "And when you're finished, you need to put a sheriff's lock on the door. On the inside of this one," and she nodded at the door they'd entered, "and a chain on the front doors." She glanced at Herrera once more. "We don't want any more surprises."

THIRTY-SEVEN

OWEN FRIEBERG hadn't achieved his status as Nate Salazar's partner at Salazar and Sons Funeral Home by being uncooperative. When Frieberg opened the side door of the mortuary in response to the bell, Estelle was sure that his head-to-toe glance was a measurement. All she had to supply was her choice of ash, oak, mahogany, or walnut for the casket, brass or wrought iron handles, and satin or velvet lining.

"Ah," he said as if that explained everything. He closed his eyes and shook his head, extending both hands in anticipation of that comforting, enveloping hand clasp he had practiced so often.

"Mr. Frieberg, I'm Undersheriff Estelle Guzman. I think you know Bill Gastner."

"Oh, yes," Frieberg said as his eyes reopened and flicked from Estelle to Gastner and then across the parking lot to where Deputy Tony Abeyta was striding across toward them from his patrol unit. No greeting hand had crept into his, and he brought them back to parade rest at his midriff.

"And this is Deputy Abeyta," Estelle added.

"Heavens, I've known Tony for years. And Bill, it's been too long." He smiled benignly at Gastner, or perhaps it was an appraisal. "Something tells me that I know why you're here, Undersheriff," Frieberg said gently. He flashed an apologetic smile. "I was catching up on some paperwork, but I'm happy for the excuse to stop. Would you like to come inside?"

"Sure." *Lots of paperwork being done tonight,* Estelle thought.

Abeyta remained on the steps as Estelle and Gastner followed

Frieberg into the foyer, where the man stood for a moment, evidently trying to decide whether or not to close the door. With the toe of an immaculately white running shoe, he nudged a small cast-iron dachshund doorstop into place. "It's really still very mild, isn't it," he said, and nodded at Abeyta as if entrusting the welfare of the door's stained-glass window to him.

"I should have called you earlier, I know that," he said. "Then you told me that you were going to try to find time to stop by yesterday afternoon, but I know how these things go. Everyone gets busy, don't they?" Before Estelle could respond, Frieberg turned to Bill Gastner. "How's retirement treating you, Sheriff?"

"Just fine."

"You were saying that you should have called us, Mr. Frieberg?" Estelle prompted. She regarded him with interest, giving him her own head-to-toe examination. He had lost weight since being captured on the videotape taken at Christmas in Acámbaro. His clothing hung a bit loosely from his compact frame, not as neatly tailored as Estelle remembered. As he turned and the light caught the planes of his face, Estelle's gaze lingered on the telltale smudge of foundation makeup in the canyon between nose and cheek, shadowed by the rims of his tortoiseshell glasses.

Frieberg shot them another gentle smile and once more closed his eyes and tipped his head back. He kept his eyes closed as he talked, a habit that fascinated Estelle. Perhaps it allowed him to talk with grieving relatives without having to watch the tears. She found herself wondering if she would be able to silently walk around behind Frieberg as he talked, without his knowing.

"Let me be honest with you," the undertaker said. "As I told Sheriff Torrez earlier, some time ago I borrowed a revolver from George Enriquez." He held up a hand for emphasis. "Now, I don't *think* that's illegal, but I'm not sure. That's one reason I called the sheriff when I did."

"No, that's not illegal," Estelle said. "And when was that, sir?"

"Oh, gosh. Sometime before Christmas, I think. Yes, in fact it was shortly after Thanksgiving. So late November, early December." He waved a hand in dismissal. "George purchased this wonderful Smith and Wesson from the gun shop some time ago. Actually, a couple of years ago, probably. I don't think he ever shot it, but he was certainly proud of that gun.''

He opened his eyes to make sure his audience hadn't drifted away, and leaned toward Estelle conspiratorially. ''I don't know why he wanted it, really. He's not a shooter. Anyway, I offered to purchase that revolver from George any number of times. I mean, it's a *wonderful* sidearm for hunting, if you know what I mean.''

''I'm sure it is, sir.'' Behind her, Bill Gastner hummed something that could have been translated a dozen different ways.

''Well…to make a long story short, he loaned the revolver to me for a while, sort of a 'borrow with option to buy' sort of thing.'' Frieberg took a deep breath, and his eyelids sank shut. ''Some time ago, I decided that the revolver wasn't something that I really needed.'' He shrugged dramatically, impressed with his self-restraint.

''Did *you* shoot it much?'' Gastner asked.

''Some. And then I discovered that I have an arthritic right thumb.'' He held up his hand ruefully, spreading the fingers. He rubbed the knob at the base of his thumb. ''The recoil just beats that to death.'' He sighed. ''So I gave the revolver back to George. I'm sorry now that I did.''

''Why is that, sir?''

He looked at Estelle with surprise. ''Well, it's my understanding that George shot himself with that weapon…that's what happened, I understand.'' When Estelle didn't respond, he added, ''I felt badly about that, believe me. If the weapon hadn't been so near at hand, perhaps…''

''When you borrowed the revolver, why didn't you take the wooden case with it?''

''Ah,'' Frieberg said, and hesitated. ''Well, the idea of a display case doesn't impress me much, I suppose,'' he said, and Gastner grinned, perhaps sharing Estelle's thoughts. The mortician sold ''display cases'' as part of his services and obviously thought highly of them. ''I happen to have a wonderful hand-tooled holster that I'd purchased years ago for another handgun. It's a perfect fit for the .41. When I returned the revolver…I think it was last week. The middle of last week. Anyway, I took the holster along, wondering if perhaps he'd like to have it to use on the elk hunt. But he didn't.''

"So when you left his office at that time, George had the revolver in his office, without the presentation case.''

"I think so. Well...I don't know about the case. At one time, he had it at home, I know that. That's where it was when I borrowed it. I went to his house.''

"And when you returned the revolver last week, did you take the weapon to his office, or his home?'' Estelle asked.

"His office. And in part, that's why I took the holster along. But he didn't want it. I don't think he could actually envision himself *wearing* the gun, if you know what I mean. It looked better to him in a wooden case.''

"What did he do with the revolver when you gave it back?''

Frieberg frowned. "Ah...it seems to me that he just slipped it into one of the drawers of his desk. I really don't remember.''

Estelle nodded. "When you heard about George's death, you suddenly decided that you should share this information with us?''

"I thought it only proper,'' Frieberg said eagerly. "Such a terrible, terrible thing. And such a waste. I knew that George had been having more than his share of troubles, of course. I considered him a good friend, but he didn't talk about himself much. But I guess everyone in town knew what was going on with his insurance dealings.''

"Did you know what was going on, Mr. Frieberg?''

Frieberg's gaze shot quickly to Estelle, and then the eyelids closed at the same time his mouth opened to speak. He hesitated, as if something had lodged in his throat. "Yes, I did.''

"Did you have dealings with Mr. Enriquez yourself?'' Investigators had spent more than nine months building a case against George Enriquez, compiling a history of insurance fraud that would have led to an indictment on multiple counts. Owen Frieberg's name had not been on the list of those duped.

"I...I did. In fact, the day he died...'' Frieberg stopped as if someone had stepped on his foot.

"Sir?''

"I went to see him first thing Monday morning."

"What prompted that?" She watched as color crept into Frieberg's cheeks. Instead of closing his eyes this time, he fixed his gaze on the tile in front of his shoes.

"I have a boat," he said. "Perhaps you've seen it, out back?"

"No, sir."

"The bass boat of my dreams. Every bell and whistle known to man."

"If only we had a lake," Gastner said dryly.

"Elephant Butte is only a couple hours away," Frieberg said. "And I pull it behind my camper, too. We've been everywhere."

"And the *we* is…" Estelle asked.

"Well, I mean *I've* been everywhere. Anyway, I insured the boat with George's agency. He found a company that didn't charge an arm and a leg, and I appreciated that."

"When was this, sir?"

"Oh, it's been a year now. And then," he grimaced, "a wheel came off my trailer. Can you believe that? That was in April. Fortunately, I wasn't going very fast when it happened…and in fact, it was on one of those gravel access roads to the Butte. I guess I should be thankful for that. But it was one of those magic moments when everything that could go wrong, did. When the bearing froze and the wheel came off, the hitch failed. I didn't have the safety chains properly connected. Perhaps you can imagine what happens when a wheel departs and then a heavy boat goes wandering off by itself." He grimaced good naturedly, pulling the corners of his mouth back and showing perfect teeth.

"So you made an insurance claim?"

"Exactly. A substantial claim. By the time the rocks in the bar ditch were finished with both boat and motor, it wasn't a pretty sight."

"And this claim was in, what, May sometime?"

"Yes. I can find the exact date if you need it."

"Mr. Enriquez paid you?"

"Ah, yes. With a personal check."

"What was your reaction to that?"

"I know that's not the way things work, Mrs. Guzman. Before

I saw the check, I had no reason to believe that George Enriquez had taken me for a ride, in company with everyone else.''

"You had a policy in hand?"

Frieberg looked uncomfortable. "No. But I didn't actually lose anything, either. He paid me, and paid me in full. Promptly, too."

Estelle studied the man's flat, bland face. "So tell me," she said quietly. "Why Monday morning? Why did you go to see him then?"

"I…" Frieberg bit off his first thought and closed his eyes.

"You knew that you didn't have a legitimate policy with Enriquez long before this. Five months before. And by your own admission, you knew about Mr. Enriquez's dealings and that the grand jury convened on Tuesday. What prompted the visit Monday morning?"

"Actually, it was the jury business, Undersheriff," Frieberg said carefully. "When Enriquez paid me for the boat, I was grateful, and…" he shrugged. "Maybe a little suspicious. But I kept paying the monthly premiums. Why, I don't know, except…"

"You got what you paid for," Gastner muttered.

"Exactly, Bill. I paid a premium, really pretty modest, and the first time I have a claim—and it was a significant one—he paid promptly. I admit it. If I knew that George was playing the market a bit, so what? I was benefiting, so I went along. But then I started to think, when I began hearing about the grand jury, that this was going to explode into something ugly. I procrastinated, I admit it. I knew George's office was closed for the week, but driving by on Monday morning I saw his car in the lot. So I stopped."

"What time was that?" Estelle asked.

"Oh, shortly after eight, I think. I went in and told him that I would need to look elsewhere for my insurance."

Gastner chuckled, shook his head, and turned away, studiously examining the glass of the front door.

"It's true," Frieberg said with a flash of irritation.

"And what did Mr. Enriquez say in response to that?" Estelle asked.

"He wrote me a check for six hundred and twelve dollars…six months' worth of premiums."

"You still have that check?"

"Well, my bank does, I suppose."

"And that's all?" Estelle asked. "You complained, he cheerfully refunded half a year's premiums, and that was it?"

"Well, in essence. We exchanged some words, of course, but I don't know how well you knew George Enriquez. It was hard to stay mad at him for very long."

"You hadn't really lost anything, had you?" Gastner asked.

"No. And I think that's to George's credit, too. I hope that comes out. I hope that what I've been able to tell you is some help."

"Well, sir, we actually didn't come over to talk about your boat insurance," Estelle said. "And I don't think that's why you went to see George Enriquez on Monday morning, either."

Frieberg cocked his head quizzically. "I don't understand."

"Let's talk about tonight."

"Tonight?" He looked around the foyer as if a wet dog had been allowed to slip inside the funeral home along with the three visitors.

"About nine-thirty, give or take?"

"I don't understand. I've been working here most of the evening. Now wait a minute. What's going on?" His eyes shifted to Deputy Abeyta, the only uniformed officer present. For the first time, he appeared to realize that there were three police officers confronting him, not just two acquaintances.

"Mr. Frieberg, did you allow someone to borrow your vehicle this evening?"

"Of course not."

"Temporary tag seven forty-one, two eighty-six, expires ten twenty-eight this month, a silver 2003 Dodge Caravan," Gastner said, looking at Frieberg over the top of his glasses. "That's yours?"

"Yes, that's mine. What's your interest in my car, Bill? I thought you were working for the state now."

"I am," Gastner said. "And your car doesn't interest me in the least. Where your car *was* just might."

"What are you two talking about?"

"Mr. Frieberg," Estelle said patiently, "earlier this evening, your van was reported at the pharmacy, after hours."

The mortician pushed up his glasses and then thrust his hands in his back pockets. "I don't see…"

"You just said that you hadn't been out all evening."

"I wasn't."

"But your vehicle was? It drives itself?"

He pulled his hands free and held them up, palms outward. "Hold it, hold it." He smiled engagingly. "I was out for a bit. All right? It slipped my mind." He took off his glasses and held them out toward Estelle. He pointed at the soft rubber cushions attached to the nose piece. "These have been driving me crazy, but I keep forgetting to get them fixed when I visit the optometrist in Deming. I knew that Guy had some in his store, so I buzzed down." He rubbed the bridge of his nose. "Like to drive me crazy. You know, something like that starts to bug you, and pretty soon you can't think of anything else."

"Guy?" Estelle asked.

"Guy Trombley. At the drugstore. What, someone thought I was robbing the place, or what?"

Estelle held up the small aluminum clipboard that she carried and slipped two documents free. "Mr. Frieberg, I have a warrant to search the premises here and at your home, as well as to search your vehicle."

"You're joking," Frieberg stammered and then promptly choked on inhaled saliva. Estelle waited until his coughing had subsided and he'd wiped his eyes. "I mean…you can look around here all you want, but," he dabbed his eyes again, "I have the right to know what's going on," he finally managed.

"Yes, sir, you do. Earlier this evening, your vehicle was seen parked at the Posadas Pharmacy and Clinic. You were seen leaving the pharmacy with several cartons that we know contained contraband pharmaceuticals obtained from a supplier in Mexico. I have an inventory of those pharmaceuticals from Mr. Herrera."

Owen Frieberg stared at her incredulously, his eyes still watering from the bout of coughing. He cleared his throat. "You're kidding."

Estelle's left eyebrow drifted upward a fraction. "No, sir, I'm not. We know about Acámbaro. We know about the Christmas and *Cinco de Mayo* trips. Mr. Frieberg," Estelle said gently, "you can either cooperate with us as well and maybe save yourself some grief, or we'll plow through this thing one step at a time. It's your choice."

The silence hung heavily, and after a moment Tony Abeyta shifted his weight. The leather of his Sam Brown belt creaked, and that small sound was loud in the foyer. "My God," Frieberg whispered. "You think that I killed George Enriquez, don't you?" Estelle didn't respond. "That's what this is all about. You think that I went to see George on Monday, and killed him."

"You didn't go to talk about boats," Bill Gastner said dryly.

Estelle watched as the mortician tried to clear his throat. He blinked rapidly but ignored the tears on his cheeks.

"Mr. Frieberg, what makes you think that George Enriquez was killed on Monday?"

What little color had been able to show through the makeup drained from Owen Frieberg's face.

THIRTY-EIGHT

ESTELLE WATCHED AS a practiced expression of glacial calm settled over Owen Frieberg's face. His elegant posture—squared shoulders, chin up—showed nothing. One hand strayed outward to rest on the ornately carved back of one of the straight chairs that lined the foyer.

"What *did* you and Enriquez talk about on Monday morning?" she asked.

"I think that I need to call my attorney," Frieberg said.

"Suit yourself," Estelle said. She nodded at the old-fashioned black telephone on the ebony foyer table.

"Am I under arrest?" he whispered.

"You will be."

He straightened a fraction more, glaring at Estelle. "You're very sure of yourself, young lady." When Estelle didn't respond, he added, "I did not kill George Enriquez. You couldn't be more wrong if you think that."

"Someone did, Mr. Frieberg."

He smiled with a touch of condescension. "Well, when you find out who, I'll be interested to read all about it in the local newspaper." The smile faded when Estelle brought the handcuffs out from under her jacket. "You're actually…"

"Mr. Frieberg, you don't leave us much choice. I'm in no mood to play games tonight. You're right…you aren't required to talk to us." She stepped close and glared into his face. "You used a busload of kids as cover to run drugs. And when things started to come apart, you killed George Enriquez to shut him up. I don't think I need to stand here and negotiate with you."

"Wait." He held up both hands again and glanced nervously

toward Abeyta. "Wait a minute. All right. Earlier this evening, I was over at Herrera's pharmacy. And what he probably told you is true. We found a source of inexpensive drugs in Mexico, and he was more than willing to carry some of them in his pharmacy."

"The we is…"

Frieberg closed his eyes and hesitated just a second too long. "George and me. Other than ducking some customs duty at the border, we didn't see it as any great crime. In fact, those drugs are a godsend for folks who can't pay the exorbitant prices nowadays. You of all people should know all about that."

"Where's the source?"

"It's a small lab. Maybe an hour south of Acámbaro. I don't know how well you know the area…San Luca? I think it's north of Chihuahua a little bit. And George said that the lab is connected somehow with a parent company in the United States."

"All right," Estelle said. "And tonight? What was the purpose of the visit to the clinic?"

"I thought it best to remove the pharmaceuticals from Herrera's."

"Why was that?"

"Well," and Frieberg hesitated. "We knew that you were investigating that avenue…that you'd discovered some connection between the drugs and George Enriquez."

"And the we is?"

Frieberg bit his lip. "I meant…Listen, I *did* go see George on Monday morning. He called me the night before and said that he had talked to the district attorney and was going to cut some kind of deal to save his skin. He was almost incoherent. Maybe he'd been drinking, I don't know. But the gist of it was that he thought he could manipulate things so that Herrera would be left holding the bag about the whole drug thing. George seemed to think that he could manipulate things so that it looked that way. He was willing to trade that information in exchange for lifting some of the pressure from him…all that grand jury mess. He figured he could make you think that he was just the poor, duped bag boy. They'd find some of the drugs at Herrera's, and that's where the blame would focus. Especially with your husband's connections.''

The torrent subsided, and Frieberg looked expectant, even hopeful. ''If that's the case,'' Estelle said, ''why would Enriquez bother to call you?''

Frieberg shook his head. His eyes drifted closed. ''I suppose so that I'd have a chance to take whatever precautions I could. To warn me about what was coming. I couldn't talk him out of it, so that's when I decided to take the drugs. If they...if you...searched and didn't find anything, you'd just think George was conjuring up tall tales to save himself.''

''And what precautions *did* you take, Mr. Frieberg?''

''I didn't do anything that night...what, was it Sunday, I think? When George first called me. I went to his office the next morning to try and talk some sense into him. He told me that he was meeting the D.A. sometime that Monday afternoon, so I felt I had time. What he wanted to do was so absurd. I mean, his insurance dealings were petty. He didn't defraud anyone. He paid any claims he had out of his own pocket. At the most, it was a case of misrepresentation. There was no *loss* that anyone suffered. That's what I tried to tell him.''

''What did he say to that?''

''He said that if his whole life was dragged through the grand jury, that it was over for him...that they'd make him out to be some kind of monster. He said that he couldn't take the chance. He was ready to cut a deal. The grand jury business had spooked him. He just sat there the whole time, as dejected as I've ever seen him.''

''So he wanted to buy his way out of it.''

''That's the gist of it. He'd look like a hero, blowing the whistle on the clinic. I told him it wouldn't work, but he wouldn't listen. In the course of our argument, he wrote me the check, reimbursing my premiums that I'd paid on the boat...just like I've already said.''

''What was the point of his doing that?''

Frieberg shook his head. ''George wasn't one for confrontations, Mrs. Guzman. I suppose maybe he thought that I'd go to the police, too. Just another count in the indictment, so to speak.

But I really don't know why he did it. I didn't demand the refund.''

"What time was it when you left his office on Monday morning?"

Frieberg closed his eyes and puffed out his cheeks. "I would say that it was shortly before nine o'clock. In the morning."

"During the time you were in his office, did anyone else arrive?"

"No." His gaze shifted back to the handcuffs in Estelle's hand, trying to judge if they'd made progress toward his wrists.

"And so, when you knew what George was planning to do, you tried to cover yourself by removing the drugs from Herrera's pharmacy."

"Well, no...I mean...I had..." He stopped and Estelle saw the muscles of his jaw set.

"You had what?"

Frieberg spoke slowly, as if choosing his words both carefully and with considerable discomfort, as if he were talking around the swelling of a recent root canal. "I had reason to believe that George *wouldn't* talk to the district attorney." He almost smiled. "And I know what that sounds like. But I had no idea..." The mortician abruptly turned away, walked three steps toward the hallway, stopped, and turned back. Estelle saw Deputy Abeyta tense and shift his weight, and she held up her hand.

"I can't do this," he said, and looked at the floor. "I can't do this."

"Yes, you can, sir. Give me a name, Mr. Frieberg."

"I've lived here almost all my life," he said, as if that somehow explained everything. "How can I just..."

"Who killed George Enriquez, Mr. Frieberg?"

"I...I can't."

"That's an interesting brand of loyalty," Bill Gastner said casually. "You're going to take the fall for the whole thing?" The former sheriff had been such a silent presence that his voice sounded unexpectedly loud in the foyer.

"I don't care what you think. But I just can't..." Frieberg's voice trailed off. "We've known each other too long."

"If you're afraid for your safety, Mr. Frieberg, we'll help you all we can," Estelle said. He shook his head, lips pressed tight. Estelle nodded at Tony Abeyta, and an instant later Owen Frieberg found himself face first against the wall, hands cuffed behind his back. The deputy frisked him quickly and then turned him around, a hand on his right elbow. The mortician faced Estelle again, and the impersonal, cold steel of the handcuffs had worked their magic. She could see it in his eyes.

"Mr. Frieberg," Estelle said, "we are placing you under arrest. At this time, the charges include illegal possession of prescription drugs, illegal transportation of prescription drugs across international borders, conspiracy to commit prescription fraud, and conspiracy to commit murder. You have the right to an attorney."

She watched his face settle as she recited the litany of Miranda. When she was finished, he nodded, the picture of dejection. "The pharmaceuticals that I removed from Herrera's are downstairs in one of the freezers," he said. "There's nothing else that would interest you or your investigation. I would appreciate it if you'd extend Mr. Salazar the courtesy of not turning his establishment inside out."

"Mr. Salazar will just have to deal with the inconvenience," Estelle said.

"May I have my jacket, please?" Frieberg nodded toward the small coatrack by the door. Abeyta reached for the windbreaker, checked the pockets, and then draped it over the undertaker's shoulders. "Thank you," he said.

"There's no reason for you to take the blame for everything," Estelle said.

Frieberg grimaced and shifted against the vise of the handcuffs. "We should never have sold the drugs to Herrera in the first place," he said. "I told Guy that at the time."

"You told Guy Trombley that?" And now that the name was out, spoken by a voice other than the echoes of her own nagging suspicions, Estelle felt her pulse slow as the finished puzzle fell into place.

"Yes. He just laughed and called it insurance." He managed a weak smile. "About as effective as some of the insurance

George Enriquez sold. But Guy didn't like Herrera much. Professional grudge, I suppose."

"Did Trombley kill George Enriquez, Mr. Frieberg?"

For a long time, Owen Frieberg studied the floor. "You just ask yourself who had the most to gain from all this," he said softly. "That's all you need to know."

"I've already asked that question," Estelle said.

"Then you know what I'm talking about," the mortician said. Estelle nodded at Deputy Abeyta and watched as he escorted Owen Frieberg outside.

Estelle puffed out her cheeks in a long, slow exhalation of relief as the door closed.

Gastner tipped his head back a bit so that he could focus on her face through the lower part of his glasses. "And now the fun really begins. Where do you go from here?"

"Trombley's pretty smooth," she said.

"Appears so."

"All the time he was talking to me the other day, he knew exactly what I was putting together. And he made sure I knew..." Estelle paused and looked at Gastner. "He made sure I knew that he didn't think much of Louis Herrera. And he made sure I knew that Enriquez had been despondent. That's when I got to thinking."

Gastner grinned. "Thinking is a good habit, sweetheart."

"With Enriquez out of the picture and no drugs in the store when we come snooping, they're home clean," Estelle said. "Or so they imagine." She reached out and squeezed Gastner's arm. "Just what old friends are for. It's not rocket science to figure out who gains from all this."

"Sure. If George was supplying Trombley as well as Herrera, why not? Maybe the whole gig was Trombley's idea in the first place." Gastner frowned. "Trombley goes to Mexico all the time. I think he's got relatives down there, somehow. He's no stranger to south of the border."

"He told me that," Estelle nodded.

"Enriquez was smart enough to figure out what he thought was a sure thing: promise the district attorney that he could deliver *Guzman*, meaning Herrera's pharmacy and the hanky-panky therein, and say nothing about Trombley. Old Guy's a big name in town. Been in business since God invented rocks, damn near."

"I don't think that Louis Herrera knew that Trombley was involved, sir. If Enriquez had handed over Herrera to the D.A., there's a likelihood that that's where it would have ended. Louis is a newcomer, working at the new clinic owned and built by the rich kids." She sighed. "Just like you said. I can see Enriquez thinking that way. I can see the gossip mongers jumping on that bandwagon in a heartbeat. *'Well, no wonder their prices are so low at that new place.'*"

"So why kill Enriquez, then? Why would Trombley do that?"

"Because he knew that when George Enriquez sat down and was confronted by the district attorney, the odds of him spilling the beans were certain. George hadn't thought the thing through…all the way to what he'd say when he was under the lights. And Trombley could figure that out, knowing George. He'd say anything to save his skin. He'd give Schroeder every name, including Trombley."

"You have a warrant to go through Trombley's store?"

"No."

"That's the next step, isn't it?"

"If Judge Hobart will give me a warrant. All I've got on Trombley is Frieberg's implication. That's not enough."

"Put him in the vise, and he'll talk."

"Frieberg? He's going to sing like a canary. But while he's singing, I don't want to go to the D.A. with just one man's word. Not yet. I need something else. Other than that, I have nothing…or at least almost nothing. If Trombley fired the shot that killed Enriquez, it's been too long to pick up any residue off his hands."

"Assuming he was too dumb to wash," Gastner said.

"And we found nothing else at the scene. Nothing that points to Trombley. Those offices are the next thing to a public place, with people in and out all the time. There's a gallery of fingerprints that would take the Bureau's computers a month to wade through and wouldn't prove anything anyway. We can't prove that he actually pulled the trigger."

"You said *almost* nothing," Gastner added.

"You're going to groan," Estelle said. "I've got Leona Spears."

Gastner didn't groan, but he looked skeptical. "Better you than me, kid," he said. "What's psycho lady have to do with anything?"

"She cornered me at the hardware store earlier in the week, and she wanted to know about everything that was going on—about the Kenderman case, especially."

"Of course. Wonderful, bonehead Leona. And like I said, better you than me."

"In the course of our conversation, she said a few complimentary things about the new clinic and the pharmacy…and about how nice it was that some of the drug prices had come down. She said that since the new drugstore opened, Guy Trombley had been forced to lower *his* prices, too. I've been thinking a *lot* about that."

"Huh. And now we know how he did that goddamn little trick. But lowered prices aren't proof that he's in cahoots with your buddy there."

"It's a place to start."

"So how does Leona Spears fit into all of this?"

"I've got something I want to try. She can help me with it."

Gastner looked dubious. "You be careful about opening Pandora's box with that woman, sweetheart. She's nuts. And we both know it. Hell, the whole goddamn town knows it."

"That's what I'm counting on, sir. Want to ride along?"

"Ah, no. Thanks. It'd be more fun to find a nice rock and drop it on my foot."

THIRTY-NINE

DESPITE HER RESOLVE, Estelle Reyes-Guzman's finger hesitated a moment before dialing. Bill Gastner was right about Leona Spears. Whether Pandora's box or the LaBrea tar pits was the more apt analogy, Estelle was loath to step too close. At two minutes after ten, the phone range twice, and when the receiver was lifted at the other end, Estelle could hear Placido Domingo's cellolike voice in the background—a familiar operatic aria that was one of Francis Guzman's favorites.

"Helllloooo," Leona Spears's rich contralto greeted.

"Leona? This is Undersheriff Guzman. I hope I didn't wake you."

"Oh! My goodness, no. Would you believe it, I'm just sitting here working on a set of bridge specs. Now *that's* excitement for you." She chuckled. "I'm so glad you called."

"I know this is an imposition, Leona, but I wonder if we could meet for a few minutes."

Leona Spears paused to think about that for a nanosecond or so. "Why of course, Estelle. Do you want me to come down to the office? Would that be convenient?"

"Actually, I'm in the car at the moment, Leona. Could I just swing by? Would that be too much of an imposition?"

"Well, certainly not. You come right ahead. I'll put on some coffee."

"No…please don't. Not on my account, anyway."

"How about some tea or something like that?"

"Tea would be nice," Estelle said, although her knotted stomach recoiled at the thought of anything, liquid or solid. "I'm on

Bustos coming up on Pershing Park. As I remember you're over on Alamo?''

"Four sixteen Alamo Drive. That's right. Right behind the high school. Third house on the right. I'll turn on the porch light for you.''

"It'll be about three minutes," Estelle said. As she clicked off the phone, she could still hear Placido Domingo in the background, heading for high C. She knew that at that moment, Leona's pulse was kicking into triple digits with anticipation. The woman had run for several elective offices over the years, but her favorite target was the sheriff's post, despite no working knowledge of law enforcement beyond what she might gain from the television. Her consistent landslide losses never deterred her from jumping into the next race. What prompted her fascination with law enforcement, Estelle couldn't guess.

In less than three minutes, Estelle turned onto Alamo Drive, the short spur running west from South Fourth Street. She saw the state truck parked in front of 416. Leona's front yard was straight from the drafting board to reality. A perfectly manicured square of crushed stone sufficed for lawn, its boundaries marked with tight chain-linked fencing. Estelle pulled in beside the pickup, thinking that a double yellow line up the driveway wouldn't be out of place. If the woman owned a car of her own, it was tucked away in the one-car garage.

Even before Estelle stepped out of the car, she saw that Leona was standing at the front door of the house. The woman loomed enormous in a floor-length, frilly robe, her corn-yellow hair gathered in complex French braids to drape over her right shoulder. She peered out over half glasses with octagonal granny frames.

"This is an unexpected pleasure," she said as Estelle approached. She stood to one side and gestured for Estelle to enter the house. "And I confess to being a little worried, too. When the law arrives in the middle of the night, it's not for tea and cookies, is it?"

Estelle glanced back at her, surprised by the matter-of-fact tone. Leona was more apt to indulge in flights of fancy, imagining herself privy to all sorts of confidences that weren't her business. "I'm sorry for the inconvenience, Leona. But I really need to talk to you."

The highway engineer waved a hand in easy dismissal. "Not a moment of it, Estelle. Let's go into my office. The tea water's on, too." She beamed. "And I've got cookies, so we're all set. Or maybe something stronger?" A hand fluttered. "But of course not. You're on duty."

They passed the living room, the furniture a metal and plastic style of decades past, all of it looking unused. Leona had turned one of the two bedrooms of the tiny home into her office, complete with an enormous drafting table wedged between matching filing cabinets. With just enough room to turn around, Leona could slide from drafting stool to the plush leather office chair that faced her computer table.

Estelle stood for a moment watching the image on the huge flat-screen monitor. The view was through the windshield of a vehicle, the black two-lane highway spooling through western prairie land, the mesa in the distance gradually growing in size.

"That's a little screen-saver program I worked up," Leona said with satisfaction. "Recognize the spot?"

"It looks like the area up by Newton," Estelle said.

"That's exactly right!" The woman chuckled. "Now I'm *really* impressed with myself for making it look so good." She rubbed her hands together. "But you didn't come over to admire my computer's screen saver." She turned the chair toward Estelle. *"Sitzen,"* and she heaved her bulk onto the drafting stool, planting one large elbow on the slanted surface. "So. May I be so presumptuous as to say that you look exhausted, young lady."

Estelle smiled faintly. "I am. It's been a long, long night, Leona. And bound to be longer before we're through." She saw the engineer rear back as if marshaling her considerable forces and held up a hand to stop the flow before it started. "I need to ask you a favor, but first, I need to make something really clear, Leona."

"Of course." Leona's eyebrows furrowed, one of them rising a bit.

"What we talk about can go no further than this room," Estelle said.

Leona nodded eagerly. "I may be a flake, Undersheriff, but I'm no gossip."

"All right. I'd like you to do a little undercover work for me, if you think that's possible." She watched the woman's heavy face, and this time the left eyebrow twitched several notches higher.

"Me?"

"Yes." Estelle could imagine Sheriff Robert Torrez's swarthy face melding to brick red as he asked, *"You asked Leona Spears to do what?"*

"Of course it's possible," Leona said briskly.

"Well, wait," Estelle said. "I need to ask you a couple of personal questions first, and *then* you decide."

Leona's eyes narrowed, and her head turned sideways so that she was looking at Estelle out of the corner of her eyes. "Personal like how?"

"And don't feel you have to answer," Estelle said. Leona nodded slowly. "Who's your family physician?"

Leona visibly relaxed. "Here I thought you were going to ask me something terribly clandestine, something from the seamy side." She smiled broadly. "That one's easy. Dr. Grona. He's over in Deming." She immediately frowned again, prepared for the next challenge.

"No one here in town?"

"Noooo," she said carefully. Her face flushed beet red, from the lace collar of her muumuu to her hairline. "Your husband is *way* too good-looking for me to be comfortable with, Miss Estelle, and Alan Perrone reminds me of a corpse. Hugh Clausen is a good Swede, but he drinks. And Kurt Baylor is in the process of moving his practice to Grants." She shrugged. "Besides, I've been going to Dr. Grona for eons and eons. I'm in Deming half the week anyway, so it's no inconvenience." She flashed the broad smile again. "And all that is probably *way* more than you wanted to know."

Estelle nodded. "Actually, it's helpful. My next question is absolutely none of my business...not that the first one was."

She hesitated, and Leona leaned forward on the stool. "My

dear, if you're here in the middle of the night asking, then you have your reasons. Shoot.''

Estelle fished a slip of paper out of her pocket and handed it to Leona. The woman scanned down the list of eight prescription drugs, frowning.

''And so? What's this?''

''Do you currently take any of those medications?''

''Interesting, interesting. What *are* you in the middle of, dear girl?''

''Please.'' Estelle nodded at the list.

''Well, let me see. I used to take Petrosin, up until about a month ago. And then Dr. Grona switched me to something else, I don't remember what.''

''You were having some kind of reaction to Petrosin?''

''No. It just wasn't working for me. Let me tell you, I wish I didn't *have* to take it, but sometimes it's just not possible to face the day without it. May you never suffer from depression, Estelle Guzman.'' She scanned the list again. ''None of the rest. Not just now, anyway. I had some Daprodin a month or so ago for a bladder infection. Great big horse pills.''

''Large price tag, too.''

''Oh, of course. Thank God for insurance, though. Still, the co-pay is enough to land you on your back.''

''Where did you go to have the prescriptions filled?''

''I've been using Trombley's for years and years.'' Leona lowered her voice as if in mid-conspiracy. ''And he's so thoughtful, you know. Like with the Daprodin? He would give me a few extra, in case the infection flared up again. That way I wouldn't have to go through the whole rigmarole again. In some ways, old Doc Grona is kind of a fuddy-duddy. He wrote a thirty-day prescription for the Daprodin, instead of the normal ten. So I just saved the rest for another day.'' She beamed smugly.

''So you still have some of the Daprodin, then?'' Leona nodded. ''May I see it?''

''Well surely.'' The woman heaved herself upright. ''And I'll make the tea. Any special favorites? I have everything on the planet.''

"Actually, I'm fine, Leona. Really."

"You don't *look* fine. How about a little cup of Earl Grey? That cures all ills. And it's scads cheaper than Daprodin."

Estelle grinned with resignation. "Okay." She felt a stab of affection for this lonely Brunhilda.

"Cream and sugar?"

"No, thanks. Just Daprodin."

Leona burst out with a hearty laugh. "Ah, yes. All right. Let me fetch that." She left the room and was gone for no more than two minutes, long enough for Estelle to read the two diplomas from UCLA, one of them a doctorate in civil engineering. A framed photo caught the former governor of New Mexico shaking Leona's hand at what was obviously an awards dinner of some sort, with *I appreciate all you do!!!* written across the top corner of the photo in heavy black marker.

"Here we are," Leona said, and handed the small bottle to Estelle. "And I'll be right back with the tea. Cookies? I've got some of those wonderful little lemon things from Denmark."

"No, please. But you go ahead."

"Well, I'll bring enough, in case you change your mind." She hustled out of the room. Estelle rolled the prescription bottle between her fingers, then popped off the top. She shook one pill out into the palm of her hand and pressed the lid back in place. She regarded the pill for a moment, reading the DAPRODIN DG on one side, the 500 on the other—identical in appearance with either set of pills she'd taken from Louis Herrera's pharmacy. *Quiero o no quiero,* she thought, and popped the pill into her mouth, letting it rest on the front of her tongue. The taste, if there was any at all, was bland and chalky.

Estelle deposited the capsule into a small evidence bag and slipped the bottle and remaining medication into another, marking them carefully. She was putting the cap back on the pen when Leona Spears returned with a tray and cups. She saw her medications now secure in the plastic bags and stopped short.

"Leona, this last batch of Daprodin DG that you purchased from Guy Trombley is a placebo," Estelle said. "That's what we're investigating at the moment."

"You're kidding." The large woman set the tray down carefully on the computer desk.

"No."

"How do you tell, then? That it's fake, I mean."

"The taste, for one. The real medication has a tart, stringent taste, like quinine."

"I've had some that does and some that doesn't," Leona said. "Now what about the Petrosin?"

"That I don't know. It'll require a lab analysis."

"I have some, you know."

"Petrosin?"

"Yes. You remember I said that Dr. Grona changed my prescription? I kept the medications." She scrinched up her face like a guilty child. "I keep things, you know." It took her only a moment to produce the bottle, still containing two dozen or more tablets.

"Also from Trombley's pharmacy," Estelle said, looking at the label.

"Now surely, he wouldn't…" and Leona let the sentence trail off. "What was it that you wanted me to do?"

"Leona, may I take these with me?" She held up the two evidence bags.

Leona Spears snorted. "I don't have much choice there, now do I." Then she smiled eagerly. "Whatever you want to do. I have other prescriptions from Trombley's as well…would you want those?"

"I'd appreciate it."

In another moment, Leona had assembled a row of nine bottles, some out of date by more than a year. She watched with satisfaction as Estelle nudged them into another plastic bag. "I hope that helps," Leona said. "If this is all you wanted of me, it's the easiest thing in the world."

"I think this will serve the same purpose, Leona," Estelle said. "I think it will. Do you understand that if this ends up in court, you'll be asked to testify about the circumstances of your acquiring these medications? And that you received them from Guy Trombley?"

Leona nodded. "I'm no stranger to the courtroom, my dear.

It doesn't frighten me one little bit. And now a fair trade, Mrs. Guzman. *What*," and she leaned heavily on the word, "is going on? I've known and *trusted* Guy Trombley for just years and years. I just can't imagine…"

"We have reason to believe that counterfeit pharmaceuticals are being brought into the country, Leona. There is evidence that some of them were dispensed at local pharmacies, including in Posadas." She smiled ruefully. "That's all I can really tell you at this point."

The engineer's eyes narrowed, and she leaned back against the slanted surface of the drafting table. "Oh, my. Don't tell me that the new place is involved, too. Your husband must be just beside himself."

"Leona…"

"What else can I do?"

"Sit tight. Do not discuss this with anyone. No one. That's really important, Leona. You really need to keep this to yourself."

"When you first came, you mentioned something undercover," Leona said.

"With what you've been able to provide," and she lifted the bags, "you've given us a valuable shortcut," Estelle said.

Leona's eyes twinkled craftily. "You were going to ask me to try and purchase bogus drugs from the store, weren't you?" She glanced at her watch as if coordinating the time for an assault. "I could go down in the morning and ask for something. I think half the time Mr. Trombley is convinced that I'm just a hypochondriac anyway."

"The thought had crossed my mind. But with this, it's not necessary."

"I'll be happy to help, if that's what you need to do."

"And we appreciate that. But the results would be the same, either way." Estelle rose. "I'll be in close touch."

"Do you have time for tea?"

Estelle sighed. "Some other time, thanks." After sidestepping four or five other conversations, she made it to the front door. The cool air outside felt wonderful.

FORTY

SETTLED INTO THE Expedition, she found her cell phone, pressed in the number, and waited.

"Yep," Robert Torrez said after a moment.

"Bobby, I just came from Leona Spears."

"You *what?*"

"Leona supplied the missing link. I need to wake up Judge Hobart for a search warrant for Trombley's Pharmacy. And an arrest warrant. I'm pretty sure how the whole scam worked. We nailed Louis Herrera and Owen Frieberg a few minutes ago."

"So I understand," Torrez said. "We're runnin' a little short-handed around these parts."

"Frieberg implicated Trombley, and now we have the proof of that."

Silence followed, and she could hear voices in the background. "Who pulled the trigger on Enriquez?" the sheriff asked.

"Frieberg wouldn't come out and say it, but he implied that Guy Trombley did."

"Maybe once he hears a cell door clang shut, it'll loosen his tongue. Works wonders sometimes."

"We need to move on this, Bobby. Tonight."

"Well, we're tryin' to move…about eight directions at once. Before you do anything else, stop by here. And by the way, the district attorney would like to talk with you."

"We don't have a lot of time to waste, Bobby. I don't want Trombley slipping away."

"Talking to me isn't a waste of time, Estelle," Dan Schroeder said, and his voice startled her.

"Sir, we have to move on this."

"Whoa, whoa, whoa," the district attorney admonished, and she heard a car door close out the background noise. "Look, I need to talk to you."

"I understand that, sir."

"It's not a 'it can wait until tomorrow' sort of thing, Estelle."

"I understand that, too, sir. If we move on this, it isn't going to take long."

"I have a couple of questions that I need to run by you, for one thing. We need to know what the little boy told you while it's still fresh in your mind."

"He didn't tell me anything, sir. He's too frightened."

"You talked to him?"

"There'll be time for that later."

"Maybe so. Something else more immediate, though. There's a fair-sized crowd of oglers here, including Frank Dayan. I figured you'd want to talk to him yourself."

"Bobby can do that," Estelle said.

"Please," Schroeder said. "Dayan's not going to settle for monosyllables, and the whole damn situation could use your touch."

"That's not a real high priority for me just at the moment, sir."

"Well," Schroeder said, "Dayan aside, I've got some questions that I'm not going to hash over on the telephone. You're heading in?"

"Yes, sir. We really need the search warrant."

"We'll get it, trust me. But will you humor me in this?" Schroeder's tone didn't leave much room for discussion. "You and the sheriff and I are going to meet for a few minutes, and you're going to lay all this out for us, one step at a time. You're going to bring us all up to speed. All right?" Before Estelle could answer, the district attorney added, "And then we're going to secure a warrant, because I have no doubt that you're exactly right. Then we're going to have a couple of well-rested, cool heads bring in Guy Trombley. Not you. Not Bobby. Not anyone who's worked thirty hours straight. All right? That's the way I want it to work."

When Estelle didn't answer promptly, Schroeder added, "Look, I talked to Bobby, and he agreed with me. We both know you're concerned about your husband and what this whole damn mess is going to do to his name. And that puts you too close, Estelle. I understand that. But I don't want mistakes. And neither do you."

"Sir," Estelle said, "if you and the sheriff want to send someone else to arrest Guy Trombley, that's fine with me. I just want it *done*. I don't care who does it. In fact, that's probably the best thing to do."

"I just think it's best if the whole town doesn't end up thinking this was some personal vendetta, Estelle."

"Which it was," she said, and almost managed enough energy to laugh.

THREE HOURS LATER, Deputy Jackie Taber's voice on the radio was calm. "PCS, three oh three is ten fifteen, one adult male." Estelle Reyes-Guzman leaned back in her chair and closed her eyes. That may have been a mistake, since it then took considerable effort to open them again. She looked across the conference table, across the sea of paperwork, at District Attorney Daniel Schroeder.

"Take a break," Schroeder said. "I know you'd like to be there."

"I don't know if I want to be or not," Estelle said, but she was on her feet and headed toward the door almost before the sentence was out of her mouth. She stepped into the short hallway between the conference room and Dispatch. Through the glass partition around the Dispatch Center, she saw Frank Dayan in earnest conversation with a state policeman. The publisher caught sight of Estelle and gesticulated urgently.

The undersheriff tried her best to keep her expression sober.

"Do you know what day this is?" Dayan asked.

"I have no idea," Estelle replied. "I've lost all track."

The newspaper publisher shook his head sadly. "You arrest practically the whole town the day *after* my paper hits the streets."

"What can I say."

"Well, for one thing, you can tell me what the deal is with Owen Frieberg. I caught sight of him being brought in. I saw the handcuffs."

"I'll do better than that," Estelle said, and then held up a hand. "Can you give me just a couple minutes?"

"I've given you the whole darn week," Dayan said. "What's another minute or two now?"

"Do you have your camera with you?"

"Sure."

She pointed at the hallway, beyond Dispatch. "Go wait in the doorway of my office, Frank. Guy Trombley is going to be coming through into booking in about," she glanced at her watch. "A minute. You might get a shot." She smiled. "Scoop time."

"You've got to be shitting me. Guy Trombley? What…?"

"Stick around," Estelle said. She patted Dayan on the arm and left him standing in the hallway, groping the camera out of his coat pocket. She knew he might have five seconds to snap a picture, during that brief moment when Trombley was led from the garage to the booking room. She guessed that if Trombley saw the newspaper man, he'd have a second or so to try and hide the handcuffs from view. In any case, the fuzzy photo would run on the front page of the *Posadas Register* in a week's time.

Undersheriff Estelle Reyes-Guzman met the group in booking, out of the range of Dayan's camera or hearing. Trombley regarded her silently, his icy blue eyes holding hers while the officers loosened the shackles. "I'm sure you're happy now," he said.

She ignored him and instead turned to Deputy Jackie Taber. "Thanks, Jackie."

"You can go home now," the deputy said, and smiled.

"I'll get Frank Dayan squared away, and then that's exactly what I'll do," Estelle said.

"The sheriff can talk to Frank," Jackie suggested.

"Oh sure," Estelle laughed. "That's going to happen in this lifetime."

AT TWENTY MINUTES after five that morning, Estelle pulled the county car into her driveway on Twelfth Street and switched off the engine. She sat for a long time, half expecting the radio or the cell phone to interrupt the silence.

A knuckle rapped on the car's window, and Estelle realized that she'd closed her eyes. "You going to sit there all morning?" Francis asked. He opened the door for her and watched as she pulled herself out. She reached out and took his hand.

"What time did you finally get home, *Oso?*" she asked.

"*Padrino* brought me home about two or so," he said. "I sent Irma home."

"Two? Ay."

He shrugged. "We had a good long talk," he said. "Your dispatcher kept us updated."

Estelle managed a smile. "I'll have to talk to Ernie about giving civilians insider information."

"Bill's only a quasi-civilian, remember. Did you talk to Trombley?"

"No…not yet. Bobby and Dan Schroeder are going to do that. I'm not sure I want to."

"There's no question in your mind that he killed Enriquez?"

Estelle shook her head. "He admitted it," she said. "That makes it easy, doesn't it? He said George threatened him, and that he grabbed the gun away during a struggle. He hit him, then tried to make it look like suicide. Trombley told Jackie Taber that George had the gun out when he arrived, as if he was thinking about it all along."

"So Trombley is going to try for self-defense?"

"Or manslaughter at the worst. He's slick. He thinks he can cut a deal." She smiled faintly. "Right now, he doesn't know that we have evidence George was collapsed backward, holding his head with both hands after the blow to the temple. That makes a claim of self-defense a little bit thin."

She linked her arm through her husband's and sighed. "It's not going to be any fun," she said. "Not for you."

Francis shrugged. "*Padrino* and I talked about that. Louis is cooperating?"

"Sure. Frieberg swears that Herrera had nothing to do with the scheme itself. They offered him the drugs, and he took them.

And that's that. The district attorney is leaning toward fraud charges at the most. If Louis handed out a fake prescription and collected less than a hundred bucks, it's a petty misdemeanor.''

"Not so petty," Francis muttered. He held the front door for her.

"That's before the state pharmacy board is done with him," she said. "On top of that, I'd expect civil actions taken by the patients who think their health was jeopardized." She turned as he closed the front door, keeping her voice down. "And that's what is going to be hard on you guys. On you and Alan."

"We'll weather it," Francis said. "We'll pull in every patient involved and make sure they're all right—and do whatever it takes to make it so." He reached out and pushed a strand of hair out of her eyes. "One step at a time. Right now, you look like you could use about thirty hours' uninterrupted sleep."

Estelle closed her eyes. "I told Louis that I didn't want to see him on the clinic property ever again," she said. "I shouldn't have said that. That's not my call to make."

"But you're right," Francis said. He took her by both shoulders, his gaze searching. "You did the right thing, *querida*. If he was willing to give patients fake meds, then we don't know how far he'd go, given the temptation. Don't lose any sleep over it. You did the right thing. As far as Alan and I are concerned, Louis Herrera is history. I'll do everything in my power to see that he doesn't practice pharmacy again. Ever. Anywhere." He turned her away from the doorway. "Right now, you need some rest, *querida*."

"Sleep," she repeated. "What a concept."

"At least until *Los Dos* wake up in an hour," Francis laughed.

HARLEQUIN®
INTRIGUE®

WE'LL LEAVE YOU BREATHLESS!

If you've been looking for thrilling tales of
contemporary passion and sensuous love stories
with taut, edge-of-the-seat suspense—then
you'll love Harlequin Intrigue!

Every month, you'll meet six new heroes
who are guaranteed to make your spine tingle
and your pulse pound. With them you'll enter
into the exciting world of Harlequin Intrigue—
where your life is on the line
and so is your heart!

THAT'S INTRIGUE—
ROMANTIC SUSPENSE
AT ITS BEST!

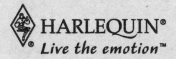

HARLEQUIN®
Live the emotion™

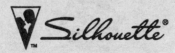